No Kiss Good-Night

KEVIN ZDRILL

iUniverse, Inc.
Bloomington

No Kiss Good-Night

iUniverse books may be ordered through booksellers or by contacting:

iUniverse
1663 Liberty Drive
Bloomington, IN 47403
www.iuniverse.com
1-800-Authors (1-800-288-4677)

ISBN: 978-1-4759-2824-2 (sc)
ISBN: 978-1-4759-2822-8 (hc)
ISBN: 978-1-4759-2823-5 (ebk)

Printed in the United States of America

iUniverse rev. date: 07/11/2012

This book is gratefully dedicated to very special people in my life. The first one not only gave me life, she breathed inspiration and wisdom into my soul and words of knowledge into my being. Thank you, Big Momma.

The second is my wife, Anna. You have inspired me to be a man, a husband and a father. Your uncompromising support truly defines the love we have for one another. Thank you for being an extraordinary wife and mother. "BWO"

And to Michael H, who is bigger than life itself and has shown me how to live it to the maximum. Our laughter will never stop, my dear friend.

Realizing I was perilously close to executing an Olympic-quality somersault, I stepped back from the fifteenth-floor railing. My second dismal thought was that no one would know if I had gone over. I was alone inside my Winnipeg apartment. On any other day of the year, the silence was an accepted normal, but today it was a defeat. Today I turned thirty-nine, and I'd had a plan to tackle the dreaded experience with a show of force. With focused determination, I'd gained the commitment of my most cherished friends, family and acquaintances to form a protective circle around me as we celebrated the end of my favourite decade, my thirties.

This morning my phone rang at 9:00 a.m., and I dashed toward it with a large grin, preparing to hear the well-wishes of a thoughtful friend. It was my sister, Julia Adams. She was flying in this afternoon from her home in Minneapolis, one of the guaranteed members of my protective birthday circle. Except today was my birthday and Julia's plane ticket was one weekend off. Julia was calling from the airport—ticket, bag and gift in hand—mere hours away from joining my circle. In her zest for supporting her brother she'd given the airline the wrong date for her day of departure. Julia had a heart of gold but her pocketbook wasn't lined with it. The airline wanted $900 to change her flight. End of the line. Julia asked if it would be okay for her to hang on to my gift until I saw her at Christmas when I came to visit. Yes, it would. Strike one from my protective circle.

I thanked Julia for calling. I still had confidence my remaining troops would take up the slack. I spent the rest of the morning getting silly from blowing up a few coloured balloons I'd bought at the Dollar Store. I chose a stack of CDs to play during the party, including my favourites by Streetheart, Loverboy, Harlequin and Neil Young; I pulled out my wrinkled Twister mat in case the party got wild and stuck 39 candles into the vanilla cake I'd bought the day before at Safeway.

Lonny Wood rang my phone at 12:30 p.m. He was my best friend, my only friend, a part of my circle, and it looked like he was not going to show up. Lonny had intended to drive in from Brandon today after selling his cell phones to various farming communities. He explained that while he was having breakfast that morning at the Double Decker Restaurant in Brandon, he'd bumped into a "harem" of girls paying their bills at the same time he did. The girls were heading off to a Passion Party one of the women at Double Decker was hosting. Thirty women equaled thirty potential cell phone sales, maybe a phone number or two for Lonny and a free sex toy thrown in by the hostess. "Business is business," he said. Lonny promised to drop off my birthday gift the next time we got together.

After Lonny bailed on my final thirties party, slight panic set in, but I pulled out the two bottles of Barefoot champagne that I had chilling in the fridge and left two champagne glasses in the cupboard. I set the bottles on the kitchen table alongside the remaining three glasses. I liked that odd number. It was lucky.

I could honestly say at one thirty when I got off the phone with my young assistant, Christy Chambers, my hands shook as I continued to tape up the banner I had made up at Staples over my patio door: HAPPY BIRTHDAY, GUS ADAMS!

Christy apologized as profusely for having to jam on my birthday bash as she did for throwing up while on the phone. She had been out all night partying at her friend's bachelorette party. The gang in their own circle of support shut down Times Night Club and then had a backyard bonfire in Charleswood that ended when each of the girls threw up into the fire. Calling from a cell phone, Christy was stretched out in front of the smoldering fire as part of her vomiting support for their soon-to-be-married girlfriend. Christy promised to bring my gift to the office. I removed her champagne glass from the kitchen table.

I heard a knock at my door at three thirty and raced from the bedroom, where I was finishing putting on my new tie with the custom-tailored mocha-coloured suit I'd had made for my birthday party. I'd had the seamstress stitch Birthday Boy on the right sleeve to impress my guests. I flung open the door with exuberance, expecting to greet my first guest. There stood my landlord, Harold Waldabowski, who'd promised to be part of my circle. With a flourish of my arm, I welcomed him inside.

Harold was cancelling. "Sorry, chum. Old Mr. Hardy on floor ten finally died." Harold had to meet the coroner in the lobby to provide access to the apartment. Harold handed me my birthday gift in an envelope. It was a ninety-day rent increase notice. Harold was giving me an extra thirty days' exception. "Happy birthday."

I closed the door, walked over to the kitchen table, removed Harold's glass and returned it to the cupboard. I returned to the table, popped the champagne, filled the lone glass, lit the candles, tried to think of a wish and couldn't. I blew out the candles in three attempts and made my way to my fifteenth-floor balcony.

Standing outside on my balcony, I stared back inside my apartment, studying my reflection in the patio door. The face of a thirty-nine-year-old man looked back at me.

I flexed my chest, and nothing changed. Where was the tapered V that led from slim hips to a flaring set of shoulders? Gone was the detailed moulding of well-toned muscles. I leaned closer to the glass. Lines. The map of my life around my eyes went nowhere. I was moving from being a ball-kicking dude to hey-old-man.

But the shit that really pissed me off wasn't in my appearance. It was the noticeably empty space beside me in my own bed. I was void of a loyal woman who would be there for each birthday and holiday—someone who cared if I felt ill in the morning or would report me missing if I didn't show up at the end of the day.

I had never been married. Years ago, I dated. Long-term relationships were never long enough to see through a season change. A nice break had now become a nine-year drought. Seeing a shimmer of grey in my hair signified the obvious: in one more year I would become *forty years old*. And I was haplessly alone.

My cavalier attitude toward sustaining a meaningful relationship had jeopardized my entire future. I'd situated myself on the cusp of the place no man wants to be. I could imagine the comments. "Don't go there, honey. Being single at his age, he must have issues." Issues? No. Boredom? *Yes.* I basically got bored. The thrill of courting created a vicious cycle of complacency and Saturday night vacuuming. I became a wheel in a relationship. Lingerie was soon exchanged for faded sweats. Eventually there was nothing left to discuss. Our pasts were revealed and mundanely reworked. Relationships became a victim of discussing the weather. I often bailed out before the rot of gangrene could set in.

I've had successes in my life. I run a private psychotherapy practice a few short blocks from the apartment. Every day I deal with the problems that invariably arise in relationships. I solve them. I admit, it was taking an abnormally lengthy time to establish my cliental base. This isn't a surprise. I have a fifteen-year plan. I'd moved from Michigan to the province of Manitoba, which meant not knowing anyone. I had a beautiful fifteenth-floor apartment that offered a spectacular view of the city and the meandering Assiniboine River below. I was only an aging loser when it came to my own love life. Go figure.

Standing on the balcony, I resolved I wouldn't become victim to turning forty alone. There was a woman out there for me. She knew it. I knew it. We only needed to make that first connection. I needed to approach making that connection methodically. I had twelve precious months to hand my beating heart over to the woman meant for me. It was that simple.

I would never be so wrong.

"Hi, my name is Bonny. I'm thirty-five years old and starting over ..."

I stepped outside my patio door and peered over the railing toward the parking lot, looking for "the car." It was hot outside even though it wasn't quite eight in the morning, a typical Manitoba day in July. A black Chrysler Intrepid had just pulled up, as it had every morning, Monday to Friday, at this time. And every morning at this time for the past year I'd stared down as I currently was doing, one hand on the railing and the other holding my cup of Starbucks coffee. I watched for the kiss. It was my love barometer for each day. I watched the couple through the windshield lean toward one another and kiss. *A simple act. Such a meaningful act of bonding,* I thought. The female would leave the Intrepid and walk across the street to the Heritage building, where I assumed she worked.

Invigorated by the morning kiss fix, I reentered my apartment and began preparing for work. A quick shower. One vitamin capsule. White shirt. No tie. I believed in casual counselling. I was ready.

During the fifteen-floor elevator ride I thought about time. I calculated if I always lived on the same floor, I was dedicating three weeks of my life to riding this elevator—time that could be spent finding my love interest. Twelve months until forty meant elevator time was too precious. I would start using the stairs.

I enjoy living on Wellington Crescent. It is in a beautiful, central, exclusive area of the city, a twenty-minute walk from my clinic in Osborne Village, a place with soul otherwise known just as the Village. I strolled along the sidewalk lined with ancient trees, always a soothing jaunt right into the mixing bowl of the Village. Everybody from the town idiot to the artistic wanna-be thrived within the one-mile strip. I ambled past pubs, boutiques, an array of ethnic restaurants, a group of tattoo-stenciled squeegee boys and a pair of skateboarders. I loved the area. My practice in the three-story building was in a street-front basement, a fluke find for me. I was the envy of local business. I didn't care. Walking down the steps always made me think of going down inside a patient's psyche putting me in the frame of mind I needed to counsel the weak.

The interior was bright: no wood paneling. Seventies classic rock music played through the Bose speakers. Dr. Hook was singing. This wasn't a funeral home. Couples came here to focus on love. I was there to adjust the lens. I closed the door and sat across from the desk belonging to my lone office assistant, Christy, a bright, vibrant and aloof twenty-one-year-old who was beautiful, too much so for her own good, I thought. She had a figure that kept endless guys calling her for dates. Trouble was that sometimes in all the mesh of testosterone and sexual lust, the good ones got away. Between appointments we convinced each other not all people were jerks. Comforting. Misguided. There was hope for us to find that special someone. What else could we do? I lived vicariously through Christy's mating tribulations. She drew inspiration from my desperation.

I was ready to be entertained by tales of her blind date over the past weekend. Kids her age didn't understand dignity. Only time and repeat rabbit punches to pride change that. I slouched into a chair in front of her desk. She could see the stress etched into my face. She placed a nicely wrapped gift on her desk and pushed it my way.

"Sorry!" Her face did not lie. She felt badly for missing my birthday. I opened the gift containing bottles of hair products that claimed to cover the grey.

"I've told you shampoos have come a long way," she teased. "You guys born in the sixties have a hard time letting go of the past, don't you? It's designer products, my dear Gus."

I nodded my head and smiled weakly. "No worries. I appreciate the gift. My birthday was a total bust. My chain of support broke at every link."

Christy looked pained. She changed the subject to save herself from watching a man cry. Her face brightened with exuberance.

"You have a new couple. First timers."

I perked up. "Great. Don't get too many of those in the summer." I smiled at her expectantly. She knew what I wanted. My stalling was killing her. I asked about her blind date. She never let me down when it came to a first date with mystery men.

"Only assholes drive BMWs." Her eyes were fiery. "The fact he didn't open the door for me was the first red flag. I don't care what kind of car it is. Show me respect and open the damn door. I knew it wasn't going to get better on the drive to Sorrento's Pizza. He offered to pay for supper. But first I had to reach into his pants pocket. If I chose the right one, he paid. If not, I got jammed with the tab. He had on khakis pants that were too small. Grossed me out. I could see the outline of his yoo-hoo. Yuck!"

I had to laugh. Christy saw life around her in one dimension. At least it kept me amused. I could never decide if she exaggerated her innocence. Who knew for sure? Women were, after all, the world's great subtle connivers. I urged her on.

"It only got worse, Gus. Honest to god. We were still in the restaurant parking lot when Steve's buddies surrounded us. He completely ignored me while they made farting noises and behaved like jerks."

I asked, "How bad could it be?" Apparently bad enough for her to walk away unnoticed. I agreed. That was bad.

Better luck next time, I wanted to offer. Somehow I knew my weak condolence wouldn't be welcome. She saved me from a response.

"Men treat me like a dumb blonde, and I'm not. Look at my hair," she said, pulling at the long, waving mane. "Brown. Not even a blonde streak. So what gives?"

She did little to inspire me to date. I was already reluctant. I grasped shreds of hope. Hope eluded me again.

Christy must have read my disillusionment. Had I become a road sign of despair?

"One of us has to get lucky, Gus. There's survival in numbers." I detected a faint trace of confidence in her voice.

I reminded her that hope hadn't helped the dinosaurs or the passengers on the *Titanic*. She wasn't deterred.

"Get off your soapbox, Gus. For a guy having an oh-my-god here-comes-forty-crisis, you're lackadaisical about it. Break the jitters with a first date, buddy. Honestly. It can't get worse than my own dates." She laughed, and I wasn't sure how to interpret it.

I told her she had me convinced until her laughter brought me back to reality. She was correct. I needed to take that first bullet. The loaded gun was out there—spin the chamber and pull the trigger.

I decided to counter with an excuse. Where would I start? Libraries? Supermarkets? A street corner and a sign? Christy found my remarks funny enough to laugh. It was different for guys. Women only had to flare a naked calf and the men came running. We had to earn trust. That took time.

I thanked Christy for sharing her latest dating disaster with Steve and made my way into my office, my spacious, radiant sanctuary. I enjoyed the uncluttered atmosphere that held two plush, white leather chairs for my clients, a coffee table with a coffee brewer for my Starbucks French roast, and my own throne. Sitting back in my reclining black leather chair from Staples, I wondered what I would encounter with my next appointment. A new couple was surprising because summer was usually a slack time. People were too busy hitting the beaches and backyard barbecue parties to spend time mending broken relationships. I had plenty of untethered time during summer months. Winter was my bacon. During the eight months of frozen hell, I generated enough working capital to carry me through a summer of drought. In my profession, it was feast or famine.

This was my only appointment today. I placed my hands behind my head. As much as I wanted to draft a plan to search for a love interest, my thoughts were scattered. I was distracted. I was also interrupted. My appointment arrived early.

I greeted Jean and Jerry Trotts with a brisk handshake in my usual manner: reserved, searching, cheerful. I sat with them in a circle. No table, no couch. I left the melodramatics for television. I instantly took a liking to the Trotts. They were mid-fifties, married for thirty-five years, financially well off and secure—everyone's ideal mom and pop. Jerry was into his first year of retirement. I was intrigued.

I urged them to speak about themselves. Jean had never worked outside the home. Instead, she had elected to raise three children at home; all were now married, with children of their own. She had no regrets. She idolized her husband. His hard work provided well for the family. Jerry mirrored his wife's respect. He praised her for raising three well-adjusted children and enduring a lot of time without his presence while he worked long hours. He was now learning to enjoy a life without deadlines and had plenty of hours to fill.

"What have you done with all this time, Jerry?" I asked. I saw a curtain tumble over both faces. Finding the trigger with the first question was rare. I congratulated myself for having a hyper-perceptive day. I inflated my chest.

Before I allowed an answer, I back-pedaled. What had Jerry done with his spare hours while he was still working? I directed the question to Jean. I held eye contact firmly, never wavering. To waver was to lose my connection. It worked. Jean was very uncomfortable. *Come on, Grandma, out with it.*

She hesitated. I leaned forward. Jerry glanced at her with a sideways look.

"Jerry worked hard. Work was all he had. It made me unhappy that he couldn't have activities outside the office. So when he first asked me to play a game with him, I didn't say no." The entire time she spoke, she stared at her hands. I could see red creeping up her wrinkled neck. *What kind of games did your husband want you to play with him?* I was curious. "Games" smelled of something grandparents were not expected to be doing. Call it a long shot, but I didn't expect to hear the word *Monopoly.*

Jean explained that Jerry liked to pretend. I motioned for her to illuminate for me. "You know," she struggled, trying to hide her embarrassment, "pretend to be people he wasn't." Jerry didn't move his head but kept his eyes locked on his wife. Jerry was doing an excellent job of role-playing as a statue.

"Give me an example," I urged. Speculation was out of the question. I needed details.

"Well ..."

I sensed, besides being awkward for her, an explanation was an act of marital betrayal. Yet the intake notes indicated that she had initiated the counselling.

Jean sought an out with her response. "Can't we just talk about this generally?"

I shook my head. "We need to break the emotions down to their raw form," I explained.

Jean continued, not fully reassured. "Jerry would wait until after supper. He'd put on my nylons. I would wear a tie and be his boss." Jean glanced furtively at her husband. He stared at her.

I didn't say anything.

Jean continued. "All these years I did it to give pleasure to Jerry. I really didn't mind. Sometimes it was fun, like the time he wrapped a white towel around himself like it was a diaper and let me wash him in the tub. He made little baby sounds while I scrubbed his back. It brought back fond memories of when my children lived at home."

I let her keep talking. Her story was putting my own life into perspective.

"Then there was the time he chased me around the kitchen on his hands and knees. He wore our shepherd's collar. I carried a rubber bone we bought at Pet Mart. I looked around and discovered our neighbour standing at the door watching us. She's ... . she's never spoken to us since."

"When did you start seeing your husband's source of entertainment was interfering with the way you felt, Jean?"

She sighed.

"I was okay with Jerry's games because he only wanted me to play once or twice a month. But since he's retired we've been playing the games almost every day. I'm starting to get worried. What if one of our daughters visits with their children and discovers us? I'm mortified by that ever happening."

Jerry finally looked my way. I motioned for him to speak.

He shrugged.

At first I thought he wouldn't say anything. But he did. Surprisingly, he failed to show a trace of embarrassment. In fact, he was quite relaxed. He explained that some men enjoy football. Others play cards and smoke cigars. He enjoyed shaving his chest. So what?

I agreed there wasn't anything odd about the activities he found pleasure in. It was the increasing frequency that was bothering Jean.

It was time to stop for the day. Since it was our first session, becoming familiar with each other was enough. I asked them to schedule with Christy and walked them to my door and thanked them for their time today. A few minutes later Christy entered my office to say Lonny wanted to meet me for lunch at Carlos and Murphy's patio. Lonny was my best friend. In fact, he was my only friend. She inquired how the meeting went with the Trotts. I asked her if any one of her dates had ever suggested she call him Fido.

"Not once."

I didn't think so. Romance hadn't changed all that much.

I walked out into the bright street and paused, taking in the loud sounds of traffic, the people, the smell of exhaust and dog shit. Squinting, I wished I had brought my sunglasses. Nowhere was the sun as penetrating as during a Winnipeg summer. Not even when I was growing up in Minneapolis did I remember the sun being this bright. Maybe it was the depletion of ozone? But all the locals said the sun's intensity had always been like this. I enjoyed it. It made my worst day feel okay.

I ambled to the corner of River and Osborne, turned right and began the single block walk to the restaurant. My eyes caught a pair of girls bouncing toward me. They each wore a coloured tank top, one blue, one red. They were both voluptuous. As they got closer I could see they were quite young. About fourteen years young. I quickly averted my eyes. I didn't want my desperation to get me mislabelled as a pervert. It didn't stop me from blaming modern milk. The girls of my teenage years never developed like the girls of today.

Cars and people sped past me as I jostled to the front door of Carlos and Murphy's and into the roar of the lunch crowd. Jocelyn, the hostess, waved me over. She was blonde and glowing and, I'm sad to report, married. I was here for lunch often enough so that she knew I preferred sitting outside on the side patio. I chose the sounds of buses and cars over the clattering of plates and hyena laughter. Carlos and Murphy's offered everything I wanted in an afternoon eatery: good Mexican food, a sombre wood interior, casual setting. The patio was a bonus. Jocelyn brought me a glass of iced tea. I thanked her.

I looked at my watch. Lonny would arrive soon. Although he was never on time, he kept his engagements ... except when it mattered most, like yesterday, on my birthday. But I would forgive him, since I couldn't hold grudges against four people without exhausting myself. Lonny was the same age as me, thirty-nine, but without any disillusions. He didn't care. At least not about his age. His body was in chiseled condition. Each sunrise presented a new day of challenges for Lonny, which is why he made a good cellular phone salesman. Ironically, he had sold me my phone. That's how we first met, and I was happy with my deal: six months of free cellular phone use. I had been nothing more than a sales transaction. Later in the week, we'd met up again by accident at a local British pub called the King's Head. The next five years were history. Lonny is everything I could have been but wasn't. Besides not caring that forty was less than a year away, he relished being single. He dated more frequently than I had bowel movements in a week. He lived alone in a two-bedroom condo named The Lofts in the Exchange Theatre District converted from a one-hundred-year-old warehouse. Impossible to buy, except for Lonny. Selling phones gave him connections. He'd been literally one phone call away from having his name on the short list. The result was an enviable sixth-story, eighteen-hundred-square-foot condo with a sixteen-foot ceiling with eighteen inch barn wood beams. The Exchange was in the centre of the most heavily concentrated nightclub district of the city.

I sipped my iced tea. A Winnipeg transit bus shot by. Lately the buses had dropped the standard orange-and-silver side panel design in lieu of advertising. Another cash grab for the transit system that was never intended to turn a profit. I couldn't miss this particular ad. The letters were large, in bold, dark colours: CALL *NOW*. U 2 CAN DATE and a phone number. The latest in discrete telephone dating services; *just like ordering room service,* I reflected. The ad made me smile. How absurd. I pictured some desperate guy in a small basement bedroom with a flickering light above his head, clutching a phone with a sweaty hand and skimming through a menu of women. U 2 Can Date. Yeah, right. I couldn't fathom that anyone with any intelligence could meet the love of his life, sight unseen, with a random phone call. No way. I let the thought pass along with the bus. I wished Lonny would arrive. I was starved. I was also beginning to work up a good sweat at the only table without an umbrella.

I looked over and noticed Lonny standing across the street, waiting for the light to change, dressed sharply in a designer shirt and light-coloured pants. I could see why women were attracted to him. He looked damned appealing. He saw me and gave a short wave of his hand. I saw him smiling. He was always smiling. Wouldn't matter if a cop were writing him a ticket, he'd still be smiling. Clinically, I would say his Axis II smile was a way to cover an inner conflict of low self-worth, but I knew differently about Lonny. He believes a smiling person is always seen as approachable. Who doesn't feel comfortable around a guy who's smiling? Right or wrong, Lonny smiled. Once he even tried to get me into the habit. I dropped it after two days. It was too much work.

"Hey, Gus," Lonny greeted me, climbing over the railing separating him from the patio. "Sorry 'bout skipping your b-day, dude. But you know what? I scored twenty-seven sales, and you should see the sex toy."

"I'll pass on that, thanks."

"Did you rock out your party?" he asked, grinning.

"Yeah, something like that." It was too painful to even get into it with Lonny. He pulled a strip of paper from his wallet.

"Hey," I said taking it from him. "A ticket for two on the River Rouge boat tour. Cool. Thanks, man." I was impressed. It was an actual gift. In past years Lonny's gift was something semi-used by him. He had stepped up on this one. "For you and me to go?"

Lonny laughed. "Hey, buddy, I don't come with your birthday gift. Find a chick, or take out your assistant, Christy. I don't know. Think water romance. A sunset. This assures you of dessert with your meal, my man." He was smiling broadly.

I placed it in my wallet, nodding. *Perhaps a tool in my quest to find my better half?*

Jocelyn came to our table and took our orders. I was sticking with my usual hot chicken sandwich with gravy. Lonny ordered a tossed salad. He had abs. I had a tasty lunch.

"Look," he said leaning forward, scanning the street. "We've got to hit the beach soon. This hot spell is supposed to hold all summer. The beach'll be loaded with women. If there's a place for you to find a kitten, it's there. They can't hide anything on the beach. It's all on display. No gel-filled bras, bulky sweaters, cellulite coveralls to keep away the bedroom surprises." Going to the beach was easy for Lonny. He was tanned, fit and seemed natural by the water. I stuck out like a bulging kitchen trash bag. But I agreed to go. I had no choice. If the possibility of meeting women existed, I was obligated. Summers in Winnipeg were hot, sunny and short. Hours became critical.

Lonny pointed to a guy in a snowsuit, the ripped sides revealing his naked ass. Bearded and clearly unwashed, he pushed a grocery store cart carrying neatly stacked packages. "When I see a guy like that," Lonny said, "I don't feel regretful about my own life." I agreed. The homeless guy had a sobering effect on our petty gripes.

"Christy had a crappy date again. Yet another arrogant loser."

Lonny knew a lot of men in this category. I knew he didn't consider himself one. Yes, he was proud of his arrogance. He was definitely far from being a loser. Lonny believed attractive girls like Christy went through a lot of chaff before finding Mr. Right.

"I've said it before and I'll say it again," Lonny boasted. "I'd take a crack at her if it wasn't for the few years' difference in age."

"Say almost twenty years," I corrected. "In my books, that's a generation, Gramps. You'd start using words like *cool* and *hip*, and she'd be gone. Knowing your ego, you'd be crushed the first time one of her friends called you a fossil."

Lonny's face went into a scowl. Apparently, I missed his point; his skill treating women as equals would be a welcome novelty for Christy. I didn't press him any further. Lonny was very protective of his sexuality. He was always quick to defend his position if he thought I was analyzing him. I never did. Nor did he believe me when I told him so.

Our meals arrived, and I attacked mine. I thought age diminished appetite.

I let Lonny talk while I ate. Another golden quality about Lonny I enjoyed was his ability to talk incessantly. All I was required to do was nod at the appropriate times and laugh when needed. He caught me off guard with a question.

"What are you doing tonight?"

I was considering going to the Cinematheque Theatre after supper. Today the new films came out. I had seen the one playing last week twice. I was also interested in meeting the ticket booth girl. She was cute and, I suspected, in her twenties. I had bought my last seven tickets from her. Yet it seemed wrong to change our relationship. I couldn't ask her to see the movie with me. But coffee afterward would be nice. She always greeted me with a smile. If she was interested in me, it might be against company policy for her to ask patrons out. It was my move.

Lonny needed to leave. In twenty minutes he would be in front of twenty-five aerobic-obsessed women at a fitness centre, giving a sales seminar on the advantages of his cell phones. Half of Lonny's sales converted into dates. He left his portion of the bill payment on the table. In typical Lonny fashion, he again scaled the railing. I was alone. I thanked Jocelyn for her service and started back to work.

Christy had nothing new to report when I arrived at the clinic. No sudden appointment had booked. In truth, I could go home, so I did just that. For a change, Christy was hitting the clubs tonight with her girlfriends. She labeled the night "Dinkless in Winnipeg."

I walked into my apartment and relished the coolness. Air-conditioning was a must in the city. I hated nothing more than resembling a sweating farm animal. I checked the *Winnipeg Sun* newspaper. A German movie titled *Bandits* was opening tonight at the Cinematheque: "An all-girl band escapes from prison and become celebrities." It'd have to do, since my evening was otherwise a bust. I flicked on the thirty-two-inch television and fell into my favourite microfiber chair, a beaten-down classic brown recliner that moulded to my body. I had actually started to drift off when the sound of a name from the television jarred me to attention.

U 2 Can Date. I focused on the screen; an attractive brunette female was on the phone to an equally attractive guy. The scene cut to them both enjoying each other's company at a dinner table. Later they laughed together in a hot tub, champagne flutes in hand. "Call now. It's easy to get set up on the System."

The System.

It seemed penal.

It also appeared simple.

And I needed easy. I didn't know what else to do. I was failing miserably in my quest to find my equal. Forty loomed closer while I languished in my chair. Still, the thought of meeting women based solely on a voice and scripted speech was too Russian roulette for me. Never mind throwing two strangers together in the hopes that their dislikes didn't strangle their likes. I wasn't sold.

Instead, I showered and changed into beige khakis and a fern green T-shirt. I had time to stop at the King's Head for a drink before the movie. Both places were less than a block apart. I had long since lost my awkwardness over seeing movies in theatres alone. Eccentric? "No date" was more like it. But tonight I might even work up the balls to ask the ticket girl out.

I called a cab, and by the time I made it downstairs, it was waiting. For six bucks, it beat trying to find parking in the Exchange District.

The drive was short and uneventful. Even though it was early evening, the sun still shone high and bright. Dusk wouldn't begin until ten thirty. I paid the cab fare and closed the yellow door behind me as I stood in front of the King's Head. It was a narrow, two story building with the pub on a raised first level. I entered and climbed the worn red carpet on the single row of wooden stairs. Inside was typical British decor: long, narrow, woodsy, smoky. A brass-and-wood bar stretched along an entire wall like a bunker. The pints were right from the barrel—ale that kicked your ass. Dart boards were on one end, billiards on the other. Steak and kidney pie was served in the middle. And the bartender really did know your name.

The patrons were scattered and few, mostly male. The females reserved their arrival for after dark, in protective groups. I'd be long gone by then.

Maybe that was my problem? My contemplation was interrupted by a voice barking at me.

"Hi, mate!" Robby had been working the kegs for as long as I had been coming. His career was pouring a good head, and he wore the kilt to prove it. "Having a Boddy today?"

I nodded. He never forgot. Here was a lesson for McDonald's.

I braced myself because I knew what was coming next.

"When are you bringing your wife down?"

Robby's little joke. He asked me every time. Asking if I was married was Robby's way of ensuring that I kept my humour. Robby tossed me his favorite Monty Python line anytime I was feeling low about myself; "Always look on the bright side of life."

I continued to joke along because, after all, laughter was all that I had left.

"Ah shucks, Robby, I desperately wanted to, but she's waiting for her sister to come over so that we can have a threesome. It was her suggestion, and it's impolite to say no." Robby found the remark extremely funny, and his face burst into a deep red. What was better were the expressions of two lonely hearts against the bar, who seemed to actually believe what I had just said.

"Robby," I challenged, "Can't you play anything but the Pogues over the speakers?" He looked at me strangely.

"Mate, there isn't any other group worthy of it." We both laughed. He wiped down the counter with a rag.

"Are you walking across for a showing?" Robby called the movies a showing. I mentioned the new release tonight. Robby always became excited by new releases. The after-movie crowd inadvertently ended up downing a few pints there before heading home. I paid for my drink and found a corner spot by the front window. I could see Market Square Park across the street, a narrow half block of green space that was lively during the summer days with musical acts. At night the drunks used it to count stars.

I sipped my beer. Why did I persist in activities such as attending films? Two hours alone in the dark. What was I afraid of? I could only blame myself for being 39 and single. I needed to grow some nuts. Why could Lonny date unfailingly? Because he didn't care about rejection, I realized. An amazing attribute, having the presence of mind to simply not care about a relationship ending.

I sat back in the wooden chair, finishing my beer and watching a middle-aged couple in deep couple talk. Holding hands, drinks between them, both leaned forward with silly, flushed smiles on their faces. A relationship. *Get with the program, Gus.*

I put my empty mug aside. I sauntered through the door.

"No worries, mate!" Robby never let me escape without it.

The air was still warm outside. Not bad for nine o'clock at night. Heading across the grass, I previewed opening scenarios with Ticket Girl. "Make those two tickets." "Do you like butter with your popcorn?" "Can I drive you home after your shift?" "What d'you say we blow this booth and hit the drive-in, baby?" I snickered. Sure, and we'll get in the taxi after she throws herself into my arms. Gay men didn't deal with this cat-and-mouse pain in the ass. Gay men knew what they wanted without the head games. At least, that's the way it appeared to me in the few movies I'd watched.

The cinema was on the second floor. I began the ascent. There she was, under the bright lights inside the booth, preparing a ticket. Her smile said she desired me. She just had to realize it first.

C'mon Gus. C'mon. My heart beat hard. *Don't hand her sweaty money.* Our eyes met. I smiled. She smiled back. I was in.

"Hi!" I spit against the glass.

"Which show?"

"Don't you know?"

Silence

"Ah, *Bandits.*"

"Five dollars."

I handed her a crumpled, sweaty bill.

She handed me a ticket.

I walked away.

Sitting down in the seat, I growled at the screen.

What had happened to my witty remarks? It amazed me I could be poised in front of a married couple, listening to them tell me he chased his wife around wearing Fido's collar, and be so useless in front of another type of stranger.

For the first time since my thirty-ninth birthday, I began to feel fear. Forget getting romantically involved with someone by forty. Conceivably I could reach my Depends-wearing years alone. Jesus. The revelation scared the hell out of my fragile reality.

The smallness of the theatre closed in around me. The screen was distant and vague. The movie passed. I snapped out of my stupor when the credits began rolling.

I felt like I had been punched by a professional boxer. A silent cab ride home followed. I rode the steady elevator up to the fifteenth floor. I stood on the balcony, naked, overlooking a city that was non-existent. A jet roared into the sky. The woman of my dreams could be on that very plane. *Come to me by sea or sky.*

A strong gust of wind made me shiver. It was late, after midnight. Six and a half hours until I stood outside in this exact location observing the morning kiss fifteen stories below me.

I walked back inside, closed the door, crawled into bed. Sleep didn't come for a long time.

3

"Hello, this is Glenda. I'd like to meet a nice man. Somebody who is a nice person. Because I am a nice person ..."

Grey. The world was reflected back to me in a dull, grandmother grey. Morning sunshine that might fool me into thinking my life was a trip to Oz was denied. The sky from my patio door appeared thick with bleak, friendless clouds. My living room was dismal.

If I thought seeing a kiss between my couple would lift my doldrums, I was wrong. They seemed as listless as I was. *The power of the weather,* I observed to myself.

I ducked outside to peer over the balcony for a moment, but that was enough for the drizzle to chill me thoroughly. Another display of the unkind extremes I had discovered in this region—it was stifling hot one day, followed by freezing snot from my nose the next.

I struggled with the idea of calling a cab. My umbrella won out. I walked the stairs, smirking that I was beating the time bandit. A blast of cool, wet air assaulted me when I opened the outside door. Not such a good idea to walk, maybe, but I was committed. The rain swept road dust and car exhaust into my nose so that I choked on it.

Crossing Osborne Street on a rainy morning was always a treat. It reminded me why I chose to walk. For as far as I could see, rows of red brake lights blinked. Traffic was not moving. It never did in the rain, and

I could never understand it. Water didn't equate to hazardous driving in a city. But in Winnipeg it meant panic gridlock. I needled my way between the bumpers of vehicles that jostled for position in the intersection. Each wanted to make it to the other side of the street, but, of course, none could. They tried anyway. Lack of patience became road chaos. A few horns bellowed.

I was relieved to finally close the door to my clinic behind me. Christy was already at her desk, reading a *Glamour* magazine. Unlike me, she wasn't stubborn and drove everywhere. This meant we had a difference of opinion on the rain's coolness. I fired up the coffee machine, listening to chatter about Christy's evening, ironically dateless and fun, just her and the girls. I congratulated her on finding happiness among hairless armpits. Before she could inquire into my heathen evening, I retreated into my office and closed the door.

My first appointment wasn't for an hour, so I had time to kill. The weather had put me in a mood where I simply struggled to breathe. I had yet to open my first subscription edition of *The Art of Psychotherapy* on my desk since it arrived last week. Sorry, it got another pass.

I grabbed *The Village Press*, an underfunded local rag. If anything, it might prove useful for a few entertainment ideas. It turned out to be a bust. Did I care where the latest rave by DJ Nobody was being held? All this changed when I turned the magazine over.

U 2 Can Date.

There it was again, that insidious ad for singles. It was everywhere. I could only afford to advertise in the Yellow Pages. This group found a way to put their stamp on my underwear while I slept.

Call Now.

What did I know about telephone dating? Rumours. Wasn't it a hidden form of prostitution? Did I want my clinic raided by surly policeman? What would the other building tenants think of me then? The headline? LOCAL THERAPIST CAN'T FIND A DATE SO ELICITS DAYTIME PROSTITUTES TO CLINIC FOR SERVICING.

Who would know about this kind of shit?

Lonny would. If there was a sin out there, Lonny craved it. I called his cell phone.

He answered with his usual zestful energy.

"Listen," I began, "I know this is stupid, but I need to satisfy my curiosity. What do you know about phone dating services?"

Lonny apparently knew a lot. He described it as the field where divorced moms were sent out to pasture. If I could ignore three screaming brats while getting it on with Mom, everything would be all right. Basically, it was the final frontier for divorcées void of pride, dressed in fashions from previous decades, with damaged, bleached hair and nothing left to lose. Beaten up and spit out by the marriage-and-baby machine, these women were desperate, a sure lay. Heels to Jesus, pull up your pants and be home by eleven. As an added bonus, it was a cheap date. The women didn't expect a fancy dinner. Forget flowers. Bring a bag of candies for little Billy. Say "Hey, baby," and all the dating prerequisites were met.

"But is it prostitution?"

"Sometimes," he assured me, "it is." But those women were too rehearsed on the phone, he explained. If the message was too brazen, it likely meant the woman had logged a trucker's mile of filthy ear talk. Otherwise, fair game—honest women embittered by love but still in need of a little loving.

I've known Lonny long enough to appreciate his expertise in flying his kite high. Somewhere in his diatribe were fact and a whole lot of fiction. It gave me the direction I needed. I thanked him for his advice. He ended our conversation by suggesting I update my immunizations.

I had to admit the chat with Lonny piqued my curiosity. What if he was right? Would I be any further behind? I had to face a fact. I was beyond desperate.

U 2 CAN DATE.

With surprisingly steady fingers, I dialed. An automated female voice greeted me. Together, we went through the System to get myself set up. All the while I was assured my information was confidential. I was given a box number. I grinned. So far, phone dating was easy.

It was time to search.

After listening to the options I made my selections. Romance. Ages thirty to forty-five. There were 490 women desperately seeking a father for little Billy.

I made my first inquiries.

"Well, hi there. You've reached a girl who's 165 pounds, long red hair and blue eyes. I like to have fun and like all the good things in life. If you think you could be the next guy to make me feel good, I know that I can make you feel really good. So, get back to me."

I hit the three key. *Boring. Pass.* What was she expecting with that sort of sell-job? No wonder her husband left running.

"Hi. I'm Lynda, and I love singing and going to the theatre and movies. I'm open-minded and can talk on any subject. In fact, I usually keep the conversation going. I'm independent and a full spirit. I love my family and friends and hope to meet someone. If my wheelchair doesn't bother you, box me back."

I hung up the phone.

What the hell was I doing? Lonny was correct that this service was a potluck soup of misfits.

I had to give this further thought. These first calls weren't what I had expected to find in romance.

And my Chow had arrived.

Ian and Lucy Chow were in a love-hate relationship. Hired the day after an ill-fated honeymoon, it had been an interesting bundle of months for me as their therapist. If I wasn't prying hands away to open an airway, I was turning my head aside to wait out a tortuously long French kiss. A progress report would show the sessions were failing to make a difference. My models of therapy were sound techniques. Ian Chow was a man who refused to change, a terrific soul mate with one problematic cross to bear. He had wandering eyes. He also had an insanely jealous wife. Petty jealousy, in my assessment, although I would never tell Lucy that, because I enjoyed the act of breathing.

Ian Chow took pleasure in the female form. He enjoyed the swell of nice hips, a well-defined calf, sparkling eyes, cover-girl hair that blew freely in the wind. He simply admired women. Ian never missed an opportunity to satisfy his admiration. If a woman caught his fancy, he would look. It was never followed by a sexist remark. Not even a remark oozing with longing. He took quiet pleasure within himself. A borderline gentleman with a nasty caveat.

Lucy Chow despised her husband's wandering eye. It was an act of betrayal. It royally pissed her off.

I needed to focus on certain facts. This was their twelfth month of marriage. They were both young: twenty-one, to be exact. Young enough to be cocky. Young enough for a lack of tolerance.

When I asked her what bothered her the most when Ian ran his eyes across the beautiful driver in the next car, the jogger in spandex or the pretty, flirtatious checkout girl at the food store, Lucy couldn't decide. We needed to pinpoint her anger.

Likewise, I found Ian evasive when I forced him to admit that he was finding these women more sexy than his own beautiful wife.

I braced myself to leap between them should he answer wrong.

Ian played it safe. I relaxed. He said each time he looked at another woman, it reminded him how lucky he was to have the wife he did. Bada bing. *Atta boy.* I heard this sappy line played in my office like old Beatles 45s. I didn't care. Lucy said it was the most endearing remark he had ever made. I might escape bloodshed. The Chows found occasion to knot tongues while I flicked through a copy of *Dialectical Behavior Therapy—Shout Out The Emotional Instability with Mindfulness Meditation.*

Halfway through the article, tongues back in place, I had their attention back.

"You see, Lucy," I tried to assert, "Ian loves you. He needs your help. It's up to you to remind him it's hurtful at the moment he gazes at another woman.'

"Ian," I declared, "when Lucy points out the pain you are causing her, avert your eyes, apologize and think about how your actions are inappropriate."

We had dished this crap out a dozen times in the past. Both would smile, hold hands, gaze longingly into each other's eyes. They'd swear eternal love. The physical assault afterward from Lucy trying to choke Ian with her hands would be clearly evident at the following session. Ian would arrive wearing a turtleneck in summer.

But therapy was a religion of forging ahead. The Chows were destined to be my patients forever. Or rather, until death would they part from me. Either way, I collected my direct billing.

The Chows had exhausted me, and I made my way to the King's Head in the late afternoon. The thought of climbing fifteen flights of stairs deterred me from stopping at home first. I had the cabbie take me straight to the pub.

Robby's banter and greeting didn't disappoint. He nodded opposite the bar. I caught the eyes of serious intrigue. She was alone. She was sipping at a pint. She smiled.

I sauntered her way.

"How's the Boddington tasting tonight?" It was innocent and it worked.

"Fine," she replied after a sultry sip. "Either you own this place or you come here too often." I wasn't sure of her angle. My confusion must have shown on my face. She explained: Robby poured my pint without asking what I wanted. Her power of observation excited me. This was a helluva girl. I pegged her at a young-looking thirty-two. Her brown hair was nicely pulled back. Her loose-fitting top couldn't hide fulfilling curves. I wanted more.

Leaning up against the empty chair across from her, I pushed on.

"Robby has a photographic memory. I was last here seven years ago." We both laughed. She understood my humour. I knew I was in love.

"I'm Gus." I held out my cold hand, wet from clutching the frosty pint.

"Jasmine." We shook. Her fingers were so soft.

"Just getting off work?" I had learned a few openers from Lonny.

She nodded and explained she worked as a motor vehicles clerk over at the Law Court building down the block from the King's Head. She came here often with the girls for lunch. The fish and chips were her favourite. I pictured how a diamond would look on her finger. I judged a size-five fit. Jasmine stated she normally wouldn't have come to the King's Head in the evening were it not for the cancellation of the intramural volleyball team she taught at a school. Fit and giving back to the community—where had she been all my life? I craved to learn more. My dedication to be custodian of the daily balcony kiss was now paying back dividends. Before me was my just reward.

I leaned forward, confident with my new friend. Long-lost lovers reunited after being separated by the sea.

I explained I came after work to unwind and people watch. Jasmine seemed genuinely interested. She even asked if I had noticed an increase in neurotic pub people. She made me laugh. I could enjoy her making me laugh for the remainder of my life.

I mentally stimulated Jasmine. She understood the person I was inside. Having an ear to bend for a change was refreshing. I used my spotlight to its fullest, signaling to Robby to bring another round. Conversation and beer were flowing briskly. I believed I was entering the intimate zone with Jasmine. She held reservations about marriage. Her aunt and uncle were divorced. I agreed. It wasn't always the means to an end.

I had made myself comfortable in the empty chair, mercilessly drawn in by her sapphire eyes. I had to meet her parents. I needed to shake hands with those masters of immaculate creation. Their daughter could define beauty.

I felt guilty that Christy would be a widowed single after tonight. She'd be understanding. Her tenacity would prevail, and a man would fall to her graces. The four of us would share Sunday dinners, laughing, watching Canadian football on CBC. Our children would grow up and play together, bonding into lifelong friends.

Jasmine's body expanded before me into a rising pharaoh I pledged to worship till my demise. She didn't have to vocalize the reciprocal feelings she had directed at me. I just knew it.

It was time to consummate beginning our existence together.

Her eyes lit up. A sea of red flushed her skin. The beauty of her lips parted fully. She spoke.

"Jake!"

I stammered. She had forgotten my name. Understandable. We had only just met. What was a name anyway? I forged ahead. Love drove my appetite.

"Jake! Come here, you crazy gorilla." Her arms parted. I leaned forward, ready to be accepted. I had already been graciously bestowed with a pet name. I was the gorilla. King of the Savannas.

The smell of auto grease cut through my smoky nostrils. Our table was violently jolted; my beer spilled.

"Jaz! There's my sexy girl." I matched grease with the coveralls. I matched the white nametag Jake with the coveralls. I matched the guy in the coveralls as the gorilla in Jasmine's life. Game. Set. Match. My wick was extinguished. I was beaten by a twenty-minutes-or-less oil-change guy. I watched Jake steal my future with a sobering hug.

"Jake," pointed Jasmine, "meet Gus. He works as a psychotherapist down in the Village. We should get Cindy and Danny to see him." Her eyebrows crinkled seductively. I didn't want to see Cindy and Danny. Let them get a divorce. Divorce was no-contest nowadays and a helluva lot cheaper than my fees. I wanted to express the twisted anguish that was swirling inside my body, let her know her choice behind door number three was Jake the booby prize. Together, our children would carry on her sapphire eyes and not stained fingernails.

"Nice to meet you," I said, extending my hand and my best bullshit smile. A hundred years earlier I would have taken him outside to let the fastest draw decide who rightfully earned Jasmine's love.

"Hey." His muscled grip was strong from cracking open thousands of 10-W30 oil cans.

I offered to buy Jake a beer. He refused. He hated beer without the fizz to make him belch. They were going to 8 Traxx, a techno nightclub two blocks over, where his bubbly beer would be served by women in heavily logoed swimsuits. A place where a guy like Jake blended in with the rest of blue-collar, pickup-driving simpletons.

Jasmine shook my hand. Her touch was electric. I thanked her for putting up with my banter. Perhaps we would cross tables again? I watched them leave. I was hoping to sniff one last, lingering scent of Jasmine's perfume. Sadly, Jake had cleansed the area with his grease-stained coveralls. A true warrior he was.

It was getting late. The pub had filled with couples and other lonely men. I felt depressed. Robby bade me a good night as I slunk out the door into the dusk-filled street. A horn blared. A small rush of cars passed. I had forgotten to call a cab. A walk suddenly seemed the proper choice. It would take me forty-five minutes, tragically elongated by the discouraged state that now saturated me. The walk was my penance. I was nothing more than an insignificant speck of insolence in a world that didn't give a shit.

4

"Are you sick of head games? Because I know I am ..."

I arrived at the clinic well before Christy. Sleep had been evasive. Instead, I heard Jasmine's cries of ecstasy, propelled by Jake the Gorilla. Christy left a message that she was running late. It was just as well. At this point, time alone was irrelevant to my self-respect.

I sat in my chair and closed my eyes, listening to Steely Dan and thought that should I reach forty still single, I would have at least tried to date. There was some level of self-respect that remained for a guy who tried. And with that wish reverberating inside my head, I picked up the phone and dialed. "I can date too," I declared.

A few System choices later, the first female voice slinked toward my ear. I held my breath. This was as profound as a baby's first steps. After all, any one of these voices could be my future wife whispering good morning to me in bed for the next fifty years.

A giggle. "Yeah, okay, Box 13339. I'm a very beautiful thirty-one-year-old female with a voluptuous build, which definitely does not mean porker. Ah; I'm in school to be a nurse. I'll be finished this year, so I'll have a good career ahead of me. I have many interests and hobbies. I enjoy playing guitar and reading a lot. I enjoy the great outdoors, love fishing and I am also a master angler and hope to find someone who's also interested in the same activities. I stand five foot six. I have strawberry blonde hair;

brown eyes and a couple of tattoos. I'm looking for an individual who has the capacity to carry on an intellectual conversation and who's not afraid of an assertive female. And by that I mean a woman who's able to give affection and receive love. I'm looking for a gentleman who knows the meaning of romance and who's capable of it. I'm also looking for a lot more qualities, so if you're interested and this sounds good to you, please leave me a message."

I searched my feelings. Was this her? Did I hear my soul mate described? Could I forgive her for the repetitious silliness of casting a glimmering hook into a billion-gallon pool of water, hoping to outsmart a prehistoric, moronic fish? Would her tattoos give me hours of viewing pleasure each night as she undressed before me? And did "assertive" mean an arm wrestle over who takes out the trash? This voluptuous non-porker deserved a pass. I saw an uncertain future with a competitive, must-win overachiever.

I hit button three.

"Hello, gentlemen." I heard a controlled, even voice. I was impressed by her introduction. Here was a woman who took this game seriously. That was worth points.

"I am an attached female, twenty-nine years old. I am five foot tall, with long, curly red hair. I am seeking an attractive, tall gentleman for an absolutely no-strings-attached encounter or two. Ah, I'm very open-minded and outgoing and hope I'm a lot of fun. At any rate, if you're interested in finding out more about me and what I'm looking for, leave me a message."

Succinct, yet I was intrigued. Not by who she claimed to be, since I knew nothing of her, but by her actions. Attached and looking for a discreet encounter? I was stunned. Who was the poor son of bitch watching hockey at home while his flamboyant wife preyed on tall gentlemen? That took balls. She was actively soliciting an affair. I'm sorry, but the need to delve more into this woman's mind was overpowering. I pressed nine.

"Hi, I'm Gus. I just heard your message and would like to meet." I left her my box number. I realized what I had just done. My head spun. I was arranging to see a married woman. I tried to rationalize. This was more of a clinical experiment than a true date. There was no future here. I felt somewhat more comfortable after my feeble justification. More importantly, I had made a move to change my destiny. I was making an attempt to date.

Christy looked like shit when she clambered into the office. Her hair was hurriedly put together with pins. Her normally smartly crafted makeup was sparse. Even her skirt was creased.

I grinned. "Did a rich playboy just drop you off at the airport on the way back from Cancun?"

"Scratch anybody with the name Rod from the date list," she shot back.

"Doesn't it rhyme with *bod*?" I asked, eyebrows rising.

"No. It's more like 'oh my god, what a jerk you are, Rod.'"

"Oh?"

"He promised me a night out of the town."

"And?"

"He meant a night *out* of the town. Literally. He drove us to Gimli in his RX7."

"That's nearly two hours straight north."

"You don't have to tell me!"

"What's out there?"

"Nothing that I want a part of ever again."

"Gimli's quaint. What could possibly be bad in a town of Icelandics?'

"Besides trying to have a romantic dinner at the Viking Bar? Bad start."

"Sure."

"Rod getting drunk before our meal was complete."

"You mean tipsy ha ha-type drunk?"

"No. I mean sourly pissed. Hammered. Whoops, I fell out of my chair again."

"Interesting."

"I could have done without the front row seat for watching him puke into his soup bowl."

"The smell of vomit dulls the romance, doesn't it?"

"Followed by being asked to leave by the management."

"Icelandics have a narrow sense of humour."

"I guess I was flustered by all the bullshit and wasn't thinking when we got back in the RX7. Rod started driving and fatally wounded a mailbox."

"They tend to jump out in front of you at the most inopportune times."

"The RCMP pulled us over. Actually, Rod struck the back of a parked truck first. It wasn't much of a chase. We were a block away from the bar."

"Too bad. Television is always looking for the next great dangerous pursuit. You could have been famous. The Gimli Viking Mailbox RoadKillers strike again!"

"You try handcuffs, buddy. Look at the bruises on my wrist."

"I guess it's only fun in the bedroom."

"I was so humiliated sitting in the police station. They charged Rod with drunk driving, dangerous driving. And, oh yeah, he already had a suspended license."

"Jail time?"

"Yup."

"Where did that leave you?"

"With no ride back to the city. His car was impounded. What was left of it. It took me hours to convince a turkey farmer to let me ride with him. Smelled like shit inside the cab of his truck."

"Did you have to perform tricks?"

"Shut up."

"Just asking."

"He dropped me off outside your clinic. The turkey farmer was adamant he needed his morning coffee and nip from the Salisbury House outside Winnipeg first. I endured another hour in a room full of stale cigarette smoke drinking sour coffee."

"Where's the decency?'

Christy wiped at a lipstick clump in the corner of her mouth.

"I dunno, Gus. Now I'm risking my life trying to date."

I stood up from my desk to look out the window at passing feet.

"Who am I seeing today, Christy?'

"I believe you have no appointments."

"Then I think I'm going to book the day off. I might saunter over to Assiniboine Park and reflect."

"Are you in a soul-searching frame of mind?"

I nodded. "Put it down to a bad experience with a gorilla last night. Don't ask. Don't want to talk about it. I need my space today."

Christy's face crunched in a look of dumbfounded curiosity that I was not about to quench.

I left the clinic and started ambling down River Avenue. With all the walking I did my thighs were nicely ripped. I admired my legs in shorts as reflected in the window of a shop. The leanness stopped at my hips. From my scrotum up was a mess of rolling tsunami flesh and coarse hair.

It was a bit of a jaunt to Assiniboine Park but a distance worth the effort. The park was the city's largest, with miles of paved walking trails and acres of open green spaces. The rest of the area was surrounded by mature trees and wildlife. I loved it. So did hundreds of other lost souls, families, single women and dogs. It was a great place to let loose with a Frisbee. All I wanted was a place to sit my sorry ass down, to admire the tufts of clouds floating past and to people watch.

I positioned myself in the middle of the largest patch of grass. From my vantage point I could laugh at the rollerblading people struggling past. Families with children barbecued hot dogs in fire pits. A couple of guys tossed a ball. Lots of people were just walking, enjoying the heat of summer. A park loaded with people in the middle of the day in the middle of the week as though it were a weekend was typical in Winnipeg.

It only took a few hours under the ozone-depleted sun to feel the urge to leave. Suddenly a pint at the Crackling Crow back in the Village made perfect sense. I began the long walk back.

By the time I reached the English pub, I was famished and thirsty. They made the best steak and kidney pie anywhere. I stood by the bar to place my order. More importantly, a Boddingtons was top priority. I waited. I was ignored. The bartender stood at the other end of the bar wiping out a mug.

"Hey," I called out. He looked me squarely in the eyes and turned away. He returned to wiping the mug.

"Hey," I tried again. Louder. He bent below the bar and began tapping against the kegs.

"Hey, when you quit pretending to play the steel drums, I'd like to place an order." I was loud enough that a couple of women on the far back of the room turned around. I waved. What did they care? They had their beers. The bartender stood up and opened the cash register. He took out a stack of bills and began counting. Slowly. Infuriated, I circled the bar until I stood directly in front of him. I was within an arm's reach, ready to grab his black shirt and shake. I took a deep breath. I was in a zone impossible to ignore.

"Hi, I'd like to place an order, please." Polite. Fresh. I even managed a smile.

He walked across and took an order from a redhead who had just arrived. I was officially snubbed.

"*Hey!*" I slapped my hand against the wood counter. The redhead looked at me as if I were crazy. I wanted service. It worked. I got the bartender's attention. He twisted around and barked.

"Wait yer turn, mate." He continued taking Red's order.

Wait my turn? I had been circling the bar like a buzzard on wounded prey. There was no turn to wait.

"I was waiting long before she got here," I heard myself shout across to him. Several more people began to take notice of my duel.

"The beer ain't going nowhere," he grumbled over his shoulder. "The lady's been waiting a fortnight."

What the hell did that mean? I began to fear my patients' psychoses had rubbed off on me. Was this really happening or was I hallucinating? Was I experiencing a persecutory delusion? I felt like I should recite serial 7's back to myself. I would give this *Twilight Zone* episode one more attempt.

"Excuse me, sir, I've been signaling you for fifteen minutes. No one else has been near the bar. Red only just arrived. Meanwhile, you've been fingertapping the kegs, teaching yourself to count money and wiping the tabletop that already has more gleam than my porcelain toilet bowl. I don't want to get to know you. In fact, I won't even approach you again after this order. All I want is a pint of Boddingtons and a steak and kidney pie. So what'd ya say, huh?" Apparently, he had nothing to say. He handed Red her glass of wine, wiped his hands on a towel and walked straight out from behind the bar toward a set of doors leading to the basement kitchen. He never came back. I stood alone by the bar. Red smirked and took her wine with her to a secluded corner to read a book. *Kiss my ass.* Beyond being incredulous at what had just happened, I was also pissed off. I went behind the bar and poured myself a pint. I pulled a crumpled five-dollar bill out of my pocket. Not satisfied, I mashed it, further abusing the innocent bill.

I had lost my mood for a beer. I finished half and left. The bartender never did return. Maybe I was overly intolerant about my wait; I watched three other patrons patiently stand against the bar to place an order that would never happen. Surprisingly, not one of them slammed a hand against the bar in a murderous fit of alcoholic need.

I left the pub hungry and frustrated, desperate to get to my apartment and lock out the world's insanity.

The walk did nothing to dull my indignation. Snubbed by a bartender. Laughed at by a redheaded Merlot drinker in a British pub. My alienation would be short-lived. I had a response in my U 2 Can Date message box. In fact, I had a date with Destiny in two evenings at Saffron's Restaurant on Corydon Avenue, a very trendy hangout for girls with very trendy names. Destiny. She apparently didn't consider her wedding vows to her husband to be her own destiny.

I fell back into my La-Z-Boy. I had a date. The word rang foreign inside my head. Was it a first step on a long road? I had to be honest with myself. I wanted the farmer's shortcut. Patience. Perhaps that bartender at the Crackling Crow was correct in his assessment of me. I had to wait my turn. Was I really like that? I waved it off. I ran a more important checklist through my head: clothing. I'd missed my womanly calling when my egg was being fertilized. I was obsessed with buying clothes. Many still had the sales tag still attached.

Restless, I hopped out of my chair. Inside my bedroom was a double walk-in closet. Except my closet couldn't be walked into. When the three walls became compressed with hangers of clothes, I began piles on the shelves. When I couldn't squeeze any more clothes between the shelves and ceiling, I went to JYSK and purchased a few closet organizers. I constructed three units that could stack, hang and fold. I filled those. Finally I had the doors taken off. It was a real bitch if I wanted something from the back. That's why clothes commandeered both hall closets. Tomorrow I would buy more clothes. The beauty of fashion was that it was in continual motion. I made no excuses about why I wore the same two pairs of Dockers to work each week. Or rotated the same five shirts. It was a comfort thing.

I left the bedroom and grabbed the phone. I dialed U 2 Can Date and found Destiny's voicemail box. I left a return message confirming our date at Saffron's. I failed to hide the excitement in my voice. Tough. It was a relief to be finally doing something about my rapidly approaching fortieth birthday.

5

"Hi, this is box 3222. I'm forty-one years old, but people think I'm in my early thirties …"

I was up early and on the balcony, waiting with a coffee that was rapidly growing cold, when my couple pulled up fifteen floors below. I gazed down lovingly as they chatted inside the car. I couldn't see their expressions. They led me along their conversation with hand movements. I let my breath release slowly, watching, feeling the kiss between them. It was beautiful. I surprised myself when a moan emitted from my throat. Satisfied, I began my day.

I bounded into my clinic, startling Christy with my vigor. She asked me if I had taken up drug use. I smiled. Did I get laid last night? I laughed.

Christy smelled an exposé and cornered me against my desk. I broke down. I explained what I had been doing over the phone. Dial a bride. I could see Christy was shocked by my brazen approach. She bit her tongue. She lost control when I mentioned my liaison with a married woman. Two hundred thousand single women within a thirty-mile radius, and I was starting with an attached female. Christy was still too pure to realize my utter desperation. A caged animal was irrational. I wanted out.

We had to cut our discussion short. Peter and Alabama Daube had just arrived for their session with me. It was time to get to work.

I waved for them to come into my office and closed the door. This was our second session. Our first had ended abruptly when Peter's appendix burst in my office. He had nearly died from the rush of toxic fluids. However, time heals all wounds. Four months had passed, and the Daubes were determined to get their counselling. Rather, Alabama was the driving force. She had been clear about one thing. In her words, "If this goddamn thing didn't work, I am divorcing Peter." And it wouldn't be a hugs-and-kisses divorce. Her intentions would be to rape and pillage him to the end. I sensed the importance of my therapeutic role.

Peter and Alabama Daube dressed as though they couldn't afford therapy. The reality was they couldn't. Peter was a gambler. Make no mistake, his vice wasn't counting cards inside a casino. His mathematical skills were frighteningly simplistic. Figuring out how much he owed the gas station attendant became a stressful event. Peter gambled on a level far lower than most: lotto draws, bingo, fifty-fifty tickets. If it could be torn, stamped or computer picked it suited Peter's fancy just fine. Peter spent a great deal of money. In turn, Alabama was humiliated into wearing thrift clothing. She did her own hair. It showed. Wispy and severely over-coloured, it was damaged and stuck out in all directions. It did nothing to complement a tired face with wrinkles and dark circles. Unsuccessfully, she applied an obscene amount of makeup in bright colours, hoping to blind those who gazed her way. What little she made as a cashier at an A&W Restaurant went toward her discount cosmetics. The Daubes were in their mid-forties and, as unwilling as they were to accept it, the truth was their life was never going to improve. Again, it was not my place to highlight this reality. Without hope there was no future, right?

Meanwhile, Peter continued to be a loose cannon with the family income. Even after twenty-four years as a linesman for the CN Railway, Peter's accumulated fortune was $38,000 of credit debt. Where they found the money for my service astounded me. That aside, I accepted the couple with open arms. I insisted on cash payment.

Peter's compulsion to gamble was in dire need of being controlled. And if I couldn't be the road to that outcome, Alabama would be running off with the next customer ordering a Papa Burger with fries. I became focused.

They took their seats as I studied Peter.

"Feeling better after the operation, Peter? You're looking good. I see the ashen skin colour last time you were here has left." My attempt at humour released the tension in the air. I continued.

"Let's see if we can start to get an understanding about your addiction, Peter. It will help me and Alabama see what we can do differently for you."

"All I want is for him to stop spending the goddamn money on those ridiculous games," growled Alabama. She was already upset.

I proceeded with extra caution.

"I should sue the goddamn government for promoting it. Don't they see how it's ruining our lives?" Her hands gripped the chair.

I held up my hand. I gave the sermons here.

"Alabama, pointing fingers won't stop Peter the next time he's inside a convenience store waiting to pay for his soft drink next to a Sports Select stand. We all know he'd put the drink down and use the money to place a bet. A losing one. No," I continued, leaning back in my chair, "we have got to take away Pavlov's association from Peter." They both looked back at me as if I were the one with the problem. Skeptics. My determination grew stronger from their disbelief in me. A defeat in my career would not come from a cap-wearing lotto loser.

I pulled out my magic wand.

Alabama sunk lower into her chair. She seemed unconvinced. Peter's eyes grew wide with longing. In my hand I held a brand-new pull ticket. I may have been sitting four feet from Peter, but I could see the sweat glimmer on his forehead. I had cast my lure. *Now bite hard, you bastard.*

"What's that for?" Alabama remained uncertain in the face of my creativity. She knew her burgers. I knew my therapy.

"Peter must learn to suppress his obsession. He is visually stimulated by certain objects associated with gambling, Alabama. This pull ticket happens to be one of those associations. What are you feeling right now, Peter?" My hand held steady.

He licked his lips. His right hand stroked the armchair. He fidgeted in his seat. I knew he wanted to caress this ticket.

"Well," he struggled, "it hasn't been opened yet. I can hear the gentle tear of paper giving way. I can picture a matching number inside. I feel excited about this. My head is dizzy. I feel funny down below." He wanted to reach for it. I pulled back. He groaned.

"Oh for god's sake," muttered Alabama. I ignored her.

"Peter, this ticket doesn't exist."

He looked confused.

"But it's right there in your hand. Please let me touch it. Just once."

I shook my head.

"It really doesn't exist." I pulled a lighter from my pants and held a flame under the ticket. The ink caught, igniting in an intense flame. I tossed it on the table, where it quickly became smoking ash. Peter looked devastated. Alabama looked bored.

"This is what I mean, Peter. Nothing changed in your life from when I had the ticket in my hand moments ago until it became smoldering ash on the table. Everything about you has remained the same. What I'm trying to say is touching or not touching the ticket isn't necessary for you to feel better." I couldn't tell if he heard me. His watering eyes hadn't left the blackened ticket. Did fat people look at dessert this way? I brushed the embers into a trashcan. Peter looked at me with hurt eyes.

I explained my goal was to wean away the urges he felt to touch tickets. It would be unpleasant. More tickets would have to be set afire.

"Gus, I'm paying you to help my husband, not to watch you burn paper. Do you think that helped Peter? See the expression on his face? The bastard's about to cry. What did we accomplish today?" She sat forward in attack mode.

I wasn't about to be outmaneuvered.

"My method will start to make sense soon when it all comes together. Right now we have a lot of pieces spread out before us."

"Cut the crap," she insisted. "I already told you if this quest for fire doesn't work, Peter's getting served with divorce papers. My marriage is at stake here." I attempted to calm her down by saying I needed time and her support. I almost broke my rule and promised she'd see results in a few weeks. Hell, I might turn Peter into an arsonist before I was through. I couldn't give guarantees. First rule in counselling is know when to fold them. I ended our session for the day.

6

"I'm looking for a professionally employed, single man between the ages of thirty and forty to do stuff with and hang out ..."

The phone was ringing. I was already on one line. Christy was on her line. The morning had long exceeded chaos. My second pot of coffee was half finished. It was accelerating from being a terrible day to an absolutely shitty day at just past noon. I swore under my breath. The ring was distracting my conversation with an hysterical patient. Her husband never returned from a stag party last night, which was his third stag party in two weeks. She still didn't get it. I tried to signal Christy to answer the ringing phone. She was studying her nails, deep into her own phone conversation. The caffeine had agitated me further. As if I needed to be more wound up. I was seven hours away from my date with Destiny. And the office air-conditioning was down and out. I was contending with massive underarm sweat stains on my Egyptian cotton shirt.

"Christy!" I barked, covering the phone with my hand. She fluttered her hand at me. I took it to mean her conversation was too important to leave to answer the goddamn phone.

I listened to my patient with waning tolerance. She was sobbing now. I wanted to scream, "You'll find your husband under soiled sheets at the cheapest hotel. He'll be the guy being violated by two artificial blonde sleaze bags." I gripped the phone tightly in my hand. After fifty rings, who doesn't hang up? The putz calling my office, obviously. Christy showed no sign of doing her job. I was left to suffer.

My patient babbled. What did she want me to do? If her husband wanted to be home with her, he'd be there. He didn't check with me about his agenda. Between her heaves I could decipher that she'd found his wedding ring hidden under his shaving kit. It still wasn't coming together for her. Could she follow a recipe? I made a mental note not to accept baked goods from her in the future.

Blissfully, the third line stopped ringing. I could almost deal with the discussion in the ensuing silence. The ringing returned. Enough. I cut the conversation short.

Slamming down the phone I raved, "Who's so important that you can't do your job?" I charged at Christy. She hung up. I was in a foul mood, and she was the unlucky recipient. Her face contorted. She looked at me and buried her head in her hands. Pity wasn't in my vocabulary today.

"Sorry. Sorry." She kept her head buried.

"I've got ranting Bev Costello pleading for me to tell her where her husband is right now. Meanwhile the office line is going nuts. Remember, you have a button called hold. Use it." I felt mean and enjoyed it. I stood over her. These were the times when employees hated their bosses.

"Gus, it was Rod on the phone. He wouldn't let me go."

I was confused. "Rod? Which patient is he?"

She spoke through her hands. "Rod, my romantic date in Gimli. You know, the jerk who got arrested."

"Why are you wasting time with him? He's an asshole." My eyes bored through her fingers.

"I'm not. He's history. At least to me he is. He's still in jail. In Gimli. He was begging for my forgiveness."

"That's the power of sobriety. It brings forward reason."

"Actually, he's asking to borrow my car. They're letting him out tomorrow. He needs to get around until his insurance pays."

I scoffed. "He was drunk!" I bellowed. "It voids his insurance."

"He drives for Meals on Wheels. He needs a car."

"Tell him to buy a pair of Nikes and learn to run fast. Don't even consider lending him your car, for Christ's sake."

Finally she looked at me.

"I told him I couldn't and hung up. Sorry again for missing the phone call."

I slumped, tired. I softened. My rage was diminishing. I waved her off.

"What's going on, Gus?" she called out to me as I was walking to the coffee machine.

"Nothing."

"You've been in your office all morning keeping to yourself. It's not exactly the exhilaration of someone who's going on a date tonight."

I poured too much sugar in my cup. "Shit." I dumped the contents out and tried again.

"See. Agitated. Unfocused. Bad sleep?"

"They didn't kiss this morning," I confessed, talking to the wall. It took her a moment to realize I was referring to my car couple.

"Really?" She was surprised; it had never happened before.

I nodded. I took a sip. Our eyes met.

"He tried but got her cheek as she was trying to escape. It rattled me."

Her eyes searched my face. She probably saw my fear. It was a bad omen.

"So that's what has gotten you all cranky?"

Sure it was. Why today? Why never before? I knew the answer. Because I had my first real date since I began seeing them kiss. They'd cursed me. I was screwed. The first call I nearly made this morning was to Destiny to say, "Forget it. It's off. They didn't kiss. We can't do this." Christy didn't help.

"I wonder if this means her husband will discover the affair? Maybe he'll come after you."

Holy Jesus. I hadn't thought of that. It would officially be an affair. I tasted bile. My coffee soured in my mouth, and I poured it out.

"Do you think that's it?" I froze, waiting for her answer. She just shrugged. What did her shrug mean? My palms were wet. I felt cold. It was a warning.

"Relax, Gus. Obviously she is skilled enough at affairs for her husband not to know."

I didn't what to be the guy to end her streak.

"Go see her. Don't have sex with her. Talk. Nothing wrong with that. You'll live to see tomorrow. Promise."

I felt somewhat relieved. I would go. But it only eased my anxiety slightly. Christy smiled at me. I went back into my office. My phone rang.

"Hey, Mr. Adams. You haven't paid your phone sex charges. You owe us double for calling our underage category. Pay up or we go to the police."

He momentarily had me. I was still shaken.

"You're a piece of work, Lonny." He continued to laugh at his joke while I explained that I was seeing a girl tonight on Corydon.

Lonny dove right in. "Listen carefully and take notes, Fabio," he urged. I leaned back in my chair. It was the Lonny Show. "Do you have a pen?" I lied and said yes.

"Okay, things have changed. Whatever you did with a chick last century, drop it. Lose it. Do you like to be laughed at?" There was no chance to answer. "The scene has become an amazing place." I assumed Lonny was referring to dating as *the scene.*

"Gus, the women of our time have evolved. They no longer want to be chased. Know why? Because they want one of two things. They want sex. Or they want commitment. There are no other options. And when they want either of these two choices, they don't want to wait. Listen up. *They will tell you.* No more guessing. You won't go broke buying expensive flowers and dinners by candlelight. They will grab you by the nuts and tell you to your face."

I was in awe. I'd had no idea.

"Ground rules. Gus, let the girl talk. She'll spout enough fluff to stuff a million pillows. Don't say much. She won't know jack about you. But she'll always get the specs she needs. Nothing more. Frankly, she couldn't give a shit. Hey, guys aren't the only callous ones in relationships. So just nod. Smile. Grunt. Laugh at anything. And for the love of God, always agree. Always. Always. Bloody always. She's not looking to debate her views. Remember, she isn't one of the guys. Agree, and she'll tell her friends you're the most sensitive guy around with a whole lot of integrity."

I broke into the conversation, suddenly wishing I had been writing this down. It was serious stuff.

"What about kissing her? Do I kiss when we introduce?" I heard choking sounds where Lonny's voice should have been.

"Gus, think about what you're saying. She doesn't even know if you brush your teeth yet. Why would she want to kiss? *Do not kiss.* Not at the beginning. Not when you're wishing her an awkward good night. When she's ready, and I stress the word *she*, you'll be deprived of air."

"What could I talk about?" I snuck in the question. I was beginning to have my doubts.

Lonny's laugh was a sharp bark. "I can tell you what *not* to discuss. Your mother. It's taboo. Never mention her. If you have a picture of her in your wallet, take it out. Flash that while you're trying to impress her with your platinum Visa and you're dead."

Mom was gone. Where was the compassion?

"If she does actually ask you a personal question, answer it with a sob story of some personal woe you suffered. Make one up if you have to. But make it heart-wrenching. You know, your grandfather died in your arms right after you told him your lifelong wish was to be just like him. They eat shit like that up. Believe me."

"I get it, Lonny. But let's suppose she decides to get romantic."

He cut me off. I should have known better.

"I was getting there, pal. Hold it in your pants. It'll happen. Look for the cues. Get in close so that you can see her pupils. She'll think you're being sweet. What you're really doing is reading her eyes. If you see her pupils dilate, she's hot for you. She's ready. But remember, this ties in with the shoes she's wearing. If she meets you in high heels with an open toe, she's come for business, my man. Hope you showered that night."

I was astounded. Where did Lonny get this material? I didn't know if I should be impressed by Lonny's powers of observation or scared. He took this way too scientifically. But I had nothing else to go on.

"And listen, Gus, don't be a nice guy." Lonny had to hang up abruptly. He didn't have a chance to explain his remark. I was left with an earful of cellular static and a head full of wild images. If this was the way things had become, why was divorce so common? Who the hell would want to reapply for this crap a second time? Or a third? I whistled.

The surreal wait was ending. I couldn't postpone my encounter with Destiny any longer. During my walk to Corydon Avenue on a beautiful sunny evening, for the first time I began to wonder what she looked like. Not that I was picturing how our wedding photos would look. Call it general intrigue. I decided to stop attempting to formulate an image. I would be wrong anyway.

I listened to my worsted wool suit pants rub together, loving the sound. It gave me confidence. I stood in front of Saffron's. The outdoor patio wrapped around the front and right side of the small building. Cars travelled bumper to bumper along Corydon. Harleys roared past. It was the strip, the place to be seen, the place to be. Dress up and dine out. Patios were sprinkled for blocks both ways. There was only one patio of concern to me.

I was early, and already every table was taken. I stood to the side and scanned the faces. *Is she here?* I felt foolish and exposed. I neared the end of the patio and began to turn away. A hand went up. I focused in. She waved, beckoning to me. Two things immediately struck me as I got closer. One, she looked young. Two, she was absolutely beautiful: tanned; brown, vibrant hair that danced around her face; white, gorgeous teeth; a wide smile. Her body was defined by her spandex halter-top. My eyes fixed on hers. She stood, and we shook hands. Her grip was firm. I broke Lonny's rule and spoke about myself.

"I have to be honest with you, Destiny. This is the first time I've tried a phone dating service. You get to be my guinea pig." She looked me over carefully before smiling. I felt overdressed in a $300 tie next to a girl in her twenties wearing Lululemon running tights.

"No prob, Gus." Her smile shined. "A lot of men do this sort of thing after the divorce. Totally." She gulped at her drink. It was a clear liquid. I couldn't tell what it was. Maybe Kool Aid? The waitress came, and I ordered a scotch.

It occurred to me what Destiny was referring to. I explained I was never married. She pointed at my clothes. Divorced men dressed in suits. She said she felt comfortable with the scene. Apparently, she was okay with my denial about being divorced. A waitress took my order, and Destiny took over the conversation. She was married. Two years. Great husband who was a long-haul truck driver. He spent three weeks each month driving. She said she was often manic because she was bipolar and was sloppy taking her meds giving her too much energy to sit at home while he was on the road. She taught aerobics four times a week and worked out five. She lived for summers at the beach jet skiing and partying. Cracking up, she reported she shopped the rest of time. Her chest bounced when she laughed. My eyes followed. I explained my work as a psychotherapist. She listened and gulped more of her drink. I leaned closer. Her eyes were a glittering green. I didn't see dilated pupils. I sat back and looked down. Reeboks.

"I wanted to call you," she said, brushing back her hair. "My entire day got totally screwed. There wasn't time for me to change after my workout. I thought we should cancel. My husband called because he cut his run short. Instead of arriving back here tomorrow night, he'll be in the city in a couple of hours. Screwed everything up." She heaved back more of her drink. It was a big glass. She definitely wasn't intimidated by it. I grew

44

more awkward each time she mentioned her husband. I felt him sitting at our table.

"Destiny." I looked around for the waitress, wondering where the hell my drink was. "You said in your ad 'discreet encounters' are your thing."

She nodded her head vigorously. She had boundless energy. She responded by saying the System gave her access to filling a gap in her life. Nothing more. She loved her husband totally. His job was his life, not hers. She giggled.

Her gaze skirted past me. "You're much older than my husband. I usually see younger men. I totally find it helps their performance." I think I knew where she was coming from. It was her young way of saying, "Wrong dance, pops." I contemplated saying I drove a five-litre rag top Mustang. My seventeen-year-old mustard-coloured Subaru Outback was sitting underground, unused, rusting and would do nothing for igniting Destiny's opinion of me. Forget pupils. She was busy studying the Generation X crowd around us. I asked her if she'd been to any concerts lately. Concerts were out, she explained, killing the remainder of her drink. Raves were the total goodies. She went to them when her husband was out of town. She and her friends would get high on ecstasy. She loved to dance. On the drug, she could dance all night. She'd come home at noon the following morning totally exhausted. I had no idea what a rave was. Nor did I dare ask. I took Lonny's advice and nodded my head like I knew. "Yeah, that ecstasy puts on the dancing mood," I agreed with her. She finally looked at me. Her fingers fiddled with her empty glass.

"I can't find our waitress. Why do they only hire two people to look after the entire place?"

I knew what she meant. My drink still hadn't arrived. I could feel my throat in a vice grip. I could use the shot.

"I hate waiting," she whined. She sat up in her chair. Her brow knotted together appealingly. "I'm sorry to cut our evening short. Like I said, I wanted to call you. I have just enough time to get home before my husband arrives. Funny, but he never alters his runs. It means less money."

I thanked her for meeting me nonetheless. And I thanked God her husband had at least warned her. Just because he drove eighteen wheels around the country didn't mean he was stupid. Christy might have been tragically correct, my corpse crushed into the concrete after ten tons of Detroit steel drove over me.

"Look." She slanted closer and whispered, "This waitress sucks. Let's dine and dash." I didn't get it. She nudged her head to the sidewalk.

"You mean ..." I began to say.

"Like get the hell out. Not pay."

I was startled. I had never done that before.

"But I haven't even received my drink yet." I could see she wasn't concerned by my loyalty.

"*Hey, Destiny!* I thought that was you, babydoll." The voice seemed to come out of nowhere, and I jumped in my seat. Did management have our table bugged? Had they overhead our criminal intentions? I turned my head in time to discover the most grisly son of a bitch roaming outside of prison walls. I wanted to get out of my chair and do my deed of crime just to escape any need to converse with this Manson follower.

"Hatch! Dudeman, what are you doing here!" Destiny jumped out of her chair and hung from Hatch Dudeman's shoulders in a hug. His beard and the wild hair around his face blotted out the horizon behind him. I began a subtle movement, shifting my chair in short lurches, pretending I was sitting at the next table.

Destiny was placed back on Mother Earth; she continued to stare up in Mountain Man's eyes, the smile etched on her face more clenched than my own butt cheeks, which I was squeezing.

"I came over here to ask you this very question, babydoll." Mountain Man circled Destiny's waist in his hands, so big that his fingers touched one another. "I was parking my Fatboy when I heard your laugh. I was surprised, since your old man is trucking. I just got off the horn with him an hour ago, and he said he was coming home tonight. He said you knew this, so here I am, wondering what the hell you're doing at Saffron's and not getting all nice for your old man at home?"

Destiny's face grew dark. "Just capping a drink before I do just what you said, Hatch." Through the corner of my eye, I could see Destiny attempt to shake her hips free from Mountain Man's grip, but that wasn't about to happen in this lifetime. I pretended to mouth a few words to the three people at the table I faced. Suddenly my chair swung around without touching the patio blocks.

"Hello," I said, gripping my chair handles.

"You a divorce lawyer in this cheap-ass suit, buddy? You working on documentation to shake her old man out of her life, huh?" Mountain

Man loomed over me. I didn't know if I was about to pee or say something to save my life.

"I'm sorry, I was at this table here," I stuttered, looking for someone at the table to nod and agree.

Mountain Man's beard dangled across my forehead.

"Yeah, and I'm a moron for thinking I saw you sitting at this table right here," he growled, smashing his fist against it without breaking eye contact with me. "Is that what you're saying I am?"

"Nope. Nope. Nope." I shook my head side to side, giving myself a chiropractic cervical adjustment. "Just sharing a drink with Destiny. Her idea." Screw it. I wasn't dying alone.

"Hatch ..."

"You dinking 'round on your old man, babydoll? After all he has done for you? Putting miles under his ass so that you have a place to stay. This the way you pay him back, with some hotshot lawyer in a suit?" A vein the size of a wiener pushed out from his forehead.

"I'm no lawyer ..." left my mouth, followed by a yelp when Mountain Man's hand crushed my thigh. How could someone's hand be so strong? I had to run hot water over a pickle jar in order to open it.

"Why don't I rip this suit from your body in order to find your lawyer cards, huh?" He pretended to tear at the fabric, and Destiny came to my defence.

"Hatch, please, he's right. He's no lawyer, and I ain't leaving my old man, okay?" Hatch seemed to relax—at least his grip on my thigh did.

"Then what's going on here, babydoll? Because I'm not liking it. Your old man is not going to approve of this, babydoll."

I flexed in my chair.

"Hatch!" Destiny pleaded with him. I imagined her Lululemons stuffed completely down my throat while I lay in a ditch outside Richer. "You don't have to bring my old man into this, okay. Why get him pissed, right? I'll make this right with him. I promise." Destiny's eyes moved from mine to Hatch's.

Hatch loosened his grip on my thigh and stood up with a smile. "Hey, why get your old man riled up, right, babydoll? Next weekend we have the Sturgis Harley rally, and I don't want him pissed for that, right? But come to think of it, I do need to detail my Fatboy pipes before we head out next weekend. Lawyerman, I know for a fact you'd like to contribute to chroming my pipes, since I ain't gonna be bringing her old man into this little soiree, huh?"

My throat was so dry. "I don't ride, so I don't have anything I can give you for your bike. Sorry. Can I get you a drink instead?" I braced to have my thigh assaulted again. Instead, Hatch laughed; it didn't sound like someone who was enjoying his present company.

"My man—typical lawyer," Hatch said, looking over at Destiny, who stood frozen in her runners, "always talking in circles."

"But I'm not a lawyer …"

My thigh convulsed, and I gagged. Hatch's forearm bulged from gripping me. "No one but an asshole lawyer wears a suit to an outdoor patio in the middle of the summer. Got it?"

I nodded agreement with extreme vigor.

"So this is what you can do for me, Lawyerman, even if you don't … *ride*. You have a bank account, right?"

I kept nodding, fearing more torque on my thigh.

"And I'll bet you have one of those fancy gold bank cards, huh?"

More nodding.

"Then you and me are going for a walk to that ATM over there, and you'll contribute a financial donation to my chroming." Hatch leered. "This might even buy my silence so I don't get her old man involved, huh? You wouldn't like her old man even as a friend. Him and lawyers don't get along at all."

I felt my foot going septic from lack of blood flow.

"Let's go, Legal Beagle," said Hatch, lifting me up and pushing me from behind as I limped forward, trying to navigate between the chairs and tables of people actually enjoying an evening out. I prayed Christy had deposited some money into my account; otherwise, I had nothing left to barter for my life.

I jammed my bankcard into the machine and looked at the row of withdrawal options. "Would forty … ?" He redirected my finger to punch the "maximum" button instead. Five hundred dollars shot out the bottom.

Hatch sandwiched my rent into his pocket. "Now you see, Lawyerman, you don't need to ride to help me out, huh? Painless." He slapped my back, and it was far from painless.

"Ciao, Gus." Destiny waved and turned away with Hatch.

I battled my emotions as I stumbled along the sidewalk like a surviving bombing victim. Was I a victim? Of what sort? Foolishness? I turned down Wellington Crescent without thinking about it. My legs were on autopilot. I felt my face flush. Tonight wasn't a march into destiny. It had almost become a march into my personal demise.

I reached my apartment just as darkness swept the streets. The weight of the day crashed down onto my shoulders. I staggered. My thigh pulsed. I could still feel the impression of Hatch's fingers. The elevator doors awaited, open, offering me the sanctuary of isolation and security. The elevator would look after my fragile esteem. It would take me home and put me to bed. I entered and poked the button assigned to my floor. The door closed. I was safe once again.

7

"I don't know if little kids will bother you ..."

If the saying "tomorrow will be a better day" required proof, I certainly wasn't finding it. Tomorrow did not feel any better than the previous day. When my appointments were finished, I kept my office door closed. I walked over and looked out and up from my basement window. The view was concrete grey or sky blue, depending on which half I looked at. I thought about the date last night. It was a failure. Besides going absolutely nowhere in my quest to find a soul mate, I nearly got myself killed by a Harley-Davidson-riding maniac. I could only blame this fiasco on myself. What the hell had I been thinking? I realized the only way I could make peace with myself was to try one more time. I reached for the phone.

"Hi, I am thirty-four years old, five seven, full-figured and wear glasses. I work full-time Monday to Friday at a job I absolutely adore. I am a fantastic cook and also the mother of three of the world's best boys. I have a wide variety of interests that include hockey, baseball and movies, and I love country music. I love life, and I am looking for someone to share it with. If you are kind and caring and very honest, as honesty is important to me, I'd love to hear from you. And if you're looking for just a friend, I can be a great listener and a great friend. Hope to hear from you soon. It's Chris."

I prepared to meet Chris.

I was getting together with Lonny for lunch at Tangos, a small, dark, very trendy, expensive Italian restaurant on Corydon across the street from the Roasting House. Lonny was paying.

He arrived before me. I slunk up to the table while he was chatting up a waitress. I surveyed the menu while he slipped her his card. Another hit.

"Hey, bud," he said to me when the waitress was gone. "Networking," he said with a grin.

I nodded smugly.

"I've ordered for us." Lonny always did when he paid. I didn't care because everything was excellent at Tangos. "So, tell me, was she the one last night?" He spread out in his chair, ready for a good story. I didn't disappoint him.

"Women are like that, Gus," he tried to reassure me. "Dangerous." He grunted. "You're lucky she was able to reason with that freak of nature. I still don't understand why you wore a tie. Think about it, dude. You were going to be outside on a patio. Casual is in."

I realized he was right. Even in her aerobic attire she didn't look out of place. I let the issue drop. I explained to him that I had left another message for a possible date.

"Not with *her* again?" He grasped the table in horror. I assured him that was never going to happen. "No kidding. You don't need 70,000 pounds of Detroit steel chasing you down Corydon Avenue." Lonny had a way with descriptions.

Lonny inquired about my latest tele-female selection.

I explained.

"Kids, huh?" He said no more.

I looked at him, but he kept quiet. I could see he fought to keep his face neutral. "What?"

Lonny broke into a wide grin.

"Tell me?"

He waved me off.

"Don't be a jerk," I threatened.

He gave a poised answer. "I didn't realize you were comfortable with kids."

"Well, it's not like they'd be going on the date with us. That's why there are babysitters."

"Don't be too sure about that, bud. Some mothers can't separate from their children. Hence the term *mama's boy*."

I shook my head. Outrageous. No one brought kids on a date. Especially a blind date.

"I'm just saying, Gus, you are not dating the mother. *You are dating the family.* Hope you're comfortable eating pie next to the smell of a shitty diaper."

I was horrified. I refused to believe that sort of thing happened. I went on to boast she had a sexy phone voice.

"Sexy by phone, ugly in person. Sorry." Lonny persisted.

"Regardless"—I defended my reasoning—"we have a lot in common. We are both looking for a special someone to share life's precious moments."

Lonny looked alarmed. "Did she say it like a Hallmark card?"

"Something like it, yes."

"Watch yourself."

"Why?"

"She probably also said she'd be your friend."

"Actually, she did."

"Hmm." He didn't elaborate.

"You're making more out of this than necessary, Lonny. Christ, at least give me a chance to meet her first. This conversation is loaded with too much speculation."

"Fair enough." He turned his attention to the arrival of our meal.

We ate mostly in silence. I think I had pissed him off for disallowing his observations. Too bad. I wasn't about to let him spook me. He didn't have a deadline to find love.

Lonny paid our bill and reconfirmed with the waitress to call him. I shook his hand and parted ways. I returned to the clinic to find a message from Chris. She had called back.

And she wanted to see me.

Tonight.

The suddenness had a certain appeal to it. I decided to go for it. I needed to rub clean the bedlam from last night. She left a number at her office. I called. Her voice was even sexier live.

"Gus! Hi! I'm glad you called. Can you make it tonight?"

I could feel her anticipation. This was the aggressiveness I needed.

I accepted. Short notice was now fashionable. Before I could ask about arrangements for meeting, Chris laid it out for me. Six thirty. My place. She'd be outside in her vehicle. Pleased with myself for choosing a self-reliant, decision-making woman, I confirmed her preference. She was quick to describe what she'd be driving before we hung up, a maroon Chrysler minivan.

I was embarking on my first legitimate date in ten years.

I hated waiting. I stood inside my apartment vestibule, waiting. She was late. I had arrived at the front doors twenty minutes early. Now it was another half hour past the time she'd promised to arrive. I had been waiting almost an hour. My feet hurt. I was tired of averting my eyes from the stream of tenants coming through the doors. I felt exposed. It was a form of public humiliation. I chastised myself for allowing this substandard existence.

Two couples who had seen me standing on their way in noticed me still standing on their way out of our building. By then the smell of my sweat started invading the scent of shower soap. There was no air-conditioning inside the vestibule. The couple gave me the strange, sorrowful look someone would give a street bum. I was no bum. I was a dating imbecile.

At that point I decided to make the trek back upstairs. Chris either wasn't coming or was going to be painfully late. At least if she called, I would be there to answer. For dating etiquette, I always left my cell phone at home. The blare of a horn turned me around.

A late-model minivan waited outside. The woman inside waved. I broke into a smile. I ran up to the passenger door and fumbled with the handle. I could feel the sweat from the heat and anxiety of my wait trickling down my back. Inside I was greeted by a gush of cold air. *Heaven.* Next came the powerful smell of female perfume. All my resentment evaporated. I got my first look at Chris. She was pretty, with brown hair that was long, full and slightly curled in a wild, abandoned way. The lines around her mouth and eyes made her look older than thirty-four. But she appeared happy when she smiled. I greeted her with enthusiasm and suppressed a desire to thank her for dating me.

"Gus! Hi! I'm so sorry for the delay," she said quickly, with sincerity I believed. I held my hand, signaling the need not to explain further. I was ecstatic she'd even showed up. But I didn't say that out loud. It was better she live with a little trace of regret.

"Hello to you, Chris. Forget about it. Nice to meet you." I offered her my hand. Her hand was soft and slightly damp, but she shook mine firmly.

"I appreciate your tolerance, Gus. I don't think I would still be as jovial." I noticed how attractive her brown eyes were. I was looking forward to spending an evening of looking into them.

"My babysitter jammed about looking after my kids tonight, and I had to make last-minute adjustments," she admitted. So there it was. Now we were set to begin our date; true confessions were over. I was anxious to get started. We hadn't left my driveway yet.

"Don't worry about it, Chris. It gave me a chance to meet all the tenants in my building." I tried to make it sound like a joke, and she accepted it that way. We both laughed. "No problem," I said trying to be understanding, "nothing goes as planned. All we can do is try and make the best of things. Listen, where have you planned for us to go? All afternoon I've been dying of curiosity!"

She had both hands on the steering wheel. Should I tell her she needed to press the gas with her foot to move the van? Meanwhile my eyes scanned what Chris was wearing: a dress that went all the way to her ankles, black open-toe sandals. She looked nice.

"I'm glad you think this way, Gus. What I'm trying to tell you is my babysitter wasn't available tonight. I'm not sure what you know about kids and sitters, but on short notice it's impossible to find a replacement. I hope you don't mind, but I've brought my kids along." She looked nervously at me. I didn't quite understand.

"Ah, do we have to pick them up?" I wasn't sure what to say.

"Boys, meet my friend Gus." She glanced back in the rearview mirror. The scream of high-pitched voices startled me. I turned in my seat to find three sets of eyes focused on me.

"Wow," was all I could say.

"I'm sorry, Gus. I didn't know what else to do. I really didn't want to cancel. They're good boys. We'll hardly notice them. They've all promised to behave. I planned to walk through the zoo. The boys would love to go there too." I could see from her expression she expected me to leap from the truck. I wanted to. But I also wanted to know more of this woman. Her voice was as sexy in person as on the phone. Sure, she looked closer to a worn forty and had probably never owned an article of spandex in her life, but she wanted to spend the evening with me. I was sticking it out.

"Hey, this is a good opportunity for us to meet. And the zoo sounds fine. Hi, boys." I waved to them.

55

"Gus, the one on the right is my youngest, Derrick. He's almost four. The little guy in the middle is Damian. He's six and a half. And next to him is Duke. He's nine." Duke? The name struck me as odd. Then again, so did spending a first date mingling with half the Brady family. I waved again.

"Alrighty," I said cheerfully. "Let's get to the zoo so Derrick, Damian and Duke can see the wild animals." She gave me a lovely, wide smile. A way to the man's heart is through his stomach. For a woman, it's through her kids. I felt satisfied with the way I had handled her accidental surprise. At least it eliminated the troublesome decision about whether tonight would progress into physical intimacy. Passion was hard to find when you were performing in front of a Sesame Street audience.

"Interesting that all your kids have names beginning with the letter *D*. Any reason?" I decided to use the situation as a conversation platform. Happily, we were finally on the move, pulling onto Wellington Crescent.

"Actually, there's nothing more to it than my ex-husband's preference for boys' names beginning with that letter. My ex's first name was Dean. Our last name is Dickson. So he found it humorous to match first names to the same character."

For a moment his name almost seemed familiar.

"Sounds as though you were the odd person out. *Chris* doesn't exactly fit your ex-husband's pattern."

"My first name is really Christine. But I've always called myself Chris. Here's the fun part. My middle name is Deborah. I never use it."

"Wild. A family of double Ds."

"It certainly isn't in reference to my chest size." The remark caught me off guard. Nevertheless I sneaked a glance, wistfully noticing she wasn't lying. But what did you expect after three kids?

I didn't want to confirm her comment either way, so I passed it by. "How long since your divorce?"

"Three years. It seems like it only happened yesterday." She looked apologetically at me. "Don't get me wrong, I'm over the break-up. What I mean is that I've been so busy working full-time and raising the boys, the years have gone by quickly."

"Dean doesn't share responsibility with you?"

"He lives in Switzerland. When it came to choosing between an aging wife with three young boys to raise or shacking up with a twenty-two-year-old Swiss Air stewardess in some mountain village, he couldn't run to the airport fast enough. He met her on a flight to Europe.

He travelled a lot on business. He's an author. Internationally his books have sold extremely well. He was on a tour promoting his latest book when they met."

"What was the book called?"

"Honestly, I don't remember. It was about discovering ways to find the life you deserve. He found his, I guess."

"By any chance was it called *Relax, Actually This Isn't Your Life*?"

"Yes! Now I remember. That's exactly what it was called. How did you know?"

"I thought your ex's name was familiar. I read that book. It's actually pretty good. Sorry."

"Don't be. I don't hate him. I just hate girls in red caps."

I laughed. "Has he ever been back?"

"Nope. Doesn't call, write or send birthday gifts. He's made himself not exist."

"Support?"

"Wired to my account without fail. That's the extent of his presence in our lives."

"Sad situation for your boys."

"It is. But he's powerless around natural blondes."

I watched as we turned into the zoo's long driveway. Trees lined the narrow roadway. Chris parked the van in front of the gates.

"Okay, everybody out!" Derrick, Damian and Duke dove from the sliding door with little war cries of freedom. I watched the boys run with abandon to the ticket booth. In their eagerness they screamed for their mother to hurry up. I couldn't remember getting this excited after my first paycheck.

"Exhausting," I commented. As adults we try to slow things down. We prefer that time doesn't hurry along any faster than it has to. But for kids, time existed in the now phase. Like "I want to see the animals, now."

"Hey, you guys! Wait for us!"

I watched Chris's large hips shift side to side under her dress as she attempted to run to the kids, who all began crying.

I caught up to them just as Chris was trying to pick up her youngest child, Derrick, from the ground. He was sobbing uncontrollably. Snot ran down his chin. Chris wiped it off with the back of her hand. I made note of which hand.

"Ah, shit," Chris swore. She fumbled in her purse.

"What's up?" I inquired, walking up to look down into her purse with her.

"Can you believe they accept cash only? Even the bloody hot dog stands on street corners have Interac machines. Shit, I don't have enough."

I sensed my moment to shine with a mother and children desperately seeking animals. I took the cash from my wallet, handing it valiantly to the attendant.

"Gus—" She tried in vain to move my outstretched arm. But it was too late, and the entrance fees were paid.

"No problem," I said in the bashful tones of a hero having just saved a drowning family from certain death. Little Derrick rewarded my efforts by cleaning a bulbous mound of snot from his finger along my wool gabardine pants. It became an impressive rope of nasal fluids stretching from knee to cuff. Only I was privileged to see Chris's son's handiwork, as she was preoccupied with pulling Duke off his brother Damian. I pretended to ignore the substance on my leg.

"Thanks, Gus." She smiled sweetly at me, squeezing my arm. *And thank your son for giving me his most prized possession*, I wanted to say in return, but I didn't. Instead, I shrugged. My hero moment had lost its glamour.

The kids ran ahead of us, pointing at the cages of animals. Their excitement brought a smile to my own face. Chris noticed it.

"Have any kids of your own, Gus?" She squeezed my arm again.

I shook my head.

"It's a big decision. When Dean and I decided to start a family, we never thought it would be three this close in age. I had my tubes tied after Duke."

I decided to defend my position.

"I haven't met the woman to share my children with so far. It's somewhat of a sombre realization now that I'll be a very old man by the time my kids reach their teens. I refuse just to have kids for the sake of their looking after me when I become decrepit. I hear this reasoning often enough, and frankly, I think it's wrong. Children aren't created to be your own personal geriatric caretakers. I would hope as a civilized society we've moved away from that need. Anyway, I should concern myself more with finding a woman who wants me to be the father of her children—a dad who'll be playing catch from his wheelchair."

Chris was silent for a moment as we strolled in unison.

"Maybe you need to walk into a family that's already there for you. That way you've bought yourself some time." I saw her looking at me.

"I've never really thought about it," I replied honestly. I hadn't. Nor had I considered three surrogate offspring, either. Three for the price of two was reserved for canned soups.

"Damian!" Again, Chris broke ahead. I watched her voluminous hips shift while she raced to where Damian had a peacock in a headlock. The bird was screeching in fright. Its tail flared as it struggled to free itself. Before Chris could intervene, the peacock sensed an opening and pecked at the base of Damian's neck. He screamed and let go. Chris reached her crying son as the indignant peacock fluttered back into the park.

There was a small drop of blood on Damian's neck from the peacock's desperate bid for survival. Damian's brothers stood around in a circle, awed by their hysterical brother and his injury.

"I need to get him bandaged and something to disinfect his wound. Birds are filthy." Chris picked Damian up in her arms and began to carry him back in the direction we had just come. I could see he was too heavy for her, and I offered to carry him. She looked at me gratefully. I could see fear in her eyes as she handed me Damian. The kid was dead weight, and I felt something let go deep inside by my hip. I wasn't exactly in shape myself. No wonder Chris was struggling. But Damian was hysterical and too shaken up to walk. Chris pointed to the zoo's recreation building. I focused my energy, trying to ignore the kid's double-digit-decibel screams.

We approached the building, and I wanted to throw the kid the remaining ten feet. I saw my reflection in the glass door. My hair splayed in all directions. Sweat stained my shirt. Duke and Derrick, their brother's abuse from the peacock forgotten, were crying about going back into the zoo. Chris herded the boys inside and held the door for me. I slumped, letting Damian stand on his own feet. He seemed fine. Realizing the attention he was getting, his screams stopped. It seemed to continue in my head. I mumbled to Chris I would be in the bathroom.

I was thankful no one else was inside the white porcelain bathroom. I leaned on the counter. In the mirror, my face was an unhealthy red from exertion. The front of my shirt was stained with blood. I looked as though I had taken a gunshot to my shoulder during a drive-by shooting. I cursed. It was the first time I had worn the finely woven clothing. I tried unsuccessfully to reduce the stain, but I was shit out of luck. Blood against white cotton spelled t-r-a-s-h-c-a-n. The shirt was a write-off. And now a huge watermark outlined the blood smear.

I was very self-conscious of my bloody badge of honour when I rejoined the rest of the members of my date in the main room. An attendant had cleaned the wound and bandaged it. Everyone seemed calmer. Chris noticed my shirt.

"Oh, Gus. I'm so sorry. I'll replace the shirt for you. Blood doesn't come out. What is it? Polyester?"

"Egyptian cotton."

She seemed unfazed.

"I've told the kids we'll see the zoo another day. I can't risk another attack on my children by a wild animal. I might even sue."

I wondered if she was forgetting it wasn't the peacock that went looking for a wrestling match.

"I have no problem with that. It's getting late, anyway." Her boys felt differently. When they were told they wouldn't get to see the animals, each boy broke into a fit. Duke swung his arms around. Damian began crying and dropped to the floor, where he proceeded to slap his hands against the tile. Derrick was too young to understand what was causing the reactions and cried in response. Chris smiled wearily at me. She gathered the boys, and we left for the parking lot. Everybody climbed into the van, and we departed from the zoo.

"I want ice cream."

I wasn't sure which kid was making the demand behind my ear. It turned out to be Duke. He led the chant as his brothers joined in and bellowed their ice-cream request. Chris looked at me.

"I know there's a place just up ahead on Broadway Avenue. It's an outdoor stand. It's good stuff."

Chris thanked me for my support.

We found the place at the moment when the chanting was reaching a feverish pitch and I was about to do my own screaming. Chris must have noticed my posturing. She reached over and put her hand on my knee, the one opposite the snot-smeared leg.

"Okay, boys, let's go get some ice cream!" Their mother's declaration as she stopped the van sent the kids into a more heated frenzy. I pitied the ice-cream man.

She opened the door, and her kids spilled out, tripping over each other. Little Derrick lost out and fell to his knee. Duke stepped on his back, not breaking stride in his race to the stand. Little Derrick screamed about his scraped knee. Chris knelt beside him. I hurried to the vendor to rescue the employee, who looked bored. The scene was probably nothing new to him.

"Tell the man what you want, boys."

He opened the freezer door for them to peer inside. I caught a faceful of icy air. It felt great. The kids grabbed at the treats. I saw the employee looking at my blood-splattered shirt.

"Sucking chest wound," I offered. His eyes widened, and he looked away.

Chris walked up with Derrick, who was in a state of simmering hysterics. He was too young to choose, so Chris got him a cone full of swirling colours: blue, red and white. The artificial colouring made it seem appealing. I had no appetite. Chris chose a Klondike bar for herself.

"Gus, this is really terrible, but there's no Interac here. Can I bum the cost off you, again? I'll make it up to you."

I wasn't too clear about what "making it up to me" meant. But it didn't sound like paying me back with cash. I was cornered. I forked over the last of my bills. If she tried this again tonight, we were both screwed.

"You're so sweet," she said sincerely. She brushed against me. I could still smell her perfume. It reminded me why I was there. I felt encouraged.

"Just don't forget me in your will." It was corny, but she laughed. It made her brown eyes stand out.

"I'll tell you what," she began, leading me and the boys back to the van. "Supper's on me tonight. I have reservations at the Royal Crown Revolving Restaurant. It shouldn't be any trouble adding three kids to the seating. How about it?"

If not for the allure of her perfume, I might have resisted. I agreed.

There was one concern: my shirt. I couldn't even entertain the thought of going to a classy restaurant with blood splashed on my shirt. Never mind the rope of snot on my pants.

"That's the beauty of children, Gus. People tolerate soiled clothing. It's expected. Things happen with kids. Nobody will even give you a second look."

I wasn't exactly convinced. "Fine. If anyone asks, I'll say it's nothing more than the final stages of a bleeding ebola."

She leaned against me in laughter.

Chris asked about my profession during our drive to the restaurant. I explained I was a seamstress. It caught her off guard, and I could plainly see her perplexed look.

"No. Really. I sew, just not fabric. Actually, it's closer to moral fabric. I attempt to mend relationships. Marriages. The couple thing." I knew I couldn't tease much longer. She had started to give me the "Oh god, I'm trying to date a freak" look. So I had to back off. She couldn't hide her relief.

"I see. You're a psychiatrist."

I vigorously shook my head. "A common blur between the professions, a distinction our professions fight to the death defending. Psychiatrists are the secondary leaders in pharmaceutical prescriptions, after your local community dope pushers. Only difference is that psychiatrists can afford to push their drugs from skyrise offices that rent at one hundred and twenty dollars a square foot, not dilapidated crack houses."

Chris was enjoying my backstabbing of the profession. She even ignored her kids' screams for attention. We let the fighting behind us continue unchallenged.

"I'm a psychotherapist. No pills. No drawings, except for maybe the odd doodle in my notebook. But that's purely for my satanic rituals later in the evening. It's a casual setting. No one takes off their clothes or lies on a couch. Although I've yearned for a few patients to be naked. That was a joke," I assured her. She nodded and grinned. "Nope. Just bright lights, music from the stereo and a cold beer in the fridge if someone really needs it."

"So what do people talk about?"

"They tell me why their marriage is not what they expected. I tell them, surprise, that's normal. What they need to do is realize how to accept each other."

Chris warmed to the conversation. "I should have used you to save my marriage."

I rolled my eyes.

"I think your dear Dean was destined to be swayed. Unless you can see yourself at home pushing a drink cart and asking him if he wanted white or dark rum, there wouldn't be much for me to do. I'm sorry. Frequent flyer points win out."

She reached over and jostled my hand. "You're crazy. I can't figure out when you're telling the truth or making things up."

"In my job, you become fast on your feet or else punched in your mouth."

I was going to tell her about some situations I had run into, but the smell of vomit suddenly stole my attention.

"Did we just drive over a skunk?" I didn't want to seem obvious, but one of her darling monsters had just splattered the back of my seat with the latest McStomach Special. The innocence of ice cream was changed forever. I would never have guessed it could smell so vile. But then again, I didn't have much experience with the expulsion of Freudian orifices. I had a lot to learn if I was to become an instant parent of three.

Chris tried to steer us in a straight line while glancing behind the seats to see who hadn't held down their ice cream. I was afraid to look behind me. I was more terrified that Chris was driving the van with one hand. I wasn't about to let myself die with snot on my pants.

"Derrick. Do you have a stomachache?" Stopped at a red light, Chris reached back with a Kleenex to wipe Derrick's face. I could see concern etched on her face. Astonishingly, the smell of the puke didn't even phase her. I was witnessing a true case of parenthood. I wished I could feel touched by it.

"Mommy, Derrick made throw up on his pants." It was a brilliant observation from older brother Damian. He just didn't have to yell it into my ear.

"Are you feeling sick?" Chris finished cleaning off the puke from Derrick's face in time for the light to change, which was followed in timely fashion by a horn behind us. I could see Chris's agitation. The odour of vomit was making my head throb.

"Chris, maybe we should just call it a night."

She jumped in quickly, saying dinner was still on. She wanted to pay me back for all the cash I spent on her kids. She insisted we go.

"Onward then," I said without much conviction. I had lost hope of catching a subtle wisp of her perfume. It had been erased by the expulsion of pungent stomach fluids.

The boys started to wrestle and kicked my seat. Chris did nothing to stop it. She concentrated on her driving. I applauded her choice. When she found a spot on the street to park the van, I hurled myself out before we had come to a complete stop. I felt there was no other choice. Either I went berserk or bailed out.

"Everything okay, Gus?" she hollered across the van. I lied and replied that I wanted to help the kids out the door. She seemed pleased to hear that. I gritted my teeth. Derrick's jeans were bleached white, a puke-acid wash gone bad.

"Come on, boys. Let's see if real food settles your stomachs." Chris grabbed hands and led them along. I followed a safe distance behind. It wasn't until we got into the elevator that I realized none of us males were in condition to be eating at the Royal Crown. I saw a reflection in the elevator's mirror of a group of people who looked as though they'd guest-starred in a double episode of the *Jerry Springer* show. Damian and little Duke's clothes were soiled from wrestling. Derrick's pants were becoming stiff with drying puke. I looked like I had taken a bullet in my chest. My hair was tousled, and the wild stare in my eyes scared me. Only Chris hadn't changed. She was as poised as when we'd first met, hours ago. If I thought my impression was wrong, the hostess at the restaurant confirmed it. She looked us over. I saw her mouth begin to move, as she struggled not to tell us to get the hell away. Chris was quicker. She mentioned her reservation. I almost laughed as astonishment raced across the hostess's face. She was done. So she grabbed an armful of menus and led us very briskly to our table. I didn't think she wanted to be associated with us any longer than she had to. The other guests watched our pioneer caravan. I nodded to one woman, who apparently forgot how to close her mouth. She actually pointed to my chest. I ignored her and moved on. We took our seats, and I hid behind my menu.

"Wonderful view," commented Chris, gazing out the window. It was. The restaurant made a continuous revolution so that the city was viewed from the thirtieth floor during the meal. Regretfully, I wasn't able to summon up the same enthusiasm.

"Yup. What are you going to eat?" I didn't bother looking up from the menu when I asked her. I didn't care about her reaction.

"The boys always enjoy chicken wings before the main course."

I nodded in response.

When our waiter approached, I slunk deeper into the chair. I held the menu close to my chest. He politely wrote down our orders and fought to remove the menu from my grasp. He left and rejoined his coworkers, and I saw him jerk his thumb back in our direction. Two other waiters glanced our way. My bloodstain felt like a beacon on my chest. Chris cheerfully hummed softly to herself, glancing over the wine list. Unless the wine came in shot glasses, we were eating and leaving. I fought to reach new depths of tolerance when the boys started a fart competition. Little Duke, who let one rip so loud I saw a chef turn his head our way, won.

"My oh my, you boys each pack a strong set of hips, don't you." I looked at them warily.

The waiter came back with our wings. I grabbed a handful for my plate. I had them nearly done before everyone else had finished taking their selection. Chris gave me a strange look. I didn't bother to wipe the chunks of sauce from around my mouth while I chewed. Etiquette was out. Wiping would keep us longer in the fish bowl I was now swimming in. Meanwhile, I kept telling myself it was not bad meat that smelled but Derrick sitting next to me. I swore off ice cream forever.

"Mommy, the sauce is too hot. It's burning my mouth," declared Derrick. He also had sauce smeared around his lips. I didn't feel bad for him. Then Duke kicked him under the table and finished his ridicule by calling him a wimp. Derrick yelped in pain, dropping his wing to the floor. He scrambled beside me, successfully retrieving the half-eaten wing, which was now acting as fly tape for all the remnants on the carpet. Derrick finished the wing, carefree. I fought back my own gorge.

"Good wing, Gus?"

I could only rock my body in answer to Chris's question.

"Wing's too hot," was Derrick's only warning before he vomited the half-masticated chicken meat and the remnants of ice cream from his guts. This time the table acted as a reflection device, sending a shower across to his brother Duke, who wasn't so tough anymore. Little more than a yelp came from his lips before he was pelted up to his neck in chunky bits. His reaction was too late, but predictable. He thrust himself back from his chair. It would have placed him safely out of the way had it not been for his knees hooked under the table. The force lifted the table, and every drink became airborne. As if I hadn't tortured my shirt enough, I now added a glass of Coke. My only satisfaction was seeing Chris take a spray of Five Alive to her hair. Now she had become a member of our food-and-beverage-wearing club. I sat back and tuned out. To hell with the people who stared. Or Duke's crying from the pain in his legs. Or Damian screaming in laughter over his little brother's misfortune with reverse peristalsis. Especially Chris, who had finally become embarrassed by her personal travelling circus. I could never come back here again. It was not a fact I accepted warmly because I enjoyed this restaurant.

Before the waiter could arrive with a cloth to remove the drinks from our skin and clothing, Chris was already herding everyone to the exit. I suppose the destruction she caused eliminated the need to pay her bill in her mind. I was left behind, watching the elevator doors close behind her, and I was jammed with the tab. I was being financially raped. But I was cornered. Our waiter ensured he caught one of us. The process of elimination left me. I reached for my wallet. My indignation was increased by being obligated to leave a tip.

When I reached the building's exit doors, Chris's van was idling outside, much like it had been hours before when she had picked me up at my place, yet circumstances were so dramatically different. I walked up to her window. She rolled it down.

"Coming with us?"

"You forgot to pay for our dinners," I said trying to keep my voice even.

"I'm sorry, Gus. I was in a hurry to get Derrick out of there before he puked again." She flashed her brown eyes. The allure was lost on me.

"Sure, but I had to pay again."

"Listen, I promise to cover the entire evening next time."

"What if there isn't a next time? Then I'm stuck paying for ice cream, zoo passes and now dinner."

"Sure there'll be a next time, Gus. Didn't you have fun tonight? I did, and I know the boys would agree." The boys were quiet in the backseat. Silence is a liar.

"If there isn't, I lose out."

She shook her head.

"You'll always know in your heart you made the boys very happy, Gus. Really."

"Is that a fact?"

"Yes." She sounded too cheery.

"I think I'll take a cab home. I'm too afraid you'll need gas along the way."

She hesitated a moment.

"If that's what you want, Gus, I understand. Do you want us to wait here until one arrives?"

I could see she wanted to leave as badly as I wanted to be left alone.

"No. I'll be fine. Besides, you need to get Derrick home before he gets sick again." She nodded.

"Bye, Gus." She kept both hands on the wheel. "Say good-bye, boys."
I received a chorus of garbled voices.

Dazed, I watched the red taillights disappear down the darkened road,
along with any hope of recouping the evening expenses. The suffering
over the loss of my favourite Egyptian cotton shirt and my trousers was
still to hit me.

I walked back inside the hotel lobby, fished a quarter from a pocket and
called for a cab. It arrived in minutes. As we approached my apartment, I
realized I didn't have any cash left to pay for the ride. I would be taken to
cabbie jail and forced to watch endless reruns of *Taxi*. Fearing my name
would be blacklisted by the cab company, I instructed my driver to make
a stop along Wellington Crescent at a cash machine. I withdrew forty
bucks. I gave the cabbie his eighteen dollars when we reached my place. I
asked for my change. No tip. The cabbie became my victim. I didn't feel
bad about it.

8

"Looking for a guy I can spend a little spare time with ..."

The session was not going well. Jerry Trotts, for his own reasons, had decided to be very uncooperative in our discussion. His reluctance to participate made his wife, Jean, noticeably uncomfortable, and together they were testing my patience. Meanwhile, I was still salvaging my ego from the dating fiasco with Chris and her when-kids-go-bad brats.

"Jerry," I said, fighting to keep my voice even. "Your wife isn't suggesting she never wants to role play with you anymore." I glanced over for Jean's approval; she nodded her head vigorously.

"You see, she wants very much to be a part of your fantasies."

The stubborn old bastard crossed his arms in defiance. I was determined to break him. "The other evening you purchased a policeman's cap. You asked her to wear it. You wanted her to pretend to interrogate you. Ultimately, you instructed her to strike you in the head with the Yellow Pages. She wouldn't do it. She can't hit her own husband. Do you agree with my recounting of events?"

He gazed first at her but gave me a short nod of agreement.

"Now, when she refused to hit you, it made you angry. Not that you tried to hit her or swear at her, but you locked yourself in the bathroom. How long were you in there, Jerry?"

He smiled. "Three hours."

"And what did you do all that time?"

"I used Jean's Nair to remove all my body hair."

"Why did you do it?"

He shrugged. "It made me feel better. So what?"

"It does matter, Jerry," I persisted.

"Didn't you ever do something just because it made you feel good?" he asked.

"Sure," I agreed. "But let's keep this discussion about you, Jerry." I wasn't letting him off that easy.

"I was terrified you were going to hurt yourself inside the bathroom, Jerry," his wife said. "I could never hit you. Not even just for fun. You're my husband."

Jerry took the initiative. "I've never asked for much, Jean. Meals. Having my clothes washed. I wasn't demanding that you crack me a good one on my head. All I wanted was the cop to punish me for not confessing."

"But I'm not a cop, Jerry! And you're not a criminal! We were in our basement. What if I had broken your neck? I wouldn't have been able to forgive myself."

I ventured. "You see, Jerry, Jean's reluctance to hit you on the head with the Yellow Pages was entirely due to her fear you might become a paraplegic. As much as she knew it was part of the game, your health was more important."

He looked over at his wife. She smiled weakly his way.

I gave each one a determined look. "I'm proposing a change. Jean and Jerry," I said, "I want you to try another game. However, I want Jerry to pick out the props and the nature of the game. Jean, you will follow Jerry's instructions when he approaches you with his game. The one rule is the game cannot potentially harm Jerry in any way. That means no hitting, stabbing or beating. I think Jean will find this comfortable. And Jerry, you will be satisfied." I looked expectantly at them both and felt they were willing to try my suggestion.

"Can I choose anything for a game?" asked Jerry. He leaned forward in his chair.

"Of course."

"No hitting, Jerry. I won't hit you," Jean said.

"Your husband understands," I said to Jean, speaking for Jerry. My smile was smug. I had gotten through to the Trotts.

I sat in the front room in one of the waiting chairs. Christy was across the room at her desk, flipping through a magazine. She wasn't going to say anything until I did first. I was helpless. I needed a release. I surrendered to the chair's plush red leather and my appetite to confess. Christy took the initiative and turned up the Starlight Band on the Bose speakers to relax me.

"Last night I went out with a divorced woman with kids. She brought all three kids along. It was a disaster."

Christy tossed aside her magazine, eagerly awaiting the gory details. "Talk to me."

"I don't know where to start. She picked me up. Said her sitter jammed on her. Derrick, Damian and little Duke were in the backseat waiting for me. I got stiffed and paid for everything last night. In return I got bled on, smeared with snot, splattered by vomit and my clothing absolutely destroyed."

"Did you get a good-night kiss?"

"Nope."

"Did she say she'd make it up to you next time?"

"Yup."

"Won't happen."

I felt dejected.

"Cheer up, Gus. This is a new century. Mixed marriages, kids bred by grandparents and raised by neighbours. Sex change operations so that Daddy was once an aunty."

I must have looked crestfallen because she was quick to add a disclaimer.

"Although, I must say, Gus, in all my dates, the kids never came along. Yikes. Are you okay?" Her concern was genuine.

I nodded.

"I just don't get it, Christy. What the hell do women expect? Has the *scene* evolved to these low levels? I swear she used me for a night out for her kids. Do you realize I had to eat in the Royal Crown with a bloodstain on my chest? It was awful." I saw Christy grimace.

"Couldn't you have picked a drive-thru?"

"No! She already had it booked! I was committed."

"And you got jammed with the tab?"

"Yes!"

"How'd she pull that one? Sick kid?"

71

"Exactly. Puked all over us."

"Sounds like she's got him trained to hurl on cue."

"Jesus." Programmed children. I shuddered.

"This could be a good thing for you, Gus. Think about it. Now you know which groups to eliminate. Married women. Divorced women with young children. Which leaves lesbians and cross-dressers."

"Shut up. I'm suffering here, okay."

"Give me a break. You've had two dates."

"Both terrible."

"Gus, I've had hundreds of dates. Dozens were bad. Hell, most were awful. And I'm only half your age. Welcome to the nature of modern-day courtship. The Cleaver family is long gone, buddy."

"Television makes it look so easy. Walk the dog. Meet girl. Girl falls in love. Boy proposes. Marriage. Kids. Freedom fifty-five on an island surrounded by green water. How come they get to make it look so alluring?"

"Because the scripts are all written by pimple-faced Generation Yers still living at home with a divorced transgendered parent."

"Jesus."

"Cheer up. This is the fun stuff you'll get to tell your spouse about one night over drinks. You'll both laugh yourselves silly, end up in bed and look back at it as a distant memory. Let's face it, Gus, it's not in our cards to find our perfect halves on the first date."

"Hell, I would settle for a situation normal enough so that I can at least have a second date."

"Second dates? Get real. Consider these dates character builders."

"I just want to find a woman to be a part of my life," I said, burying my face in my hands.

"Listen, I can't accept your suffering alone tonight. Let's hit Papa George's for supper. I have a feeling if I send you home alone, instead of calling the Mobile Crisis Team for help you'll fling yourself into the Assiniboine River."

Her comment made me laugh. I took my hands away from my cheeks, ready to face the world again.

"There you are," she said, smiling at me. "You can't say no to me."

"At least when I'm with you, I know that you can relate to what I'm saying. You can't imagine how comfortable a feeling that is for a guy like me."

"Please, you're making me blush. Besides, I work for you. We have to remain professional."

"The rules are only what we make them."

Christy took my remark as silly banter, although I wasn't really sure what I meant by my comment. I shut up.

Christy walked around the room, turning the lights off by sweeping her hand against the switches. I studied her walk. I was intrigued by the sleekness of her hips. Her body flowed as she moved. I looked away when she turned toward me.

"Ready?"

"Let's go." I couldn't help myself; I intentionally fell behind her in order to observe her exposed calves. I had to admit, I mostly saw Christy's top half from behind her desk every day. Her effect on me as a woman was new to me.

We walked outside into the hot air. "Don't you just love Winnipeg evenings, Gus?" Christy asked, twirling her arms around in a circle. She wore a huge smile.

I grinned.

"This is my favourite time of the day. Right before the sun starts to set, the air becomes still and has an alluring, heavy scent." Christy clapped her hands. "I always feel like it's the day starting all over again. Don't you find the dusk mysterious? Like anything can happen?"

"I've always said it's like a vibration in the air."

"Yes! It's all around us. I can feel it now. Can you feel it, Gus?" She spun in a circle on the sidewalk as we approached the corner of Osborne where Papa George's was situated.

"Watch yourself, or you'll spin into traffic. You know those express buses don't stop for fallen pedestrians."

"Just let yourself go, Gus. Nothing bad happens."

"Yeah, well, you're forgetting in my world the sun doesn't always set in the west."

She laughed at me and continued to spin as she walked in a weaving line.

"Enough with all this extra energy, Christy. When you get to my age, just sitting up hurts."

She waved at me.

"Remember this isn't on company time. If you sprain an ankle, I expect you back at work tomorrow. No compensation claims." My warnings went unheeded. "Just promise me no spins when we're in the restaurant. I do not want to be the centre of attention inside a public venue two days in a row."

She finally stopped when we got to the door.

"So should I clutch your arm and fawn all over you? Tossle your hair? Grab your ass? Shout out, 'Oh you make me *so* hot, Gus'." She grabbed my bicep in both hands, looking up at me. "I can pretend you're my boyfriend, and we can be all over each other when the waiter is trying to take our order. Then we can duck under the table and see how long before anyone dares to look."

I had to laugh. It was funny. But I ate here often and wanted to come back again. I declined her daring offer.

Disappointed, she pulled away as we made our way inside. It was obviously a slow night. There was no wait, and half the tables were empty. We got a table in the far corner. Alone. No kids close enough to need to be concerned about projectile vomit. We took seats across from each other. The dark walls and dim lighting relaxed me immediately. I began to unwind. The day was officially done.

"Here's to surviving another one in the trenches," I said, saluting her with a water glass. She joined me in the toast.

Christy put down her glass and looked around. "Before I started working with you, I never came down to the Village. Winnipeg isn't a big city, but everyone keeps to the community they live in. I grew up in Fort Richmond, and, basically, the Jubilee underpass was as far away as I needed to go. My sister and I would hang at Boston Pizza, Monty's on Friday nights, Scandals or Strawberrys on Saturday and come downtown only for Oktoberfest at the Convention Center. Look at all the culture I've been missing!"

I followed her eyes around the room and felt ashamed. Christy had been working for me for nearly three years. I didn't know she had a sister. I inquired further.

"She's actually five years older than me. Naomi moved away to Toronto after two years at Red River College. She's a marketing rep for a pharmaceutical company. I was her bridesmaid a month before you hired me. The timing was pretty good, because I didn't think an employer would give me time off for her wedding."

"You're probably right," I said, nodding my head. "If you would have asked me, I might have told you to tell your sister to get a proxy."

"Come, on," she said, jabbing at me. "Don't play tough guy with me. You couldn't have said no. I could have asked you for two weeks off with pay and plane tickets and you'd have agreed. It tore you apart when you asked me if I minded stopping for the clinic's mail the time you went away for that seminar. I was starting to get scared you were having a stroke."

"No worthy ocean shows a sailor its strongest wave until the boat is hopelessly afar from shore. Your pay would have been docked."

"I'm on salary."

"A demotion then."

"There's no lower position for me to go."

"Well then, no lunch privileges for a week."

"Good luck. Labour laws."

We placed our orders with the waitress. Twelve-inch pepperoni pizza for me, chicken souvlaki pita for Christy and a pitcher of draft beer between us. I held a special appreciation for any woman who drank beer.

Christy had piqued my interest in her personal life. It was unchartered ground for me.

"So you were close to your family growing up? I find it rare that sisters five years apart hang around each other."

She shook her head. "When I was only in junior high, it was cool having an older sister in high school. Everybody left me alone. It was like having a brother or sister in high school gained you respect."

"Older sisters tend to lead the young astray."

"We didn't do anything illegal. All I meant was Naomi taught me the ropes for dating."

"I can see you've learned well."

She shot me a sour look. "What I mean is, I was able to see what dating was all about. I started when I was fourteen. He was eighteen."

I nearly choked on my beer. "Your parents felt okay letting you date at fourteen? And a guy who was old enough to be charged? Give me their number. I need to speak with them. Any more younger sisters still at home?"

Christy laughed at my concern for her. "Get real. We went on one date. He dumped me."

"Good!"

She shrugged. "Four years difference in age isn't a big deal now. But when you're fourteen it is. He picked me up in his dad's car. I was still riding my bike. I didn't know what to expect. We ended up at a bush party in Kings Park, my first one. I remember all these older kids standing around a bonfire, smoking cigarettes, passing around a bottle of booze. I was offered but passed. I was young and too naive to have an interest in alcohol. My date wandered off to hang with his buddies. I didn't know anyone else, so I sat down by myself and took out my doll."

"Christy, you brought Barbie with you!" I had to laugh.

"Sure. I carried her everywhere with me. When his buddies saw his girlfriend playing with a doll, he got really embarrassed. He grabbed my arm and drove me home. My sister was in the same grade at school with him and heard about all the teasing he took for it. They called him Ken for the rest of the school year." She shook her head, grinning, sipping at her beer.

"Good. The pervert got what he deserved. That's just plain wrong."

"My sister and I still laugh about it. I didn't date again until I was almost sixteen. That relationship lasted three months."

"At sixteen, three months is an eternity."

"I was late leaving puberty. My problem was that nothing was happening with my body. Meanwhile, all the girls were moving into B cups. He left me for Jacqueline. She was all boobs and bum."

"Men," I said, shaking my head in disgust.

Christy took a long swallow of her beer and sat back in her chair. Her face took on a blissful expression.

"What are you thinking?" I asked. I could see her mind had gone to a happy zone.

"You're lucky, Gus. You're doing what you want to be doing."

"What do you mean?" I was puzzled.

"Your job, helping people. It fulfils you."

"It pays the bills, yes. Fulfilling might be stretching it."

"Whatever. But you're doing what you like. I don't want to be answering phones and booking appointments for the rest of my life."

"And the solution is?"

"My fantasy has always been to work on a cruise ship. Travel the world, see every country, have a guy at every port."

"You're sounding like a long-distance trucker and his clan of truckstop whores."

"You know what I mean. Visiting exotic locations—think of all the people I would meet. Thousands! Every cruise would be different. All that traveling, plus getting paid for it."

"So do it."

Her shoulders slumped.

"What?"

She leaned her head back against the booth.

"I don't know why I just dream about it. It's not like I have anything to leave."

"You're at the right age to do these things, Christy."

"You'd be left without a receptionist." She looked at me with remorse.

"Don't be crazy. I may not find another person as skilled, but I'd find someone. I'd keep a picture of you on my desk, a personal shrine so that you're never forgotten."

She grinned. "You're too sweet." She finished her beer and refilled her mug. Our food arrived. We ate without speaking. Christy broke the silence.

"Sorry to carry on like this, but even you made a big change in your life by moving to Canada," she said envious. "I've never left the province."

"It was easy for me. I was a loner. I had good friends back in Minneapolis and a sister I was pretty close to. But when it came time to make the decision, I didn't think twice. I was more daring back then. Age breeds caution. Just look at my love life. I'm too scared to say good morning to a female mail carrier."

"Haven't you missed your old friends?"

"Not really. By the time I was thinking of relocating, all of them had gotten married and were beginning to raise kids. Single men and friends with families don't mix. I was the odd man out. The hardest was leaving my sister."

"Julia?"

"Yeah. We were close, like you and your sister. I still miss her a lot. I guess a person never really adjusts to things like that."

"Are you afraid of loneliness?" Her question caught me off guard. I wasn't sure. I thought about her question.

"Maybe? Who isn't?"

"Do you think force-feeding yourself into a relationship will stop your fear?" She picked at the chicken inside her pita.

"To be honest, I won't know until I'm in one."

"For a guy who can talk to strangers about their love lives, it's plain weird you're single. Sorry. Don't you think?"

"Perhaps. I've always considered myself a bit of a voyeur. I'm quite comfortable watching and not touching. Like the old sales pitch—if you touch, you buy it. I think my profile fits a person in my profession. We're all watchers. We study people in motion."

"Oh, but not the type of guy in a raincoat peeping through a partially closed window blind." She smiled with her mouth closed and signaled to the waitress for a new pitcher of beer.

"I don't know. I've never tried it yet."

"My fingers need to touch things," she said, fondling her mug of beer. It captured my attention.

"The way things feel tells me a lot about them. My mother told me I was like this even as a baby. She would have something in her hands and I would reach out for it. I'd cry until I was able to hold it, and then I'd shut up and smile. I cry less nowadays, but I still need to grab on to things."

"Interesting," I said. "I look, you touch."

"I also taste. It's very important before I can really become comfortable around something new."

I was confused. It must have showed on my face because Christy explained.

"Not that I would drink gas or anything rotten. If it's an object that I can taste, I do, because it helps me really identify with it. Actually, I think it makes me obsessed with it. That's why a good kisser with a tasty mouth can steal my heart."

"You're grossing me out now."

"Sorry."

"Smell means a lot to me," I explained. "A lot can be known about a woman from the way she smells. The soap she uses, the perfumes, freshly washed hair right from a shower, a fresh sheet of Bounce. Smell's a powerful sense, good or bad. It can define an entire emotion, an experience that will last a lifetime. In my opinion smell is the most important aspect of sparking a relationship." We paused our discussion while the waitress placed the new pitcher of beer between us and refreshed our mugs.

"It's all about chemistry, Gus. My sister swore by it. No chemistry, no deal. It's either there or it isn't."

"Which means if you can taste a chunk of flesh from a prospective date, then spit or swallow will tell if there's more to follow."

"You're very poetic tonight, Gus."

"You should hear me when I can rehearse first."

"Save it for your wife."

"Right now I'd take a lazy weekend on the couch next to any woman. Her title is unimportant."

Her eyes lit up. "Do you like snuggling on a couch too?"

I nodded.

"I can't do it without a bag of Doritos and a Coke."

"Let me guess," I said, leaning closer to her. "Coke in a can, not a plastic bottle, and the Doritos have got to be Cool Ranch."

"Wow! You really are a voyeur; you've been looking in my window."

"If I remember correctly, you're on the sixth floor. I'm not Spiderman."

"Then how did you know what I enjoy?"

I could see she was still convinced I had scaled her apartment wall. "It's what I enjoy. So I said it."

"Funny how you and I have similar leisure habits," she said.

I could see she was thinking about it, but she said no more.

"I suppose we're both looking for the same thing, a person to enjoy life with," I suggested.

"It's no fun on our own," she added, agreeing. She looked at me carefully. "Gus, tell me about you."

"Tell you about me what?"

"Do you really believe having a woman in your life will make you happier?" Her question seemed serious.

I thought about it. "Yeah I really do."

"Why?"

I paused. "Did you ever have anything really good happen to you? I mean, like passing a tough exam, or getting a great deal on a new car, or winning an award? Hell, even a person at work telling you she really appreciated your dedication? This really good thing happens, and your chest is bursting with pride and excitement, and you need to tell someone to make you totally complete. But there's no one to tell it to. You know your friends really don't care. They have their own lives. Your family is long out of touch. So what happens? You come home and say it aloud. Of course, there's no response, because there's no one else there. No one who knows you well enough to realize how important this new thing is to you, no one who can share your enjoyment in your success because the person knows how much this means to you. Let me tell you, Christy, there's no better feeling in the world than opening the apartment door to find that person sitting in a chair, smiling, loving you, waiting to share that joy with you. All I want is that person. Conversely, I also want to be the same thing for that person. And I need to be there before I'm forty. Does that make sense?"

"I think so." She sipped her beer. "It's a little deeper than I thought it would be." She giggled. "I'd be happy with a phone number for a guy I can call on a Friday night who I can count on not being an asshole."

"Nothing wrong with that, Christy."

I reached across the table to grab the pepper shaker. Christy was doing the same thing, and my hand grabbed hers instead. There was something odd when my hand touched Christy's. It was no more than a second before I pulled away, apologizing, but for the first time I realized that despite all the time we'd spent working together in the same office, this was the first time our flesh had met. She was warm and soft, and she became a real person to me, no longer just the person answering the phones. Strangely, I didn't think only I felt the connection. A mystified glance crossed Christy's face. I could see it. Plainly. Our eyes locked, searched and shifted away in different directions. I didn't feel awkward, and she didn't seem to either. I watched her spread pepper on her food before she passed the shaker to me. I was careful not to touch her a second time. I was wonderstruck about how little I could know someone despite sharing the same room for years. It left me questioning how well we ever know another person.

"Glad you came out?" These were the first words spoken since our hands connected. She said it without looking up from her plate. I nodded.

"Maybe I shouldn't be saying this," she said, fidgeting in her chair, "but I once overheard you talking to Lonny about a girl you almost married."

"The walls have ears," I replied, grinning, pointing at her playfully.

She was relieved I wasn't mad at her for eavesdropping. "I'm sorry, Gus. I heard you talking about it last year. It sounded like she had something to do with your reluctance to date again. Did you get burned?"

"That's putting it mildly." I sat back in the chair, thinking, holding my beer in one hand.

"Did you want to marry her?"

"Yes, I did, very badly. And I thought she wanted to also."

"And? What happened?"

I took a slug of beer. What happened? I was still wondering myself.

"One of those things, I guess." I shrugged my shoulders. "Didn't work out."

I could see the need to hear more was killing Christy. Ironically, after all those years, it still killed me inside to think about the whole chain of events. More than anything, I was afraid I might cry in front of Christy if I tried.

"It was a long time ago, Christy. Years. Ten? Another lifetime. A past I want to forget."

"Have you?'

"Yeah," I said, lying.

Christy was silent. Thinking.

Like I just said, how well do we ever really know someone?

"It's so sad to see a person still hurt after all that time has passed," she said, finally.

"Amazing, really," I added. "By now it should seem so insignificant. In many ways it does. I never think about it ... I've moved on."

Christy looked skeptical. "The way you're reluctant to trust women, I'd say you're bullshitting me *and* yourself."

"It's called learned preservation."

The waitress interrupted our conversation with the desert menu. We both declined. When she walked away, Christy bounced up in her chair.

"Hey, what do you say we hit Club Happenings? I don't feel like going home yet."

If I hadn't been half drunk, I would have said no. Whether it was the atmosphere, the conversation, the feel of Christy's hand or the beer, I accepted her offer.

I was going to my first gay bar.

We took a cab out to Sherbrook Street. Club Happenings was inside the basement of a two-story, shit-kicked building. The upper floor was a bar for lesbians. For all the years I had lived in the city, I hadn't been aware of the location. The steep, narrow stairway down into the pit of every father's worst nightmare heightened my anxiety. We paid the five-dollar cover charge and entered a large, low-ceilinged room that blew me away with sensory images.

"One thing about gays," shouted Christy into my ear, "is that they know good dance music." And apparently enjoyed it very loud, I quickly discovered. Speakers hung from the ceiling everywhere. I felt the need to crouch. We bought ourselves drinks and huddled in a corner of the room. Now I had a chance to see what kind of nest I was in.

"I didn't expect to see any women," I tried to yell to Christy. She nodded, taking a mouthful of her drink.

"Fag hags."

"What?" I shouted back.

"The girls you see are called fag hags. Straight women who are gay groupies."

"Gay groupies?" I laughed.

"They can party without the threat of being hit on. They have no interest in picking up guys. All they've come for is to drink, dance and have a good time."

"A female safe haven," I yelled.

"Yup!" She bent closer to explain more, her hot breath against my ear making me shiver.

"The gays don't care. All of them are here to get laid. It's a tight group. Most know each other. Probably have slept with each other twice over." I was astounded by Christy's revelations. Just when you thought you knew the rules, the glass was turned upside down.

I swallowed half my beer and looked around. I nearly choked when I focused on two guys a few feet away from me. It took a second to convince myself I was seeing properly. Both were young, both handsome, as far as guys went. One sat on a barstool. The other straddled him. Their lips were pressed tightly together. I was transfixed. Never had I seen two guys kiss, and the sight held a perverse fascination. I wanted to look away, but I couldn't. Both had their eyes closed and, astonishingly, their mouths never came apart. I'd never kissed a female for that long without coming up for air. I glanced over at Christy, who smiled at me, observing the same episode. She had obviously been down this road before. This was true passion.

I felt a tap on my shoulder and turned.

"Cigar?"

"No." I couldn't say anything further. It was the first time I had been approached by a guy wearing a black maid's uniform and dark fishnet nylons slinging a tray of cigars across his hairy chest. He walked steadily away in high heels and a garter belt.

"What the hell was that all about?" I asked, but Christy didn't hear me. She had her eyes closed and was moving to the music. The pounding beat shook the floor. My heart vibrated with the intense bass rhythm. I felt like I was on exhibit, the straight guy trying to seem at ease. Whether anyone knew I wasn't gay, I had no idea. My suspicions were quickly exposed.

"Nice arm," came a voice, followed by a hand around my bicep. My head shot around, and I faced a blond guy. My first impression was that he was wearing a light shade of lipstick. My second was the look of hunger in his eyes.

"Thanks." I didn't know what else to say. He let go and walked away. I had officially been hit on. Why was it that it took a man to do so?

Christy missed my moment of rebirth. She was still absorbed in the music. Much to my amazement, Mr. and Mr. Kisser still hadn't broken away to swallow. Saliva dripped from their chins.

I averted my eyes. Across the dance floor in a corner stood a well-muscled male dancer. All he wore were a pair of cutoff jeans, work boots and a dreamy smile. I sent my eyes to safer horizons.

"Not as weird as you may have thought, huh, Gus?" Christy was back.

"I wouldn't exactly say I've seen this kind of stuff before on *American Bandstand*," I admitted. *What?* I could see her soundless lips say. I let it go.

She pointed. "Twenty minutes, and those two are still going at it." She was referring to my dynamic kissing duo. "Listening to Bronski Beat will do that to people."

"Yeah. Just watching them is giving me chapped lips."

The closer I studied the other patrons, the more normal everyone seemed. Jeans. Short hair. Only a few guys wore outfits I would equate with gay culture, like frilly shirts in opaque material that displayed nipples. Otherwise, nothing seemed out of place except the high ratio of men grinding on the dance floor.

Without warning, the marathon slobberfest was over. The two guys broke apart to rest heads on each other's shoulder. *It's a highly romantic Kodak moment,* I snickered to myself.

"Let's dance! Come on!" Christy grabbed my arm, pulling me into the middle of whirling bodies. Incredibly, the music was louder. My skull vibrated. The music was far different from the days of Lynyrd Skynyrd's "Free Bird." I had no idea what to do. So I tried to mimic the spastic movements around me, and I stuck close to Christy.

"Follow along, Gus!" urged Christy. "Move your feet. Sway your hips! This is a great revamped Pet Shop Boys version!"

I turned at the caress of a hand on my ass. I wasn't fast enough to see who had copped a feel. Surrounding me was a mass of sweaty bodies. I felt flushed. It was sweltering under the strobe lights. The twisted reality coming through my drunken eyes made me laugh out loud. I picked out within the smoky room the French maid handing out cigars. I could vaguely see his hairy forearms and well-muscled calves in the sleeveless dress. It made me laugh again. I really was having fun. Another beer was needed.

The naked dancer changed my mind. Suddenly, a mash of men and women crowded the dance floor. The male stripper was wearing ball-crushing jean shorts and CAT boots. His body looked heavily oiled, lean and well muscled. He moved in circles, his hips grinding the air around him. His eyes shifted to those watching him. He placed one hand behind his head and another on the side of his shorts. I couldn't grasp the emotions that moved as fast as the dancer's jiggling pecs. Was I going to hell for watching this? Didn't this cross the boundary between attending a gay bar and participating? Would I feel shame? Should I feel repulsion? The dancer ripped away his shorts, and I felt fear. His goods sprang forward. Despite the loudness of Diana Ross over the sound system, I was certain I could hear his manhood slap against each of his thighs as he swung his hips back and forth. I broke the locker room rule and stared. I countered that under these circumstances, all bets were off. I watched with grisly fascination as the dancer clutched his goods and removed a pink ring that a moment earlier was staunchly encasing his manhood. Hypnotized, my head snapped back when the pink device struck me in the forehead. I felt wetness. I *was* going to hell. Christy squealed and kneeled down beside me. She stood back up and slapped something spongy into my hand.

"*A souvenir, Gus!*" Christy screamed into my ear. "*You've now been initiated!*"

To what club, I wanted to bawl back. This was not a membership to brag about. Christy took my hand and shoved it into my pocket, where I mercifully let go of another man's sacredness. My knees felt weak, my hand sticky. Christy looked my way, bouncing to the music.

"*You want to go?*" she yelled

"*Yeah. I'm partied out. If you don't mind.*"

She shook her head. We made our way up the stairs, feeling the cool air. Once outside, I realized how hot it was down there. I was drenched. My ears rang.

"Cab?"

I agreed. Sherbrook Street was a main expressway. Even at one in the morning there was traffic. I held out my hand to the first cab I saw.

"Thanks for the night, Christy. It sure as hell was more entertaining than a few hours in front of the television. Let's do it again sometime." I meant it. I couldn't remember the last time I had been out to bars to drink and dance. Actually, I distinctly remembered, but that memory was locked away with the same person Christy alluded to earlier in the evening. Yes, it had been a long time.

"Just ask me anytime you want to do this again, Gus. I come here every couple of weeks with the girls. You're welcome to join us." Her voice was hoarse.

"You're flushed," I said, seeing how vibrant it made her seem even in the darkness of the cab's interior.

"Too much booze and dancing," she said. She lay back in the seat and closed her eyes.

"Hey, no excuses for being late tomorrow," I joked. "Staying out with the boss doesn't entitle you to free privileges." I forced a laugh.

"I'll be there," she mumbled. "Wake me when our cab reaches my place, okay?"

"Sure." I leaned back in the worn seat. Through drunken eyes I watched the lights of downtown sweep past. I rolled my window down so that I could smell the dampness of the nighttime air. It relaxed me. I felt confident. Tomorrow I would try to arrange another date.

We reached Christy's apartment, and I walked her to her front door. I returned to the cab and rode home in silence. I put it down to the drinks and being tipsy, but the whole world looked damn good.

9

"And I'm considered a little on the shy side ..."

"Gus," Christy called out from the main room. I was sitting in my office chair, drinking water and trying to remain as still as possible. Moving hurt. I knew the suffering it took for her to utter my name. We were both paying our dues from our evening of drinking.

"Yeah?"

"Mrs. Jean Trotts is on the phone for you. She doesn't sound too good."

"Okay. Transfer her to me." I hoped this wouldn't take long. My own voice reverberated inside my head.

"Hello, Jean. What can I do for you?" I reached for my glass of water. It was almost time for another Advil.

She sniffled loudly in my ear. I grimaced.

"Gus, I'm sorry, but your therapy suggestion is not working." I could detect she was crying. I hoped it was the result of a heart-wrenching book she was reading; however, I suspected I was somehow involved.

"Why is that, Jean? I thought we all agreed the other day what we would do."

She sniffled louder this time. I wanted to scream. My finger found the volume control and lowered it.

"I ... only agreed because you said I wouldn't have to hurt my husband anymore. I ... won't hit him."

"Did he ask you to?"

"N ... no."

"Well then, you should be fine with it."

"He brought home a new game."

"Did it involve hitting him?"

"No."

"I don't see what you're upset about, Jean. Jerry is following the rules we agreed upon. I would suggest you go along with it. It's the only way everything will get better. Trust me, Jean."

"But—"

"Please, Jean. This is what therapy is all about. At times it's going to seem crazy. This is one of the times you have to jump through a thorny rose bush to get to the open field, Jean."

"You don't understand—"

"What don't I understand, Jean?" I was exasperated.

"I can't play Jerry's game."

"You're right, Jean, I don't understand. He's not asking you to hit him, so what's the problem?"

"He wants me to be a farmer."

"A farmer? Farmers grow crops, Jean. They plant seeds. They make us bread. Everybody likes a farmer, Jean. Don't you like farmers?"

"Y ... Yes—"

"Well, there you go then, Jean. Be Jerry's farmer for him, will you? And next time we all get together we can talk about it."

"I—"

"No. Really, Jean. We need to discover this game together."

She blustered and burst into tears. "Jerry's pretending to be runaway livestock, and I have to use an electrical cattle prod to keep him in the corral."

"*What!*"

"He's making me shock him. The first time he passed out."

"*The first time?* He made you zap him with the prod a second time?"

"He didn't pass out the second time. He went into convulsions. I wanted to call an ambulance, but he begged me not to."

"Is he okay now, Jean?"

"He's resting in bed. He has a bad burn on his hip."

"Anything else?"

"And a bruise on his head where he banged it on the floor during the seizure."

"You used a cattle prod on your husband?"

"I did what you said in therapy. I didn't know what a cattle prod was!" She began to cry harder.

"We agreed in therapy, Jean, that you wouldn't have to do anything that *hurt* your husband. You said yourself hurting Jerry was out of the question."

"I know!" Now she was sobbing heavily.

I couldn't make out the next few sentences.

"Jean. Please. Control yourself. Everything will be fine. Jerry sounds fine. I can't talk to you if you're hysterical. Please."

"I ... I can't do these games anymore."

"Okay. No more games until we work out ground rules. Do you understand me, Jean?"

"Y ... Yes."

"After we hang up, Jean, I want you to remove the batteries from the cattle prod and put it away. Promise me if Jerry begins to turn grey, take him to the hospital." I took Jean's thunderous sniffle as acceptance.

I hung up the phone. This guy used to build aircraft for a living. Now he was having his wife zap him with electricity. It was moments like these that shook my faith in humanity.

I settled into a plush chair inside Second Cup on the corner of Osbourne Street and River Avenue. Sipping my coffee, I remembered the drunken promise I'd made during the cab ride home last night.

"Dammit," I said, loudly. A cashier looked my way.

I pulled my cell phone from my belt and jabbed at the power button. No kids. Single. I repeated my vows again.

I rejected the first couple of selections. A 250-pound divorced mother of four was out. Instead, I left a message for "Zoe," who sounded like she knew how to have a good time and did not have any children or a current husband.

I listened a second time just to make sure I wasn't missing a red flag. "Well, hello there. In this voice box you'll find a five-foot-nine, green-eyed, slim blonde who is a smoker and a social drinker. She likes to play slow pitch and pool. She is professionally employed, but there is one hangup.

Because she is tall herself, she prefers to date guys who're taller than she is. So there you have it. This girl also likes to be goofy. She's outgoing but in certain circumstances she can also be shy. She likes to go out and rip up the town, but she likes to stay at home some nights as well. So if this sounds like the girl you might want to hang out with and get to know, box me."

I brushed aside the height requirement. How picky can you expect to be when you're lowered to picking a date by touching the number two on your keypad? Get real. She'd have to learn to deal with it. I was a little vague as to how to interpret her reference to ripping up the town. Then again, any girl admitting to being goofy was probably far duller in person. Mercifully, she was single, childless and sounded like fun. *Time to wrestle life my way.*

I still wasn't ready to return to the clinic. My curiosity to browse another U 2 Can Date category won. I punched the numbers on my cell phone, choosing "romance for women thirty years old and up." The first female voice quietly spoke. She pulled me into her world.

"Well, it isn't really like me to want to do something like this, but my birthday is in a month and I'm going to be thirty-five, and I just need some excitement in my life. I'm five-four, one hundred twenty pounds, with hazel eyes. And I think I have a wonderful personality. It's just, ah, you know, that to get me out there, I, ah, I'm very shy and quiet and … and I don't know, I'm … not just the person to go out to the bars and be wild and crazy. I'm … like I say, I'm quiet. But I need change in my life, badly. If you can break that shell, my box number is 5552, and my name is Marcia." I was leaving a message before realizing I had done so. Her voice sent a message mere words couldn't achieve. My heart thumped in my chest. Who was this girl? Yet it seemed as though I knew her soul. It was naked for me to see. The anguish of her loneliness became tentacles surrounding me. There was no escape.

I powered off my cell phone and leaned back in the chair, letting a long trail of breath whistle out between my teeth.

I had to meet Marcia. It was not a question of *if* but *when.* I hated waiting. Now that I'd set things in motion, I was restless.

A movie was in order. Subtitled. Reading would take all my concentration. I would walk to the Cinematheque tonight.

My cell phone rang. I jumped. *How did Marcia get my number?*

"Hey, dude, did I catch you in foreplay with one of your dial-a-dates?"

"Lonny?" I whispered, trying to catch my breath after being startled by the call.

"Don't sound so disappointed, dude. I can be your friend, but making love to you is out of the question."

"I'm at Second Cup right now," I confided.

"I'm heading over to the Shark Club tonight. Thought you might want to meet women without chipped nail polish."

I considered my foreign movie versus a confidence-builder night with Lonny. I could use new techniques if I was to be serious about this dating thing.

To get to the Shark Club, I crossed Main Street, turned left on Lombard Avenue and skipped up the steps into the lobby, the Liberty Grill restaurant on my right. I turned left. The club façade was encased in grey stone pillars. A beautiful hostess in a black skirt greeted me at the Shark Club door. In fact, all the female staff in the Shark Club were stunning. That was worth the five-dollar door charge.

I enjoyed the club's decor. The main room was wide open with cathedral ceilings. A large painting of a woman with a cigar in her mouth, poised with a pool cue, hung high on a wall. Leather couches were scattered around the room. A standup bar was on one side, full-size billiard tables on the other, plus a beautiful girl to rack your billiard balls. Delightful. In the back was a separate gentleman's smoking room for serious cigar aficionados. Having never smoked a cigar, I had never been inside that room.

I didn't see Lonny anywhere, so a drink was in order. The bartender opened a tab for me. Scotch. I leaned against the bar. The club was very busy. People surrounded the pool tables and gathered in tight groups, occupying all the chairs. I decided to look for the group with the most bleached blondes. And there was Lonny, zealously chatting up five women, all dressed in leather. So was Lonny. I laughed. He leaped into every fashion trend. I once saw a pair of brown cords inside his closet.

He noticed me and nodded for me to come over. I sauntered his way, drink in hand, a smile lifting my cheeks. The five girls all looked like models. *Only the best for Lonny.*

"Hey, bud," Lonny said, tapping my shoulder. "Girls, this is my friend Gus. He's a shrink, so watch what you say. He's been mandated by the

Manitoba government to report any person he fears is a nymphomaniac. I do the arresting." The girls giggled.

"Lonny has mental health issues," I observed. "Some of things he says are unfortunate side effects of his psychotropic medication."

"Thanks, pal."

"Are you really a shrink?" a cute blonde next to me asked. Her complexion looked very healthy.

"Actually, I'm a psychotherapist. I counsel married couples."

She seemed genuinely impressed.

I flashed a broad smile.

"Gus uses his practice as a front to pick up unhappy housewives," said Lonny. He poured his drink down his throat.

"That's his medication talking again."

"All joking aside, Gus is one of the best in the city," admitted Lonny. "He's been so busy helping everyone else that he's paid the price by sacrificing his own love life. Can you believe he's still single?"

The girls shook their heads.

"This guy should be recognized for his dedication." Lonny grabbed my shoulder and shook me.

"I did go out last night to Club Happenings." I thought about what I had just said. Lonny took his hand away. "You aren't going gay on me, are you?" he asked.

The girls all stared.

I held out my hands in self-defence.

"Christy took me there to cheer me up." I took a sip of my drink and added, "I had a bad day."

"Hear that, girls?" Lonny asked. "His bloody secretary has to take him out. She sees his daily emotional sacrifices. I'll tell you this much, ladies. If Gus wasn't the age of Christy's father, she'd marry him in a heartbeat."

I heard one of the women snicker.

The blonde cutie next to me shoved her glass into my hand.

"Buy me a drink, and we'll talk about your bad day." Her remark caught me off guard.

"Good for you, sister," Lonny remarked.

I led my new friend to the bar. We stood there.

"I'm Gus," I offered, shaking her hand.

"Serena."

She was as tall as I. I glanced down and noticed her boots: knee-highs. I quivered.

"What can I get you?"

"Shipwreck."

I ordered her drink and another for me. I wondered if I'd wake up on a desert island.

She leaned against the bar, drink in hand, her right hip thrust out to the side.

"So tell me about your bad day."

I wanted to. But my eyes were glued to the diamond stud beckoning to me from the middle of her tongue. Her mouth closed.

I returned to answer her question. "Wasn't so much that it was shitty," I explained with a flourish of my hand. "It was frustrating." I suddenly had no interest in crying about my woes. I wanted her to do the talking.

She kept her lips sealed and listened.

"Here's the thing. A patient was having a hard time adjusting to my therapy. Let me just say he has issues that place his wife in situations she's not comfortable in. His last request made her very upset. Fact of the matter is she cattle-prodded her husband into convulsions. Frankly, I was rattled that my suggestion nearly caused a client to choke to death on his own tongue. So Christy, my secretary, took me out for drinks after work. She thought I needed a release."

"People who care mean a lot," she said. Again, her tongue was framed within her lipstick-painted mouth, the stud glittering a sweet hello.

I nodded. I guessed she was twenty-one. I fumbled for a whimsical retort and came up with rehashed crap.

"Do you come here often?"

I watched her gulp her drink. It was going down fast. Either she was nervous or simply enjoyed being shipwrecked.

"Yeah. I actually work the odd evening here as a hostess. I've been doing it off and on for the past year. I've seen your friend in here often."

I took her to mean Lonny. He got around.

"He's a funny guy," she added.

A thought occurred to me. Did she mean Lonny had been in her bed? The image soiled my enthusiasm. I couldn't stomach sharing Lonny's lunch. She eased my fears.

"He's too aggressive for me. I enjoy the soft-spoken, mellow type." Serena took a quick sip and continued. "I do this job for fun." She finished her drink. I lifted my eyebrows to ask if she wanted another. She held out her glass. The bartender poured a replacement.

"During the day I work as an apprentice hairdresser."

"Where abouts?" I asked. I decided to refocus my thoughts on her diamond.

"At Salon Nookie Nook on Broadway."

"Do you like it?"

"It's fun." She grabbed her new drink.

"Busy there?"

"Very. Samantha—she owns the place, she's cool. Now she's letting me do the colouring. She'll be here later tonight. She's older, in her thirties, but she can still party."

I felt relieved that she considered a thirty-something someone could be cool.

Then I noticed her tattoo, a starfish, situated in the tantalizing zone between the top of her knee-high boots and her miniskirt.

"When did you get that?" I pointed, feeling my question gave me an excuse to legally stare at her slim thigh.

She smiled slyly. "When I was eighteen. My boyfriend was a tattoo artist. He gave me two more."

I was privileged to see her hip when she hiked up her skirt so I could admire the tattoo, a heart split in two. *Poetic.* My own heart jumped when she lifted her top. I was about to receive the coup de grace. She stopped short under her bra, where I saw nestled three roses.

"Nice." What else could I say?

"If I hadn't dumped the asshole, I would've gotten more. I like the feel when they're being done."

I was speaking to a hair-dying masochist. "What made you dump this guy? Did he demand his name be stenciled into your back?"

"He beat me."

"What?"

"He drank a lot. Started pushing me around. I dumped him. He was a real asshole."

"Good for you," I complimented. "Too many women tolerate abuse."

"Not me," she said defiantly. She downed half her drink.

"How about the stud in your tongue?" I broke down and asked. I felt we had reached a new level.

"Last year."

"Doesn't it hurt?"

She shook her head.

My courage didn't extend to asking why she needed it.

"I went crazy after Joey left. Started partying really hard," she admitted. "I worked as a go-go dancer at Coattails."

"Don't you have to do that in the nude?"

She nodded.

I drank some more.

"There was always a party to go to. I'd never get home before seven the next morning." She smiled during her description.

"Sounds like fun."

"I was a mess. Did a lot of drugs. Cocaine."

I was staggered. I had to keep reminding myself this girl still wasn't legally allowed to drink in some American states.

"I've cleaned myself up. Been drug free for more than a year now."

"Good for you." We banged knuckles.

"What do you do for fun?" Her question caught me off guard. I didn't do much.

"I like going for walks." She stared at me after my reply and then smiled.

"I feel like a cigar," she said, suddenly looking around. "This happens every time I start drinking. Let's go have a smoke."

I said nothing and sipped my drink nervously. Where was Lonny? I needed his intervention before I looked like an idiot. I had never smoked a cigar.

"Come on, Gus," Serena said with authority, grabbing my arm and leading me into the smoker's den. It was a small room behind French doors. The woodwork was dark along with the swanky leather sofas set in a circle.

"I've never been inside here before," I admitted.

"Usually it's full of old men during the daytime because their wives beat the shit out of them if they try to smoke at home," she said. She moved us toward the counter. She held up her hand, signaling for two cigars.

There was a haze of smoke and the rich smell of tobacco. Serena handed me an obscenely large cigar. In her hand were two oversized matches. The games were about to begin.

"After we finish these," she said, the cigar filling her mouth, "we're heading over to my apartment. We'll party there." Too many things were happening at once.

"Puff at it while you keep the match in front." Serena coached me as I struggled to suck air through the long tube of tobacco. She already had her cigar going, and smoke billowed around her face. Finally, I had an ember and away I went. I puffed vigorously.

"Don't inhale it, cowboy. Keep the smoke in your mouth." She laughed at the smoke coming out of my facial orifices.

"Thanks," I coughed. "Tastes like vanilla."

"It should, because it's vanilla flavoured. Smells better than most cigars. These are my favourites."

"Mine too." I felt it best to be a team player remembering Lonny's advice to always agree.

She grinned. "Are you up for my plans after the cigars?" Her eyes glimmered at me.

"Oh yeah," I said, squinting at her. "What are we going to do at your apartment?"

"Mr. Psychotherapist, when I'm through with you tonight, I promise you'll have a whole new book of sexual techniques to coach your clients," she said intently. She blew a long mouthful of smoke into the air.

My knees wobbled, and I wasn't sure if it was from what was about to be inflicted on my body in mere hours by this girl or from the smoke stuffing my lungs.

"You've got a long way to go," she said, watching my cigar burn.

I did. I was only a quarter of the way done.

"Let's go sit down on the couch," she suggested.

I agreed. My head felt light.

We shared the narrow couch together, and she moved in close. I tried to concentrate and not inhale the smoke, as Serena suggested. But it was obviously a skill honed with frequent practice.

"Enjoying it?" she asked.

"Yes. I like the taste. It reminds me of those vanilla fudge bars."

She leaned against me. "Cigars always make me feel devious," she said.

I tilted my head to look right into her eyes. Her pupils were dilated.

"I'm feeling mellow myself." I gasped. She placed her hand on my thigh. Her nails were wine-coloured. I admired her long fingers. I took a long drag on my cigar and blew the smoke out above my head.

"So, Serena, where do you live?" My throat felt raw.

"On Garry Street. Twenty-fifth floor."

"Roommates?"

"None. I need my space."

I was nearing the end of my cigar. My lungs burned.

"Hurry up," she urged. She butted her cigar in a silver tray. "I'm making us belly-button shooters as soon as we get to my apartment. We're starting with my belly button. And you have to know, Mr. Psychotherapist, I have a huge belly button."

I wished I could suck harder. My interest in the cigar was over. I wanted shooters. I ground it into the tray next to Serena's. They seemed a perfect pair together.

"Let's blow this joint," she said, standing up. She looked beautifully sexy in her black knee-high boots and skirt. I wondered if she would let me take pictures of us together. I made a note to stop and pick up a disposable camera on the way to her apartment.

I stood. My legs disappeared. The room leaned forward. I felt the single malt drinks rising from the depths looking for a return to Scotland. Serena pushed me back into the couch. I coughed. My mouth filled with vomit. I closed my eyes and swallowed. I tasted vanilla.

"Jesus, Gus, you've gone white." Serena's voice was concerned. "Did you just puke?" I saw her boots take a careful step back.

I held up my hand and waved. I'd seen athletes do this after a crash, signaling they were okay. I was not okay. I feared picking my head up. The room rolled to the left, pulling with it more scotch.

"Gus?" Serena's voice was annoyed.

I desperately craved air to purge the vanilla. I slumped forward, hunched in a fetal position.

"I'm okay," I said, forcing my voice to sound confident.

"You look like shit."

I needed to be very still. I was sweating heavily, and my shirt clung to my body.

"Come on, Gus. Are we going to my place or not?" She shoved my shoulder.

Everything inside my stomach rose, and I blew scotch and snot from my nose.

"Can't hold your liquor, buddy?" somebody asked me, followed by a slap to my back.

"He's choking or something." Serena was discussing my symptoms.

"Leave me here. I'll be all right ..." I didn't dare look up. I could see a trail of substance hanging from my nose. I flailed at it.

"Listen, Gus. Maybe some other time. I need to get another drink after seeing you throw up. Sorry." I saw her boots turn away. Her tattoos went with it.

I have to get the hell out of here. I didn't want to puke anymore inside the smoking room of the Shark Club. I also had to pay my tab.

I stood up, ignoring the sweat running down my face. My hair was matted against my head. I did yoga deep breathing to stifle the rolling waves inside my stomach. When I handed the bartender my credit card, he looked at me warily. He put on a plastic glove. I scratched out my signature on the Visa slip and lurched past the door, no longer interested in the outfit of the girl collecting the cover charge. My fantasy was clean air.

I found it.

Leaning against the railing, I closed my eyes and mastered the art of serenity. I needed to get home. I flagged a cab.

All the way to my place, I kept my window wide open. The air was divine. And by the time we reached my building, I was feeling better. Even my sweat-soaked shirt was drying out. Exhausted, I handed the cabbie my fare. I took the stairs up to my floor. The exercise helped clear my lungs. The clock on my table read 1:00 a.m. I stripped off my clothes and walked naked onto the balcony. I peered down and looked at the location on the pavement where my kissing couple parked each morning. It was empty. I swept my eyes across the horizon. Lights defined the activities of life below me. In response, I heard nothing but the night wind. I closed the patio door behind me.

I felt totally wiped out. The booze, cigar and sickness had won. Defeated, I walked in darkness to the bedroom. Stretched out on top of the covers, I bashed my hand around on the nightstand and found the phone. I put the receiver up to my ear and listened to the recorded message. It wasn't Marcia. I knew if I could have spoken to her at that moment she would have understood everything. Sorely, it was the other U 2 Can Date woman replying back to me.

"Hiya, Gus," spoke the voice. "I got your message. You want to get together? Sounds good. Tomorrow works for me. The day after, I'm leaving with the team for a baseball tournament in Brandon. I'll be gone for five days. I'll tell you what—I've got plans for you. Meet me at six thirty inside the Legion on Regent Avenue. I get off at six, but it takes me a half hour to cash out. Don't worry if you don't have a membership. I can wave you in as my boyfriend. You can always play shuffleboard with the geezers if you have to wait. I'll be driving my Jimmy. You won't miss it. It's baby duck yellow. I named it after my favourite champagne. Get it? It's parked out front in case you don't know where the Legion is. Oh, shit. Jeez, I forgot. You don't know who to ask for. Silly. I'm Zoe. 'Kay, Gus? Call me if you can't make it. Gotta go. The girls are waiting. We're playing a double-header tonight. Ciao."

I clicked off the phone. *A Transcona girl.* I shuddered. I craved a glass of water. My body refused to move. I fell asleep.

10

"I'm just looking for someone to go out with and have fun ..."

The morning was frenetic. I was hung over and still weak from the cigar. Tales of my showmanship at the Shark Club produced a healthy laugh for Christy. She suggested I leave smoking to the men. Peter and Alabama Daube waited in my office for their appointment.

I quickly discovered the Daubes were in a foul mood. Alabama Daube was dumping the contents of her purse onto my floor as I walked in the room. The mound of papers turned out to be torn pull-tab gambling tickets.

I decided to try some humour. It wasn't appreciated.

"Any winners in those?" I sat behind my desk.

"Gus, are you shittin' me?" Alabama Daube had no shame about what came out of her mouth.

"No! No!" I held up my hand. "I'm sorry, I was only trying to make light of the situation."

"Yeah? Well, we don't have *lights* at home because this asshole I call a husband spent our hydro money gambling. They cut the goddamn power."

"Peter," I said, looking at him with dismay. "I thought we had an agreement—no more betting?"

He shrugged. "I tried. Honest. I made a mistake. Some of the guys at the shop, they lied to me. They told me I had a sure thing."

"Of what?"

Alabama snapped. "This asshole believed he could win at the track. He knows shit about horses. He bet it all on the long shot. Why? Because his asshole buddies at work told him the horse was being doped."

"Where did they get this information, Peter?" I asked.

"Tom knows a mechanic who overheard two guys talking in the parts section inside the Canadian Tire store over on Nairn Ave."

"What an asshole," Alabama said, shaking her head.

"You agreed betting was off," I insisted.

"I know. I just wanted to win a little cash. It's our anniversary this month. I wanted to treat Alabama to the Cathay House."

"Chinese food?" I asked.

He nodded.

"I don't have power and I don't get a meal," Alabama said angrily. She gripped the chair so hard I though her nails were going to puncture my leather.

Alabama was ready to walk. Her marriage was done. She came today to rub the therapy in my face. I did something that went against all ethical principles of treatment. I bribed my patients. I paid them enough money to get the power restored. I wrote out a cheque. In return, they both promised to stay together until at least our next session.

Harold approached from inside the building as I stood waiting for my cab to meet Zoe at the Legion in Transcona. Harold was the superintendent of my building and lived on the first floor. Retired, bitter and never without an opinion, he was everyone's grandfather. I liked Harold.

He walked up and said, "Dressed like that at this time of the evening, either you going to someone's prayers, or you courting a woman. If you was married, I'd put my money on the prayers. No husband dresses for his wife like that. Since I know you still a single buck, then you courting tonight." He smiled, displaying his nicotine-coloured teeth.

I laughed. "Never could fool you, Harold. Your power of observation is astounding. Didn't you say you were once a police detective?" I nudged him with my arm.

"Yeah, and I also designed rocket ships in my evenings," he replied. "Forty-nine years of marriage makes a man see things different, boy. I swear you get to see behind you own head. Is a survival instinct to know when Mama's coming and you shouldn't be doin' what you be doin'."

"I'm going on a date. Tell me, Harold, do I look ready?"

He gave me a complete scan from my shoes to my hair before saying, "Take dat price tag off your cuff, for a start."

I reached down and removed it. Embarrassed, I thanked him.

"You owe me a coffee."

I agreed with him

Transcona is a city within itself. It's located at the most eastern side of Winnipeg, with Lagimodiere Boulevard drawing a line between it and the rest of the city. Transcona was said to be defined by idiosyncrasies like snowmobiles in the front yard, pink flamingos and pickup trucks outfitted with every Canadian Tire accessory. The cab drove down Regent Avenue. I was officially in the hands of Transcona natives. My chest tightened. I was greeted by Hi Neighbor Sam, a twelve foot, 3,000-pound statue of fiberglass and concrete.

The Legion was near the corner of Regent and Day Street in what I considered the heart of Transcona. No three-headed monsters appeared, but I did see a woman dressed in a zebra-print tube dress with white Reebok runners walking down the street.

True to Zoe's description, I couldn't miss her lemon-coloured Jimmy. I walked to the front doors of the Legion, a windowless two-story building that hid years of stories inside the faded brown walls.

Inside it was dark and loud. I picked my way carefully because I didn't want to trip over a veteran's walker. Looking at the woman working beside the bar, I knew instantly it had to be Zoe. Her tortured brown hair stuck out in a hood around a face stenciled in garish colours of blue and green. A top that was cut low and wide revealed vast amounts of quivering womanly cleavage. She wore stiletto black knee-high boots. And the fit of her leopard-skinned pants came in one size: tight.

"Gus, goddamn you, you've made it!"

I know had the attention of every World War Two veteran.

"Zoe?" I played coy.

"Of course! Do you see any other females in this joint?"

To be honest, I didn't. I was in her personal geriatric harem.

"How'd you guess it was me?" I asked.

She planted her hands on her hips. "You're the only guy in this joint younger than ninety. Go figure."

I walked over and shook her hand across the bar. Any one of her inch-long fingernails could have severed my finger. I pegged her age at the mid-forties.

"Meet the boys, Gus," she said, pointing around the room. "I could name them all, but half would be dead by the time I finished."

I gave a universal greeting. One guy piped up that he'd take seconds.

"Shut the hell up, Sidney, or I'll tell your wife what you said the next time she's in here. You'll be changin' your own enema bag for a month." Zoe meant business.

She looked me over and gestured. "Suit? Last time I went anywhere with a guy dressed like you was to my father's funeral in '83. Can you have fun in this getup?" She flipped my tie up over my shoulder.

I assured her the suit wouldn't impede my ability to enjoy myself, gently bringing my tie back to its proper place. I began to wonder if there was no place left in this world for an Armani-dressed man. I decided to show my wit. "Armani was designed with the intention of pairing it with leopard-skin pants," I said, flatly.

"Who's he, Gus?" Zoe asked while she filled two shooter glasses. She handed me one and tilted back her head for her own. I finished just as she did her second.

"A ritual of mine," she confessed. "Signifies the end of another shift and the price of my tips from these cheap geezers. Give me a few minutes to finish cashing out." She handed me a set of keys attached to a miniature six-pack of Labatt's Blue. "You can wait inside my truck if you want."

I walked outside and headed toward the parking lot. The glare of the sun against the yellow paint of Zoe's truck hurt my eyes. I squinted. Opening the door, I was overpowered by roses. The culprit was the largest sack of potpourri I had ever seen hanging from a rearview mirror. It was from Costco. On the seat and floors was an assortment of hairbrushes and combs, five cans of VO5 hair spray, various nail polishes and, to my astonishment, a hair dryer with a cigarette lighter adapter. I was inside a mobile cosmetic caravan. I flickered through a beaten copy of *Cosmo*. Zoe strode up to the driver's door, gobs of flesh bobbing out from her open blouse.

"Hiya!" She overpowered me with freshly poured perfume.

"I like your truck colour. Very vibrant."

"Thanks. The girls tell me it helps them find out which bar I'm getting loaded in."

I asked her what she wanted to do.

"First I need to stop by my apartment. I got so hammered last night, I left my purse in a friend's car. We won our baseball double-header. Didn't finish our celebration until four this morning. Sylvia dropped my stuff off at my place. Actually, it's my brother's pad. He's on disability. Hurt his back five years ago at work. On the side he does small-engine repairs for his friends. Gives him a little extra spending cash above the compensation cheques. Helps him afford his smokes. Our place is on Kildare Avenue, so it won't take us long to get there. Afterward, I'd like to shoot a few games of pool. I love it. You choose the location."

I suggested the Shark Club. Zoe had never heard of the place. I explained where it was, and she seemed to relax once I told her it was licensed.

I waited inside the truck while she ran up and retrieved her purse. I took the man who followed her outside to be her brother. He wore ragged pajama bottoms and was shirtless. He needed a shave. He nodded my way. I nodded back. I noticed Zoe still wore her leopard-skin pants.

En route to the club, Zoe talked about her job. I managed to conclude she had been there fifteen years. She said she loved flirting with the geezers.

We walked inside the Shark Club, and I swiftly understood this was the wrong venue for Zoe. I defiantly ignored the glances suggesting I was being accompanied by a prostitute. I selected a pool table in the corner of the room.

Zoe was already ordering drinks for us by the time I had chosen a couple of cues. I handed Zoe her cue.

"Here's the deal, Gus. Loser drinks the shooter chosen by the winner. Believe me, you don't want to be the loser." She barked out a laugh.

The girl who racked our balls removed the triangle and stepped aside.

"Hey, honey, I think we can manage that ourselves," said Zoe. She pushed the girl aside with a shove of her hip.

"It's her job," I explained.

"Yeah? Well, I guess she can dab me off in the bathroom."

The girl's face went red and she turned away.

"I'll break," I said, trying to steer the conversation.

"Say, Gus, you look mighty cute in your armageddon suit."

I wasn't sure if Zoe was complimenting me or just making fun again. She gave me a crooked smile. I broke apart the balls.

Our drinks came just as Zoe was about to take her shot. She threw the cue on the table and grabbed at the tray. She handed me shot glasses.

"Don't you drink anything that takes more than one mouthful?" I asked.

She looked at me funny. "Yeah, but that's my good-night gift for you."

She spread our drinks of shooters and beers on the table beside us. Zoe grabbed her cue and bent over the table. I watched her skirt ride up her legs. I also saw her stomach resting on the table. I looked away.

Zoe shouted. "What a nice shot! I'm feeling lucky tonight, Gus."

I prayed she meant the game.

Zoe sunk another ball. This time she jumped up and down. I admired the bounce to her cleavage.

"Dammit, these things are pissing me off."

I wasn't sure what she meant. "Problem?" I asked.

Her face was crunched together. She vigorously shook her shoulders. She leaned down for her next shot, abruptly pulling up.

"That's it," she snapped. "They've gotto go."

I balanced myself against my cue and waited for her to explain.

Zoe flung her cue on the table. She gave me a huge smile and reached inside her blouse. Her hands emerged after retrieving a flopping rubber sack. Without hesitating, she performed the miracle again, this time with her left chest. Now she held two jittering rubber masses in her hands. She turned and placed both along the table's bumper. I stared at them. It still didn't make sense. But suddenly Zoe's chest wasn't bulging from her blouse anymore.

"They get in the way," she confessed. "Now I can get serious." The cue ball stopped in front of her artificial cleavage after her next shot. It was my turn. I walked up to the table and tried to maneuver between the two rubber breasts. Focusing on the ball, I put aside the aroma of heated rubber and made my shot. I quickly stepped back.

After each turn, my eyes preyed on Zoe's artificial chest, resting on the pool table.

"You lose," came Zoe's announcement. She didn't even wait for our waitress. She went and got our drinks herself.

"Punishment shot," she said, handing it to me.

"We're here to have fun, not kill each other," I ventured.

"Drink. It's the rules."

I drank.

The liquid burned my throat. I felt sick.

"Game two," she shouted. Our racking girl approached our table and saw Zoe's tip resting on the bunker. She turned and briskly walked away. Zoe laughed.

"If they get in your way, Gus," Zoe said, pointing to her expunged chest with the tip of her cue like a college professor, "just move 'em aside."

I lost the next five games. My enthusiasm for the game waned. I wanted out. The rejected implants looming in my vision had become too much. Her shooters were killing me. My apprehension grew while I debated if Zoe had another section of her body to remove.

Zoe suggested we leave. I gratefully agreed. She was pushing me from behind when she said, "I can only imagine what the girls are going to say when they see me with you wearing a suit."

"I guess we're not meeting them at the ballet?"

She snorted.

I decided not to say anything more until we arrived at her surprise destination. It turned out to be the Palomino Club. I'd heard the legends: cougar heaven, the divorcée bar. Boys in their twenties who wanted to take the belt for bedding the oldest woman. There was a line of people worming outside the front entrance. Zoe led me past them all.

"Zoe, honey," said a bouncer with a shaved head and no neck. They hugged.

"Tony. This here is my date. Gus." He nodded at me and said, "Nice suit." I thanked him.

"The girls are inside," he said, flashing her a smile with a few toothless spaces.

Inside, the bar was a sensory zoo of loud music, flashing lights, gyrating half-naked bodies and the haze of cigarette smoke. Zoe led me straight to the drinks.

"Bottoms up!" She raised her glass and said, "Here's to you, here's to me, and should we ever disagree, screw you!"

I could only sip at the shot. The alcohol was starting to rival Serena's cigar.

"Come on, wus." Zoe poked me hard in the stomach. I flinched. I watched in slow motion as the creamy liqueur in my shot glass splattered my suit jacket.

"Uh oh," remarked Zoe. She laughed and said, pointing to my jacket, "Now you have a reason to throw that away."

"I just bought it!" I pleaded, fighting to control my anger.

"Yeah, right. Pinstripes went out with flashbulbs. I'd take it back and complain to TipTop." I was about to explain this was no graduation suit but rather handcrafted when I lost her attention.

"Zoe! Girlfriend! We thought you'd never show." Three women slinked toward us, balancing on high heels. All I could see were legs and hair.

"Gus, these three bitches are the craziest milfs you'll find in this city, and I'm proud to say they are my best friends! Girls! This is my date, Gus. Ignore the suit—he isn't my attorney."

My eyes watered from the assault of three pungent perfumes that combined into the perfect nasal storm. I shook hands with long manicured nails, assorted rings and cosmetic bracelets that ran up to the elbows. These chicks were decked out with twenty pounds of stainless steel. The redhead named Kat had to be over six feet tall in her heels. The second friend was black, and she wore her name around her neck on a steel collar that said *Kitten.* The third girlfriend was called Sammy, and her hair was a two-foot beehive. I wondered where she withdrew her honey from and was about to ask as a joke, but I feared being shown. Between all three women there was enough material to make one legal-sized skirt. I was about to break away for the bathroom when all four women screamed in unison.

"Bo!"

I looked to my right to see a guy fast approaching, furiously shaking a champagne bottle. I joined the squealing woman as the foam arched and fanned over the five of us. As if I needed to punish my suit any further, Bo made sure it was becoming a Laundromat special clean.

"Hey, man!" I shouted, angry. "You'll be footing the bill to clean this," pointing to the pink foam all over my suit jacket and pants.

"Relax, dude," he said, slapping my back, laughing with the girls.

"Go easy, Gus." Zoe defended her friend. "Bo does that every time he sees us Wolfettes together. It's tradition. Usually, we give him a good ole-fashioned wet T-shirt cougathon!" They all laughed.

"Well, that's just great," I spat, not accepting the rationale of the Wolfettes, "but do you think with me standing here between you all he'd have the brains to maybe think for a minute that his champagne entrance might not be a good idea? Do I look like I want to give anyone a wet T-shirt contest?" I looked at each of the women, and they continued to laugh.

"Listen," suggested Beehive Girl, pushing her body up against mine and grabbing each of my shoulders, "how 'bout I lick off all this yummy champagne to make it all better for you, huh?" She flicked out the longest tongue I had ever seen not coming from a reptile.

"Go for it, buddy," shouted Bo for encouragement. *"She won't stop at your suit either!"* he added. They all laughed, but I scowled.

"No thanks," I said, pushing her away. "I don't know where that tongue has been."

"I sure do," piped in Zoe.

"Listen, pal," suggested Bo. "I'll get you a drink to make up for this, okay? Buds?" He held out his fist, and I tapped it back. It was no use arguing with a meathead who sported a mane of permed hair from the eighties and wore black faux-leather pants with a vest.

"That's our boy!" said Zoe, body rubbing against Kat while they each held their drinks above their heads. They gyrated to the thump of remixed country tunes with rave-injected synthesizers. Dry ice swept over our feet, and the spinning lights overhead bounced off all the stainless steel hanging from the Wolfettes. I looked around, amazed, wondering how the hell this date had started out with seniors on life support at the Legion. I did not understand how my dates were veering off on such cockamamie tangents. I seriously needed to rethink the selection formula if I was to continue my quest to find a soul mate through my phone. I was certain being deemed high risk from this lifestyle would jeopardize my ability to qualify for a life insurance policy.

"Here ya go, sport," said Bo, handing me a large Caesar.

"I don't really drink these," I started to say, but then I thought, *Why turn this group any further against me?* and I added, "without all of you toasting together!"

Kitten came over and lightly hip checked me.

"How's that for a toast, Suitman?" she purred.

I tried to swallow, but her perfume made me sneeze. I blew a shower of Caesar into the air and across Kitten's cleavage in her low-cut top. Flecks of salt glistened from her tanned skin.

Bo shouted. *"See!* I knew Gus wanted that wet T-shirt after all, ladies!"

Before I could even object to the statement, both Zoe and Beehive Girl bent down in front of Kitten and did multiple licks across her chest, scooping up the bits of salt. Bo pulled out a camera from somewhere and took a photograph. *"That's one for my bathroom mirror!"* He grinned devilishly and gave me a wink.

I wanted out of the bedlam and was working furiously at finishing my makeup drink. I was nearing the bottom when I noticed the girls and Bo smirking at me.

"What?" I asked, suddenly feeling like I had become the centre of attention.

"How you feeling, Gus?" asked Kitten, scoping me with her eyes up and down.

I frowned.

"Any ... urges?" suggested Zoe.

I stared at them.

"Feeling like a stud?" inquired Kat.

"What the hell are you all talking about?" I was starting to become very self-conscious about something that I was obviously missing.

"Dude," Bo said, grinning, not making any sense to me.

"Okay, already. What's up? Why are you all looking at me like that?" I scanned my body.

"Bo's given you a little helping hand," Zoe said with a silly smile, downing the shot of tequila she had in her hand.

Bo fist-punched both Kat and Kitten and said, "I gave ya a little extra in your drink, dude. You know, to help you when you step up with Zoe tonight."

I looked at him blankly, having no clue what he was talking about. Bo read my confusion and clarified.

"Dude, I put a Viagra in your Caesar! No worries for you sporting timber!"

I was horrified. I had been drugged! I was appalled.

"What the hell were you thinking!" I shouted, trying to be heard above the pounding music.

Bo came over and put me into a headlock. "The least I could do for you, dude. No worries." He fake-wrestled me for a moment; I was actually trying to break free for real. I pushed myself clear and put my drink down on the table.

"This is bullshit, you guys! I don't need Viagra. That's not cool, slipping that shit in my drink!"

"Relax, man," breathed Zoe, "you don't think you need it now, but let me tell you, Bo did you a favour." She tried to run her fingers through my hair, and I ducked away.

"Zoe doesn't have heavy-tuned suspension in her four-by-four for nothing!" squealed Kitten, making all the girls join in.

I looked at them hopelessly.

"I'm going to the bathroom," I said, turning my back and tuning out their laughter.

I searched for the washroom. Once inside, I walked on a urine-soaked floor that smelled just as bad. I watched the patent leather on my Florsheim shoes absorb the secretions. I looked in the mirror. My face was red from rubbing against Bo's imitation leather vest. *What a bunch of goons!* I had no desire to go back to them or even say good-night. *Lord knows what else they might try to slip into my drinks.* I wondered what side effects I would suffer after having "dropped a Viagra." I prayed it wasn't one of those "four-hours-and-still-erect, consult-your-doctor" side effects. I'd bathe in a tub of ice and shock myself with electricity before I explained my problem to the triage nurse at the ER.

The thought of returning to Zoe and her sorority of cretins made standing inside the bathroom's urine soaked floor seem like the better option. I glanced at myself in the mirror. I looked shell shocked. My eyes told me the answer. *Run.* I pushed my way through a group of guys standing outside the bathroom door and did my best exit stage left out the Palomino's front lobby door. The air outside was humid. I immediately began to sweat. Without thinking about how to get home, I started walking. I embraced the silence of the darkened streets compared to the thumping music inside the Palomino Club with Zoe's clan of eighties cut-outs. An inviting green Perkins Restaurant appeared, and I was suddenly very hungry. It occurred to me that all Zoe and I had done all night was drink. Apparently eating was far down on Zoe's list of priorities.

The restaurant was very busy. I managed to find an empty booth, and after waiting twenty minutes for a waitress who looked weary after being heckled every minute of her night shift, I ordered a plate of fries. Evidently, this was the place to be after an evening of drinking. The castaways from the surrounding bars laughed and swore from their tables. Shouts preceded the fight that broke out in the booth behind me. I stood

111

up and was hit in the chest by a bottle of mustard. Now a rope of mustard sectioned me like a slab of beef. The lone waitress stood back while the two fighters were grappled apart. Peace among the patrons resumed. My appetite disappeared. I left without paying. *Screw it.* I defied anyone to try to stop me. I couldn't suffer any more indignation tonight.

It was raining when I walked outside. In seconds my wool suit sagged with water. I conceded—it was officially ruined.

I sank into an intensely antisocial mood. For self-punishment, I decided to continue my trek home in the rain on foot. Forty-five minutes later, I was cutting through the legislative parking lot, still a half hour from home, now cold, the booze flushing from my system. I simmered in my foulness on the vacant streets.

A man inside a parked Cavalier rolled down his window and called out. I intended to ignore him. His voice carried in the dark a second time. I twisted to my right and stopped a few steps from his open window. He looked to be in his mid-thirties, clean cut. I leaned and looked inside his car. He was alone.

"You're wet," he said, grinning. I nodded while he added, "I thought you could use a ride. I was just leaving."

"I know Winnipeg's a friendly place, but I would think picking up strangers for midnight rides is beyond the call of duty," I said.

He chuckled.

"Yeah, well, there were a few times I was the one walking, wishing anyone would do the same for me. Just thought I could help. Besides, you look like you need to get out of that suit. Whadda you say?"

I considered. I had another thirty minutes' walk. My feet were beginning to rot, and I was tiring.

"Tell you what," I offered.

"Shoot."

"Let me ride in the backseat."

"Deal."

I opened the door and checked that the door handle worked. It did. I noticed his strange look.

"Saw it once in a movie. The couple didn't check the door. Couldn't get away when the driver turned out to be a psycho. Killed them both."

He laughed, started the car and responded by saying, "That's old tricks. Now I just turn around and shoot."

"Okay, enough said before I change my mind," I replied, not sure if he was joking. I trusted my judgment and climbed into the car.

"I promise to get you home safely. Where are we going?"

"Wellington. Drive east, and I'll tell you when we get there. Thanks." Now I felt the cold wetness of my suit. It was going to be a total loss.

"Do you mind if I remove my jacket? I'm going green with moss underneath." He said it was no problem. I peeled back my jacket and unbuttoned my shirt. Although I was half-naked inside a stranger's car, I felt slightly better. He turned the heat on.

"So what do you normally charge strangers?" I asked, amused.

He inquired about what I meant.

"You know, to drive a guy home. I can offer you twenty bucks."

He looked back at me strangely through the rearview mirror. We were idling in the lot.

"Let's go before I lose my nerve," I urged.

"Just sit tight, Romeo," he remarked.

I was about to ask him what the problem was when both passenger doors opened and I felt strong hands yanking me from the car. I was hauled outside, my face pushed into a puddle of water on the asphalt, my arms twisted behind my back. I tried pulling away, and a knee began to grind my head into pepper. I was about to scream when someone spoke.

"Take it easy, playboy," I heard a man's voice say. I felt cold metal around my wrists. I was about to yell for help when I was lifted to my feet. I was staring into a group of policeman.

"You're being charged for soliciting a prostitute for sexual favours. I am about to read you your rights. Afterward, you will be taken and booked at District One." Another man began reciting the all-too-familiar speech that I had heard countless number of times watching *Cops* on Saturday nights. Then I would laugh at the mentally challenged perps squirming in front of the cameras. I wasn't laughing now.

"Hold on a minute—" I began.

"Tell your story to the sergeant at district. We've heard all the bullshit, bud."

I was shoved into the back of a squad car. I was astonished to see that the parking lot was scattered with police cars and flashing lights. As my head was being pressed into the backseat of the car, I caught sight of my friendly Winnipeg driver. He was joking with another policeman beside the Cavalier. I felt foolish with my shirt undone. This didn't look good. I glanced around the car's interior. The doors didn't have handles. I really was dead.

The cab dropped me off in front of my building just before five o'clock in the morning. I beat the sunrise by fifteen minutes but not the rap for being formally charged with soliciting prostitution. I was sent home with a future court date, along with a brassy warning that should I fail to appear, a warrant would be issued for my arrest, and I'd be apprehended and jailed. I hoped the ink smeared on my fingers would not become a lingering tattoo of guilt.

Harold was sneaking a smoke in the lobby when I did the walk of shame.

"You look like shit, friend." Harold never believed in tact.

I didn't have the energy to attempt a fake smile. Even a simple response seemed mountain-like.

"Suit's shot," he said, pressing on, pointing at my tattered Armani with his cigarette. "Dis why I stay married forty-nine years. Sometime I think I'm the fool fer keeping with one woman. Den I see a guy like you coming in after chasing women—takes away the itch to remove the ring." He puffed at his cigarette.

"Shouldn't you be doing that outside?" I asked.

He ignored my comment. "She was a hellcat, eh?" He grinned, smoke clouding his face.

"I'll give you the highlights later, Harold. It's been a long night." I walked away and rebelliously took the elevator. I shoved my suit down the trash chute. If the evening hadn't been demeaning enough, when I was trying to vocalize my innocence at the police station, during the inspection of my belongings, out came the penis ring from the dancer at my initiation night at Club Happenings. Also found inside my pants pocket, compliments of Bo, was one more of his extra-strength Viagra tablets. The circle of policemen laughed and pointed while taking pictures with their personal cell phones, mixed in with evidence photos for my new file that further deflated my pleas of morality and integrity and earned me a nickname from the desk sergeant: *Stud Cock.*

11

"I've joined this service because I've found it hard to meet new people between home and work …"

I stumbled through my life for the next three weeks. I hadn't been outside since my arrest, other than for the walk between my apartment and work. I hadn't told anyone, including Christy. So the sun above felt good on my face as I sat with Lonny outside the Muddy Waters Café patio at the Forks. It was my first chance to speak with Lonny since our night at the Shark Club. He had been travelling for work on a cell phone sales campaign to the Manitoba farming communities. Speaking about my ordeal was the therapy I needed. Lonny gave me his listening ear.

"When are you seeing a lawyer about this?" he asked, sipping his iced tea. His skin was bronze after taking full advantage of the summer months. I hadn't been in the sun long enough to develop a hint of a tan line.

"I have an appointment with a lawyer who's downtown in the TD Center. I don't have a clue how competent he is. It isn't like I asked for references for the best lawyers to defend gay johns." Somehow I managed to join Lonny in a laugh.

Lonny shook his head and replied, "I can only imagine the expression on your face. You're sitting in the backseat of the car, soaked from rain, your shirt undone, and suddenly, bam, you're being hauled out on your ass and booked on charges for wanting man sex in your booty."

"I told you it was a bullshit setup. If the cops have to resort to that low level of deception for sting operations, I want to sue. Nothing happened to indicate I was there for anything other than the ride I was offered. Remember, he approached me first. What a huge, ridiculous embarrassment."

Lonny's gazed into the blue sky, and I asked him what he was thinking.

"About the broad you were dating earlier that night …" Lonny began.

"Zoe?"

"Right. Lives in Transcona and drives a canary-yellow Jimmy?"

"Baby Duck."

He grinned and said, "I dated her."

I looked at him carefully. He wasn't joking.

"What—?"

"Yeah. Last summer, at the former Rolling Stones bar. She's got an amazing chest, right? Well, I spotted her bouncing around on the dance floor. We left in her truck after exchanging a few words and shooters. Gus, she drove us out to the floodway. Next thing I know, she's slammed it into four-by-four, and we're off-roading up and down the hills through the freaking water in the middle of the night. Scared the shit out of me. She said it was sexual foreplay. What the hell, you know?"

I rolled my eyes and responded, "I go out with her and get arrested. You get lucky. Was she wearing her rubber implants?"

Lonny eyebrows furrowed, and he shrugged. "Implants? Does she have any? Who knows? It was dark. We were drunk. There's not a lot of room inside the truck. All I remember were limbs everywhere. My feet kept sliding on cans of V05."

"I'm losing hope, Lonny."

Lonny brushed my remark aside and said, "You've only started, dude. Trust me. By the time you're through, you'll be carved up like an old school desk."

"Thanks for the encouraging outlook."

"Deal with it."

I nibbled at my chicken fingers. I wasn't hungry.

"Guess what?" Lonny said, suddenly.

"What?"

"I've got to get another swab done. Chlamydia, this time. Got it from a university football cheerleader. Shit. You never can tell. She seemed clean."

"Clean means nothing."

"I mean, you'd expect a girl to look after herself."

"It's a two-way road, isn't it?"

"I'm going to start asking for a bill of health. This is getting stupid. My second test this year, you know."

"Start protecting yourself."

"Yeah, right. It's a sad day when I've got to start wearing an Hazmat Suit when I want to be with a woman."

"Then don't bitch about having to get swabs."

Lonny leaned across the table and disclosed in a low voice, "I'm on to a new thing, Gus." Lonny confessed, "Cyber chats."

"You mean online chatting?"

He nodded. "It's great. You should read what some of these chicks write. Filthy! I've been exchanging words with this one sick mother who blows me away with the shit she types. I'm trying to convince her to meet me in person. If she's anything like what she writes about, you may never see me again." We laughed.

"I'll wait for your confessions in *Penthouse Letters*," I said.

Lonny sat up in his chair. "If you're this despondent about finding a decent woman, let me try reading your hand."

"What the hell are you talking about?"

"I met this girl in Dauphin last week in the lounge of the motor inn where I was staying. We got to chatting, and she mentioned she reads hands as a hobby. She read mine. Said I have an extraordinary sex drive. How about that? She also showed me how to understand what some of the lines mean. The only one I was really interested in was the love line. I call it the 'getting lucky' line. Want me to read yours? Believe it or not, this shit actually works. She said it's all connected to the development of our personalities and nervous system. I wasn't really paying attention. She had nice breasts, and I'd listen to anything to keep her talking."

"So now you're an expert?" I asked, skeptical.

"Like I said, dude, it's the basics."

I held out my hand, and Lonny grabbed it and looked at my palm. He was quiet while his eyes darted up and down. He ran a finger along a grove on my palm. Uncomfortable, I glanced to my left and noticed a familiar face. Jerry Trotts. He was walking past our table. Our eyes met. He ran his eyes down to where Lonny held my hand. Jerry Trotts raised an eyebrow. We locked eyes again, and he winked. Without breaking stride, he reached down and lifted his pant leg to reveal fishnet stockings. He nodded briefly, lowered his pants and left the area.

"Okay, forget it," I said quickly, pulling back my hand from Lonny's. He looked at me, startled.

"What's up, man?"

"Forget it. I ... let the future happen as it will." I sucked at my drink, refusing to look at him.

12

"Looking for a couple of young, well-endowed guys to have some intimate fun with. Must be clean, discrete and know their way around the bedroom ..."

I should have felt some eagerness, even a twinge of curiosity. Surely not emptiness, a vortex of blackness. Was I that tarred with bitterness and detachment? In a few hours I'd arranged to meet Donna Jean Reynolds, who was divorced, in her late-thirties, with two teenaged daughters, self-described as full-figured, with soft features, someone simply interested in conversation and getting to know one another on the road to friendship. To me this had safety written all over it. And at that, point I needed a date inside the back of a Red Cross truck. I was developing a twitch above my right eye.

Donna Jean had invited me to her place for supper. Her offer left me with an easy escape should the evening turn sour and little chance of adding to my criminal convictions. More importantly, it eliminated an opportunity for me to run up my credit card. The summer of dating was quickly draining my monetary resources.

I slammed the fridge door. I heard a bottle crash inside. Instead of checking to see what destruction I'd created, I walked out onto the balcony. It was a toss-up whether it was hotter inside my apartment with the broken air-conditioning or outside under the sun in the ninety-degree humidity. We were being treated to one of Manitoba's famous heat waves. It would likely last for weeks. Harold wouldn't promise when a technician could look at my air conditioner. I threatened to hold back rent. He countered with eviction.

I opened my windows. I discovered the glue in freshly laid carpet reacts with humidity to produce noxious plumes of gas that I loudly claimed were silently killing me. Nobody cared. The heat created the driest summer in twenty-nine years. Even the green tree leaves were showing pain by turning yellow. The longest day of sunlight for the year was coming up. For me it meant summer was half over. The days would begin to get shorter. My chest tightened. Shorter days brought me closer to spending my fortieth birthday alone and single. I hadn't grasped an encouraging shred of substance in any of my dates yet. I wallowed in the same frenzy for escape as a trapped animal. I contemplated stepping in front of a car. In reality it might be the easier choice.

The Fringe Festival was starting, I read in the newspaper. Two weeks of amateur acting, plays, tricks, treats and all kinds of shit, scattered around the city. I would go again this year and beg Lonny to come with me again. Like last year. I laughed alone in movie theatres. I was the freak sitting between boys and girls engaged in healthy social interactions. I was the perv on the precipice of life looking in, glaring, ogling those I couldn't have and wanted to be.

Fed up with the wait for a breeze that wasn't about to come, I walked back inside the apartment and caught my reflection in a mirror. The elastic band on my underwear was torn, and a huge section of pubic hair was exposed by the sag. I didn't care anymore. The underwear was coming with me on my date with Donna Jean.

I pulled out the bottle of wine chilling inside the fridge, a red suggested by the clerk. It was also coming with me tonight. I saw what had broken inside the fridge: a bottle of HP Steak Sauce. The contents were now coating a plate of shriveling spaghetti. I closed the fridge door.

I sported a new approach for dressing for the evening's date—abused underwear, creased jeans, faded T-shirt, runners. *Take it or leave it, baby.* I called a cab.

The short drive to River Heights was pleasant because of the mature elm trees that lined the streets. The canopy of green was almost tranquilizing. It put my mind at ease. My head rested on the worn seat cushion. Through the back window I saw the full moon. I disregarded any astrological connection and closed my eyes for the remainder of the drive.

The car stopped. I wanted to tell the cabbie to keep driving. Instead, I sat up, paid my fare and walked up the cement path to the house. The grass was cut, the gardens sprinkled with flowers. A girl stood behind the glass door. For a second my breath quickened, thinking it was Donna Jean. But the girl looked way too young. Oddly, I felt a fleeting disappointment. As I got closer, I saw the sensually firm lines of a body only someone hitting their twenties can have. Her nipples were clearly defined behind her thin white top. Her feet were bare, and when I reached the door I noticed her hair was wet. It had to be a daughter. I forced myself to wipe the lust from my face and force a smile.

"Mom, I think your date is here," I heard the raving young goddess call into the house. I opened the door, and she stood blocking my way, her breasts inches from my face. I was swarmed by the smell of a ripe apple orchid. My entire body flushed and tingled. She stepped back.

"Hi, I'm here to see Donna Jean," I said, doing an impressive job of sounding casual. Meanwhile, I was wallowing in her arousing scent. I fought to get a grip on my emotions. The girl gave me a glossy smile, and I watched her walk away. I didn't think she wore anything under her grey sweats. I pretended to be looking the opposite way just as Donna Jean approached from around the corner. This time I knew it was her. She was more of what I expected: my height, brown hair that was dull but nicely pulled back. All her subtle curves had long filled out, but she still retained the shape she had gifted to her daughter. When she got closer, I saw that even makeup couldn't hide the years on her skin. But her eyes glittered, and she held out a hand that was soft, warm and firm. She leaned nearer for a partial hug and said, "It's a pleasure to meet you, Gus. Supper will be ready in half an hour. Can I get you anything to drink?" She stepped back, and I said a scotch would be fine. I needed something strong to numb the images of her daughter.

"Great. Follow me into the living room then."

She pointed to a chair, and I sat down. The house appeared much larger now that I was inside. Next to the living room was the kitchen, and on my other side was a rec-room with a television running. The furniture was dated, dark and floral. I found the decorations too much: pictures, statues, plants. While Donna Jean reached for a glass in the kitchen, I caught another set of eyes looking at me from the hallway. The girl was wearing jeans and had blonde hair. However, she was every bit as stunning as the other. I looked away. Donna Jean had a wonderful genetic pool.

"Very nice house, Donna Jean," I complimented. And I meant it, despite the busyness. It was clean and organized. It even smelled womanly. I felt at ease. She scored a point.

"Did you bring us wine for the evening?" asked Donna Jean, pointing to the bottle in my hand. I nodded and handed it to her.

"Red. This will go excellently with our meal. Good choice," she told me.

"I had the kid at the store pick it out for me," I admitted. "I don't buy wine often."

"We can't be experts at everything," she replied, moving efficiently around the kitchen.

I studied a series of framed school pictures of two young females on the wall in front of me. They had to have been taken years ago; the girls sported thick black eyeglass frames and wore braces. Acne pitted their faces.

I decided to open a conversation. "Was that your daughter who answered the door?"

She laughed. "Isn't the resemblance to my striking beauty remarkable? That was my oldest, Natasha. There's another one around here somewhere. I think she's watching TV. If you see her, it's Shannon. I've been told they're both going out together to a movie in a couple of hours."

"No problem," I said. "This beats the noisy restaurant crowds."

"Annoying, isn't it. I took a chance you might also be one of the disenfranchised, fed up with waiting in lines, sour waiters and inflated prices for dressed-up Kraft dinners." She handed me the scotch. She held one of her own and sat down across from me. I was impressed she drank scotch. Now she scored a major point.

We were both quiet for a few moments, reflecting on our own thoughts. I took a sip and finally asked, "Have you been using the System for a while?"

She knew what I meant and replied with both a smile and a laugh. "You're my first. Do I seem that nervous?" She put the glass to her mouth and looked my way.

I returned her smile. "No. Not at all. In fact, I would never have guessed because you actually seem very relaxed."

"That's called showing my years. I believe it's the one positive thing about age. The grey hair and cottage cheese are negatives." We both laughed. It was a pleasing sound. Point number three scored. I loosened up.

"How about you?" she asked.

I smirked. "You're number three."

"So far so good … ?"

"If I can walk out of here with the clothes on my back and a good-night hug, you'll be awarded my undying affection."

She grinned. "That bad, huh?"

"It's changing the way I counsel my patients in their treatments. Honestly. I've seen the other side of women, and it's frightening. I can stand in line at the bank and have a totally pleasant conversation with the woman next to me. Put her in a dating situation and she becomes this raging, predatory hormone. It's taken me four weeks since the last experience with a girl I've now nicknamed 'Medusa' to recover enough guts to arrange this date."

"I can believe it," said Donna Jean. "The men I've been dating were blind dates, compliments of the people I call friends. You've been an absolute bonus, Gus. Really. First, you've been the only gentleman to bring over a gift. Second, I didn't detect liquor on your breath. And you've even shaved!" We chuckled and drank our scotch.

I felt the warmth spreading.

"My friend Lonny tries to keep me focused. He's famous for saying dating is a game of chess. A lot of playing pieces are going to be kicked out of the game before checkmate is called. I don't think I have as much time as in a game of chess before my patience runs out. Or the money in my wallet."

She nodded and said, "A million years ago when I was dating my husband, he paid for everything. I've discovered what women have done to themselves with liberation in the last twenty years. Now I'm splitting automobile gas! What a crock. Where's the chivalry?"

"Here's to the sanctuary of a good book," I toasted, and we banged glasses.

I turned when I caught movement coming from the hallway.

"Sorry!" came the throaty apology.

"Well, since you're cutting through and interfering with my entertaining, I guess I should introduce you," said Donna Jean, feigning that she was resigned by the intrusion. I could see she was immensely proud of her daughters.

I stood and held out my hand. Donna Jean introduced me to her daughter Shannon. We shook. As she was removing her hand, I took notice of the smoothness of her skin. Life hadn't yet maliciously inflicted the telltale lines of compounded work. It advertised her innocence. Ashamed, I kept my observations to myself. Minus bonus point for me.

"Nice to meet you, Shannon. Don't worry. It's no bother to me where you walk in this house. I'm the stranger here, remember."

"Sorry again, kids," Shannon said, laughing. "I have to start getting ready. Nice to meet you, Gus." She disappeared.

"Well, I'm sure to get a full report on their impressions of you tomorrow, my man," admitted Donna Jean. "They've got to make sure their mom isn't getting involved with a nerd or something."

I laughed and said, "Good thing I left my pen holder at home." Donna Jean grinned, stood up and went back into the kitchen.

"I think our food is just about ready," she said.

"I can't wait. If it tastes anything like it smells, it's going to be amazing."

"Don't flatter me until you've tried it. I thought my ex enjoyed my cooking. Look where it got me."

"He was a fool for leaving a woman who can bake and shake in the kitchen. I think it's a dying art."

"Unlike food, adding spice to a relationship requires more than just a sprinkling of curry."

"Exactly. It's a helluva lot more complex. If you don't mind my asking, have you been divorced for long? I realize this is a sore topic for people. I'm reluctant to ask during a non-professional talk."

"Not at all. Hey, being divorced is a fact of my life. I'm not ashamed of it. Nor do I try to hide it. Gary is a great guy. I still love him. But not in the way you need to love somebody in a relationship. We never were the right match for each other, not from day one. I think we got married just because it seemed like the right thing to do. Then Natasha came along. A couple years later it was Shannon. By then we were so entrenched that breaking apart wouldn't be fair to the girls. We did all the things families do. Parent-teacher. Sports. Gift-filled Christmases. We gave our girls tons of love and support. By the time they were in their teens, even they could see the cracks in our marriage. Separate beds can be a huge giveaway. So it wasn't a great shock when we sat them down and discussed a divorce. We felt it was important they assisted in the decision. Gary and I were willing to stay married if a divorce would have created serious problems for the kids. Amazing thing about your children—they know a lot of things about their parents we don't realize or want them to know. Unanimously, they said they would accept any decision we made. It wasn't completely easy. But it was still better than continuing the fake smiles and orgasms for another twenty years. It's been three years now."

"I'm guessing you're not about to rush into another marriage."

"Funny you should say that, Gus. However, I would gladly walk down the aisle again if I found a man I loved. Absolutely. I still have feelings, you know." She laughed. Her back faced me while she poured the steaming contents from a pot into a bowl. I turned and looked into the shadowy hallway in time to see Shannon, naked, in the doorway to another room, about to wrap a large towel around her body. She looked my way and held the towel open a moment longer before pulling it closed. She disappeared.

I groaned.

"What was that, Gus?" Donna Jean's back was still turned to me.

"Ah, do you need some help?"

"No, thanks. I've just about got it wrapped up."

I drained the last of my scotch. *Yeah*, I thought to myself, *so does your daughter*. I craved a bigger glass of scotch. I furtively glanced back down the hallway. Mercifully, this time it remained empty. I focused my attention on Donna Jean and tried to erase her daughter's naked image.

"Another one?" she asked holding up my glass.

"Please."

"How about yourself, Gus? Ever married?"

"Nope. I realize it's a bit of an oddity for a guy my age not to be married. Then again, I've never been involved to a degree that I've even lived with another woman. I can't begin to imagine how I'd cope trying to share the television remote."

"Or with a perpetual shortage of toilet paper. Did you think of that one?" She handed me a fresh drink, and I gulped it.

"See, it's things like that you don't find out until you're in it neck deep."

"All right," she said, pulling a chair back from the kitchen table, "come and get it." We settled in, speaking little while we ate. The food was very good. Another big bonus point for her. They were adding up.

Donna Jean raised her glass, filled with the wine I had brought along. I followed her lead.

"Here's to a wonderful tonight and finishing everything on your plate." She grinned and pointed while we drank. I enjoyed her humour. She was aloof and at the same time sharp. I was impressed and said so.

"Gus, you're more of a gentleman than I'm used to. Just not having you ask me who my favourite wrestler is moves you to my he's-a-great-guy bonus round." She blushed.

"Please, I think we're both finding a level of comfort in each other. We've been with enough losers to recognize the flower in a field of weeds. And now you've shown me there is food outside of McDonald's."

She reached out her hand and touched mine. I didn't mind. Nor did I attempt to move it. We stared into each other's eyes. There was a conflicting mixture of vibrancy and sadness in hers. I could only wonder what horrors my own displayed. Disconcerted, I prayed it wasn't a burning image of her naked daughter. I became spooked.

"Thanks for the meal," I said, pulling away and sitting back in my chair. Her expression loosened while she mimicked my posture. Our connection was broken.

"You're welcome," she said, standing up. "Listen, if you want to move down into the rec-room, make yourself at home."

"Actually, I'd like to wash up if I could."

"Bathroom's down the hall to the left," she said, moving our plates to the sink.

I walked down the hallway, already forgetting whether Donna Jean had said left or right. I turned right.

I pushed open the door and stopped. Natasha stood in her bra and panties. She looked up at me and smiled. Her tan skin defined her black attire.

"Sorry," I said, starting to turn away.

"Lost?" she asked, and suddenly she was beside me.

"Uh huh."

"If you're looking for the bathroom, it's across the hallway." She brushed past me and her full breasts pressed into my arm. I went into the bathroom and locked the door. I looked at myself in the mirror. I saw the face of a thirty-nine-year-old man having illegal thoughts.

I turned on the taps and let the water run. I needed to regroup. *What the hell is going on?* Was Donna Jean in on this grotesque display by her daughters? I couldn't accept such a depraved plot line. Donna Jean was too sweet for such perversion. I was already dancing a thin line with the law with my current charges. I'd heard that in Canada sexual criminals get "dangerous offender" status, meaning no parole, and I needed parole.

It had to be the daughters' own doing. To scare me off? Vengeful daughters were not uncommon. I had treated a few. I contemplated my next action. I didn't have any. I splashed cold water on my face. *It's the damn full moon.* I knew it. Signs could never be ignored. I thought about my kissing couple. Where had the fuckers misled me?

I must have been in the bathroom long enough for Donna Jean to become concerned. She knocked.

"You okay, Gus?"

I called out over the running water, "No problem. I'm just a bit of a freak when it comes to scrubbing my hands. I'll be right out." I looked at myself again in the mirror. I didn't recognize the person with wild eyes and burning ears.

"C'mon, dammit," I mumbled under my breath. *Ignore the girls. Concentrate on Donna Jean.* She was a wonderful woman, actually worth a second and third date. I cautioned myself not to screw this up.

I left the bathroom.

Donna Jean was by herself in the rec-room. The television was on, and she sat forward when I walked in and parked myself beside her.

"Don't worry," I said, holding up my hand, "I take my time when I wash my hands. Moreover, I don't like to rush when I dig through the cabinets."

Donna Jean hesitated a moment before she realized I was joking. There was notable relief on her face. She relaxed. We both leaned back in the softness of the couch, and she said, "Thank God, I thought you hated my dinner so much you were trying to drown yourself in my sink." We both laughed.

"So tell me," I asked, looking around the room, "besides cooking, what else do you do for entertainment?"

She smiled and stretched out, obviously over the tension of my marathon bathroom break.

"During the summer I try to do as much as I can outside. My girlfriends and I go to a lot of the patios. The Fringe Festival is coming up, and I'll be seeing some of the events. I did it for the first time last year and enjoyed it tremendously."

"Hey, I was thinking about going myself," I admitted, secure that I wouldn't mind leaving an opportunity open to see Donna Jean again.

"Listen, if you don't come down with a major intestinal illness from tonight's supper, perhaps you'd consider going with me to the festival? I'm not fussy which acts I go to." She studied my face.

I grinned and said, "I think it's a great idea. I was dreading convincing Lonny to go with me. I knew he did it out of pity last summer."

"Is this the friend you were referring to earlier?"

"Yes."

"Is he married?"

I squinted at her and asked, "Are you thinking of dumping me for him? He's a salesman. So he's sleazy."

She laughed and said, "I didn't mean to sound like a desperate, backstabbing bitch. I just found it strange he hates going to the Fringe. Singles go there in droves in the hope of meeting someone. At least, I think someone once told me that."

I shook my head. "Lonny was into this cyber-dating gig last time I spoke with him. He gets off on the things women write to him. He's actually trying to meet one of the girls in person."

"Good luck to him," Donna Jean said, taking a sip of her drink and beaming. "The women are *never* what they claim to be. Trust me. If I used the computer, I'd have Britney Spears's body with Rosie O'Donnell's wit."

"No, you wouldn't," I said, brushing my hand against her shoulder. "You're a woman who can be herself online and in person." She gobbled up my compliment and thanked me. I gave myself back the minus point from earlier.

"Mom, we're getting ready to leave and wanted to let you know," piped a female voice from the kitchen.

"Then come over here and do it properly."

Donna Jean's daughters walked into the rec-room, their manner of dress far from what I would think going to a movie would entail. In defiance, I made sure not to give them anything more than a casual glance.

"Gus," said Donna Jean, "I don't think I formally introduced you to my daughter Natasha. You met her at the door when you first came in."

I did not add the other occasion, when she was wearing her black-lace underwear. I waved a silent hello.

"Nice to meet you," she replied. Her lips were outlined in bright, glossy lipstick. I looked back at Donna Jean. The sight of her two daughters, dressed in miniskirts and shiny black knee-high boots I swore were made of latex, was killing me. Worse, I could now smell the tantalizing blend of perfumes. I found a clock on the wall and saw it was nearly nine thirty. I decided I had taken the evening as far as I could on a first date. What I really needed now was an empty room so I could put this night in perspective. I was beginning to feel claustrophobic.

Donna Jean spoke, "Well, you two girls be very careful out there. You know how to avoid questionable strangers. I'll leave the back door open for you. The keys to the car are on the hallway counter. Have fun," finished Donna Jean.

I used this as my own cue to make my exit. Placing my empty glass on the coffee table, I stood and faced Donna Jean.

"It has been a fabulous evening, Donna Jean. But it's also been a long day. I'd like to end it on this wonderful note. I'd also like to think this isn't the last time we'll see each other."

She stood up, surprised by my sudden announcement but also understanding, as she had been all evening.

Showing her true skill at hospitality, she said, "Girls, why don't you drive Gus home on your way out? It's late for him to take a taxi. And Gus, I'd feel better if they gave you a ride after the efforts you made taking a cab here."

I was quick to refuse. "Please. That's too much to ask. Really. Believe me, I'm used to cabbing it. I do it so often I don't even notice it anymore." I could see Donna Jean wasn't going to accept my rebuttals.

"Gus, just this time, okay? Next time we get together, I'll drive. If the girls want to use my car, then they have to earn it. Don't feel bad. I'd be driving you home myself if they weren't going out tonight with it."

I looked hopelessly at Donna Jean and saw her determination. I felt trapped. She had no idea how much I didn't want to get in the car with her two she-devil offspring. Their faces portrayed nothing but pure, lying innocence.

I caved. "Okay. Fair enough. I still don't agree with this whole thing. As long as you understand it isn't expected."

"Agreed," she said.

"Agreed," I repeated.

"All right. Girls, go get the car ready. I'll walk Gus out to meet you in a few minutes. Thanks." The girls turned and swaggered away.

My heart was already racing. *What the hell just went wrong?* Where were my balls to say no? I chastised my chicken-shit demeanor. Christy would be so disappointed.

"Gus," said Donna Jean, moving close beside me, "you've been a fine gentleman tonight. I find you very interesting. And I would love to see you again. How about it?" Her eyes searched mine.

I nodded. I thought I should say something.

"Definitely. We'll make the arrangements to see some fine local entertainment at the Fringe." I did what felt right and shook her hand. She held mine firmly in her own, just long enough to send me a message, before releasing it.

"Let's go. The girls get impatient fast." She grabbed my arm and walked me to the curb.

A Ford Taurus idled on the street. I couldn't make out either Natasha or Shannon in the front seat through the tinted windows. Nevertheless, that didn't alleviate my trepidation because I knew they were both in there.

"Thanks again for a wonderful evening, Gus," said Donna Jean, leaning forward and hugging me. I tried to loosen up in her bear-hug grip but was unable to.

"Take care, Donna Jean. Great meal." I forced a smile. My mind was blank. I entered the backseat. Inside, I was met with an overwhelming rush of perfume. No sooner was the door closed when we were pulling away. I had infiltrated the lair of Natasha and Shannon.

I needed to say something, so I did. "Look, Natasha, I want to apologize for stepping into the wrong room. I was looking for the bathroom. I apologize for making you uncomfortable." I felt better pleading my case first.

Natasha giggled.

"Funny, I thought it was you who looked uncomfortable," she replied. She turned from the passenger seat and smiled slyly. "I kind of thought you liked the bra and panties I was wearing."

I shook my head.

"No," I denied, "I felt bad for intruding in your room."

Shannon piped in. "Strange, Natasha, it's not the way you described his reaction to you. You said Gus had his tongue hanging out. Leering ..."

"I did not leer," I asserted.

"You leered," contended Natasha.

"No, I did not," I persisted.

"Why fight it, Gus?" asked Shannon. "You wanted my sister, and that's that."

"No. It's not that way," I contested.

"Really? Then why did you touch her?"

"*I didn't touch her!*"

"Yes, you did."

"She rubbed her body against mine!"

"You leered, and then you touched her. Admit it, Gus. You want my sister."

"This is stupid," I said. "I'm not discussing this further."

"Fine." Shannon kept one hand on the wheel while she pulled a bottle from her purse. She passed it to her sister, who opened it and drank. She gave it to Shannon, who did the same.

"Have a sip," she said, offering me the bottle.

"What is it?"

"Gin. It puts us in the mood."

"Mood for what?"

"To party."

"Just take me home, all right? And while we're at it, you might want to know my address."

Natasha lit a cigarette, filling the interior with smoke. I rolled down a window.

"Actually, Gus," said Natasha, "we need to make a stop first. I know you won't mind."

"As a matter of fact, I would."

Shannon drank from the bottle. "You have to understand two things, Gus."

"And what is that?" I snapped.

"First, you are not in control of this car."

"I can get out anytime," I sneered.

"Second, before you leap, think about this—"

"What?" I broke in.

"We are in control of whether our mother finds out about your sexual attack on Natasha in her bedroom. You fondled her breasts and demanded sex. Knowing our mother, she'll go to the police."

I sat back in my seat and sputtered, "*So you'd actually tell her bullshit to coerce me? Blackmail? Why?* I don't understand. I don't even know you two."

131

"You know my sister well enough to know what colour underwear she has on right now," Shannon stated.

"C'mon!" I shouted. "This is ridiculous. Take me home, all right?"

"All you have to do to earn our silence is come with us tonight, Gus."

"And where would that be? I thought you two were going to see a movie?" I was starting to take their threats seriously. These girls were nuts.

"The Glory Hole."

"What? I've never heard of it."

"After tonight you won't be able to stay away."

"I'm sure. Buy me a season pass. Now what movie is that?"

"It's a private bar, Gus. Each night is based on themes. Tonight's theme is a surprise for you."

"Girls, I think I've had enough surprises tonight. Let's forget it. Just take me home. Okay? All is forgotten."

"Do you think my sister will forget your fingers trying to penetrate her?"

"*Bullshit!*" I shouted.

"Then shut your mouth and come along. Easy, isn't it?" Shannon smoked the cigarette her sister lit.

Natasha drank from the bottle and said, "I've been traumatized, Gus. This will make me feel better. Who knows? It might even erase my memory of your attack."

"You know that's total crap!" I snapped.

"Gus," Natasha said softly, "the police treat sexual attacks by pedophiles very seriously."

"What the hell are you suggesting? I'm not a pedophile."

"I'm seventeen. A minor. You touched me."

"*I did not!*"

"Actually," claimed Shannon, "I'd consider Gus a hebophile. Pubescent girls are more his hunger."

"You like 'em young, huh, Gus?"

"Yeah, you go through the mothers to get at us unsuspecting girls."

I nearly gagged. I was done.

"You understand now, Gus?" asked Shannon. The cigarette was hanging from her mouth. "I'm nineteen. As the older sister, I have to protect Natasha from perverts like you. So you're coming with us."

"Fine." I crossed my arms in anger. I was furious. Complete lies. Yet, I was fucked. I was already charged with prostitution. Christ, I could go straight to jail based on nothing more than a statement by a lying seventeen-year-old. So I'd play their game. Once we were inside the club, I'd leave and find my own way home.

"Have a drink, Gus. Relax. Enjoy the splendid evening we have conceived for you."

"I'll pass. Drinking with minors is against the law. And so is while driving a motor vehicle," I added.

The two girls laughed. I wondered what they found funny about my comment.

We pulled in front of a building void of any signs. I saw that we were on East Provencher Boulevard in a seedy, rundown industrial area of the city. We all got out of the car together. Natasha threw the empty bottle on the front seat.

Inside the building door, I was assaulted by darkness, black lights and thumping, jungle-like music. When I heard the screams, I jolted to a stop. Shannon, who was walking behind me, gave me a sharp nudge. I kept going. We walked into a room shrouded in mist so thick I couldn't see past anyone's torso. The place was freaking me out. I had enough. I turned.

"Sorry, girls, this journey ends here ..."

I was tackled from behind. Surprised by the swiftness of the attack, I was quickly subdued. My screams were lost in the blaring music. While I was on the floor, I was disorientated by the cold whiteness of the dry ice. I tried to struggle, but it felt as though someone was sitting on my back. Then my shoes were yanked off. My pants came next. Followed by my shirt. Harsh material gripped my wrists and ankles. I thrashed. I was yanked to my feet and carried by two large men. All they wore were thongs and black hoods shielding their face. Natasha and Shannon led the way for my kidnappers.

"*What the fuck are you bitches doing?*" I protested, wriggling to get free. The grip on each limb remained firm. I was moved across the room and strapped to a large, horizontal wheel. "Enough already," I pleaded. Now I was getting scared. I was immobilized against the cold wood.

"You are now a slave under the power of Mistress Natasha and Mistress Shannon," purred Shannon, leaning over me to adjust one of the straps holding my wrists.

"Do you see, Mistress Natasha?" Shannon asked her sister. "Our slave has chosen to wear faulty underwear. He must be punished."

I thrashed. There was no give in the straps. I felt exposed and vulnerable. People in various dress walked past me, casting bland glances my way. No one offered help. I stopped my struggle and took in more of the room. I was in a chamber of misfits. At least that's the way it looked to me. Across the darkened way I saw single cages containing standing men and women. Some were semi-nude and guarded by women wearing only leather hoods. They were spraying the prisoners with oil from a fire hose. A woman spanked a man who stood against a blackboard, writing out the words BAD BOY over and over in chalk, with a ruler. To my other side, three slings hung from the ceiling. Each sling held a man secured by handcuffs. A group of people stood around beating them with pillows. Feathers filled the air in a floating, white surrealism as the pillows burst. I saw another woman sitting in a chair, with two other women standing beside her blowing up balloons and popping them. My attention was brought back to Donna Jean's daughters.

"Attach the rings," I heard Shannon command. Her sister approached me, carrying glittering metal chains in her hands. I screamed. She squeezed the metal clips secured at the end of each chain.

"*Are you girls crazy?*" I shrieked, watching in horror as she applied the clamps to my exposed nipples. The metal was cold. It hurt. I screamed again. "*Take those things off me right now!*" I insisted.

"Punishment for careless dress," snarled Shannon. I didn't recognize her. Under the black lights, fog and my fear, her face became misshapen. I was staring at Satan.

She raised her leg. "Lick my boot, slave," she commanded, shoving the sole of her latex footwear in my mouth. I could smell plastic and leather. I wrenched my face away but couldn't escape; she pressed it harder against my cheek. I'd had no idea I'd be licking the boot I had innocently admired only hours earlier. I obeyed. I ran my tongue along the filthy bottom sole. The girls squealed with delight. I had satisfied their demands.

"Take off the clamps," I pleaded to deaf ears.

"Silence! Or I will summon the Dungeon Master," Natasha snapped. "Whining will only result in further punishment. I must congratulate Mistress Shannon for her victory in breaking your spirit." She removed a stubby handle from her belt. There were a dozen leather tassels on her flogger. Shannon bent over while her sister pretended to fail her with the prongs. I squeezed my eyes shut. *This is insane.* I strained against my bindings, which only gripped harder. I felt my hands grow cold. When I opened my eyes again, I wished I hadn't. Even with the billowing waves of dry ice fog, Jerry Trotts was easily distinguishable, despite the diaper he wore and the oversized crib he was being pushed in. He was looking right at me. Apparently, he had recovered from his cattle prodding. I yelled to him. He shook his rattle in response. I watched helplessly as Jerry Trotts rolled past, sucking vigorously on the soother inside his fifty-six-year-old mouth on the way to the other side of the room. He then climbed on top of a changing table.

I had regained the sister's attention. They stood on each side of me, examining my body.

"Too much body hair," observed Shannon.

Natasha nodded her head. "Hair is disgusting. Fix it."

Shannon bent to the floor and retrieved a shaver. It jumped to life.

"Enough! Stop it! You've had your fun. Shannon! Put it down!" My pleas had little effect except producing a tight grin. She was intent on fulfilling her sister's command.

"Silence!" Natasha growled, hitting me on my thighs with the whip. I shut my mouth. The clippers did their job. In three quick passes my chest hair was gone. Years of pride and proper shampooing and grooming now lay on the floor, obscured by the dry ice.

"*Are you bitches happy now?*" I cried.

Shannon ran her hand gently along my stubbly chest. "Better. You've now passed the initiation into the Black and Blue Ball." Her hand moved along across my face, around my ears and through my hair. "Your status as slave has now been elevated to server."

I could only wonder what other appendage I'd have to have sacrificially removed for my promotion. Without warning, I was turned upside down. Donna Jean's meal rose to the back of my throat. I couldn't scream as my mouth filled with scotch. My world righted itself again. I felt my hands and feet being released, and I dropped to the floor. It still seemed as though I were spinning. I heard laughter as I hunched on my hands and knees. Somebody walked past, clearing a trail of fog. I saw my clothes spread a few feet before me. I scurried forward, grabbed my pants and slipped them on. I couldn't find my socks, so I put my shoes on without them. I had my shirt in my hand when I was lifted to my feet. Natasha faced me, her hands grasping my shoulders. Neither her perfume nor ample bust jiggling from her skimpy top had any sexual effect on me.

"Servers get treated to their mistress in a private room, Gus. Come back with me." Her eyes glimmered dangerously. She was a sick fuck. "Just you and me. My mother will never know."

"Get lost," I told her flatly. I shoved her backward. "Just be thankful I don't charge you with kidnapping," I warned, turning away to find the door. She must have read the seriousness in my eyes because I heard no response behind me. This time I was prepared to start swinging if I felt arms tackle me again. I stumbled past a man and woman being dunked into a tank of water. I pushed a door and was greeted by cool, nighttime air. Instantly the music beating into my brain ceased. I had found my savior—silence. I began stumbling down the sidewalk, delicately unclasping the nipple hooks and tossing them to the ground. I pulled my shirt around my body. My chest itched. My nipples ached. I swore.

There was little traffic, and I began to realize it must be very late. My hair was matted against my scalp. Sweat saturated my body. I tried to walk a steady pace despite the wobble in my legs.

A breeze rushed past me, and it felt purifying. *Where have I gone wrong in my life?* I knew what I meant by the question. One missed opportunity long ago had careened me to my fateful humbling at this very moment, forced to cascade with reckless abandon down the pathways of debauchery. I felt I should be upset about the evening. Outraged. And yet I was more wistful than angry. Despondent? Of course. Donna Jean was a woman with plenty of potential. In this case, the monster under the bed were her two daughters. I scratched at my chest.

I secured a cab at the corner of Lombard and Main.

13

"I'm not going to tell you what you want to hear. So take a chance ..."

"I didn't know whether they could see me, but I cursed and waved my arms at them this morning." In our office I explained to Christy how I took out my frustration from last night on my kissing couple. "I totally blame them for the debacle." I rubbed at my chest.

"From fifteen stories up you'd look like a deranged social assistance recipient on crack," said Christy, calmly sipping her coffee. She sat back in her chair across from me at her desk, grinning. "Lighten up, Gus. Talk to me. *It's Christy here, remember? We talk to each other.*"

I let out a long breath of air and stared at the ceiling. Even the Starbucks coffee in my cup wasn't soothing me. "Sadly, what makes this situation so bizarre is the fact is it had started to evolve into an outstanding evening with supper at her house. She was everything a guy could want! Attractive, responsive, compassionate—qualities I could grow to appreciate. And then it quickly progressed into the perverse. To put it all bluntly, Christy, I was attacked by her two teenage daughters, kidnapped and beaten. I escaped without my socks. And, oh yeah, minus my chest hair. Look at how raw my nipples are too." I opened my shirt and displayed my tortured skin. Christy's eyes grew wide.

"All I can really tell you is that I was held hostage in some weird, ritualistic worship they called Black and Blue. But I'm beginning to get the idea. I saw things that will haunt me forever. To be honest with you, it's rattled my faith in the moral state of this city."

Christy put her hands to her face and burst out laughing.

"Glad to see my misery is your laugh of the day. Thanks."

"Sorry, Gus. I know exactly what you're talking about. Have you checked yourself for tattoos? Piercings? Any rings hanging from your testicles?" She burst into a fresh round of laughter.

"Just forget it," I said, leaving the chair to begin pacing the room. "Everything's ruined. Donna Jean called me this morning and left a message. She wanted to let me know she had one of the best evenings in years. She wants to get together again. She asked me how I thought our evening went. What do I tell her? Oh, your daughters happen to be Satan's offspring in miniskirts, and they tried to crucify me on a wheel? Shit. I can't see her again. In fact, I can't risk *speaking* to her. Can you imagine what her daughters would try to do to me if they got a second chance? For the love of God, I have a feeling it would involve me being in a room alone with a goat. Honestly."

Christy laughed harder, until she fell from her chair.

"Are you through yet?" I asked.

She stopped, wiping at the tears streaming down her face. "Just be lucky it wasn't enema night, Gus." She lost control, laughing even more.

"I'm stressed. Isn't losing my beloved chest hair enough? I had to shave the rest this morning to make it look better. I'm still astounded a classy area like River Heights houses such vice."

"Never forget, Gus, finding love is easy. The hard part is keeping it."

"Cold comfort."

She snickered, still wiping at the tears on her cheek.

I shook my head. "You won't guess who I saw at the club dressed in a diaper."

"Who?"

"Jerry Trotts."

"No way!" she squealed.

"Yeah way! He was being pushed in a crib, diaper on, soother in his mouth and a rattle in his hand."

"Wow!" Christy's eyes were wide.

I left Christy with that morsel of scandalous behaviour and sauntered back into my office. I closed the door, turned up Fleetwood Mac on the stereo and sat back in my chair.

Marcia.

She had yet to return my calls. Her voice message had intrigued me. I found that the tones in her voice struck something inside me. I decided to leave another message. So I picked up the phone, dialed and heard her now-familiar dialogue. I spoke along, having memorized what she said. I asked her to please call me. I hoped she'd believe me when I said I wanted to share her upcoming birthday with her. I finished and hung up. Restlessness tore at me.

I felt at a loss about Donna Jean. There had been a connection between us. I didn't have the courage to call her back, which I realized wasn't fair to her. Neither were the blackmail and assault by her daughters. But a mother always believes her children. If they lied, I was cooked. She'd let me disappear after a few unreturned messages. Maybe Marcia felt the same way about me. I hoped not.

14

"I'm not obese by any means ..."

I overslept. When I woke at eight, I realized two things. First, I had missed my kissing couple in the car. Second, I forgot I was due to meet my lawyer in an hour. Getting downtown was as troublesome as dialing a phone in winter mitts, so I took a cab directly from my apartment. It was a pre-trial meeting to discuss the charge that I'd solicited a male prostitute, my first meeting, which I'd arranged with the lawyer's assistant.

I paid the cabbie and ran into the TD Tower and up to the twelfth floor. The woodwork in the waiting area was a rich-toned cherry with dark, bamboo wood flooring. The seating was plush black leather. I was impressed by the bucks that went into designing and furnishing the room. For me, this meant serious billing from someone who got results. I had chosen a guy from the Yellow Pages. His ad sounded tough. It was what I needed.

I expected a tall, silver-streaked hawk of a man to be my bulldog. Instead, I shook hands with a man who had a set of eyes that needed an additional two inches of space.

"Gus, hi, I'm Cletus Jack Colby. Let's sit down. You've gotten yourself into a heck of a mess, fella."

I followed him to a round table. I sat. He stood. Behind him was a wall of windows that provided a spectacular view of the city below.

"This is all bullshit, you know," I protested, eager to set the proper tone of injustice.

He looked up from the papers in his hand.

"I've seen the videotape that was recorded from the car."

I stared up at him. "I was recorded?" He nodded.

"Then, goddamn it, that proves it all! I'm innocent."

Cletus smirked. "You gave a star performance on camera, cowboy. Allow me to tell you what you are, Gus, and it's not Snow White's brother. Let me be blunt. The prosecution has you cruising in a notorious gay pickup area during the hours when respectable people are home with their families. They have you clearly explaining to the driver what sexual depravities you want him to perform on you. They have you removing your clothes in preparation for your sexual romp. What they have is a classic case, textbook, all nicely documented on video. Gus, the camera tells no lies. Unfortunately for you, I can't dispute the facts displayed on video. Plead guilty. Accept your sentence. Don't do it again. Divine intervention was all that kept your mugshot from being the *Sun*'s front-page cover story. I'll prepare the paperwork for you." He walked to another desk.

My anger boiled. "Hold on, Mr. Colby. Mr. Jack. Whoever you are. Guilty? *No way*. I was walking through the parking lot on my way home. It was raining. He offered me a ride. I accepted."

Cletus glanced up from the paper he was writing on. "The mayor wants the area cleansed of this sexual filth. The parking lot you so innocently walked through is rife with sexual activity during the late night. Personally, how anyone finds a parking lot and a subcompact car sexually arousing mystifies me. Nonetheless, if you try to contest this charge, the penalties will be severe. Believe me."

"Believe you? You won't believe me!"

"I've seen the tape."

"*It's bullshit! I'm not gay!*"

"Neither are half the sicko male perverts charged. If I could be blunt, your sexual orientation, deviation, hidden phallic lusts, whatever they are, are frankly of no importance to me."

"Pervert? *Are you not getting it?* I am innocent!"

"Perhaps *you're* not getting it, Mr. Adams. The case is airtight. If you plead not guilty, you will lose. Pack your toothbrush and tampons for a five-year term in prison."

"How can justice be so blind?"

"Please, Mr. Adams. May I remind you of this device found on your person?" With a grimace, my lawyer held up an eight-by-ten colour photograph of the c-ring from my pocket. "This, sir, clearly depicts the depravity you sought to achieve with the police officer. He could have been seriously injured and not gone home to his family that night," spat my lawyer. "Personally, I am offended at having this pornography inside my office." He looked me straight in the eye. "I go to church."

"*That's not mine!* I was carrying that thing, but it was a stupid joke that I forgot about!"

"Your source of humour, Mr. Adams, is questionable at best. Your need for the male enhancement medication found on your person is pathetic. The evidence is indisputable. I am strongly advising you as your counsel to plead guilty with a cause."

"A cause for what?"

"What I am suggesting is that you admit to soliciting the undercover officer with a request for sexual pleasure in exchange for money, but ..."

"Get real."

"You realize you need help and will undergo corrective treatment for your addictive lusting for male sex, in lieu of prison."

I squeezed my eyes shut. "I don't understand your point."

"John school."

"Now you're really not making sense."

"Mr. Adams, john school is where people like you who are caught in these sting operations go for reform, rather than becoming someone's niece in prison. It is a one-day course set aside by the court to rehabilitate those who need help." He was silent, and then he added, "They say it inhibits the cravings."

"*I have no cravings.*"

"Attend the class, avoid prison and your record will become a suspended sentence. Four years of probation. Do it clean, and nobody will ever know it happened."

He stared intently at me.

I silently cursed. This was a farce. The real crime was the bullshit plea-bargaining. So I asked suspiciously, "How certain is it I would be put in jail if I'm found guilty?"

Cletus put down his pen and sat back in his plush leather chair. "Everything in our lives have odds, Mr. Adams," he replied banally. "Your chance of winning a lottery is one in ten million. Your chance of getting

143

struck by lightning is one in ten thousand, being in a car accident one in a thousand. For you to be incarcerated after being found guilty of soliciting a prostitute is a sure thing. If I were a gambling man, Mr. Adams, knowing these odds I'd be folding."

I knew I was beaten. I conceded. Cletus had me sign papers declaring my guilt. He would have his assistant arrange for my class. I was going back to school.

I returned to the clinic and hid inside my office. I didn't care about the strange look Christy gave me. I wasn't about to volunteer my recent experience declaring my confession to having male sex.

I flipped through the mail on my desk and skimmed a couple of journals. I thought about rearranging the office furniture but gave it up when I tried picking up the table.

I noticed the phone and grabbed it. I hadn't checked my messages today. I dialed into U 2 Can Date, and there was a message. My heart sped up. It had to be Marcia. *Finally.* She had come to her senses and realized I was the only gentleman for her. She would ask for forgiveness about dating other men before me. I would laugh it off. One often had to taste the competition in order to appreciate the real deal. I was willing to let her experiment. My time to shine had arrived. *Hello, my wife.*

The voice I retrieved was male.

"Er, listen, I'm not sure how this works. My name is Richard. Ah, this is awkward for me. Er, I'm calling for someone named Gus. I hope this is the correct number. Ah, I am calling on behalf of my sister, Marcia. Gus has left a number of messages for her. Ah, how do I say this? Jeez, this is rather uncomfortable, so I hope this message will get to Gus. I'm not sure if I've said it already, but I'm Marcia's brother. Well, I don't know how else to say this, so I'll just come out and let you know. There's been a terrible accident. Ah, my sister has died. She ... she died by suicide last week. Please, this is really hard for the family. I'm ... trying to arrange her affairs. I found this number on her desk and have since spoken with the company operating this ... service. They will be removing her account. Uhm, I thought Gus should know about my sister. If someone could pass this information along to him, our family would really appreciate it."

I listened to the silence and tightened my grip on the phone. I couldn't remove the receiver from my ear. The room swirled, and I leaned against my desk. Finally, I hung up, silencing the shrill tone. I desperately wanted to hear her voice again. I needed to. I glanced around the room. I felt hysteria rising. I felt defeated. A horn sounded outside my window. Suddenly, so much seemed so insignificant, such as my guilty plea, joining john school, Donna Jean's flogger-carrying daughters or my own insignificant search for love. What did it all matter when compared to the loss of a life? I desperately craved to know why she did it. How? I needed answers I knew would never be settled. Would her picture be in the obituaries? Did I miss her prayers?

My office walls closed in around me. I needed to get outside. My appointment book was empty for the afternoon. I didn't care if it was full of meetings. I was leaving and staggered up the stairs to the main door. Once out on the street, I started walking. People I passed gawked at me strangely. I ignored them. The traffic at Broadway and Donald impatiently waited while I crossed on the DON'T WALK signal. By the time I entered the parking lot of the Forks, my shirt was saturated with sweat. I saw my reflection pass in a building's window. My skin was flushed and perspiring. The wild craziness in my eyes peered back at me.

Groups of people swarmed around the buildings and river walk. Small clusters of children gathered around the amateur performers to witness their acts. I realized how tired I was from walking for over an hour. I sat down on a series of cement steps. Beads of sweat ran down my back. I wrapped my arms around my legs and looked around. Couples danced to bluegrass, plays were performed and the smell of food filled the air. The Fringe Festival was in full swing, and I didn't give a shit.

I watched a person wearing an A&W Restaurant bear costume outfitted in an orange sweater and hat. I became the person inside the huge grinning head, and it was a living hell. In the distance, I watched the bear amble in my direction.

The bear was waving to a group of children and didn't see the man eating an ice-cream cone. The bear's ass nudged the man, and it knocked the bulbous scoop of ice cream from his cone to the pavement, where it immediately started to melt. The bear kept walking, oblivious to the accident. I watched the man look at his melting ice cream and go berserk. Things happened too fast for me to yell a warning to the bear. The man ran up to the bear from behind and leaped, executing a majestic flying drop kick between the bear's exposed shoulder blades. The bear didn't have a chance. I could hear the bear grunt, and then he was propelled into the air. He hit the ground hard on his snout and didn't move. Meanwhile, the Chuck Norris wannabe brushed the dirt from his pants and made a run for it. No one had to tell him his retribution didn't fit the crime. He came right toward me as he fled the scene of his crime.

I wasn't thinking of getting involved. There was a sickening pleasure in watching someone other than myself suffer a misfortune. Why I stuck my foot out, I'll never know. But I did. My timing was impeccable. The fleeing man didn't see it coming. One minute his Nikes were pushing hard at the pavement, the next his face was smearing concrete with a trail of his own skin and blood. He didn't get up either.

Apparently I wasn't the only person watching the entire progression of events. So was the Downtown Biz Patrol, volunteer citizens who donned red shirts and walked the streets to give directions or hold down a perp until the law arrived.

The man's whose face made a bloody landing strip was rolled over by three Biz Patrol behind me. I heard him moaning. A fourth patrol was trying to gently unhook the hood from the bear. The crumpled snout had bent the latch. The bear still wasn't moving. I decided to slip away from the scene of the crime. I got up to move to a less eventful part of the park.

A red shirt blocked my way.

"Excuse me, sir, I've got to ask you a couple of questions." The voice was female, but with the sun behind her head, all I could see was a ball of white. She noticed my squint, apologized and shifted to her left. Now I could see my investigator.

"Am I being arrested?"

She looked at me blankly and then smiled.

"Oh, no! I'm only trying to get an idea of what happened. The police will want to know, that's all. I have no power to arrest or carry a tazer, much to my chagrin." She laughed.

"Good, because I'm already out on parole, and this could jeopardize everything. This is the first time I'm able to sit down without pain." I gave her my biggest set of baby eyes.

She grinned and then laughed, realizing I was joking with her.

"Fair enough," she said. "There's too much paperwork involved in sending a con back to the joint. I'll let you walk this time, jailbird," she threatened playfully.

"My bum gratefully thanks you," I said, and this time we both laughed.

I couldn't see her eyes through the sunglasses she wore. So I looked at my soulful reflection and wished her luck with the bad guy once she had taken my statement. She nodded and turned back to the rest of her team. I heard her speaking into a microphone attached to her shoulder as I walked away to a quieter area.

I tried to show an interest in the performing arts, but I couldn't muster up enough enthusiasm. I had to accept the reality that my day was a write-off, and I headed home. This time I jumped on a dreaded transit bus.

There was a message on my home machine from Christy, telling me she'd locked up the clinic early. She also hoped everything was okay. She left her cell phone number in case I needed to talk. I wrote her number down, even though I had no intention of calling. She was a sweet person. I appreciated her concern. In reality, there was no one else who gave a shit about me. I could die and rot in my bed, the next person to find me would be Harold, showing my apartment to new renters. Even then, I suspected he'd roll my corpse under the bed.

I poked around the kitchen, thinking I should eat. Everything I had was either in a box or a can, and that required turning on the stove. I passed on eating. Instead, I poured a glass of milk. The chunks falling from the container into my glass splashed milk over the counter. I passed on the milk. I found a half-empty bottle of orange liqueur and took a sip of the sour liquid from the spout. I took the bottle with me into the living room.

I went to the stereo and turned on Van Morrison's *Moondance* CD. The news about Marcia had sucked the interest from me to continue dating, but I was at a loss how else to continue. Maybe the local bookstore? A Saturn owners' appreciation picnic? I'd heard rumours only single women bought Saturns. Then again, I didn't own a Saturn and had no intention of doing so. Did I have to cruise the Soby's grocery aisles in the afternoons? Funerals for grieving widows? The YMCA pool area? Perhaps the answer was volunteering at the local community centre Friday nights?

I picked up the phone and dialed the service. I flicked through a number of female voices until I settled on Petulla. Her message captured everything I had now whittled down to necessities in a female.

"Do you want a monogamous relationship with a very intelligent and sensuous woman? I am looking for a man with a big heart who is not afraid to treat a woman like a woman. I am attracted to many types of men, but a real turn on for me is a man who is physical—a blue-collar worker with strong hands who isn't afraid to get dirty. A man who is happy, active, trustworthy and stable. A man with a strong sexual appetite who loves living life to its fullest. I am a single white female, no kids, age thirty-five, employed full-time. I have shoulder-length auburn hair, brown eyes, nice skin, nice white teeth and a wonderful smile. I carry extra weight on my frame; however, at five feet eight inches with large breasts, my body is well proportioned. I am healthy, active, confident and love life to the fullest. I am just missing that special someone to share all this with. If you enjoy the outdoors, wining and dining, walking and sports, then we have a lot in common. I am only looking for that one special man to feel love, and if you think you could be this man, call me."

I was impressed with Petulla's profile. I made a mental note to smear motor oil on my jeans. Blue collar I could become. I thought of Jake the Gorilla and envisioned cracking cans of 5W-30 motor oil with my teeth. Frankly, I didn't care if she was three hundred pounds. I was content with all her flesh … provided it was her own.

I left a message.

15

"I'm looking for an individual who's not afraid of an assertive female ..."

"Ian," I said from inside my office, "I want you to sit on this chair while your wife sits on the other side of the table." I waited patiently while they followed my seating instructions.

"Great. Today's session is about acceptance. It's about understanding ourselves better so that we can accept the ones in our lives we love without prejudice." I ignored the skeptical faces. They were still young enough to be impressionable. I played on it.

"Lucy, accepting Ian's indiscretions without violence is your goal today. And Ian," I said, turning his way, "accepting a beautiful woman passing by without the need to look is yours. Understand?" Both nodded.

"Good."

I held up a picture.

"Ian, look at the photograph." It was a cutout from the Sears catalogue of a woman in a bra.

"See how beautiful she is?"

He nodded his head vigorously.

"Think of your wife instead. I want you to feel the anger she feels at seeing you ogle this beautiful, young model. She hurts from this anger, Ian. Do you understand?"

He nodded his head.

I put the picture down and picked a different one. This time I directed it to Lucy.

"This page is pink, Lucy. Right now you're mad at your husband. He just looked at another woman in her underwear. And he did it sitting a few feet from you. Focus your anger into this picture. Embrace the calming effect of this colour."

She glared at the picture.

"Now, Ian," I said, placing another picture in front of him. "What do you feel seeing this woman? But first, remember to think about what I just told you about Lucy's feelings." The photograph was the Canadian Tire pool girl.

"Aroused."

"Wrong. Think about your wife's feeling."

"I'm sorry, the girl's splashing in the water—"

"Ian!" Lucy half stood out of her chair. I motioned for her to sit down.

"Lucy, look hard at this picture." It was a deeper shade of pink. "Let the colour absorb your anger. Think of nothing but the colour."

She lashed out and smacked the picture from my hand.

"He's hopeless," she shouted. "How sick do you have to be to get off on a catalogue slut?"

"He made me!" Ian said, making me the bad guy by pointing his finger my way.

"Hold on—"

Lucy cut me off. "Show *him* the shitty colours," she hissed. "Let's see him get aroused with *that* picture instead, huh."

"It's only a goddamn picture, Lucy, for Christ's sakes," Ian shrieked at his wife.

"And your jaw's still dragging on the floor like a schoolyard pervert."

"Lucy—"

She stood up and pointed. Ian and I flinched, waiting for the punch. Instead, she said, "I'm wearing black stockings and garters with this ridiculous mini, and you haven't looked at me *once* today. What does *that* tell you?"

"It's not the same thing," he pleaded.

Her arms shot upward. "I'm a woman! I shave my legs. Look at my junk, Ian! What the hell gives?"

I had lost total control of the session. This was my time to remain unobtrusive.

"Lucy, I can look at you anytime," Ian blurted. "These girls are once in a lifetime, baby."

"You jerk-off," she shouted. "Maybe you should marry a piece of paper next time." This time she did strike him. I winced at the sound.

"Ah, shit," Ian cried out, holding his hand to his face. "Do ya gotta do that, Lucy?"

"*That* pain," she accentuated harshly, "is a fraction of what I feel when I see you getting off on another woman."

"Enough, Lucy." I flinched, holding up another picture. I reared back, judging how far her arm was from my face. This picture was a couple holding hands and walking along a beach. It was my failsafe. "Study this photograph to feel the serenity. You should—"

For the first time in my career, I was struck by a patient. I dropped the picture. That time I saw Ian wince.

"Don't try these heebee geebees with me," Lucy warned me. "All this crap you've been treating Ian with, and he still loses control of the car whenever we pass a Guess Jeans billboard. I'm fed up being the backseat bride. Fix my husband, you jerkwad," she ordered, "and if that means removing a piece of his brain, then do it. Understand me?" Lucy vibrated in her seat.

I rubbed my chest after Lucy's punch. Her petite size belied the sheer power she possessed. The room was silent except for the heavy breathing coming from three of us. It was a Mexican standoff.

Ian broke the showdown.

"Lucy, I love you. No one can change my feelings for you." Ian looked apologetic. Lucy's expression softened.

I was about to add to the conversation when Lucy's manicured finger pointed at me. I bit back my words.

"Do you mean what you say, Ian?" she whispered.

"Yes I do, sweet pea," he replied carefully.

I could sense we were on the cusp of peace. I dared not move.

"Then come over here and hug me, you idiot," she ordered.

Ian knew best when he'd said enough, and he complied with his wife's wishes. He stepped on my photographs and wrapped his arms around Lucy. It was a Kodak moment.

I bade the Chows good-bye and chalked up the therapy as a success, despite Lucy's fists of fury. When it came to positive results, I didn't care how we arrived at them. For me and Ian, the wounds would heal in time.

Christy gave me a questioning glance when I left my office to grab a coffee. My door was thick but not thick enough to stifle the shouting and slaps of flesh on the other side. I held up my hand, shaking my head. She understood.

I went back inside and closed my door. It was late in the afternoon, and I hadn't checked my messages. There was a reply from Petulla. She had Goldeyes baseball tickets for a game in four days. If I was interested, I was instructed to leave an answer on the System and to meet her at the front gates of the stadium. I accepted.

I completed my notes on the Chow session, and I decided to call it a day. I instructed Christy to activate our prerecorded message and lock up a half hour early.

I walked home, enjoying the sun on my face. It suddenly occurred to me that I had zero activities planned before my date with Petulla. On one hand, I was grateful for the opportunity to have a few quiet evenings alone. Conversely, in my pursuit for romantic attachment, solitude was self-defeating. Therefore, I committed myself to going to Muddy Waters Smokehouse, located at the Forks, for a solo supper on the patio. It was better than watching birds from my patio. At least I would be around people.

Muddy Waters was busy. I was fortunate enough to find a lone table by the edge of the patio. I ordered a Moosehead beer, fries and a double cheese melt. The location did offer ideal views of all the people milling about the Fork's river walk and green space. I concluded I was the only single guy there.

I sat at the restaurant until it grew dark, ignoring the hostile glares of the waitresses. They desperately needed my chair, and I wasn't about to give it up. When it was time for me to leave for the fireworks show, I left the exact amount of my bill. I believed in equal opportunity. The only tip I'd received that day was a punch to my chest.

The main field hosting the fireworks show was nearly full to capacity, and I had to struggle to find a piece of land big enough for my ass. Once I settled in near the back edge of the crowd, I got as comfortable as I could on the damp grass.

The show started, and I watched the bursts of lights shine on the faces around me. I was the only person without a head resting on my shoulder. Even a pair of dogs had each other. I focused my attention on the sky above. I momentarily wished for one of the fireworks to go errant and slam into my body. It'd be the only time in my life I'd become the centre of attention as a human torch.

A finger tapped at my shoulder. A voice was saying, "I didn't think they let cons around explosives." I turned.

I geared up, preparing to dish out a punch to the drunken bum's groin.

"Move on, will you?" I said, giving my best threatening face.

"Is this the thanks from an ex-con for the pity I took on you the other day? You're a real compassionate guy, you know? I could have you sent back to the slammer, buddy." In the darkness, a flash from the fireworks lit up her face, and I realized who was talking to me. No longer able to suppress it, she grinned. It was the Downtown Winnipeg Biz Patrol girl who'd quizzed me for helping stop the guy who'd drop-kicked the bear.

My expression relaxed. "Oh shit, I thought you were going to pester me for a couple of bucks. I didn't recognize you without your sunglasses. The red shirt should have clued me in," I said, smiling up at her.

"That's okay, I don't often leave a lasting first impression. I'm told I'm ordinary and blend in well."

"Well, if it's any consolation, I remember you quite well. You took pity on an ex-con who sends most shrieking away. I am forever grateful."

She laughed along with me.

I said, "But I have a prison confession to make to you."

She gulped.

"I'm not really an ex-con. In fact, except for a recent misfortune, and injustice, may I add, I've been the ideal citizen. Sorry. I hope it doesn't shatter my bad boy image." I looked at her apologetically.

She laughed softly. "I'm relieved. Mother always warned me to stay away from dangerous men. They'll only break your heart in the long run."

"If I may correct your mother, all men will break your heart, honey. By the way, how's the bear doing?" At first her face was blank, and then she realized what I was referring to.

"Not so good. He's been unable to sit up since the trauma to his back. I think it's going to be a long recovery for Yogi."

"See what happens when you bump another man's ice cream?" We laughed.

"So did they put you on the twenty-four-hour shift?" I asked. "Or are you trying to be nominated for Biz Patrol employee of the year?"

"The psychiatric doctors said this was my next step to being integrated back into the community. Because I don't get paid, they abuse my hours, but it's better than having to go back on the medication."

I pointed my finger at her and said, "You're good. I was actually starting to feel sorry for you. My mind was made up to call my city councillor tomorrow and demand an inquiry into the exploitation of the mentally ill. I guess we're even now."

"Fair enough," she said, nodding in agreement. "Are you here alone for our grand hour of Winnipeg's finest fireworks?" She waved her flashlight.

"Isn't it obvious?" I asked. "Was it my pass-for-one entry badge, or were some of the husbands complaining that I was leering at their wives?"

"Quite elementary. It's couples' night, and you're not holding hands with anyone but yourself," she explained.

I burst out laughing and said, "Pretty pathetic, huh? And I thought people were looking strangely at me because I'm wearing socks with my runners and shorts."

"That's also part of it," she admitted, grinning.

"How's crowd control tonight? Saved any lost children?" I asked.

"Nope. But I got a woman trapped in the restroom a fresh roll of toilet paper."

"The mayor will be calling you in the morning with a key to the city."

"Yet again ..."

"It's tough being a saint, isn't it?'

"Such a bore after a while. All those shrines built around my portrait ... The city's running out of parks to name after me. When does it all stop?"

"Believe me, it doesn't. You're cursed with leading society down the path of righteousness."

"Oh great. When I grew up listening to Zeppelin's 'Stairway to Heaven' I thought it was a cool dance song. I didn't realize it would be my calling in life."

"We were warned of the dangers of rock music. Now you pay the price of fame."

"In that case, how about letting me lead you to the world's greatest coffee house, Starbucks. Do you dare to share a cup with a saint? You might never be the same after the experience."

"If there's even the slightest chance of my body undergoing a metamorphosis, then count me in. I need all the help I can get. And I love Starbucks."

"You're easy. I didn't even have to wave my magic wand, namely my flashlight, to alter your mind."

"Your smile is more than enough."

"Flattery like that might get your coffee paid for by a humble Biz employee."

"I'd consider the evening a success if you don't fling your mug at me."

"You've got to have faith in yourself."

"That was wrung from me like a squeegee long ago. However, someone once said I was more stubborn than the roots from a prairie weed."

"Then I'll meet you after my shift at Starbucks in the village. I'm off at midnight."

"I'll look for the lady in the red shirt."

"You do that, jailbird."

"I will, Ms. Narcissistic Personality Disorder." Laughing, she bade me good-bye and disappeared into the night. I watched her until I couldn't see her anymore. She was gone before I could ask her name. I sat back on the grass and laughed.

When I reached the Starbucks and walked inside, I didn't see her, and it all finally made sense. I had been set up to waste my time. My anger grew quickly; my face flushed. Why had she lied to me? I was determined to return to the Forks until I found her and gave her a flying dropkick myself. My day had already been scarring, and now it had become a complete shit-show.

I turned to leave.

A whistle pierced the crowded room.

I looked around and saw an arm waving at me. Squinting, feeling foolish, I recognized the Biz Girl seated in the far corner. She was disguised because she was no longer wearing her red shirt. I walked over.

"Thought you were leaving?" she said, sipping a cup of coffee.

"I was," I admitted. "Didn't see you here."

"Fooled you by changing my shirt, didn't I?" she said, grinning behind her cup. "I don't wear it all the time, you know."

I nodded. I was trying to simmer down from not being stood up.

"I do have other clothes, especially when I'm meeting strange men for coffee."

"I was so focused on looking for someone in a red shirt that when I didn't see anyone, I thought I had been set up," I explained.

"Set up for what?' she asked, sipping at her coffee. "You got people after you?"

I could see her smirk behind her venti cup.

"I wish it were something so *Bourne Identity*," I confessed. "I don't know. When I didn't see you, I was suddenly thinking you had played a joke on me. I realized on the way here I don't even know your name."

She put her coffee down. Smiling, she reached over to shake my hand. "I'm Mitch." Her grip was firm, her fingers long, the nails unpainted.

"Gus."

"Now we're friends. Tell me how you'd remember me now. It would be for my outstanding beauty and irresistible personality, right? All the boys tell me this. And I mean dozens of them."

"Well," I said, "I don't count Hutterite villages, so your dozens don't bother me. But if I were to give a true confession, I wouldn't forget your eyes. I find them penetrating and entrancing."

"Very good," she said, clapping her hands. "You haven't had a coffee yet, so I can't blame your comments on a caffeine-induced lie."

I leaned back in my chair and smiled. "Okay. I confess. I have a thing for women in red T-shirts."

I watched her nod as she admitted, "I guessed you were the Freudian type. Your own eyes have that lost, dreamy look. Probably raised on a bike with training wheels until you were fifteen, weren't you?" She hid behind her coffee mug.

"Hell," I confessed, "I still look both ways before I cross the street."

She looked up again. "Which means you either share an apartment with your mother or call her once a day."

"You're close," I retorted. "I usually check in once an hour by phone. It's a comfort thing. In fact," I added, looking at the empty space on my wrist where a watch would fit, "I have to call her in ten minutes." We both laughed. I ordered the extra-bold French roast coffee from the employee making her rounds.

"Now that we've got the introductions done with, Gus," said Mitch with a bemused look, "do you make it a point to go to couples' night to watch the fireworks alone?"

"Only when I'm single."

"Which means there isn't a Mrs. Gus expecting you home right now," she said, playing along.

"All that awaits me at my place is silence," I confessed.

"Very sad, Gus." She frowned. "I give you points for your admission. Most real men have too much pride and self-worth to make such a truthful confession."

"Thank you. It has been my lifelong mission to stand proudly single. By the way, I lost my self-worth when I had to undergo my first penile swab for an STD."

"I'm honoured for your disclosure that you are disease-free and won't taint my virginal body."

I warmed to her easy demeanor. She had a sense of humour that worked well with my own. I gave her credit that a half hour into our conversation, she hadn't removed any rubberized body part. I awarded her a point.

"Actually," I said, focusing on my napkin, "this has been a rather sad week for me. A girl I was hoping to make arrangements with for a date killed herself. I'm still trying to deal with it."

I could tell by her reaction that my confession startled Mitch. But she regained her composure quickly and asked if I minded telling her more about it.

"There really isn't a lot to tell," I said. "I've been trying this phone dating service thing, and her message caught my attention. Something in her voice grabbed me. I left several messages asking her to call me. But as things turned out, I never got the chance to speak to her."

"How awful," Mitch said sincerely.

I nodded, appreciating her sincerity.

"It's tough when I think that had I heard her message sooner, I might have been able to intervene. Maybe she wouldn't have taken her life. I guess I'll never know."

My coffee arrived, and we quietly sipped our drinks, assessing our situation. I broke the silence.

"This has been a one-way conversation," I said, and I saw she was relieved I had changed from my morbid topic. "Besides busting bad guys beating up on Yogi Bear and leading lost souls on the path of righteousness, what else does Mitch do to fill her days?" Her expression was quizzical and remote.

"Haven't you heard of me? I'm Winnipeg's I'll-do-anything girl. If a volunteer is needed, I'm there. Last summer I worked the events for the Pan Am games. You can find me cruising the stairs at football and hockey games. I've even poured a mean sample of liqueurs at the liquor commission during the Christmas season."

I was impressed. A modern-day saint sat across from me.

"Your tan speaks for itself," I admired. "And when you end your days saving humanity from the mayhem, is there a special someone to rub your feet and tuck you in at night?" I asked, chuckling.

She snickered, and her crystal eyes glimmered. "I've no time for men after spending a day keeping section ten at the stadium safe." She smiled faintly. "Actually, men don't have time for a girl who hasn't drawn a regular paycheck all her life. See what a material world it has become? I'm judged on my net worth. Nowadays, I travel with my financial statements."

We both laughed, understanding the absurdity that perceptions held.

"I'm a native Winnipeger, born and bred," she said. "Raised in the North End by Ukrainian parents as an only child."

"North End?" I said surprised. This was considered a tough section of the city.

Her eyes lit up. "Our reputation precedes us." She winced and said, "Mention that area of the city, and we're automatically labeled as the *bad apples.*"

"I wouldn't say that," I insisted.

"No?" she retorted.

I shook my head, smiling. "I moved here from Minneapolis. Therefore, I am without a bias. Although, I have to admit I've heard the talk. Perhaps you can dispel the rumour."

"The toughness we grew up with over the years has evolved into an image that we're all hard-drinking, blue-collar labourers, ready to fight from the wrong look. You have to remember, I grew up when the Savoie was as mellow as Earl's is today."

"So this was before the No-Knives-Allowed sign was hung by the door," I stated.

"Yes." She laughed.

"So I shouldn't fear for my life with you," I insisted.

"I'm a pacifist."

"Prove it."

"I sometimes work as a camp counsellor for children at Lake of the Woods."

"Good enough for me."

"I'm glad. I thought you were ready to ditch me with the tab tonight."

"No. I'm the sap whose bank account gets pillaged."

"How sad. It must be because of your puppy-dog face. I could never take advantage of it."

"Even pups can nip."

"No. I can't see you being the type," she clarified.

"I thank you for the vote of confidence."

"You're welcome."

I sat forward. "You and I are both hapless singles trying to find one tiny shred of acceptance in this world of wolves and carnivores."

"Or a good cup of coffee," she giggled, raising her mug to her mouth. I admired her relaxed demeanor. Mitch exuded the take-me-as-I-am-or fuck-off attitude. It was a precious gift.

"What brings a patriotic, I'd-die-for-my-country US boy into our fair, wimpish country? Are you on the lam?" She grinned crookedly.

"You must have missed last week's *America's Most Wanted*. I'm on the run for burning the flag."

"Oow," she purred, "a fugitive of the worst sort. How exciting. Talking to you makes me an accessory to harboring a fugitive, I suppose."

"I won't give you up when they come to waterboard me. I promise. I swore to my mother I'd never allow a wholesome girl to sink to my level of despair."

"How noble."

"All I ask is for you to send a yearly Christmas card to me in the pen."

"Consider it done."

I sat back in my chair.

Her eyes never wavered.

"You don't mind being single?" I asked, curious.

She shook her head, suppressing a smile. "Why should I? It's never made sense to me to be with someone I really didn't care about just to say I'm attached. That's ridiculous. It's a waste of my time. I'm saving all my energy for the guy who's going to add the missing pieces to my life. The rest I can do myself."

"Such as?"

"Laughter."

"Excuse me?"

"I need someone who can make me laugh. Not polite laughter to make him feel good about a stupid remark. But the kind that rips me apart from inside. I find the ability to make someone really laugh a precious asset."

"Interesting," I said. I could tell she was sincere.

Our drinks were finished, and we held empty cups.

"So are you glad you came out? I can take the truth," she asked. Her eyes squinted in preparation for my response.

I spoke truthfully. "Yes. I don't make a habit of letting myself be picked up by women at fireworks shows. But it's been an absolute treat."

She seemed pleased by my response. "In that case," she said, "let's exchange numbers. I can always use a companion for nights when I need to share a cup of coffee and a cheap laugh."

I agreed. We wrote our numbers on an available napkin. She got up and reached across the table. We shook hands.

"On that note, Mr. Gus Adams, I thank you for a fine evening. A hot bath awaits me at home." She grinned, and I did too.

"I'm going to stay for another round of brew," I said, noticing her surprise. "All I have at my place is a shower and air-conditioning that works only part time. And besides, in a few hours I'm off to work again, so anything I can do to prolong tonight, all the better."

She shrugged.

"Cheers!" she said and walked out the door, disappearing into the night.

I finished my second drink and walked home an hour later. The air was hot, humid and still. Not many people or cars were out. I realized it was two in the morning. I didn't feel tired. I strutted with a bounce right up to the front of my building. Harold stood outside smoking. I stopped for a chat. I felt sociable.

"Hey, Harold. Keeping an eye on things?"

He scowled, and inhaled a long drag of smoke from the cigarette dangling from his lips.

"Bloody Hodgetts in 101 got themselves a newborn. Bloody kid's got a set of lungs on him. I guess if it was your own kid, the screamin' would sound like music. I gots that kid screamin' on one side of me and Mama snoring like a lumberjack's chainsaw on me odder. Out here, at least it's just me and the cats. Unless they fightin', they quiet."

He went on. "You been seein' another girl tonight?" He looked me over, squinting, chewing on the cigarette's filter.

"I was at the Forks watching the fireworks."

He jerked the hand holding the cigarette. "Was over hours ago. Get lost comin' home?"

I was feeling too good for Harold's comments to jar me. I was about to answer when we were startled by a woman's voice.

"Harold?" asked his wife, now standing at the door in her plain housecoat. "Are you staying out all night? Come back inside before you catch a chill."

I restrained a laugh at her motherly tone. Her husband looked at me, momentarily speechless.

"Has dat screamin' in 101 stopped?" He drew in the final embers of the cigarette and threw it down by his feet.

"Never you mind. Babies need to cry to clear their tiny lungs."

Harold mumbled something I couldn't hear, but I couldn't resist seizing the moment.

"Sounds like, old boy," I said, slapping his shoulder and walking past, "it's beddie time for you. I'm going upstairs to watch satellite TV. Good night," I said to his wife, who smiled at me.

I took the stairs two at a time. I didn't stop until I reached my floor. Then I had to rest until the grey fuzz left my eyes. I had been over-exuberant. My vision cleared, and I entered the motionless tomb of my apartment. I turned on all the lights in an attempt to make it feel like someone actually lived inside, but all it did was make the emptiness seem bigger. It was still just me. Every direction I looked accused me. I took a chair out on the balcony and sat there with a can of Pepsi that felt cool in my hand. I looked in a northerly direction. Somewhere out there lived Mitch. She would have long ago toweled off and gone to sleep, her red shirt neatly folded beside her bed for the next day. I always held tidy views of people. I gave them the benefit of the doubt. I thought back on our conversation. Then an odd realization struck me. I hadn't gone out on the balcony to watch my kissing couple this morning. Strangely, I felt okay about it. It was another hour before I made it to my own bed.

16

"I would like to find someone to cuddle up with and start the millennium off on the right foot ..."

The next couple of days went by without event. Two days fewer of summer, two days closer to forty. I had two fewer days to find and develop a relationship. It was too much to think about, and I didn't.

I ran into Donna Jean quite by accident while picking up a dessert. I had gone to Baked Expectations on Osborne to get Christy and me the mocha cake we both craved that morning. I was walking out the front door with the cake in hand when a familiar voice called out my name. I searched my internal data bank for recognition. Even when I turned her way it didn't click.

Her voice faded back in. "You said you'd call me. The Fringe Festival is on, and I'd like to go with you."

Donna Jean. I felt my face flush. Feeling guilty, I looked past her to Mistress Natasha and Mistress Shannon, who were both smirking. I was cornered. What happened to Mitch's theory about never meeting someone you know in this city by accident? If I ever spoke to her again, I'd be bringing this example up.

I forced my best smile. "Donna Jean! Nice day for a cake."

She wasn't about to be swayed by my cavalier declaration.

"I'd like an explanation, Gus. That's all. What happened? I thought we had gotten along at my place," she said sharply.

There was no mistaking the anger in her voice. And the disappointment. How could I tell her the truth about her psychopathic daughters? They stood behind her in their yellow and white sun dresses, prissy and proper. I had little difficulty remembering them decked out in leathers and latex, Natasha flogging her sister's behind. The craziness of the evening started reliving itself, and my armpits released a torrent of sweat.

The daughters gazed at me smugly. There was only one possible escape route in such a bad situation and that was to lie. The huge, juicy sort that make fables.

"Things around here have been a real mess, Donna Jean. Two days after our supper at your house, my sister was run over by a hit-and-run driver in an SUV. All four tires drove over her body. She had just finished her volunteer shift at the Salvation Army, feeding the homeless and hungry." The tears in my eyes were sweat running down from my forehead.

But Donna Jean was old-fashioned. She bought it and looked horrified by my story.

I decided to use it to its maximum. Second-lie rule of thumb: if the lie is smoking, empty the clip.

"They didn't find her for a while. Her battered body lay silently on the wet pavement in the light rain along the darkened street. They didn't find her until the morning …" I stared at the sky with distant eyes, bringing back the harsh memories. "Her bones crushed, unable to shout for help, my dear sister was determined to live. By the grace of God, she was found by a van of Cub Scouts going home from a jamboree. They saved my sister's life.

"I was devastated by the news. So I've been flying back and forth between the rehabilitation hospital and here. They tell me she'll never be the same again." I looked up at her with watery eyes helped by the sweat running down my face and said gently, "I'm sorry I forgot to call you, Donna Jean. I kept thinking about it while at my sister's hospital bed." She moved closer and hugged me.

I held the cake to the side. "Thank you," I offered softly.

"Oh, Gus. This is terrible. My prayers are with your sister."

I thanked her again. She offered me another meal when I was available. And she gave me all the time I needed to heal with my sister. I felt victorious. Natasha and Shannon looked bored.

"Enjoy your dessert," I said weakly. She nodded and gave me a pitiful smile. I stood aside as she led her daughters into the shop. Watching Natasha's hand coming, I was trapped against the doorframe and defenceless. Her fingers grasped my crotch and tightened sharply. I gave a yelp. Before her mother could turn around, the vixen's fist was long gone. I limped away.

Christy asked me what was wrong when I got back to the clinic. My face was still pinched, and I waddled. I told her I had just been assaulted. Her concern was immediate; she was already dialing 911 when I explained the identity of my assailant. She laughed. I asked her what was so funny. Apparently she found my vulnerability to such young girls endearing. I threatened to withhold her portion of the cake. She apologized.

The phone rang and Christy answered it. She cupped the receiver with her hand and said it was for me.

Who is it? I mouthed while chewing on cake.

She shrugged. I gestured for her to find out. I didn't want to leave my cake if I didn't have to. I was the type of eater who had to go all the way with a meal or my momentum was lost.

Christy swallowed the remainder of her mouthful and asked the caller's identity. She cupped the phone again and told me it was a woman called Mitch.

I froze. Her call was unexpected. I hadn't thought much about her since our late-night coffee rendezvous. Nor had I told Christy about my experience. She asked me if I wanted a message taken. I shook my head and made a decision. I signaled her to transfer the call to my office. I put my cake down and closed the door. My palm was sweaty when I grabbed my phone.

"Hello?"

"I've got bad news for you, Gus. The Forks community has reviewed your file. You've been banned from returning alone. From now on you must be in the company of a woman. I've been selected. Sorry."

I laughed and played along, agreeing to go with her if that's what it took to visit the Forks again. I mentioned that it was an invasion of my solitude, but a small one. I was willing to make the sacrifice. She said she'd pass along the information to the committee.

"But first," she said, "I should test out your suitability to be seen in a public place during daylight hours. How about coming with me to BDI around seven tonight?"

"You mean that ice-cream place on Jubilee?"

"Yup. Best in town."

"So I guess you're not hiking the grasslands of the Forks seeking lost children?"

"Nope."

"On that note, let me brush up on my etiquette for ice-cream dates. You can consider your offer accepted."

I also discovered she was more transportation handicapped than I was and didn't own a car. She biked and bused everywhere. And if she couldn't reach her destination through those two methods, it wasn't worth the effort. Although I didn't say it, I thought how awkward eating our ice cream on the transit system could be, so I offered to pick her up in my vehicle. I got her address on Lisgar Avenue in the North End.

I hung up and walked back to join Christy. Her cake was long finished, and she was working on mine.

"I've never seen you run that fast except for the night at Happenings when you were about to be fondled by your first naked man."

I could tell she was dying to know who had captured my attention. So I explained, starting from the bear attack, my role in the apprehension of the perp and our later discussion at Starbucks.

Christy was appalled. "I'm disappointed in you, Gus. You become a hero, meet a downtown biz gal, get asked out for coffee during the fireworks and say *nothing* to me? I'm shocked." Christy shook her head, scooping the final remnants of my cake into her mouth.

"You've got to understand," I pleaded, "all my dates have been huge disappointments. I didn't want to add another one."

Christy laughed as though she didn't believe me.

"You sure moved your ass to the phone when I said who was calling. I'd say you were holding out on me."

"*I've never had a woman call me back a second time!* What can I say? It feels kinda good."

"Fair enough," she conceded. "But from now on I want full disclosure."

I agreed.

"I was thinking about asking you to join me at Kokonuts tonight," Christy teased. "However, I see someone's got a date to share an ice-cream cone."

I waited until she was finished giggling before offering my defence. "We'll be having separate cones, thank you. And I would have passed on the bar, anyway. What I don't want is a night of that pounding dance music and young teens hopping on my feet."

Christy wore a shrewd, schoolteacher's smile. "So you're *driving* tonight. Do you remember the little *D* means you go forward? The *R* means you go backward."

"Shut up. I'm not a moron with everything, you know. Christ. It's been a few years, but so was the last time I went swimming. I can still dog paddle. Give me a break." I walked over to the stereo and ramped up the volume on Bob Seger.

I broke away from the office an hour early. I knew I'd need the time to make my car roadworthy. I stood looking at the silently rusting exterior, now covered with a light blanket of underground parking dust. It had been what: three, four, hell, maybe five years since I last drove it? I started it from time to time just to keep the battery active. But it still held a tank of gas at the lovely single-digit inflation price of seventy-seven cents a litre. I figured the octane level was as strong as a glass of water by now. I always knew a sudden emergency would arise when I would need to drive my car at a moment's notice. I could forgive myself for the five-year hiatus.

I ran a hand along the puke-coloured hood, relishing the memories of my beloved 1985 Subaru that showed a bruised 270,000 kilometres on the odometer. Seats were split at the seams, and the driver's side mirror was long ago removed by a cyclist who misjudged while trying to pass me on Arlington Street.

I hopped inside the interior that smelled of old car. I rolled down the windows. I put the key in the ignition and, after a quick turn, the car hesitated and then started. I listened to the four cylinders hammer away in front of my feet. I grinned. This was the only reliable friend I had.

I was off to meet Mitch.

The excitement of driving was quickly lost while I waited in traffic construction, and I soon realized why I had hung up my keys. Never once while walking had I ever become agitated like while driving. However, I was committed to another small sacrifice that would go unnoticed by a woman. But it was exactly this kind of thing guys kept tallies on. Then one year we'd spring it on an unsuspecting girlfriend as a backwater defence during some silly argument about commitment.

The fastest way to the North End where Mitch lived was straight down Portage Avenue, left up Main Street and right on Euclid a few blocks after crossing Higgins Avenue. The area was expansive with pre-war homes, some over one hundred years old and once filled with proud European immigrants. Now the parents had long died off, the children lived in LindenWoods designer homes and the solvent-sniffing homeless roamed the streets. Family homes had become dilapidated rooming houses, burned down and beaten down by years of neglect.

I found Mitch's house near the end of the street. It was quiet, the houses in better shape than most. She was sitting on the wooden porch, and she waved when I pulled up. In her hand she held a beer. She was dressed casually in red shorts and a halter-top that complemented her lanky frame. Her tan was very dark, and it gave her an athletic appeal. I enjoyed the way her brown, tangled hair blew around her face in the wind. I opened the wobbly chain-link gate, walked up the wood steps that screeched under my feet and greeted her.

"I didn't hear any gunshots, so I assume you made it here uneventfully," she laughed.

I grinned and accepted the Moosehead beer she handed me. I took a seat next to her. I could smell fresh soap on her skin. Now that I sat close under an evening sun, I pegged her age to be in the late-twenties; she was still too young to appreciate that her laugh lines were to become her nemeses as wrinkles. We clicked bottles in salute. She gripped her bottle, her nail polish a chipped and faded bubblegum colour. I admired her defiance not to be held hostage to womanly perfection.

"So," she began, "I've been curious all day. What kind of place do you work at? The girl who answered the phone made it sound pretty official. Are you a covert operative with the government?" Her brow furrowed, and I laughed.

"Christy is my sole secretary, a naive young gal who answers my phones and books my appointments. I run a little clinic in the Village. I'm a psychotherapist for couples. Our association is still lobbying for us to be allowed sidearms. Pretty unglamorous, huh?"

She seemed impressed, despite the fact I didn't perform wiretaps or save jumbo jets from terrorist attacks.

"Have you been doing it long?"

I told her I had been in the profession just under fifteen years.

Her eyes widened. "I can't imagine myself doing the same thing for that long," she admitted. "After three weeks at the same job, I'm already chomping at the bit. Especially if it means being locked inside a room."

"I do have a window," I reasoned.

"Does it open?"

"No."

"Then what good is it? You're not able to smell the scents the wind brings if it doesn't open."

"I'm more worried of the wind blowing in old syringes," I said, making her laugh. I pointed at her bottle and asked, "Do you often drink beer alone?"

She was chuckling as she said, "Nope. But I knew you were coming, so that makes it allowable. Besides, if the locals don't see you holding a beer, then you're not tough enough to be living in this area."

"There's some more of that North End folklore coming out again," I ventured.

"Followed by 'we don't raise children ... we raise pit bulls instead.'"

"And ... ?"

"And I'm allergic to dog hair, so I'm not included. I did try raising fish for a while, but the damn things are so quiet I forgot about them. A few weeks later I noticed a bunch of floating, shriveled corpses."

"It happens," I said, trying to sound supportive. "I never could understand the desire to raise fish, which is more of a pain in the ass than entertainment."

"Here, here," she offered, and we clinked our bottles again.

We sipped our beers, enjoying the feel of the sun. The rays caught one of the lone pieces of shiny trim still remaining on my car.

"The guy charged with assaulting the bear mascot has taken a strange turn," said Mitch.

"How so?"

"He's now pressed charges against the bear."

"What?"

"I know it's absurd, but he's claiming the bear purposely ran into him and gave him a crippling whiplash."

"Holy shit. He's saying *he* got whiplash. The poor bastard in the bear suit was drop-kicked! He's the one in traction."

"This nutjob is claiming his inability to work. I've heard he hasn't worked in five years anyway! The judge will likely dismiss the case. Strange world, isn't it?"

"Oh, yeah, it sure is."

"I guess we should get going before BDI runs out of ice cream."

"There'd be a revolution of the underclass."

"Led by us, of course."

"Of course."

We finished our beers, and she placed the bottles in the corner of the porch. I questioned her when she didn't lock her front door. Apparently, if the bandits wanted to get in, a lock wasn't going to stop them. Besides, her greatest asset was an empty fish tank.

Mitch was either a tactful person or just didn't give a shit about the dilapidated condition of my car during our drive to BDI. She tried the radio, realized it was broken and hummed a tune instead. We arrived at BDI, ordered our cones and sat down by the river. A few scattered people were doing the same thing.

"This place reminds me of Scotty's Island in Lake of the Woods," Mitch said suddenly.

"How so?" I asked, having never been there.

"I used to take the day-trippers to the island after our tour of the lake." She saw my look of confusion and grinned.

"Sorry. I forget our lingo doesn't always make sense. *Trippers* are the name for the kids we take out on canoe trips. I've canoed up to six weeks on some tours. Sitting along this riverbank reminds me of those times on Scotty's Island. I don't think the kids ever appreciated the beauty of nature."

"Unfortunately," I began, "the concrete jungle is my Scotty's Island. I trade the smell of pollen for exhaust."

We watched the flow of muddy water at our feet and ate our ice creams silently. Her experiences canoeing raised a thought.

"Mitch, about those canoe trips you went on—I'll bet you had your choice of chiseled Tarzans to help you portage?"

She grinned and tossed a wiry strand of brown hair from her eyes. "Not likely. Those trips didn't exactly attract a romancing type of guy. I suppose if I didn't mind settling for unwashed, unshaven, heavily calloused males who had extensive foot rot, I'd have been perfectly happy. No. I never got involved with any of the male crews." She shot me a comical look and then asked, "So how does dating in big-city USA compare to an inbred place like Winnipeg, Gus? Have you found any nice girls to write home about?"

I glanced out over the river, watching the brown water flow past our feet. Did I admit the shambles my love life was really about? Or did I fake it? There was no question I wasn't about to expose my freakish passion for stealing a peek at two strangers kissing every morning.

I cast my pride aside with my answer. "I haven't had a successful relationship in ten years. Nor did I made much of an effort to date since then. I've never been engaged. Have no illegitimate children in another country. This summer I made a pact with myself to make an effort to date. So far, all the dates I've been on have been complete disasters. Women have gone nuts in the last ten years. Christy says that's the way it is. I say she wouldn't know, since she was twelve years old ten years ago. I know this sounds absurd, but you're the first woman I've met this summer I've been able to see twice. So either I'm really bad company or just old-fashioned in my standards." I was afraid to look her way and see disgust etched onto her face. Her remark surprised me.

"I don't think you're such bad company."

She fell silent. I couldn't determine if that was a good thing or not.

"So I'm not crazy for being picky and judging people?" I asked, deciding to get her to elaborate.

"Personally, I would never allow myself to settle for someone just to settle," Mitch clarified. "I think you're being fair judging people the way you do. I'm happy being single. Sure, there are plenty of guys I can hang with and have a good time. But at the end of the day, I'm going home alone because none of those guys share the same chemistry. To me, a man should bring out my best, make me feel good about myself and respect who I am as a person. And personally, I have no problem drinking a beer alone." She brightened.

"Does this mean your roommates have a strict no-boyfriend-in-the-house policy to adhere to?' I asked.

"Ah, Gus, it's so much simpler than that. I don't have roommates, period. Share the same coffee mug with a roommate? I don't think so. Why do you think I live in the North End? It sure as hell is not for the collection of bloody bandages on the sidewalks. Two words: cheap rent. The landlords practically pay you to live there. I've heard the city waives the property taxes. This low-cost housing allows me to live alone with my dead fish."

Mitch went on to say her parents had moved to Victoria, BC, on the west coast three years ago, after her dad retired from driving city transit. I had probably ridden on his bus at some time. Now all she had for family was the twice-a-year phone calls, on her birthday and Christmas.

My ass was starting to get sore from sitting on the riverbank, so we decided to leave.

On the way back to her place, Mitch thanked me for picking her up. We pulled up in front of her house, my brakes squeaking.

"Keep saving those marriages" were her parting words before she closed the car door and bounded up to her porch.

I watched her collect our empty beer bottles and disappear inside. She never looked back to notice my wave.

17

"I'm on the System looking for erotic phone conversation to get me off now, so if you're interested give me a call ..."

The following morning I waited on the balcony like an ambush squad long before the car pulled up. I had already showered, dressed and was on my second cup of coffee. For the first morning in weeks, the sky was grey with clouds. Rain was in the forecast for today. I made a mental note to bring my umbrella.

The car pulled into the driveway and parked. My heart sped up. I vaguely made out the tops of their heads as they spoke. I thought I saw their hands embracing. After a brief talk, their mouths met for a kiss. It was long, and I felt the passion from my perch. I envied their existence.

During the walk to work, my umbrella swinging beside me, I could taste the heaviness in the air. I was hoping the rain would hold off until I got to work. All I wanted was to get through the day unscratched, go home, shut the door and hit the couch. In essence, I wanted zero brain simulation.

And then I remembered my date with Petulla. I was to meet her at Canwest Global Park for the baseball game tonight. I'd need to bail out of it. I'd already fallen in love with my couch. I'd postpone. I simply didn't have the energy to engage myself in conversation. I was discovering I needed a break from my rigorous dating agenda. I'd just have to accept the lost day in my pursuit of blissfulness.

There was a message from Christy on the machine at the clinic saying she wouldn't be in today. She justified her absence as a womanly issue. That was good enough for me. I'd manage alone.

The first task was a call to Petulla. No one answered her phone. She also appeared to be the only person in the city without an answering machine. That pissed me off. I'd keep trying, but if I didn't get through to her, I'd be obligated to be at the game. The thought soured my positive mood.

Shortly before lunch I received a call from Lonny. He was on his cell phone outside of Winnipeg. He wanted to meet. He wouldn't accept no. He suggested the Crackling Crow. I agreed to meet only at the Coyote Café. It was closer to the baseball stadium, should I not be successful speaking with Petulla. And unlike the Crow, we'd actually get service at the Coyote Café. Lonny wouldn't admit to the nature of this urgent meeting, but it was something big. This was classic Lonny. He never just had a story to tell. It was an epic adventure. I deduced I was about to hear passages from his love-in trip to Piney with his cyber-sex kitten.

I called Petulla's phone again and let it ring until the phone became hot against my ear. Did I want to get involved with a woman who didn't own an answering machine? What further issues would I uncover? Eight-track stereo system? Flashbulbs? Knee-highs? This gave me something to contemplate during a no-appointment day.

I couldn't lock my door fast enough when the time arrived to leave. I felt obligated to stay until four thirty because Christy wasn't around, on the chance a walk-in couple came to inquire about my services. None did. I caught the bus outside my clinic and waited out the fifteen-minute ride.

Lonny was already at the café when I got there. I quickly noticed two things about Lonny that weren't typical. He was unshaven, and his eyes looked haunted. I knew I was in for a damn fine story this time.

I slid on a stool beside him.

"Hey, Killer," he said, giving me a quick sideways glance.

"What's a good-looking guy doing in a shithole town like this?" I replied. My remark promoted a very forced smile from Lonny. He really was as down as his face suggested.

"Should I cancel Neil Diamond's performance at your wedding?" I asked.

"The whole world's a farce, Gus. I can tell you that much with absolute certainty."

"Hell, I realized that when Ford gave the Mustang a four-litre engine for the conservative customer."

"What the hell is wrong, Gus? Why do people have to play games? Just for once, I'd like to not dig away twenty layers of crap to get to the core of who someone really is."

"Does this conversation in any way relate to your visit to Piney? Or is your return from there strictly coincidental?" I waved off the bartender who came our way.

"She lied to me, Gus. *Freaking lied to me.*"

"The Internet Queen of Piney, a liar?" I proclaimed. "That's like accusing the Hi-Neighbour of being a pedophile."

"I'm not joking, buddy. She pressed all my buttons. The more I think about it, I'm probably one among a hundred of her pawns."

"Or thorns in her bush."

"Jesus, this makes me mad."

"Why don't you tell me the sequence of events rather than throwing me chunks of beef like a caged lion?"

"If you haven't tried the Internet, don't do it."

"Does this mean I should cancel my Internet banking account? Tell Uncle Gus what happened to you out in Piney." I placed my hands against my cheeks and listened.

"I pulled into a driveway covered in wild brush and watched a fleshy human Smurf waddle over to my truck, trying to convince me she was Morgan. I took one look at this circus freak and laughed, thinking it was a joke. I knew Morgan had a wicked sense of humour from our 'net chats, so I played along. I'm thinking she'd convinced this friend who'd been involved in a serious farming accident to pretend to be Morgan."

"You mean the badass tattoo on her forehead didn't give her away?"

Lonny ignored my comment, the hollowness in his eyes deepening.

"By the evening I'm still hanging with this pint-sized Sasquatch and starting to get pissed off that the joke is still going on. So I tell this fatty fuzzball I'm leaving unless Morgan gets her ass over there."

"Did you have to tap your heels three times?"

"She grabs my arm with a six-fingered paw and takes me to a computer, where she shows me transcripts of our conversations. *All of them!* Now it occurs to me this fleecy broad *is* my Morgan."

"Okay, so it wasn't love at first sight. I've been a firm believer that love starts from the brain."

"Yeah? In walks her brother. This aberration must have been an extra in the movie *Deliverance*."

"The twang of a banjo didn't alert your senses that something was amiss? What happened next?"

"These two clowns sit me down and lay the deal on the table."

"Let me guess? You'd be spared getting bent over a log by modeling a sleeveless black wet suit?"

"Gus. Please. This is difficult for me." Lonny rubbed his eyes and continued. "Outside behind the trailer was a twenty-acre *grow operation*. I'd get a 20 percent cut of Manitoba's finest, selling it from my truck on my cellular sales route."

"Great way to start a little nest egg for a down payment on a cabin up in the mountains. Think of your future, my boy."

"There I am, sitting with two poster victims for fetal alcohol syndrome, the smell of sweet leaf burning in the distance, thinking that I should shitkick them both. You know I'm fully against violence toward women, but Gus, no woman has a mud flap of hair groomed on her chest."

"I wonder if she uses a conditioning shampoo on it ..."

"Somehow I managed to keep my anger in check. I'm sure I did the right thing by tactfully declining their offer. These people looked like they'd be comfortable chewing on a man's leg."

"Just for the hell of it, you didn't notice George Romero lurking around with a camera crew?"

"No. *No.* Just the laughing lettuce swaying in the wind like corn stalks. What kind of idiot was I to believe she was legitimate?"

"Does this mean you're going to the police? Maybe you can clear up my prostitution charge while you're at it?"

"I'm junking my computer. The entire system is cursed. I'm getting totally sloshed tonight and erasing the images of her nostril hair dangling past her lips. Drink with me, buddy. Help a chum tip a few dozen back."

"Can't. Sorry. Got a hot date with Petulla to watch baseball. You know I'd be here with you helping to scratch out your last will and testament in the carpet. Just stay away from parking lots."

Lonny nodded, his head hanging. I slapped him on the back and told him I had to go. I'd call him tomorrow to make sure he survived the night. Lonny was quick to rebound. He got over Bernice, a former girlfriend, who turned out to have Coke can–sized testicles under her dress. Lonny was a survivor.

The air was heavy when I walked outside. I was sure it was going to piss down with rain. I remembered the stadium had no roof. I didn't look forward to sitting in wet underwear for three hours.

The threat of rain couldn't dispel the swarm of baseball fanatics from shoving their way into the Canwest Global Baseball Park. I fought against hotdog-carrying, coffee-spilling parents and screaming kids just to find a single space to stand. Finding Petulla in the rush of the crowd was a challenge. I had to admit my surprise the city could support a bush league baseball team. Secretly, the actual reason for the fan support wasn't the love of the game. It was the free giveaway of cheap gifts that shut the kids up and earned the parents three hours of peace. Winnipegers were staunchly renowned for seeking the thrill of cheapass freebies.

I scanned the bedlam of people for a confident, shapely woman with white teeth. She found me.

Petulla deserved credit. She'd described herself as honestly as one person could. She was tall. She held a few pounds of very evident roundness. Yes, it did fill her out in a girly sort of way, like after an eating binge gone bad. She did exude an imposing confidence that almost scared me. And a final truth—her breasts were huge. Disconcertingly huge. My head disappeared somewhere in the fleshy mass when she grabbed me in a bear hug. I suppose any blue-collar man would have happily burrowed a new home in those few seconds. But my blue wasn't etched into my collar. I held my breath and waited it out. I made sure to eject myself with a smile. I remembered her ad saying she relished a man with big, strong hands. I reached out to prove the strength in my digits, only to have them lost in her fleshy mitts. I conceded. My ally would need to be intelligence. I summoned within myself every reserved cell.

"I think we might get rain," I said, proudly displaying my umbrella.

"Good thing I put my bra on today," she retorted.

"Where're we sitting?" I asked, changing directions.

"Follow me," she said, dragging me by my forearm. We plowed through the children and elderly until reaching our destination. The seats behind the home team's dugout weren't that bad.

"So what'cha do, Gussy?" Petulla asked, at the same time negotiating with a snack vendor.

"I'm a psychotherapist."

"My sister saw a shrink once."

"Good for her," I replied, watching Petulla stack her purchases in the empty seat next to her. She'd cleared out the vendor's tray for him.

"I always told her, she shoulda had him put those electrode thingies into her head. Dumb as a stump, she is. A good zap mighta put some sense into her."

I nodded, not sure who needed the zap. "How about you?" I asked.

"How about me what?" she replied, looking at me strangely while she ripped open a jumbo pretzel bag.

"Your job? Where do you work?"

"Oh, that," she said, shoving three pretzels into her mouth before replying. "I work at the cosmetic counter at the Bay downtown. Here," she offered, leaning closer with her neck, "smell me."

I took a whiff. I recognized lilacs. I thought of my grandmother's bathroom spray.

"Love this scent," she said fondly, spitting bits of pretzel into the hair of the woman sitting ahead of her.

"Do you come to these games often?" I felt empty-handed, having not bought any treats. Petulla didn't seem about to offer me any of her own stash. I feared to ask.

"Only when I need sex," she asserted.

"Pardon me?"

"I take my guys here because it gets my juices flowing. Then we go back to my place to tear the walls down."

"Do you do that with every guy you come here with?"

"Yup."

I stared at her. "Yeah, but there has to be forty homes games in the season. Some of those weeks have eight home games in a row!"

"I've got needs, Gussy. That's why the hockey season suits me even better. *Go, Jets, go!*"

My concentration on the game folded. I didn't want to visualize Petulla naked. Was it even possible for her to remember the names of all those men? I was horrified. I couldn't visualize a naked Petulla without a rolling belly covered with Doritos crumbs.

"Next weekend you and I are going camping," Petulla said, sucking on the straw in a two-litre jug of Pepsi. "There's a great spot at West Hawk Lake that rents hump shacks to couples in love. We'll spend all weekend with my eyes looking up into the stars and your ankles bent behind your ears."

My own eyes shot around at the people near us. Many were obviously tuned in to our conversation judging by the large grins pasted on their faces and the odd snicker. I shrank in my seat. There was no way in hell I was allowing myself to be locked down in a hump shack with a hormonal Petulla. My face flushed. My ankles couldn't reach behind my ears without a hip transplant.

"*Come on, you stupid bastards! Hit the goddamn ball!*" Petulla suddenly shouted at the field. Several players turned around to stare at her.

"They're trying their best ..." I offered.

"*For Christ's sake, if you watch the ball you'd hit the goddamn thing!*"

One of the players actually pointed our way. I couldn't make myself any smaller in my chair. I heard thunder in the distance. Maybe it was Petulla's voice echoing inside my head

"How's your nachos?" I asked.

She flung herself to her feet and catapulted a hotdog onto the field.

"*Eat that, you stupid son of a bitch, if you don't wanna play ball!*"

One of the men sitting with his wife in the row ahead of us apparently had enough of Petulla's foul language and turned around to speak. He got no further than opening his mouth before Petulla shoved her second hotdog into it.

"Mind your own business, jerk-off," she muttered, taking a chomp from a Hershey bar. I wasn't sure if she had removed the wrapper.

"Boy, nothing like a relaxing game of baseball, huh?" I asked, hoping it'd take her attention away from the field.

"Hold on a sec, Gussy," she frowned, stopping me with her hand. Apparently, she wasn't done with the players yet.

"*I saw you holding hands with your mother today, number forty-two! What kind of athlete are you, Jennifer!*"

I didn't know what to say. Petulla caught the attention of the Goldeye's fish mascot, who made its way over to our row and began waving and pointing an oversized foam fish our way. With surprising agility for a big girl, Petulla grabbed hold of the fish, yanking the mascot into our row.

"*Oh yeah, you wanna play, Big Boy?*" Petulla jumped up and landed her knee on the mascot's head.

I could hear the groan from inside the hood, and I flinched. *Is it open season this year on mascots?* I wondered.

I felt a whack in my lower back that buckled my knees. I turned around, grimacing, wondering who'd sucker-punched me. I was staring into the feral eyes of a man pointing his cane at me.

"Control your bitch," he growled, flicking his dentures back and forth from his gums.

"Mom! Look at what that lady is doing to Fishy!"

I looked to my side and watched a seven-year-old break out in tears as he pointed our way.

Petulla raised the mascot's head over her shoulders in victory.

"See if you blind mice can hit this thing, losers!" she screamed out, and she shot-putted the head well into middle field.

"Petulla! Calm down! Calm down!" I begged her. Suddenly our brawl was being broadcast on the ballpark's mega-screen, and I was twenty feet tall.

"Fight for your rights, Gussy! Fight for your rights!" Petulla panted. She noticed that I was clutching my back.

She pointed a meaty finger at the senior behind us, her eyes open and wild.

"Hey! Did you attack my Gussy! Try that again and I'll smack your dentures out to first base!"

The fight went out of the pensioner. He quickly sat down next to his horrified wife, who grabbed his hands.

To my left the mascot was trying in desperation to drag himself away from the killing field. Petulla's attention was diverted to the ball players scrambling toward us from the field.

One of the stand attendants was jogging up the stairs, heading our way. She was nearly at our row when the rain burst from the sky. I was instantly soaked by two months of pent-up water. The female attendant reached our row and wiggled next to Petulla. I couldn't make out the conversation over the roar of the rain slapping against the concrete. Whatever the attendant said apparently didn't sit well with Petulla, who threw her nachos into the row ahead of us. The female attendant reached out to grab Petulla's arm, but she couldn't hang on. Petulla's skin was slippery from the rain and nacho cheese. Petulla used her greatest asset. She twisted her body violently to the side, swinging her pendulous breasts at the attendant, who took the full brunt on her shoulder. The impact knocked her over two rows.

Now I could see a platoon of attendants hurrying our way. We were done.

This time Petulla was up against three burly ballplayers who withstood the powerful impact of her breasts. She fought hard and valiantly, even managing to stuff a handful of popcorn between her lips while wrestling with one of the men. One ball player attempted a bear hug, but her breast size made it impossible for him to close his arms. She reached out and ripped the jersey right off the first baseman, sending the crowd into roar. I was knocked to the side by the remaining baseball player, landing in the row ahead of us. A little kid poured his carbonated Coke over my head and said, "*Boo.*" His sister followed by dumping her vanilla ice-cream cone into my hair. I heard the crowd roar out once again, and I wasn't sure if that was one for the home team or Petulla. I fought my way to my feet in time to see Petulla being led up the stairs, still clutching the torn jersey and waving it above her head. I followed the remainder of the crowd and scurried to get out of the rain. It took me a few moments to find my bearings and located a bathroom, where I wiped the vanilla ice cream and Coke from my hair. My back hurt, and I made a mental note to visit an emergency room if I pissed blood.

I exited the bathroom and wandered among the crowd until I exited outside toward the parking lot. I wasn't sure what had happened to Petulla. I assumed she was locked away in some room awaiting a police escort downtown. Maybe I could refer my lawyer to her. Someone grabbed my arm.

"*There you are, lover. I knew you'd wait for me!*"

I jumped. It was Petulla.

"What are you doing! I thought you were taken away by the ballpark staff to the police!" I stared at her glowing face.

"Ah, shit, honey. They can't control a woman like me. I broke loose and made a run for it." She flipped me around, giving me a power hug. Her breasts felt like oversized therapeutic pillows. Moments earlier they had been lethal weapons.

I was about to convince Petulla to turn herself in when she tossed me against a green 1999 Nissan Frontier pickup truck. I was pushed inside the driver's door by Petulla and then squeezed along the bench seat to the passenger side.

"Come on, lover. Let's go have the last laugh."

"Huh?" I tried my door. It didn't work.

"Handle's broke, honey, that's why we came in my side."

"Petulla, let's call it a day, all right?" I begged.

She laughed and burrowed her hand into the supersized bag of Dorito chips next to the shifter. "It's third inning, and we need to make sure those ballplayers take the game seriously."

I shook my head vigorously. "We don't need to do anything, Petulla."

"Shush, sugar." Shards of Doritos fell from her mouth. She shifted into four-wheel drive.

Petulla focused ahead. "Now, if this doesn't get their attention ..." We charged the backfield fence and plowed through, the green wood spinning sideways into the grass. Out of the corner of my right eye I saw clods of sod sailing past my window. I cried out and grabbed the dash. Players fled as the Nissan burrowed donuts into the fresh turf. Once again we were highlighted on the mega-screen. The ballpark crowd was standing on their feet. I put one hand over my face. The right fielder dove to his left and was pelted with wet soil.

"Catch that in your glove, Wonderboy," Petulla shouted at her closed window. She reached down and grabbed another fistful of chips, shoving most of them into her mouth.

"I love a day out at the ballpark," she wailed, splaying chips across the front dash and window.

"Personally," I said, "I prefer stadium seating."

"Nothing like being up close and personal with the players, Gussy," Petulla gasped, finding a Reese's bar somewhere and plowing it into her mouth.

"You mean like the short stop hanging from my side mirror, Petulla?" I asked, staring in disbelief into the wild eyes of the player as he dug in while Petulla spun the Nissan in circles. I rolled down the window, shouting, *"Let go, you stupid idiot!"* He still had a hand inside his glove gripping the mirror, and I wiggled it loose, using the momentum of the vehicle. The player fell free of the vehicle; I held on to the glove.

Petulla shouted, *"That was the only thing you could ever catch in your glove, Jacko!"*

We both laughed, and Petulla headed the Nissan out the same battered hole we entered. We squealing and wobbled on to Waterfront Drive the wrong way. Petulla cranked the wheel to the left and entered Provencher Boulevard, and we shot over the bridge above the Red River into St. Boniface. I hung on to the side of my seat with my left hand, and my right hand grasped the dash, the grin across my face the size of a pizza. Despite the swath of destruction behind us that we had just inflicted, I felt a sense of wild excitement I didn't know was inside me. *The devil in us all*, I reasoned.

Petulla spoke with relish. "I feel like Chinese. How 'bout you, Gussy? All this drivin' has depleted my MSG levels." Petulla was sucking furiously on two straws stuck inside a 7-11 Big Gulp.

I laughed and shook my head. "I think I'll cash in my chips at this point, Petulla. Thanks. Seriously. This has been a date I will never forget. In fact, if I get arrested later for it, I'll be able to keep the striped wardrobe as a souvenir." Petulla reached over and slapped a chocolate-stained hand on my thigh.

"Suit yourself, Gussy, but let me tell ya, once I get a few wontons down my mouthpiece, I'm a woman who can't be wrestled off the satin." She squeezed my thigh and smiled at me, a ring of nacho cheese around her lips.

"Let's leave something for next time; how does that sound?" I smiled back.

"Nasty, Gussy, making a woman wait like this. You're gonna give me sleepless nights playing coy." Petulla's hand ran past my groin and up to my neck, where she tried to bend my head forward for a kiss. I closed my eyes and tasted feta.

"Can you drop me off at VJ's Drive Inn, Petulla?" I asked, spying it as we drove up Main Street.

"Anything for you, sweetcakes. You call momma when you're ready to be sprayed with whip cream and have me crush bananas over your body for the ultimate lick." She ran a long tongue over her lips.

I tensed in my seat but managed to smile and laugh.

"Absolutely, Petulla!" I remarked. "Here," I said tossing her the ball glove belonging to the shortstop as we pulled up in front of the restaurant.

Petulla lit up. "These make great holders for my Jello snacks."

I slammed the door and watched the Nissan pull away. The reality was that I wanted out of her truck before every single Winnipeg police car was on the road looking for it. Petulla's baking timer was on borrowed time. We were officially fugitives.

I looked around me. My clothes were damp from rain. My back ached from the cane driven into it. My hands still shook from what Petulla and I had done to the ballpark. I walked up to a pay phone next to VJ's, and the smell of juicy burgers made my stomach rumble. I was planning to call a cab to go home, but I thought about calling Mitch instead, to see if she was around for a bite to eat. I grabbed a quarter from my jeans and punched out her number on the phone. At the tenth ring Mitch's voice came on her machine, and I started to leave a message. I was disappointed she wasn't around.

I was in the middle of my speech when her real voice took over. I discovered she screened all her calls. That way the phone solicitors could waste their time and not hers. I applauded her phone defiance.

She asked me what I was doing, and I explained the entire Petulla incident and explained I was a fugitive on the run for real this time. She laughed and mentioned she was glad I had called. She had just been thinking about me. I asked for further details, but she wouldn't elaborate. When I asked her why she wasn't working, it turned out the rain warning had cancelled her shift at the Forks. When I told her I still hadn't eaten, she suggested a meal at Kelekis, a few blocks from her place. I explained I didn't have my car and would be in a cab. That didn't bother her. We'd work around it.

I got to her place forty minutes after my call. I was wet and I was shivering. The rain had sapped the humidity from the air. The last vestiges of the summer heat wave were gone.

I rushed up to Mitch's door, and it opened before I could knock. Mitch took one look at my wet clothing and ordered me into her kitchen. Before we went anywhere, she explained, she'd dry my clothes. Meanwhile, I got to wear a pair of her sweats and a sweater that said Downtown BIZ PATROL.

The rain stopped, and my clothes were still drying, but we decided to hike to the restaurant on Main Street. We had the place to ourselves. I ordered a double dog with fries, and Mitch did the same, except she added cheese. I enjoyed watching her stretch the cheese from the bun to her mouth like a bridge. We drank Cokes and laughed ourselves silly describing our worst dating experiences.

"I've dated men who often want to sack the girl within the first few dates, Gus," explained Mitch, sucking at her Coke with a straw without the intensity Petulla had earlier. "My philosophy has always been if the hormonal needs are satisfied first, the relationship is doomed by the sex. The sex will taint a person's ability to not only see a person for who they are but also put blinders on what's really there, good and bad."

"Like an emotional condom," I added, seeing her nod while she laughed.

"Truly it is, Gus, no joke." Her soft eyes held my attention. "Sex is going to feel great no matter who the person is, and you know it releases enough hormones to make us believe this is the greatest person in the world. Well, guess what?"

"What?" I asked, popping a french fry into my mouth.

"Instead of finding out if this person is truly compatible sooner in order to cut loses, it takes longer, like years longer, and by then the entrenchment makes it a messy, painful separation. Sex will mislead you into believing this is the right person."

"That's it, no sex for us, like for at least two decades. I will not budge my stance," I stated strongly.

Mitch grinned. "You'll succumb when I'm ready." We both laughed.

I sipped at my pop. "I've been sexless for so long, I've been revirginalized, if that's even a word."

"If it's not, it doesn't sound good."

"Believe me, it's not a badge of honour."

"But it's an honour to be with a virgin."

"So be gentle with me," I whimpered.

"I can not make you that promise. But I will promise to use my advanced CPR if you go into shock."

"Shock! Seeing me naked with this body will shock you, all right."

Mitch burst out laughing.

"That bad, huh?" she said, still laughing.

"I'm banned from removing my shirt at any Manitoba beach, and indoor pools provide me with a one-piece to wear."

"Gosh, that sounds *really* bad, Gus. Gee, I don't know if I can handle being with such a flawed man. This perfect body that I have will only make you look worse, you know."

"I bet every construction worker you pass makes a call out your way," I said.

"You bet, but that's usually because I've driven a car too close to the work site, endangering a worker."

"Speed kills."

"I drive like a turtle."

"Perhaps stick to a bicycle."

"Which is why you don't see a car in my yard."

"And here I thought you were into being green. What a disappointment."

"Stick with me long enough and I'll disappoint you many more times," Mitch assured me.

"Flaws." My eyes lit up. "Sounds like I'd be in for a lifetime of hurt with you. And yet," I teased, "I'm strangely drawn to spending all the time necessary finding out about these mysterious flaws."

Mitch looked mischievously at me. "You better watch what you say, to this girl, cowboy. You let me latch on, and I'm digging my heels and heart into you."

"Those words don't scare me," I boasted.

Mitch looked dreamy, and she said, "Really?"

"Really," I said and nodded.

"I'm a handful, cowboy," Mitch said softly.

"I have big enough hands."

Mitch's eyes worked over my body and face. "I find you a complex guy, Gus Adams."

"I'm really a softy behind this professional demeanor. I cried during *Titanic*."

"Softy." Her face glowed. She smiled. "I'm glad you called me tonight." She reached out and held my hands across the table.

I savoured their softness and warmth.

"Such gentle hands for a person wrestling bear-beating bandits," I said to her, and she smiled and handed me a Kelekis monogrammed napkin.

"A keepsake of this wonderful evening."

I accepted her gift.

When the waitress finally came around to tell us the time had come to close the joint, we couldn't believe it was quarter to one.

We walked back to her house, and although I didn't say so, the dark journey was nerve-splitting. Every shadow jumped at me, ready to make me a morning newspaper statistic. Mitch laughed at my unfounded fears. We made it back safely and uneventfully.

My clothes were dry. Mitch handed them to me. I promised to bring her sweater and sweats back cleaned. We sat and talked for another two hours. Already a false dawn glowed in the sky. I finally felt my first twang of tiredness. Mitch agreed. Waiting outside on her porch for my cab, we huddled close, slapping at the odd mosquito that ventured out from the shrubs. All I could see was the silhouette of her face; all I heard was her husky voice as we spoke. She never seemed to be without a story to tell or a point to exchange about a topic I mentioned.

The cab pulled up, and our time was over. I felt the need to shake hands, hug or touch her arm, but I left with a salute that morphed into a partial wave. She leaned against the doorframe, a darkened figure watching me leave. I saw her hand waving while we drove off.

Oddly, as I got closer to my place, I didn't feel the sense of emptiness I usually did after arriving home from somewhere. I paid the cabbie and walked to the front door, inhaling the freshly cleansed air. I loved this hushed hour of the morning. It supercharged my energy, and I made it, two steps at a time, to the fourteenth floor before I became winded.

I burst into my darkened apartment, not noticing the quiet stillness greet me as a usual companion.

18

"I want you to know you're good-looking and not hope it ..."

The next morning I described my baseball experience with Petulla to Christy. I spared no details, right down to Petulla's breasts as weapons and the two of us tearing up the Canwest Park's outfield in her Nissan. Christy remained the model friend by agreeing with every complaint that women had become simply weird. There was no technical, medical or educated term more appropriate then *weird*.

Christy, playfully sitting on the corner of my desk, asked, "How was your time with Mitch? *Shame on you for coming home three o'clock in the morning!* Girls need their beauty sleep, you know. I'm sure she was politely trying to get you the hell out of her house so she could go to bed. No girl wants to sit with a guy doing nothing but talking. Boring ..."

"What's wrong with conversation? Talking can be as stimulating as physical activity," I assured her.

"The language spoken is with the body," she insisted, swaying her shoulders. "It's much more expressive. You should try it sometime."

"I don't think Mitch is the body rhyming type. She appears very comfortable using her lips."

Christy shrugged her shoulders, not convinced. "Perhaps she is for now, but give her a few more evenings listening to your phobias and other tales of woes, and she'll be the one signing up for a telepersonal account."

"Hey," I said, hurt, "what the hell's happened to your support? I'd have thought you'd encourage me about actually talking to another woman. What gives?"

Christy scrunched up her face. "Ah, I'm happy for you Gus. Really. Now I'm the one left alone. This sucks."

"She's only a friend, Christy."

She wasn't satisfied with my reply and made that known by shaking her head. "You know boys and girls can never just be friends. Eventually, we all end up in the sack."

"Perhaps that's how you operate, but I can hold a friendship together with a woman without getting more involved."

"Yeah, right," she spat. "You'll say anything right now so that I don't feel alone. So cut the crap, all right? I mean it when I say I'm happy for you. This is what you've been looking for all summer. A girl who doesn't have a cross to bear or a cross burned into the flesh of her back. And not only did she give you her correct phone number, she actually invited you inside her house. You've made great strides, my love-stricken friend."

"See," I said, stabbing at the air with my finger, "I'm your friend."

"You're also my boss. That neutralizes everything."

I laughed. "You make this shit up as you go along, don't you?"

She nodded. "This girl intrigues me. I've got to meet her."

I held up my hand and responded by saying, "She won't be coming around until I confirm she's actually a friend on her own accord and that Lonny hasn't been paying her."

"Would he do something like that?" she asked, horrified.

"I wouldn't put it past the bastard," I said ruefully.

The main office phone rang, and Christy ran to her desk to pick it up.

"Gus," she shouted, "there's a man calling for you."

"Who is it? Did you get a name?" I shouted back.

"Yeah. It's ... Cletus Jack Colby."

My heart raced. I'd signed my innocence away. What could he possibly want now? I thought about whether I had neglected to pay his fee. I grabbed the phone and signaled Christy to turn down Seals and Croft so that he didn't think I was partying at work.

"Hi, Gus here," I said banally.

"Mr. Adams, Cletus Jack Colby. We meet earlier about your solicitation charge." He stated this as if I wouldn't remember who he was and what he had done to me.

"I know who you are," I replied dryly.

"Very well," he said, clearing his throat in my ear. "I'm following up about your court-mandated enrollment in john school in exchange for pleading guilty and eliminating an incarceration period. I'm calling with the date and location of your class."

I could detect a level of repugnance in his voice, as though he were speaking to a child molester. On paper, I was a proven gay felon, but in my heart, I knew my injustice would someday be reprieved.

I was dutifully warned that if I skipped the class, a warrant for my arrest would be issued, and I would earn a straight-to-jail pass. Just as I was about to hang up, Cletus decided that I should understand that without a change in my covert homosexual lifestyle, I'd be dead in five years of an incurable disease. I hung up without saying good-bye. Or thank you.

Mitch called me a few days later, asking if I wanted to join her for a movie. I agreed to pick her up at her place in my Subaru.

My car was getting the most attention it had in years. I was starting to wonder if my rusted gas cap would unlock after all this time.

When I pulled up at her house Mitch signaled me to come inside. Down the street two women fought over case of Club Beer, rolling on the grass and then over the curb into the middle of the road. A car skillfully steered around their withered bodies. This was business as usual in the North End.

Mitch was dressed in a skirt, tight blouse and the current fashion of high-heeled boots. This was the first time I had ever seen her dressed up, and she looked good. She was a woman blessed with naturally flowing curves. I complimented her appearance, causing her to blush.

"Listen," she said once we were inside her living room. She handed me a Moosehead beer. "I've had a change of heart about a movie. It's such a wonderful evening, I can't justify spending it inside a dark theatre. I'm thinking we are now down to the final stretch of an Indian summer. Let's save the cinema for another time."

I concurred and asked what she had in mind. She said earlier that day she had seen an advertisement on the television for the River Rouge boat cruise that does a tour of the Red River, combined with a meal and dancing. I thought it was an excellent idea. The birthday gift Lonny had given me suddenly occurred to me: tickets to the River Rouge! I searched my wallet and found them. Mitch was ecstatic. She hadn't been on the boat since her high school graduation. I'd never been at all. Our decision made, we finished our drinks.

Luck was on our side that clear, sunny evening. A last-minute bus tour from Kansas City had booked nearly the entire boat. There was a single table for two left. So we boarded the cruise boat with seventy hard-core senior citizens who still knew how to party.

We spent the first hour on deck watching the scenic shoreline of the city pass leisurely by. I mentioned that it made me feel like we were in a different city all together.

"This is beautiful," Mitch admitted, the warmth of her body next to mine feeling serene and peaceful. The only other sound was the paddlewheel slapping at the water behind us. We watched deer feeding along the shore.

"All these years I've been in the city, and I'm still discovering hidden treats," I exclaimed. "This was a great idea." We toasted with our wine glasses.

The captain of the boat approached us just as we were admiring the sun's fiery red ball while it set ahead of us. He was carrying a camera.

"This deserves a romantic picture," the captain politely interrupted.

"Of course," Mitch said enthusiastically.

"Grab your man in nice and close," he insisted with a smile. She didn't hesitate and pulled me against her. I turned my head to stare directly, intimately, into her face. My knees weakened when I saw that her pupils were wide and dark.

"Okay, here I go," the captain said from behind the camera. Mitch and I gazed at each other, a silly smile etched onto my face. The flash lit the sky, and the captain thanked us for our participation. He walked away, but Mitch refused to let me out of her arms. I didn't resist.

"Did you know you have perfect facial features?" she asked sincerely, and all I could do was raise my eyebrows.

Suddenly, she kissed me, right on the lips. I finally managed to find my voice and thanked her for the compliment.

"Actually," she replied, "it's my pleasure kissing someone as beautiful as you." Before I could sputter out another response, her lips were on mine again. We broke away, and I noticed the approving smiles of a couple shuffling past on their walkers. They must have known something I didn't.

"Well, now," I announced, "this has become one of those moments I'll be thinking about during every lonely night."

She grinned and pulled me into a hug against the boat's railing. I could feel her heart beating hard in her body. She felt good in my arms, and I reciprocated her passion. Our sudden intimacy didn't seem awkward. It felt right. I buried my nose in her hair, inhaling the perfumed strands. She pressed her face against my neck, and I could feel each breath. An unobstructed realization ensued: I was falling for her.

When the dinner bell chimed, we broke apart and retained our interlocked hands while we headed downstairs for dinner. We were asked to join the seniors' party from Kansas City, and we accepted their offer. The meal was superb, and Mitch and I worked our way through three bottles of wine. It turned out that the theme of the bus tour was couples married a minimum of fifty years. A standing ovation was made for the oldest couple, who had been together for sixty-nine years. When the dancing started, those two had more energy than Mitch and I combined. A live swing band played all the forties and fifties tunes I had grown up with at my parents' house. We quickly realized both of us lacked the coordinated skill needed to dance without a lot of toe stepping, so we learned as we went along. We both laughed ourselves silly at our clumsiness.

Afterward, everyone proceeded to the top deck to watch the stars and were treated to a spectacular prairie evening.

The captain found us again, leaning against the rail near the bow.

"Still taking pictures, Captain?" asked Mitch, grinning, saluting him. He returned her smile, stopping in front of us. He held a photograph in his hand.

"I've been taking pictures for the thirty years I've been operating this vessel," he said proudly, "and this picture of you is simply too precious for me to keep. I'd like you both to have it." Mitch accepted the photograph. He was right; it captured an outstanding backdrop of the setting sun and two fools who seemed a natural fit together. I had never taken a good picture, but there was something visceral in this one. At its barest level I saw two people who looked very happy. We thanked him, and he left to mingle with the other guests.

"We make a beautiful couple, cowboy," Mitch purred while we admired our picture.

"It looks like we have been taking pictures together for years," I commented. We really did photograph well. I was pleased the captain had given the snapshot to us.

"Why do I feel so special around you, Gus?" Mitch asked suddenly. I could see she was serious as she studied my face.

I shrugged. "I am a professionally trained counsellor skilled at the touchy feely ..." She mock-punched my arm.

"No, really," she pressed. "I've never felt this way about someone before. You make me laugh. You listen to what I'm saying. And if you're just putting on your listening ear, you're a true gentleman for your kindness. I don't know exactly what it is about you, but I feel like you are genuinely interested in who I am and what I have to say. You have a comforting decency about you."

"I can reply to that easily enough," I replied. "You're also easy to talk to. And it helps that we share a lot of interests and opinions."

"I guess so." She was quiet and reflective for a moment.

"What're you thinking?"

Mitch smiled sweetly at me again. "I want to spend a lot more time with you, Gus. Since I've been hanging around with you, I've found myself drawing closer to you. I hope this doesn't scare you, but I kinda like you."

I laughed and said, "If that scares you, then don't worry about it. Because you're giving me the same warm fuzzies." I couldn't believe I had just said that, but it must have been the right thing because Mitch ran her hand along my arm.

"Life's got a strange way of leading to what we think we want to happen," I said, staring at the black water moving below our feet. "All summer I've been calling mysterious women and judging them only by their voices in my pursuit to find eternal love. Meanwhile, it only took a walk to the park and an encounter with a bear."

She gave me a gentle nudge with her elbow. "Hey, just remember it was me who found you."

"How could I forget?" I replied. "And I never thought I'd fall for a woman in uniform."

"It was the tight shorts you liked. Admit it," she teased.

"Actually, it was the walkie-talkie strapped to your waist. I like the look of authority."

"You should see me with my flashlight," she said, laughing.

"I'm still suspicious of how you stumbled on me in the dark during the fireworks show. There must have been a thousand people there."

Mitch suddenly looked uncomfortable.

"What?" I asked.

She shook her head.

"Spill it," I said, grabbing her around the waist.

"Okay. I'll confess," she said, looking me in the face. "I saw you come into the park. I followed you the rest of the time, and believe me, that was pretty hard to do wearing a bright red T-shirt. It took me until the fireworks to build up the courage to approach you. Actually, my partner finally kicked my ass for me to talk to you. He threatened to do it for me."

"What do you mean?"

"Well, after I met you the day before, I couldn't stop saying how gorgeous I found you."

"Oh, please."

"It's true. You are a hunk."

"Okay, Joanie Cunningham. Whatever."

"So the real hero is my partner. If it weren't for him, I may not have spoken to you."

"Like two ships passing in the night. But you did, and here we are."

"Here we are," she repeated, kissing me once again.

19

"I know on the exterior you're so strong and in control but inside is just a shy, scared little boy ..."

Walking through the St. James Community Center on Ness Street to honour my agreement for john school wasn't my proudest moment. I still firmly held I had unjustly been lured into a bogus arrest, but I wasn't about to vocalize my accusations in enemy territory. My sole plan was to nod when I had to, fill out the correct forms and get the hell out, unscratched. My greatest relief was surveying the room full of misfits and not recognizing anyone I knew. I grabbed an empty desk near the back of the class and hunkered down for the next eight hours.

I had time to look around while we waited for the instructor to arrive. I was amazed by the cross section of society that was packed into the large room. Men from eighteen-year-old pizza delivery boys to one guy I thought ran a mutual fund investment column in the local paper sat around me to be converted away from the sins of convicted gay johns. I wondered how many of these men had graciously accepted this assignment in exchange for avoiding the truth with their wives. I concluded that today there were a dozen housewives thinking their husbands had gone over to help a nameless friend from work finish the basement. I laughed silently to myself. I was no better. Mitch had no idea I was a convicted pervert either.

The middle-aged instructor walked into the room looking bored. I knew exactly what he was feeling. After a while, spinning the same yarn to a group of hormonal men became monotonous. He carried a stack of handouts under his arm. Class had begun.

The instructor summarized that our urges for illicit gay sex had nearly caused embarrassment to our families and colleagues, as well as jail time, were it not for this reform class. He brought out coloured charts showing close-ups of diseased male organs resulting from sexual relations with prostitutes. We got to watch video confessions of men dying of AIDS, apparently contracted in the same way. Within our folder of handouts were half a dozen condoms for protection, as well as a chapter copied from *Good Good Lovin'* on how to reignite romance in the relationships at home.

We went over the various medications to control our sexual urges, including a detailed explanation of the benefits of castration. Finally, the instructor passed around one complementary gay nudie magazine for our viewing pleasure during bathroom use at home, as well as a Jeff Stryker video sponsored by the City of Winnipeg. We were told to use these tools to relieve our sexual tensions when the urge arose. Finally, near the end of our day our knowledge was tested. We were instructed to place our course material at our feet while the instructor gave us our exam booklet, full of neat little pictures; we had to match the venereal disease to the correct dripping sore. The last page consisted of a two-paragraph assignment. We had to explain how this course alleviated the need for parking lot sex. The last form to fill out was our evaluation on the instructor's performance and the course material. I gave him an A plus.

20

"I am part of a couple, and my partner would like to see me with another male ..."

Lonny's Ford Escalade skidded to an aggressive stop in front of Mitch's house, signaling that he had arrived. He waited inside the vehicle, the music blasting what I thought was Notorious B.I.G. rapping. I wasn't going to complain. He'd offered to pick Mitch and me up from her place and take us to Branigan's Restaurant at the Forks. I rarely had the luxury of riding inside a leased $60,000 vehicle.

"Hiya, Mitch," Lonny called out over the thumping street gang rhythms as we climbed into the cab. It was the first time they had met in person.

"Hey, Lonny," Mitch yelled in response.

I got into the large backseat and looked around. "Where are the gats so that I can put a cap in a pedestrian's ass on a drive-by?" I bellowed to Lonny.

He glanced into the rearview mirror and grinned. "Not today, brother. We're on a different mission."

We made the drive in record time, and Lonny even managed to find a parking stall close to the restaurant. Silence was welcome when the music stopped. We headed inside.

"Gus tells me your cell phones have the longest-lasting batteries around," stated Mitch as she took her seat at the table opposite Lonny.

Lonny's eyebrows lifted, and he smirked. "Endurance kind of goes with the territory," he said and winked.

"Cut it out," I said, holding up my hand. "Don't get Lonny started, Mitch," I warned. "It's going to be bad enough having to sit here watching him get the phone numbers for the waitress, hostess and salad chef."

"Please," boasted Lonny, "you give me too much credit. Remember—those who ask, receive."

"See," pointed Mitch, "I did that by asking you for coffee at the fireworks show. Look at us now."

"You're forgetting I was in a desperate time in my life then," I said, grinning.

"Whoa," said Lonny, sitting back in his chair. "That kind of statement earns a man a week's worth of lonely nights."

"Damn straight," agreed Mitch. "See how tough he's talking now that he's involved in a relationship. When I found him, he was a lost little puppy dog looking for a home. He would have licked the cracks of my toes for attention."

"Okay. Hold on," I said, laughing. "Now you're getting gross. I draw the line at lapping toe lint."

"Please," squirmed Lonny, "this is a place serving food. Toe jam is not on the menu here, I can assure you that much."

We all clinked water glasses.

"All right, guys," said Lonny, setting himself up for one of his entertaining stories. "I heard a good one the other day at work. There's a technician who works out of our satellite office in Portage La Prairie named Leonard. He's been divorced twice already. The first time his wife left him for his younger brother. He still goes over there for Christmas, for Christ's sake. Anyway, he got married last fall. He claimed a third time would put the odds in his favour. Well, unfortunately, Leonard was wrong. Not that there's anything about Leonard that drives his wives away, other than the fact that he's boring. Zero personality. He's what we call a 'classic techie.' Blah. If we have a system go down, Leonard can get up it again. But what woman wants a guy who speaks of nothing but Ethernet bridges and megabits per second? Get my point? He unwittingly drives them to cheat. It only took wife number three six weeks to realize she had married a semiconductor. So in keeping with today's technology innovations, she started calling phone sex numbers. She's smart—set up a separate credit card account so that Leonard would never see any billings. He comes home thinking it's business as usual while his wife finishes wiping the saliva from the phone receiver.

"I told you Leonard doesn't have much personality, but he's not dumb. Having been served with divorce papers twice before, he's developed a sense for when things are amiss in the household. Although he can't prove anything, Leonard started to have his suspicions about what his wife did in his absence. Trouble is, there's no one to catch her with because she's playing it smart by keeping her affair 100 percent electronic. But Leonard, being the crafty bugger he is, decides to follow his intuition and buys his wife a new 1.6 gigabyte cordless phone from Radio Shack. She thinks he's wonderful. Now she can make her sex calls from the bathtub, laundry room—hell, even when she's neatly stacking Leonard's clean underwear in the dresser.

"A week goes by. Leonard comes home from work as he has every other day for the last six weeks. Kisses his wife. Tells her about his day programming hard drives. And asks her how *her* day went. Well, she gives her husband the regular canned response: cleaning house and watching soaps. *Bang.* Fatal mistake. Leonard walks up to his wife and starts reciting passages of heated conversation that would make a Catholic priest turn red in the face. He reads passages and passages of smut his wife spent the day breathing to strange men, whose names Leonard also recited. Horrified, his wife knew she was fingered—so to speak. The one question she wanted answered before she packed her bags and became ex-wife number three was simply "How?"

Leonard just smiled and took hold of the Radio Shack 1.6 gigabyte portable phone. Always remember this, folks—when it comes to electronic geeks, the motherboard is their friend. His wife's downfall was simple. When Leonard purchased the phone he made a few adjustments so that he knew the phone's frequency. That means anyone with a radio scanner, say, parked outside the house, would be able to pick up entire crystal clear conversations when tuned in to the same frequency. Leonard had a scanner. And now he also had another court date. Fellows like Leonard need to understand the only person who will ever be able to love them in life is their soldering gun. Sad, but true." Lonny took a long pull from his water, nearly draining his glass after another Lonny classic.

Mitch looked at me and said, smiling, "Guess what I'm getting you for Christmas?"

The waitress came to our table; we fought to stifle our laughter while she took our orders. I used the opportunity to use the bathroom, and when I returned Mitch did the same.

"So what'd you think so far?" I asked Lonny. Before he even said anything I could see he was busting to tell me something.

"Great girl," he said. "I like her sense of humour. She can banter with the best of them."

I nodded my head in agreement.

"Apparently you've done a number on her," Lonny said, sipping water from his glass. He studied me above the rim.

"What do you mean *a number?*"

He looked around first, I assumed to see if Mitch was coming back. She wasn't.

"Come on, bro, what are you getting at?" I asked. Lonny loved building suspense, especially when it came at my expense.

He leaned forward in confidence.

"While you were in the crapper she said a few things about you."

My heart sped up. I had no idea what she would have said to Lonny. "Well, are you going to tell me, or do I have to reach across the table and slap your bitch ass silly?"

Lonny laughed. "Good one, tough guy. You'd throw out your back just getting out of your chair too quickly."

"Jesus Christ, Lonny, tell me before she gets back. Otherwise you won't be able to tell me until tomorrow."

"Maybe it's best that I wait. This might spoil your evening."

"You already have if you don't tell me," I warned. I was breaking into a sweat.

What? Did I screw up already?

Lonny sent one last glance over his shoulder and finally confessed.

"Did you know this girl is all goo-goo over you?"

"What's with the Flintstone expressions?" I asked, not sure what he meant.

"Open your eyes, jackass. She's fallen big time for you. I don't know what you've done to convince her you're the guy to sign a lifelong contract with, but she sure made it clear that you're *that guy.* "

I fell back in my chair. "What'd she say?" I was relieved I hadn't blown it just yet.

Lonny grinned. "I guess you two had a moment on the River Rouge. She said she saw inside you that night. I didn't ask for details how she did this. Whatever, she has very strong feelings for you, buddy-boy. Now I'm going to go out on a limb here, but my impression is she could be the one and only."

"I don't get your point. The one and only what?"

Lonny laughed and said, "Your bloody wife, man. This chick sees you as husband material."

I felt dazed. "She told you all this?"

"In so many words."

"But she doesn't even know you, to be telling you this stuff."

"Women feel comfortable telling me things."

"So what should I do?"

"Oh, why not do something silly, like love her back?"

"Are you sure she feels this way? You didn't read more into it than was said?"

"She was pretty blunt about it. 'Gus is a guy I could grow old with'. Take it as you will."

"Wow."

"Yeah, wow. *Just look at her eyes, man.* Pure buffalo."

"Huh?"

"Every time she looks at you, it's like she's waking from a hot dream."

"Do you think ..." I stopped myself when I saw Mitch exit the washroom. "Shh. Shut up. Here she comes. Act normal."

"What ..."

"Hi, boys," Mitch said, taking her chair.

We remained silent.

"You both have that guilty look, like when I pick up shoplifters from the Forks Market. What gives?"

"Oh, nothing," said Lonny. "I can't convince your hubby here that Labatt's Blue is a better beer than that British crap he drinks. What's it called?

"Boddingtons."

"Yeah, right. So now we're fighting."

Mitch reached over and took our hands. "Shake and make up, okay. I want no bloodshed on our first group date."

203

I looked over and smiled at Lonny. He was always able to think up excuses faster than I ever could. We shook.

"Good boys," said Mitch. "Now let's eat this fine meal."

"I would think after eating so many lunches here you'd be tired of this place," I said to Mitch, who shook her head.

"Since they took away the hot chicken sandwich I haven't come here as often. But it's never about the food as much as the company you keep."

Lonny looked my way and nodded.

"Gus mentioned you managed to buy one of those condos on Bannatyne, Lonny," Mitch said while scooping a forkful of food from her plate.

"I happened to know the right people, who put my name on the list."

"I expect an invite to see the inside of it. I hear it's very unique."

"Lonny enjoys the seven nightclubs that surround his building. That's the only reason he lives there," I teased.

"Consider yourself invited anytime, Mitch," offered Lonny. "And bring this lump along, if he's not too cranky."

We laughed. After our meal was finished, we sat around, before Lonny drove us back, the music as loud as before. I felt unsteady on my feet from the pounding bass. Once we reached our destination Mitch helped me into her house and onto the couch.

"Great guy," Mitch offered while she opened two beers. "Type of guy you really feel like opening up to."

I sat up. "What do you mean?"

She came into the room and sat beside me.

"I just mean I feel comfortable around him. I'm glad we got together."

"Yeah, he's all right," I said sipping my beer.

"Listen," Mitch said, tenderly, "I want to give this to you." She handed me a small box. I studied the carefully wrapped offering finished with a red ribbon.

"Mitch. What are you doing buying me gifts? There's no need to be spending money on me."

She waved me off. "Don't be silly. I was walking past the store, and when I saw it, I knew it would look amazing on you."

I peeled back the wrapping and opened the black box. Inside was a silver bracelet. There was an engraving on the inside. To Gus, ALL MY

Love. I glanced at Mitch, who had her hands braced against her excited face. She urged me to put it on.

"Wow. This is nice," I said, meaning it.

"See what I mean about it being you? Enjoy it, Gus."

"The best part," I said, moving closer so that I was able to kiss her mouth, "is the engraving. Did it come with it or did you put it there?"

She pushed me away, smiling.

"I did it all myself," she said proudly. "And I mean it. You're a terrific guy, Mr. Adams. Since we met, you've shown me what it is to be happy. I love waking each morning. I can never wait until the next time we talk. The funny thing is I never thought I could feel this way about someone."

I blushed. It had been a long time since I'd heard a woman tell me I made her feel so good. It made me feel good. I could see a future with Mitch. And I told her that.

She reached across to kiss me passionately. "You're wonderful, Gus. Meeting the way we did was the greatest act of fate." She buried her head on my chest.

My heart was beating hard. My quest to clock in at forty with a woman to love was actually going to happen. There had been a period after Donna Jean's rabid daughters that I began to seriously doubt if there was a woman out there for me. Marcia's death had cast a bitter pallor over my motivation. At that point, I was resigned to forfeiting my crusade and living life through my satellite television. But Mitch came along.

"I am very much enjoying every minute with you, Mitch," I admitted candidly.

"Be with me forever, Gus. I mean it. I want to share my life with you," whispered Mitch.

I swallowed, trying to contain my admiration for Mitch's conviction.

"I'm not going anywhere, lady."

"Good," she said, squeezing me tightly.

21

"Why am I in this category? I'm not really sure ..."

My life changed that night following the dinner with Mitch and Lonny at Branigans. During the next few weeks we spent hours on the phone talking about a whole lot of everything. The days we could spend together, we did. Christy, never one to stifle her opinions, was blunt: she enjoyed the new Gus.

Surprised, I was sorry to let her down: I still wore the same underwear.

"You know what I mean," she contended, cracking open a Diet Pepsi in my office. Dan Folgelberg played quietly over the speakers. "The sullen, bitter, shaven-chested Gus has been transformed into a swashbuckling stud. Now I can only pray there's a guy waiting for me at the next fireworks display, ready to take me away from all this."

"All this what?" I asked, laughing, looking around. "You make it sound as though you're working in a shit pit from hell."

"Well, you know, this isn't exactly my dream taking place here."

"Hey, it's what you make it to be."

"I know. I keep closing my eyes, and when I open them, you're still here bent over the coffee machine, showing me crack."

"I've never heard you complaining," I said sarcastically.

"Consider it now said."

"Fair enough."

"But, Gus, now I have to survive single life alone! Think of the pressure, man!"

"Listen, honey. You've only been single on and off for maybe four years. This old son-of-a-bitch junkyard dog has seen ten years shoot past. You could use a few more scars."

"You're forgetting it's a different world for me. Time moves a lot faster, which means my years are condensed."

I snickered. "Christy, my dear, your life isn't made from Campbell's chicken soup—you'll say anything to have the last word."

She shrugged.

Mitch opened the front door. Christy swirled around to look at me.

"That's my woman," I announced.

"You didn't tell me she was coming here today!"

"I didn't know," I responded honestly. This was Mitch's first visit to my clinic. She hadn't mentioned stopping by, but the sight of her generated a healthy stir within me.

"Behave," I playfully warned Christy as she stood up from her chair.

"Get real."

"She doesn't like to be kissed like you Europeans do."

"I'm not European. Relax."

"Then make me look good," I whispered.

She huffed. "Yeah, right. I'd have to knock her unconscious."

"Hi, Mitch!" I shouted across the room. "Come on in and join us."

"Not bad," I heard Christy mumble as Mitch approached.

"Howdy, guys," greeted Mitch. She extended her hand to Christy. "I'm Mitch. Pleased to meet you."

"I'm Christy."

"Oh, I know."

"You do?"

"Listen, Gus has talked about you enough so it's like I've personally known you."

"Is that so?" Christy shot me a look.

"You've been an inspiration for him."

"He's a good guy. He won't do you wrong," whispered Christy to Mitch.

"All right, ladies, we've all been introduced," I said, breaking up the conversation. It called for serious intervention. "Nice to see you in our humble work environment," I directed at Mitch. "This is where Christy and I make the magic happen every day for couples," I said, sweeping my arms in a broad circle.

She folded her arms and looked around. "I needed to assure myself there really was a clinic for the relationship-challenged that my lover talks about each day."

"Right now, you're standing in the bear pit," commented Christy, referring to the reception area.

"Oh," said Mitch, closing her eyes and shivering, "the walls are speaking to me. The pain. The cold. It's all coming to me now. The spirits are alive."

"Knock it off," I said, pulling her into a hug. "You're scaring the young girl here."

"Speak for yourself," defended Christy.

"I'd say she's battle-hardened from working alongside you," Mitch ventured. Christy reached over and they smacked hands in the air.

"All right, you two. While you jive-slapping ladies double-tag me, I have to remind you this is a place of business. There are clients to attend to."

Christy and Mitch looked around at the empty room.

"Then there are phone calls to answer," I added. This time Christy put her hand to her ear.

"Seems pretty quiet to me," she remarked to Mitch, who nodded in agreement.

"Fine," I conceded. "Go do your nails then."

"You're scrambling now," said Christy.

I led Mitch away by her hand to my office and leaned against my desk.

"Now back to the more important matters at hand," I said, not breaking my hug. "What's up?"

Mitch pushed me aside and opened her purse, withdrawing two slips of paper.

"Tickets to Jazz on the Rooftop at the Art Gallery. Coming up next week. I'm looking for a particular guy to take me." She pretended to glance around the room.

"I've got a great idea," I said loudly. "Why don't we go see that thing, what's the name, Jazz on the Rooftop? Would you like to go?"

Mitch laughed. "I'd love to!" She did a little victory dance.

"Then it's a date," I confirmed. "I've got to hand it to myself, I'm good. Another fantastic occasion I've planned. Anytime you want to offer some input into our relationship, feel free. I can't carry us alone."

"Please. I love you to be master of my domain. Rule my every thought, master." She pretended to walk like Frankenstein.

"Enough! Stop it," I brushed at her arms. "All I need is a patient to walk in seeing you do that, and they'll be thinking I'm using some type of zombie therapy. You'd be surprised what people assume. Worse, they'd demand I use it on them!"

My remark caused us both to laugh.

22

"I'm a very dominant female, and my name is Mistress Tyra. And this ad is for men who seriously crave, desire and obsess about being dominated, controlled and disciplined. I know this is what you want …"

Even though I would do nothing more than sit and watch television alone, Saturday afternoons remained sacred for the frivolous do-nothingness I adored and treasured. I was on par, once again settled in my chair next to a mug of iced tea and the satellite TV. So when the phone rang, I made no move to answer it. I rarely received calls on a Saturday. Lonny couldn't be bothered, since Saturday was his day to play sports. That left Harold occasionally calling to say something utterly unimportant, like the new garbage disposal rotation, or solicitation from companies that left me wondering how the bastards got my number. My phone number was apparently passed around like a lost FedEx package. I finally answered the intrusive call because Mitch had a sweet habit of calling me just to say hi.

My entire life was forever changed by *the voice.* I had not heard it in ten years. One word was uttered in my ear.

"Hi."

One word, and I knew who it was.

One word.

It crushed the safety gate I had erected. Behind it came roaring all the poison that had destroyed me. All because of *the voice.*

My heart started racing. I didn't want this. *Not now. It's over.* I had locked it away.

The voice.

One word said so much: teasing, electric, playful. Through the distance, the fog from the many years began reforming into memorable shapes.

Why did I answer? Why? Why now? I never do.

Hang up.

"Hello," I said flatly. The room became unfocused and grey and surreal. In ten years I had worked over hundreds of scenarios for what had gone wrong and what I would do if given one more opportunity to find out. No answers emerged from the grey as I clutched the phone.

"Hi, Gus! I thought this number had to be my Gus!" Zestful, possessive—I resented everything in her voice. I hated her for the invasion of my recovery.

Hang up.

"It's me!"

Silence.

Her German accent was thicker than I remembered, her words slightly harder to pick out after having long lost my ability to translate. But it was still *her voice,* with its heavy European pronunciation of each letter, ending each word in her secret, vivid way that only she understood.

"Peta?" I knew, but I still asked.

Even her squeal of delight at my correct guess possessed a German flair.

"Of course! You must be delighted to hear my voice?" she asked in her deep, German drawl.

Last chance. Hang up.

"Why would I?" I asked.

The years hadn't changed her laugh, and I listened to it fill my ear.

"Oh, Gus, that's what I loved about you—so, how do you say it, serious."

I still wasn't sure what was happening and if this was really even happening, so I didn't respond. She ignored my silence.

"It is so good to talk to you again, Gus. It has been too long."

I snickered. "What happened, Peta? Did you accidentally hit my number on your preset? Thought you were ordering a pizza? I don't think Domino's delivers in thirty minutes from Canada to Europe."

She breezed over my comments, saying, "Crazy you are! I am here in the same city as you. Just like old times."

I choked. The grey over my eyes grew deeper so that I couldn't make out the television I had been enjoying minutes ago.

"What do you mean?" I stammered.

"I am here, you silly, in Winnipeg. I flew in a few hours ago." Her voice sounded thrilled, as though she expected me to whoop and yell.

"Why are you here?" I asked, confused and uncertain. "After ten years you suddenly reappear, and I should celebrate? Give me a break."

She ignored my hostility. "I want to see you."

Now it was out. She had said it, and it pissed me off.

"What makes you think I want to see you? Ever think I might not want to?" I challenged. "Maybe you're forgetting, but I woke up one morning to find you gone, never to hear from you again. Do you expect me to forget how it happened and come crawling over on my knees for you?" I spat out bitterly.

She hesitated.

I could almost see her lips working to form the words she needed.

"I can explain. I want to explain. We can do all that when you come over." Peta hadn't shed her cockiness.

"No, it's not going to happen," I stated blandly, shaking my head. My refusal felt good. I kept up my attack. "I don't care anymore what happened. Frankly, it's not even a memory anymore." *A lie.*

Peta wasn't about to be deterred. She pressed on.

"Then we won't discuss anything except the future," she insisted, adding, "I've come a long way to see you, Gus."

I stopped. Was it her cue to lie?

"I don't get it. Suddenly, without a phone call, a letter or even a shitty Christmas card, you woke up yesterday and decided, hey, I feel like visiting Gus in ole Canada? Gee, I think I'll fly out tonight. What the hell, won't he be surprised. Get real, Peta. I don't buy it."

She scoffed. "Gus, always so cautious, like a wild animal. Come over and talk. I promise there are no games. I am sorry about the way things were left."

She sounded sincere. I almost believed her. I agreed to meet.

Before we disconnected, I found out she was staying at the Hotel Fort Garry. Peta, as elegant as ever, only stayed at the best. Peta expected six stars with her hotels.

I stood in the middle of my living room, dazed. Peta's voice still reverberated inside my head. However, this time it was alive and real. This time I didn't have to pretend to remember how she sounded. Contrary to my declaration, I did want answers. In fact, I would insist. She owed it to me, especially after returning to blow open the safe in which I had secured my shattered emotions for nearly a decade.

I dressed. Looking in the mirror, I contemplated shaving. I passed. There were no impressions to make. Studying my reflection, I saw the skin on my face was worn. I had aged. I wondered how Peta would look? She had been five years older back when … my thoughts drifted. *Don't go there.* Damage control was in order, and the less I revisited, the faster I could walk away.

The traffic was light, and I made good time. The Hotel Fort Garry was a majestic twelve-story building with an emerald-coloured roof, constructed by the railway in an era of detail long tossed aside for efficiency and budget constraints. I stood alone in the elevator, amused to find I was nervous. It was difficult to comprehend who I was about to see. I had convinced myself I would never be in the same room with her again.

I stepped out of the elevator and strode down the hallway; the door to her suite was open. I could hear her singing. She had a natural voice for song.

She was across the room when I entered, and her face lit up as she closed the distance quickly. Her arms stretched out before her, her long, brown, naturally curly hair waving behind her. Her eyes captured mine, and I accepted her hug.

I pulled away, allowing her little control. But not before I caught her familiar Peta scent. The years hadn't been able to pry that away from her. She had kept her body in great shape. Even her face didn't show the harsh lines of passing forty. I felt as though I had stepped back in time.

"Gus, you came!" she yelled with delight, as though she didn't expect me to actually show up.

"To be honest, I don't know why I came," I said, crossing my arms.

She stepped back and grinned.

"Of course you do. To see me!" She laughed as though she didn't believe me.

"So what brings you back to Winnipeg?" *Get right into it.* I walked across the room and looked out at the city below. Fall had stripped the trees of their leaves, and everything below had gone from green to grey. I felt depressed.

"Business," she stated. I heard her pouring liquid into a glass. She came over and handed me a large flute of champagne.

I took it, and she noticed my curious expression.

"You look good. I would not expect so much time has passed by your features. I will explain soon enough your questions. But first," she said, taking my arm and leading me beside her on the couch, "tell me about you. What has your life been up to?"

I shifted to the far end of the couch.

I shrugged, sipping from my glass. "A little bit of this, that and the other thing." Her eyebrows furrowed, trying to understand my expression. I waved her off. She always had trouble understanding our slang. I tried again, this time more civilly.

"Same old things, really. I haven't changed my practice in the Village, although my client base has grown."

She suddenly leaned forward and asked eagerly, "Do you still have the loft apartment?" She was referring to a bachelor apartment I first rented when I moved to the city. It was a third-story walk-up for two hundred and fifty bucks in Fort Rouge. The location was terrible, but the place itself was cozy. The other tenants were students, and Peta and I spent many nights drinking beers in what we came to call loft crawls. I pushed the memory from my mind.

"No, I finally moved to a larger, cleaner place on a thoroughfare called Wellington Crescent. It's closer to work … and nicer. I don't have anyone knocking on my door at three in the morning with a keg strapped to their back."

She laughed and gulped her champagne. "Too bad. We had so much fun, especially when you set up the hot tub in the living room." She giggled.

I had to smile. It had been a crazy arrangement. The living room had also been my kitchen and bedroom, and the inflatable tub took all the meagre space. I managed to squeeze my mattress in the hallway to the bathroom. It made those late-night pee breaks a challenge. The tub stayed for five months until a party one fateful night. Travis, who lived in the apartment directly below mine, was wrestling with Peta in the hot tub when they both slipped and fell against the tub's lining, tearing it wide open. In seconds, all the water poured out and disappeared down into Travis's apartment. Drunk, we laughed ourselves silly. We didn't realize the extent of the damage until the next morning, when Travis made his way back to his apartment. The few possessions he owned had been destroyed by the water. We snuck the tub out, and I claimed that my fish tank had broken. The landlord never gave a shit, and until the time I moved out months later, I just sprayed cans of Lysol each time the mould starting gathering momentum.

Peta reached over and refilled my glass, along with her own. As she stretched, her developed legs were revealed as her skirt pulled up. Her calves were still a satisfying feature. I was busted by Peta, who caught my eyes and pointed.

"Gus, this is a social visit," she said. She paused, pulling down her skirt. "Tell me more. What else has my Gus been doing?"

I felt uncomfortable. She was asking all the questions. I was the one who wanted answers, so quiz time was over.

"I'll tell you what," I began, putting my drink down, to her dismay. "Ten years ago we were two lovers discussing marriage and the logistics of your relocating permanently to Canada. One morning I wake up to meet you at your place, and, instead, your goddamn landlord is telling me you'd given him your notice the previous night and had vacated a few hours before I arrived. All I had for an explanation was a fucking letter from you scrawled on some shitty real estate pad of paper." At first I had thought it was a joke. Peta always enjoyed teasing me. But the hung-over, unshaven landlord assured me it was no joke: a cab had taken her and her suitcases away three hours earlier. The note was simple, maybe something you'd give a casual friend you had no intentions of ever seeing again. There had been no forwarding address or phone number or even a reason why she had done it. *Not even an apology.* I spent the next five months trying to piece it all together. I suspected it had to do with an old boyfriend Peta was never fully able to shed. Yet, I would never know for certain.

Peta tried to put her hand on my leg, and I brushed it aside. She realized there would be no easy out for her. So she brought out the businesswoman. Still, she wasn't able to hide the sheepishness in her response.

"Gus, I hurt for years over what I had done to you. It was awful. I wanted to call you, but I couldn't. It would not have helped."

I shook my head vigorously. "Maybe not you, Peta, but I still don't know why the hell you left me. Was it Lars?" I braced myself.

She nodded her head, biting her lip.

"He wanted me back. Begged me to try once more. Gus, we had five years, remember." I remembered. Me and Peta only had eight months. Still,

Lars was an asshole, a womanizer who hadn't given a shit for Peta when she lived with him in Germany. She was convenient only when he needed her. In reality, his non-participation in the relationship was what drove her to Canada. The company she worked for had an exchange project, and she took it. One year in Winnipeg. Peta found it refreshing and challenging. She was a woman who could walk into a room of ten strangers, and by the time the evening came to an end, she would leave with ten new friends. So she left behind condescending Lars and his hoodlum friends and came ashore to North America.

We had met at a Winnipeg Chamber of Commerce function during a cold snap in January. She had joined to develop ties to the business community that would lead to ideas she could bring back to Germany. Her stay in Winnipeg had been in its third month when we shared a few drinks in what developed to be the most provocative conversation I had ever shared with a woman. She had reached inside and pulled me inside out with her hazel eyes and mocking smile. In those four hours, I had been hooked, netted and filleted by her easy conversation, European wit and tantalizing aroma. The winter she chose to spend in Manitoba was the coldest in 110 years. Purchasing a car was first on her list once the temperatures warmed, so I offered to take her home. She accepted, and we made the drive to a house she was renting out by the Pan Am Sports Clinic, engrossed in comparisons between our countries. Skip ahead dozens of meals, social gatherings and staggering sex to eight months later, when the phone calls from Lars started arriving. There was also a call from her father, whom Lars had approached to talk some sense into her. Germany, I discovered, was one big boys' club, and the men stuck together. Peta reassured me that she was in no way influenced by any of Lars's phone calls. But I didn't quite believe her. In some small way I knew she still had strong feelings for him. I guess it was loyalty in the end. So when she disappeared from my life as quickly as she had entered, unfortunately taking with her my dreams, inner peace, belief in women and love, I fingered Lars for the blame.

Now she was about to reveal the cause that had haunted ten thousand sleeps.

"You know how Lars felt about me," she said carefully. "He promised me things would be different. I believed him. He said he loved me."

"So did I," my voice hissed in response.

She looked hurt.

"Please, Gus, this is not easy for me. I did not like myself for what I had to do. My difficulty is confronting bad things. I had to make a quick decision. I did what I thought was the correct one."

I exploded into my champagne flute. "What you did was the cruelest act anyone could do to another person they love. I'm a big boy. I could have accepted your choice. All I asked of an empty room is why you didn't give me that respect and tell me? I'll admit I still would have suffered. Who wouldn't? *We were talking about getting married!* You don't just walk away into the damn sunset." I poured myself another glass of champagne and stayed silent, stewing in the sensations that had been suppressed for so many years.

"Please, Gus, do not be angry with me. I cannot ask for your forgiveness, but I will ask that you don't be mad. I understand I have made mistakes in my choices. Let us see if we can carry forward."

"What exactly are you back here for?" I spat.

"Later. There will be time for us to talk about it."

We silently acknowledged our standoff, warily sipping our drinks while I glared at the woman who had robbed me of my self-esteem.

I decided to break the heaviness in the air. Peta looked like she was fighting back tears. "You're pretty confident we'll be seeing each other for a second time? If I were you, I wouldn't put much faith in it. Over the years I've also developed a good technique for disappearing."

She looked hurt. "There has to be a second time. So much of today has been in anger. This is not the proper way old lovers are supposed to behave with each other." She appeared to be genuinely upset.

Seeing her sweat made me feel better. I hadn't decided if I ever wanted to see Peta again after today's gathering. But it still felt nice to exude some control for a change.

"Does this mean you will be in the city for a while?"

She nodded, wiping a tear from the corner of her eye.

I looked away. Her puppy-dog face was too much to look at. Now I felt like the asshole. *How did this turn around?*

"As I said, there is business for me to do. My company has international contracts with a manufacturer here."

"How long does this mean you'll be in the city?"

"I do not know yet. I do hope it is long enough for you and me to make amends and have good times like we once shared."

"Well," I began bitterly, "isn't it something the way things go?"

"How do you mean?" she asked tensely.

"You can walk away from me without a goddamn look back and then return a decade later and make up over a couple of bottles of champagne."

"But it is good champagne, is it not?" she asked wide-eyed, obviously completely missing my point. "This was the one you and I enjoyed so much over good times."

"I noticed your choice. I haven't forgotten," I added. I let my breath out, and I suddenly felt very tired. Dealing with Peta had drained me. My emotions were still strong. Yet, I did find some satisfaction in finally knowing what the hell had happened. Admittedly, she still possessed whatever it was that attracted me to her. I relaxed.

"Okay. Maybe we will see each other one more time before you go back to Germany. But it will be on my terms. My call. Understand?"

She nodded enthusiastically. "As long as I can see you again, Gus. Yes. As you wish." She suddenly didn't seem as menacing as a powerful businesswoman. Now she was just Peta.

I looked around the room and realized it was dark outside. It was late. Our conversation had taken us through the afternoon and long into the night. We were also more than a bit drunk. I told Peta it was time for me to go. She walked me to the door. I could see by her posture that Peta wanted to kiss me good night, but I was already making my way down the hallway. I heard her door close.

Inside the elevator I came apart. I slumped against the wall. Inside I was scrambled, unable to put any order to my thoughts. All I wanted was my bed, the sanctuary of my four walls. Tomorrow I would not be venturing outside my apartment. I needed time to work my way through the soup inside my brain. Mitch would probably want to get together tomorrow because she had the day off.

Mitch!

My gut burned. The elevator doors opened, and I staggered to my car.

We were supposed to watch a movie at her place tonight! I hadn't called her to cancel. I instantly hated myself. Again, Peta fucked up my equilibrium.

I debated whether to call her when I got home. The clock in my car said eleven thirty. Too late. I'd explain everything tomorrow. Mitch was easy about things. But still, I felt damned.

219

23

"Hello, guess what? Today is your lucky day …"

In the morning I awoke to the sun warming my face. I had fallen asleep on the couch, the television still on. Half a bottle of Jack Daniels remained on the coffee table. Mitch had indeed called, looking for me. Although she didn't leave a message, her number was recorded on my call display … three times. Technology and its wonders. I had only meant to have a nightcap to settle the shake in my hands. Half a bottle later, I couldn't pull myself from the couch. I'd slept soundly. But now as my mind reactivated itself, clearing away the aftereffects of the booze, Peta's return came spiraling down on my shoulders again.

I decided a shower would start getting my ass in gear. I'd call Mitch right after and explain the situation. I had never gotten around to telling her about Peta, but now would be a good time to say hello and good-bye to the past. I considered asking Mitch if she'd want to hit the mall today for some Sunday shopping.

I finished brushing my teeth, put on a pair of pants and a light sweater and prepared to call Mitch. Instead, the phone rang and I eagerly answered it, ready to apologize to Mitch.

I was disappointed when I recognized the voice.

"Didn't I make it clear last night I'd be the one to make the next call?" I tried to keep my tone even with Peta. Obviously my message for her to respect my privacy wasn't being taken seriously. She started talking before I could continue to chastise her.

"After you left all I could think about was us," she spoke heavily. "I've been up early and wanted to call … I couldn't wait any longer. Our agreement just won't work. I need to see you today."

"Impossible."

"Why?"

"I have other obligations."

"Can they not be changed?"

"No."

"Then we will spend only a few hours together. I promise."

"Peta." I tried to keep the exasperation from my voice. "I have made plans I intend to keep. You're forgetting that twenty-four hours ago you walked back into my life. My life revolves around the people who don't play disappearing games with me."

"Please, Gus, we need to talk. If only for a brief time. Then you can go do your plans, and we never have to see each other again. If that's what you want …"

"No. Yes. I don't know anymore. Look, Peta, it has been really difficult having you jump back into my life after all these years without a single sign that you were even alive. I really need time to adjust to the fact you're here." It still didn't seem real that Peta was a few short miles from me. I had spent ten years convincing my tortured soul she no longer existed. I had to. My survival demanded it. Otherwise, I agonized over seeing Peta's image in every girl with brown hair and hearing each song we'd danced to. I wasn't prepared to go on like that any longer.

"Gus," Peta persisted, "let's meet at that place we did when I was here. What's its name … ? Bombay Bicycle Club, I think it was called."

"Yeah, that's the place. Trouble is after it was closed for a third time by the health inspector, it never reopened. Sorry."

I heard Peta's grunt of disappointment. "Gus …"

"Meet me at the Martini Bar in an hour," I said, caving. "Look it up in the book." I hung up. I'd give Peta her hour of talk time and then be done with her. There was a threshold I dared not cross. No way. I had a great girl now. Mitch was where all my chips were played. She was here to stay in my life. Peta was a migrating goose.

I decided to call Mitch when I got home early that afternoon. We'd make plans for the remainder of the day together. We'd share a drink somewhere and laugh about this whole bullshit episode.

To save time I drove to the Martini Bar. It was in the Village, next to the Second Cup, in an old brownstone building. Inside was open and narrow, and it specialized, as its name stated, in every goddamn martini available. Upscale and expensive, it was an ideal place to sip one drink and get the hell out. My cunning excited me.

Astonishingly, Peta was already sitting at a table when I walked inside. It wouldn't have surprised me if she had a cab idling outside her hotel when she called me. Points for her tenacity.

"Gus!" she said, rushing up and placing me in a hug. Again, I was swarmed with her aroma. It was unlike anything I had smelled before. This time I let her finish the hug. *Give her the opportunity to work everything out of her system*, I reasoned.

"This place is unlike Winnipeg," she remarked as she released me and took her place on a barstool.

I didn't understand her comment, and she explained.

"It has character. The stone walls give it a European air. I love it! What better place to share a martini with a friend." A waiter dropped off two drinks.

"I ordered for us," she explained. We clicked glasses, sipping the fiery liquid. Just past noon, and here I was, drinking. I promised myself only one and then I would leave. I needed to explain my absence in the last twenty-four hours to Mitch.

"I expected you to wait for me to call," I said, deciding to take the lead.

Her face broke into a smile behind the oversized glass. "I was so excited seeing you yesterday, I didn't sleep at all last night. I could not wait for your phone call."

"Ten years will do that to a person," I said, smiling faintly. "I guess after the next ten years we may have to schedule three days in a row to catch up."

Peta gave me a puzzled look but didn't comment. Instead, she switched directions.

"When I got back to Germany, I bought myself a motorbike. You should see me, Gus. Every Sunday I drive for hours in the countryside. I feel free when I ride. It is exhilarating. My neighbours all think I am crazy for driving such a dangerous machine. No one will ride with me. They are all scared!"

"Shouldn't they be?"

"Of course not! I am a good driver!" She laughed loudly. I smiled.

"You would ride with me," she stated.

"Sure. As long as you don't go past thirty kilometres an hour. And I would want a helmet," I added.

"No one rides with a helmet," she teased.

"I'm not shocked you drive a bike, Peta, because you always did enjoy being in control. Riding is just one more thing for you to dominate."

She touched my forearm and kept it there. Her fingers felt hot and dry. I didn't shift my arm.

"You are too silly at times, Gus Adams. It is just a bike. Besides, it keeps me young at heart." She looked at me closely. "What do you do to keep young?"

"I don't eat. I find the digestive process uses up too much energy. It'll shorten your life."

She laughed again, giving me goose bumps like her laugh used to in another lifetime.

"My business takes me away from home for many weeks at a time. Often I do not even have a decent meal," she confessed. "Perhaps your theory is correct, and I will never age."

"I'd say you're doing okay," I complimented before I realized it was out of my mouth.

Peta's face brightened, and she ran her hand up and down my arm.

"The last two years I have been opening franchises in Bangkok. The culture there is unique. You would love it, Gus."

"What makes you say that?"

"They live a simple life," she explained. "You are who you are. No one pretends to be someone else, like we have to do in our cultures. I remember you always talking about finding a place where you could live a life like that," she said softly.

I was impressed. "I'm amazed you heard me say that, Peta. I was just blowing off steam the night I ranted aimlessly."

"I have always thought about what you said."

Her statement hit something within me. I never once considered she might have thought about the conversations we shared. This was a new revelation. It chipped away at my anger toward her.

"Really?"

She nodded her head, her eyes wide and honest.

"That's funny, because I always thought when you left me you threw out every memorable scrap between us. Why else wouldn't you have called me?"

"You are wrong, Gus. I thought about you a lot. *About us.* I never stopped thinking." She brightened. "How about that night we rented all six *Friday the Thirteenth* movies, drank beer, ate chips and watched all of them in a row! Then you thought you would scare me by putting on a mask and hiding inside the closet, but you were drunk and fell through the door instead!" We both roared, remembering the evening. That apartment took a lot of abuse.

"Still," I said, "nothing beats the time you tried putting new brakes on your car. You were so proud when I got your call to go for a ride. I think I had bet you couldn't do it."

"A three-hour body massage."

"Right! You had never fixed brakes before. I felt my odds were good."

"But you lost."

"Only until we came to the first stop sign and drove right through it. The only reason we stopped was because the street ended and we hit the snow bank!"

"You were screaming for your life."

"No kidding! It scared the shit out of me!"

"I think we decided to call our bet a draw."

"Only by default. I gave you credit for putting the shoes on the brakes because that did show initiative. You just put them on upside down."

"You still gave me a wonderful massage."

"I was a sucker for any reason to touch your body."

"You mean my body doesn't arouse you anymore?" Her hand ran gently over my bicep.

"Sure it does. Not a day over thirty, right?"

"Twenty-nine," she grinned.

Maybe it was Peta's eyes pulling me out of my dark room. Or her hand that never stopped stroking my arm. Likely the seven martinis were guilty to a large degree. But the afternoon turned into evening, and the Martini Bar turned into Peta's hotel room. I didn't resist. My body couldn't protest. I let go of the last ten years. Peta was here, now, and I was taking back what she had denied me. We hardly spoke. The lights remained off, and only the nighttime glow from the windows silhouetted our bodies. In the bedroom we found ourselves where we had left off a decade earlier. Any awkwardness was erased when our lips touched. For the next three hours we focused on each other. Only after did we sleep.

24

"Stop. Don't let this ad pass you by ..."

Another of Peta's habits that hadn't changed was her resistance to mornings. She grunted, her face buried as I dressed and left. My head pounded, and I was unsteady from lack of sleep and the martinis. I was also going to be late for work. First, I needed to stop at my place to change and clean up. I wasn't able to make it in time to see my kissing couple. The car was just pulling away as I flung my upper body over the balcony. Funny, but I had been downstairs only moments earlier and would have been sprinting right past their car. I was left with an eerie, taboo feeling.

Peta had scrambled my life when she left me. Now she was back, and she threatened to destroy everything I had rebuilt. My worst guilt was for Mitch. She was the innocent party. We were just starting to develop something really special. I needed to sort out where I now stood. Last night had changed everything.

Checking my machine, I saw two messages from Mitch. Now there wouldn't be any laughing over a beer about the last two days. I felt too wasted to think any further ahead. I'd deal with her tonight.

Christy took one look at my disheveled entrance, grinned and said, "You must have one helluva story to tell me, buddy. Two hours late. No phone call warning me about it. When you were dating you were always on time. Give you a steady girlfriend and you forget about everything else.

Besides, you look as guilty as a cat that's just killed the family pet rabbit. Now that Mitch is in your life, weekends have a whole new meaning, don't they!" she baited, grinning, following me into my office.

I sat down and signaled her to do the same.

"I wasn't with Mitch."

It took a second for Christy's face to cloud over. Finally the realization popped into her head. A look of shock burst across her face.

"*What!*" She leaned forward and whispered. "You were with another woman? Ah, Gus! And she did this to you?" Her eyes were wide. This was the kind of juice Christy had spent years waiting for from me. She urged me to expand. Her arms wrapped around her body and shivered. She was forgetting that this latest gossip lottery happened to come at the scandalous expense of myself.

"You remember the few times I eluded to an experience I once had with a girl a long, long time ago?"

Her eyes lit up. "You mean the one who fucked you right up? Of course! I've been waiting for you to tell me about it. All I get from you are pieces the size of Smarties," she chastised.

"Fair enough. I slept with her last night."

"*What!*"

I let Christy relish in the moment. There weren't many impressionable moments in her life, but I was sure this was going to become one of them.

"Does Mitch know?" Christy asked.

"Yes. Actually, she told me to do it. Helluva reasonable girl, Mitch is," I said sarcastically.

Christy realized I was mocking her ridiculous question.

"You know what I mean," she said again.

"Here's the poop. The woman I keep alluding to called me Saturday afternoon."

"You haven't spoken to her in years, right?" Christy asked, cutting in.

I nodded and told her exactly how many years. "She invited me to her hotel, and I went. I got home later than I had thought I would and realized I missed my date with Mitch."

Christy looked horrified. "Now you're starting to sound like *my* boyfriends."

"This was an accident. The guys you date are just plain assholes," I justified. "I meant to call Mitch Sunday and resolve the entire incident."

"And did you?"

"No."

"Who's the asshole now?"

"Hold on. Let me finish."

"Carry on."

"The phone rang, and I thought it was Mitch, but it wasn't. It was *her* again."

"The other woman?"

"Yes."

"She said you forgot your watch at her place and would you mind coming over to get it."

"Have you done this before?"

Christy nodded her head.

"Actually, she said she couldn't sleep all night because she was thinking about me."

"All you guys fall for that tired line."

"This time she meant it."

"Gotcha."

"She wanted to get together one last time for a drink."

"Why 'one last time'?"

"She's here on business."

Christy smirked.

"I didn't want to because I was committed to seeing Mitch."

"But you went anyway."

"I had to."

"Oh?"

"To say good-bye."

"Sounds more like you ended up saying good morning."

"Ah, shit. We drank at the Martini Bar and ended up back at her place. Next thing I know there's a woman beside me in bed for the first time in years."

"Who wasn't plastic," she finished.

"You're sick."

She shrugged.

"Now I've royally messed things up. I've got to think of a way to explain this to Mitch before our date tonight."

"Perhaps you could do this right now."

"Why?"

"Think fast. She just walked in." Christy saw my face harden and quickly evaluated her course of action and left the room.

I heard Mitch greet Christy as she came into my office.

"Hey, stranger," she said, coming over and sitting on my lap. "I had to come and see if you've just been in my dreams all these months or you really do exist. Where were you this weekend? I was trying to call. I thought we were getting together?" She looked at me, smiling.

I felt like I was about to have an ischemic stroke.

I did the next best thing to telling the truth.

I lied.

"Slept most of Saturday. Wasn't feeling too well. I think I was catching a bug. Then on Sunday Lonny showed up unexpectedly and wouldn't leave. By the time he grew bored, it was too late to return your calls. I was going to give you a shout this afternoon."

"You know I work Mondays."

"I had a note ready to tie to a pigeon's foot. I find it more personal."

This time Mitch's smile was more forced. She knew I never saw Lonny on weekends. If he wasn't playing sports on the field, then it was games under some bimbo's sheets. Except last weekend I was the bimbo. However, Mitch appeared to accept my response and didn't press it.

"All right. I really wanted to confirm if we're still on for Jazz on the Rooftop. It's tonight. Are you still going, or do you think Lonny will make another unexpected stop at your place?"

I felt her body stiffen as she waited for my response.

"You bet I'm still going. If he shows up, I'm walking right over him. There's no way he's keeping me from you two days in a row."

"So I'm still your girl?"

"Of course," I said, trying to keep my eyes from wavering.

"Good response." She bent over and kissed my lips. They had a different taste from Peta's.

"You're still my number-one girl." I gave her a hug. My arms didn't have the strength to squeeze hard. I felt like a total shit. What the hell was I saying to her? Mitch didn't deserve for me to break our bond of trust. I was weak. In reality, I was no better than any of Christy's boyfriends. I knew I should tell Mitch something about what had happened, I just didn't know how. I promised myself I would explain everything to her tonight. I could now add my recent lies to a growing list of why-I'm-an-asshole charges.

"That's good, because I didn't just pick you out of a crowd for your looks. You also had a glimmer of integrity," she said, squinting at me.

I nodded my agreement. I was starting to get spooked by her inferences. The irony of her timing seemed like an act of fate. Then again, I had disappeared for two complete days. During the last few months we'd spoken at least once every day, even if it was a quick phone call to say hi. Which left the old adage that only two circumstances could cause a guy to vamoose without a trace for more than a day. The first was NFL Sunday double-headers. The second was a clandestine tryst with a woman. I wondered if Mitch was aware of this adage because if she was, I was done before I could plead my case.

Mitch rose suddenly from my lap and stood across from me.

"Are you picking me up tonight?"

"Seven o'clock," I said too quickly.

"See you then," she replied, displaying her former cheer.

I let my breath out. I heard the outside door close. I had bought myself a few hours. This evening was not looking pleasant. I hoped the jazz would be more uplifting.

Christy popped her head in my door.

"Did you tell her?"

"Nope."

"Chicken shit."

"Hey," I called out to her disappearing form, "it's all in the timing. One day you'll know what I'm talking about."

"She'll be double pissed at you for lying," she shouted back from her desk.

Christy was right. I should have said something while I had the chance. I could have left out the climactic bedroom scene. Naturally, in hindsight it seemed foolishly easy. It's a heck of a lot harder when the enemy is glaring eyeball to eyeball.

I still wrestled with my emotions from the last couple of days with Peta. It felt like old times again. In fact, that simple five-letter word I long ago gave up believing in spread across me like a euphoric blanket. *Happy.* There. I had said it. It was as though Peta took that feeling with her when she left ten years ago, and she now brought it back.

Yet I realized it was a false dawn. Peta was going back. This time I wasn't in for a total shock because I knew it up front. She was here for a short time on business. I didn't know if there would be a third affair before she flew back to Germany. Although I wouldn't say it aloud yet, if she gave her commitment to return, I would wait for her. So my answer was simple. Mitch had to know the truth on where I stood.

Still, for a guy who had just made his first major relationship decision, I didn't feel too good about it.

When I left my clinic, the walk home helped me work off the growing tension that was building inside me. I took the stairs at my apartment block two at a time trying to burn away more. Finally, I stood in the shower for an hour, gradually turning up the temperature until my skin became red.

I stepped out of the shower, naked and dripping, listening to Lonny speaking into my machine. I streaked into the living room and grabbed the phone before he finished. We needed to talk.

"Lonny," I gasped into the phone from my short burst of exertion.

"Hey, dude, screening your calls now?"

"Hosing myself down in the shower."

"Don't tell me if I'm talking to a naked man, all right, buddy?"

"Why? Does it bother you?"

"This is not the image I want of you, okay? We share lunches together."

"Fine. I'm wearing a towel."

"Are you prepping your body for Mitch tonight? Don't give yourself razor burn downstairs."

"Yeah. I also need to talk to you about that."

"Ah, I don't give shaving tips, bud."

"Not that, Lonny. I'm in deep shit."

"What's up?"

I summarized the last couple of days, ending with my encounter with Mitch this morning. Lonny seemed to enjoy my predicament and even agreed to confirm that I was with him Sunday. I didn't want Mitch to know I'd slept with Peta.

"I've got to say, Gus, I find your situation amusing. This summer you couldn't get a date with a hooker, and now you're a sold-out show. Keep this up and I'll have to get my tips from you for a change, buddy."

I pulled my Subaru up in front of Mitch's house and turned off the key, staring out the windshield. I hated confrontation. Especially when the end result was guaranteed to be shit-show. I kept assuring myself that this was the only way to do things. Mitch would appreciate my candor.

I forced a smile when she hopped into the car. If she had any suspicion from the afternoon, she didn't show it. I felt more like a bag of shit. I had crushed the innocence of our relationship.

I drove to the Art Gallery, and I listened to Mitch describe her weekend. I filled in with the appropriate nods and grunts, pairing each of her activities to the stages I was at with Peta.

The auditorium at the Art Gallery was nearly filled to capacity; we held hands and listened to the jazz groups perform. At the break, we got a drink and then resumed our seats until the end of the show. My apprehension grew as the evening moved closer to conclusion. I searched for an opportune moment to broach the subject of Peta. My fingers grew colder and my palms wetter while we walked back to my car. The air was chilly, signifying fall was finally taking over summer. I was now edging toward forfeiting my confession for another night. Mitch made the decision easier for me.

"You seem distant tonight," she said inside the car, gripping my hand while I let it warm up. I shivered, but not fully from the cold.

"Really? I thought I was just being myself tonight." I kicked myself for still struggling. *Say it, you asshole. This is your doorway right now.*

She shrugged. "You've been like this all day, even when I saw you this morning. To be honest, I've never seen this side of you before."

I put the car into drive, and we started to move. I recognized this was the opening I had prepared for, but the words froze on my lips.

Mitch said it for me.

"Is there something you want to tell me?"

I could feel her hand stiffen in my own.

Then she added, "Is it something I've done?" Her voice seemed strained, not really wanting to hear an answer.

I wished I could tell her everything was fine, but I couldn't. It was time.

"No. Nothing about you at all, Mitch. It's about me."

"Oh?"

I glanced over; she was staring straight ahead. Dammit, women could always sense when things were amiss.

"I …" My voice started to break so I stopped. My mouth was dry, and I craved a drink.

"Yes … ?" Mitch's voice was flustered.

"Ah, shit," was all I could say.

"Come on, Gus," she urged. "I'm a big girl. If something's bothering you, I can take it. Let's talk about it. That's what couples do."

She was so innocent. Caring. It wasn't fair.

"I had something very unexpected happen to me this weekend. We need to talk about it." There. It was out. I had triggered the avalanche.

Her body shook. "I knew it. You've never been like this before. It's … so out of character."

I nodded and continued.

"About ten years ago, I was involved with a woman from Germany. She was here for only a year on a business exchange program. We met. There was a connection."

Mitch's hand gripped mine tightly. I could feel her anxiety.

"Anyway, we got involved romantically, and everything seemed to be going along fine. Until the day she mysteriously disappeared, and I never heard from her again."

I met Mitch's eyes, searching hers and seeing the pain. It was easier to continue without looking her way.

"I never knew what happened to her. I suspected she went back to Germany. It had something to do with a man she had been involved with prior to coming to Canada. It left me fucked up for a very long time. In fact, until I met you, I had become a self-proclaimed recluse because of it. She had stripped me of the faith I had in relationships."

"I don't understand," Mitch said suddenly. "What's this got to do with this weekend? With us?"

She was staring at me but I couldn't meet her eyes. I pretended to focus on the road.

"On Saturday she called me. I hadn't spoken to her or received a letter or anything for *ten years*. But here she was, back in Winnipeg, wanting to see me. I knew you and I had plans, and I only wanted to see her so that she could look me in the eye and tell me what the hell happened ten years ago."

"So you saw her?" Mitch's voice was barely a whisper.

I knew she could see where this was heading. She needed to hear me say it.

"Yes. And I'm glad I did, because it brought all the things I needed to know in order to bring it to closure. For instance, why she left without saying good-bye. It turns out her boyfriend begged her to come back. So she did out of loyalty."

"But that has nothing to do with us," Mitch reasoned. "It's good you had a chance to resolve this. It must have been torturous for you not knowing."

I realized then how good a person Mitch really was. She still cared enough for me to see my meeting with Peta as a therapeutic session. It only made it harder for me to continue. I felt like steering our car off a bridge.

"We had a good talk. And I did feel better afterward," I admitted. "After all these years, I still held in a lot of anger."

"Is she here to stay?" Mitch knew how to come to the point. And that would be a true concern for Mitch and her relationship with me. But it was so much more.

"I don't know. She's told me she's only here for a couple of weeks on business. I believe it."

I felt Mitch's body go limp with relief. It was the answer she wanted to hear.

"I can see why you felt so torn, Gus," reasoned Mitch. "You probably felt like shit rekindling with an old girlfriend while I'm in your life." She looked at me and smiled.

"The thing is, Mitch, I spent some time with her yesterday, and it's messed me up."

Mitch instantly looked devastated. It was not the answer she wanted to hear.

"How do you mean?" she managed to ask. "I thought you were with Lonny yesterday?"

We pulled up to her place, and I parked the car. No one made a move to leave.

"I was," I lied. "I saw her after." I couldn't refer to Peta's name.

"So what are you saying, Gus? Do you want to begin where you left off? Is that it? As though the last ten years of abandonment means nothing? I'd say ten years of silence is her way of saying just how important you really are to her." Mitch was mad. Her voice broke from her anger.

"This is where I'm confused," I admitted. "I never thought I'd feel the same way for her. You know, after all the bitterness I've suffered during these years.

"So do you?"

"Do I what?"

"Still care deeply for her?"

I hesitated. "Yes."

Mitch pulled her hand away. "Where does this leave us?"

"I don't know," I replied honestly.

She looked at me with hollow eyes. "You said she wasn't staying in Canada. What do you expect from her then?"

I was startled by her venom. "Mitch, I don't know the answer to that question either. I just don't think it's fair to you if I have mixed feelings for two women."

"Gus, I'm here now. I live here. I won't be flying out of your life. This isn't a difficult decision." Mitch didn't try to hide her despondent face.

"It's not that simple," I said.

"I get it then," she replied. "I can't compete against a ghost from the past. Is that it? After ten years you expect to start where you left off? Do you actually *trust* her? Think about it, Gus. Want to have your heart broken again?" Mitch was fighting back tears. She was also fighting to keep the man she loved in her life.

"It's different this time. I think she's come back for more than forgiveness."

"She's told you this?" Mitch spat.

"No. Not yet, at least."

"Then you're living on pure hope, Gus. Make decisions with fact."

"I realize this is hard for you ..."

"Hard? It's brutal. For Christ's sake, Gus, I'm starting to understand you've got intense feelings for this ... woman ... I just hope you understand this is all new to me. Personally, I'd never let an ancient relationship influence a current relationship."

I let her vent. I deserved it. Mitch had put everything into our relationship, and here I was, jumping at shadows.

"Mitch, I wanted to be up front about this. I don't know where it's going to go. What I want to avoid is getting you jammed up with it."

I watched as she opened the door and got out. She looked defeated as she faced her house.

"You see, Gus," Mitch said sharply, turning to look back at me, "this is why I don't mind living a single life. At least my heart doesn't get, as you would say, 'jammed up'."

My mouth opened to say something, and nothing came out.

Mitch's torso was rigid as she slammed the door and walked away. She went inside her house without looking back.

I idled outside for a few more minutes, wondering if I should make an attempt to go up and discuss this some more. But the lights inside Mitch's house went out, and all was dark. I thought I saw a momentary glimpse of her looking out a window, but I wasn't sure. I decided any more discussions would only further ignite the situation. We both needed time apart to analyze our feelings. I had hurt Mitch. I felt terrible about it. Once again, Peta had managed to sabotage my life. Now I was second-guessing my choices. Maybe Mitch was correct in suggesting I was foolish to allow Peta back in my life after she walked out of it the first time.

I parked behind my building, ignoring the cool air around me. I was too preoccupied with the way I had left things with Mitch. I'd call her when I got up to my apartment.

I walked up to the front doors and met a figure who was fast becoming too familiar.

"Hi, Gus," Peta greeted me. She was obviously cold from standing outside the locked doors. From the way she had her arms wrapped around herself, it looked as though she had been outside a long while.

"Have you been waiting for me, Peta? I could have been gone another couple of hours. Maybe I wouldn't have come home at all tonight. Were you that determined to wait in the cold?" While I was astounded by her stupidity, her tenacity did affect me. I grabbed her arm.

"Come on," I said, leading her inside, "at least warm up a while."

"Just a while?" she purred, grasping me in her arms as we got inside the elevator.

"I need to be alone tonight," I said. "It's been a shitty day."

"I am the opposite, Gus. I have been going stir crazy from the quiet inside my hotel room. I could not take another hour alone. Besides, I have not spoken to you all day. I tried calling tonight, and your machine answered."

"Like I said, I've been busy today."

"Have I come between you and a woman? There is great sadness in your face. Only a woman can bring such sadness to a man's face."

I ignored her observation. We got off the elevator and walked down the hall into my apartment. Peta closed the door behind us. I heard the lock fall into place.

I went to the kitchen and fixed a couple of drinks. I made mine extra-strong.

I turned to Peta and said, "As a matter of fact, my emotions involve a very special woman. And you happen to be a big part of the problem, thank you."

Peta's face brightened, and she kneeled on the couch to listen. "Really? Do tell."

"Contrary to what you may believe, I haven't exactly been sitting alone in my apartment for the last decade waiting for you to come back."

Peta actually looked disappointed.

I continued. "For the last few months I've been seriously involved with a wonderful girl.

"Is she as sweet as me?" Peta mocked.

"Better."

"I do not believe you," she said with exaggerated outrage.

"Believe it. She's loyal and loving and happens to adore me."

"Then why are you here with me?" Peta asked bluntly.

Her remark stopped me. I handed her the drink and flopped down beside her.

I shook my head. "I really don't know. By all rights I shouldn't even be speaking to you after what you did to me."

She slid up to me. "But I'm back now, and we're having fun again."

"Well, tonight I hurt a very special woman. I feel shitty about it." I took a sip of my drink.

"I can make you feel good," Peta said softly into my ear, gently biting it. Her hot breath felt good, and I relaxed.

"Peta ..."

She ran her fingers across my mouth. "Follow me. Let me show you why you're here with me and not with her." Peta's voice was light and playful.

I allowed her to lead me to the bedroom. I let her lead me away to another place.

I woke up and stared at the ceiling. Turning my head, I read the clock. Four a.m. I looked the other direction, into Peta's sleeping face, her brown hair a mass of curls on the pillow around her. Even in this disheveled state she was beautiful.

I got up quietly and walked out onto the balcony. I was naked and it was cold, but I ignored the temperature. I knew I was slipping in deeper with Peta. In fact, I was on the dangerous edge of falling completely over the other side, to the point of no return. My instincts told me to run. For too many years I had listened to them and had gotten nowhere. This time I was determined to do what I wanted. And what I wanted to do was stick this out with Peta to see where it went—all the way to the end this time. I realized she filled something within me even Mitch could not.

I was cold.

Peta's voice called out to me from the darkness.

She urged me back inside.

She had something to warm me.

I closed the patio door.

She showed me her warmth until it was time for another day to begin.

25

"Hi, I have curly dark hair, a big smile and big eyes. I'm assertive but not pushy. I'm open-minded but not loose ..."

I allowed Peta to sleep in a while longer, so I left her a spare key and walked to my clinic. Once there, I didn't have time to update Christy on the recent events, despite her desperation to know. My appointment was waiting. I needed the few minutes available to review my notes on the Trotts. This was our first session since Jean zapped Jerry with the cattle prod.

While I cleared my desk I came across the ad for U 2 Can Date. I stared at it a few seconds before pitching it into the wastebasket. *What a crock*, I thought to myself, laughing. The time and money I'd spent all led to shooting blanks. *Look at me now*, I boasted. I'd broken one woman's heart and was falling back in love with another, who'd previously thrashed my own.

Jerry and Jean Trotts entered my room.

"Good to see you both again," I said, shaking their hands. "How have you been since ... the accident?" I asked Jerry. I wasn't sure how to label his mishap. I noticed the shame cross Jean's face. Jerry mumbled a response that I accepted as an okay.

As I sat down across from them, I could swear I caught Jerry looking at me differently. Then I remembered he had seen me impaled on the wheel at the bondage club. I contemplated clarifying what he had seen but decided against it. Jerry was my patient. My private life was not open to discussion. I really didn't care what impressions he drew. Besides, I had been there against my own will. He had been happily perched on a changing table with a messy diaper. I knew from now on Jerry and I would hold a special bond. It was an honour I chose to ignore.

"Jean, let me ask you first," I said forcefully, taking charge of the session. "At our earlier therapy sessions your biggest concerns dealt with pleasuring Jerry in his retirement without allowing the frequency of his games to become unmanageable. So we agreed to limit the role-playing to a couple of times a week. What we forgot to do was apply boundaries to the physical allowance. Look what happened. Jerry got hurt. Update me. How's it been?" I stared flatly at Jean.

Jerry looked bored. He gazed around the room. I was certain his wife knew nothing of his extracurricular activities.

Jean looked troubled. I coaxed a response from her.

"Things have been good," she replied. "The peeper game is fun." She looked bashfully at the floor and added, "This one I kind of enjoy."

I was delighted by her response. The power of therapy is wonderful.

"How so, Jean?" I asked, passionately. "Jerry should know how his pleasure becomes your pleasure. Tell us, Jean."

"Well," she said, glancing around, "Jerry plays peeper …"

I held up my hand. "Sorry, Jean. What is 'peeper'?"

"Ah," she hesitated, trying to find the right descriptive words.

I plastered intrigue across my face.

"A peeper spies into the windows of a person's house. Jerry pretends to be a peeper by going outside and spying in our windows."

I attempted to restate what she'd said, "Jerry plays a Peeping Tom who looks into your windows. He stands outside and looks in?"

Jean nodded and smiled.

"And …" I urged her to continue.

"I am supposed to go from room to room, while outside Jerry follows me, looking through the windows."

"And what is Jerry to see, Jean?"

She shrugged. "Oh, nothing. I'm just supposed to walk around and pretend I don't know he's out there."

"Do you have to perform certain acts for Jerry?"

Her face became pinched. "No. Only after a while I have to turn to the window and catch him looking."

"Looking at you doing what?" I asked, confused.

"Looking at me looking at him, I guess."

"So, Jerry," I asked, turning my attention to my Pampers-wearing client. "The act of being caught really is the game, isn't it?"

He nodded. He scratched at his leg, and I noticed he wasn't wearing his nylons today.

"Good for you two," I applauded. "It may not seem like much, guys. However, there is an understanding growing here. This is very important for a healthy relationship. Believe me. Consider your progress to be tremendously successful. I know I do." I looked smugly at them.

Jean glanced nervously at Jerry and smiled briefly. He flashed her a courtesy smile in return.

"We're on a healthy path, people," I said standing up. "Keep it up, and I'll see you in a month." I led the Trotts to the door and watched them leave.

I began to turn around when I saw Mitch in her bright red Downtown Winnipeg Biz jacket fight her way past the Trotts on their way out. I froze. Her visit was unexpected. The call I planned to make last night had not happened. I remained at ground zero.

She waved at Christy and stepped past me and inside my office. I caught Christy's paralyzed glance.

Mitch carried a Safeway bag in her hand. "Your stuff," she said flatly. I peeked inside. A couple of shirts, toothbrush, socks, the few things that had slowly been collecting at her place. A sure sign of a blossoming relationship. These same collectibles inside a Safeway bag signified the end of a relationship. I glanced quickly at her, noticing her unkempt hair. The red around her eyes struck a chord in me. She probably had as little sleep as I did last night, although for much different reasons.

"You didn't have to bring these back," I said, trying to strike a neutral tone. Despite this being the ideal opportunity to explain how terrible I felt for hurting her, the empty wall between my brain and mouth stopped me from going any further.

Mitch pressed on. "I don't want them." Her hostile stare didn't go unnoticed by me. She continued. "Who knows, maybe this toothbrush was your favourite? I've discovered that you have strong attachments to things. I wouldn't want you knocking on my door ten years from now asking for it. Unlike you, I don't carry around baggage for that long."

I moaned. She was making this painful. "Look, Mitch," I said, finding strength in my voice, "let's be fair about this. I didn't ask for a girl I once loved to come back into my life."

Her body shook. "Nice job passing the buck."

"You know what I mean," I said, pretending to brush dust from the tabletop.

"Gus, what I don't get is your rationale. She's given you nothing yet taken away everything."

I thought about what Mitch had just said. It would have made sense, except last night Peta had given a lot. I refrained from voicing my thoughts.

Instead, I said, "Fair enough. I was only trying to be candid with you. Staying friends is very important for me. My feelings for you haven't changed, Mitch. Believe me." This wasn't a lie. I think it showed in my face because Mitch dropped her stony glare.

She began pacing the floor.

"She hurt you bad the first time she left, Gus. I don't want to see you bleed again. I fell in love with you."

Hearing her say that word cut me deeply. Normally, those very words would have been enough for me to grab Mitch in my arms and hold on to her forever. But these weren't normal times. Ten years of soul-searching told me my gut choice was the correct one. I was sticking to it.

"Mitch, this is doing us both no good."

"I know," she said, her voice a whisper.

"Then let's try to move past it."

"It's hard to lose the guy you love to a woman who has not been a part of his life for ten years."

"Mitch. Please."

She looked fragile. I had sucked the vibrancy that once exuded from her. Had that been me all the years after Peta abandoned me?

"Okay, Gus. I'm not here to beg you to come back or to feel guilty. I do want to say after the relationship we established, I was more hurt that you never called me last night. Hearing from you would have gone a long way to helping me cope. But you didn't call." Her voice trailed off. "I thought you cared about me."

I wasn't sure she wanted an answer. I didn't want to lie, so I didn't want to answer. Instead, I gave a misdirection.

"I went home and straight to bed. I found the entire evening traumatic." I stopped there before I said something incriminating. There was nothing more despicable than a lying ex-boyfriend.

I walked next to Mitch and put my arm around her. She didn't raise her head to look at me. I leaned close and lightly said, "I'm sorry, Mitch." She just nodded. I think she was fighting tears. I thought I should say something else to let her know how big an asshole I really, but the front door opened and a familiar voice exploded into the room. Mitch looked in the same direction, and I lowered my arm from her shoulders. She turned her head and saw my face, and realization spread across her own. She turned back, focusing hard on Peta. Christy's attempts at stalling Peta were in vain; she clearly thought Peta was a client. Christy trailed behind, pleading with Peta to wait out front while I was with a client.

"Gus!" Peta rushed to grab my head and placed a kiss on my lips. "I am being treated like a criminal by this … girl," her accent thick with indignation.

"Sorry, Gus, I didn't know she was a friend," said Christy. She still hadn't made the connection about who Peta was, despite the German accent. I shot a quick look at Mitch, who knew Peta's relationship to me very well. She stood silently, absorbing everything about Peta: the black business skirt, heels and flawless makeup were difficult to ignore. It was typical Peta—explode into a room, command it, sweep everyone into a bag and carry them away.

Peta finally noticed Mitch and stood back. "You *are* with someone—how thoughtless of me," she said, not convincing anyone she actually cared.

"Peta, I was just finishing up," I said pointing to the Safeway bag on my desk. Peta looked from the bag, scanning Mitch's red outfit. I could tell by her expression she would never allow herself to be seen in public dressed in such a fashion. She was likely wondering why anyone else would.

Just then, Mitch's cell phone rang, and she answered it. We all waited while she spoke to a delivery driver and confirmed her home address. I wanted to ask what it was she was expecting but didn't feel it was appropriate. Mitch clicked her phone off.

"Yeah. Right. I guess that concludes my visit," remarked Mitch, tucking the phone into her jacket. She kept glimpsing at Peta.

Peta stepped aside, giving Mitch room to pass by.

"I'll be in touch," I called out to Mitch, getting no reply.

Christy finally tuned in to Peta's identity and, sensing the potential for disaster, wisely left for the bathroom.

Peta and I were alone.

She gestured to the door through which Mitch had just left.

"Would she be the woman competing against me for you?" Peta's expression was smug.

"It doesn't matter," I said, briskly. I wasn't about to justify myself to her.

"Not bad. A little roughness that could be improved if she wanted to," Peta conceded, tossing a lock of brown hair from her eyes. I found the movement sexy. Then I saw the bag on my desk, and it brought me back to reality.

"Leave her alone, Peta. Okay?" I didn't hide the annoyance in my voice. Mitch was innocent. She didn't need her character slandered.

"Don't be silly, Gus," she said, moving next to me and putting her arms around my neck. "She seems sweet for a young girl." She nibbled at my ear, and I pushed her away before Christy came back into the room in time to see her boss being eaten for dessert.

"Shy?" she grinned slyly.

"This is a place of business," I said, trying to sound official. She didn't buy it.

"Then let's go somewhere it's not business." She sat down on the edge of the desk, her skirt riding high on her thigh. She noticed my eyes flicker along her legs.

"I'm working."

"You are the owner. Call in sick," she persisted.

"I'm already here. How can I be sick?"

"You look green to me. You're sick."

"What do you have in mind?"

"I want to go betting."

"At the track?" Peta loved gambling. Especially when it came to horses. We had spent hours and money I didn't have back in the old days. It had also been tremendously fun. Her offer was tempting.

"I'd have to check my schedule. I do have patients, you know."

"Then check." Her dark-coloured lips broke into a tantalizing smile. She was breaking me.

"Christy!" I called out.

She had finally returned to her desk. "Yes?" she asked tentatively.

"Who am I to see this afternoon for appointments? I'm sure I have patients booked.

"No one."

"Are you sure?"

"It's empty, Gus."

Peta sneered at me.

"Aren't Peter and Alabama Daube supposed to see me?"

"Next week, Gus."

"So you're free to go," Peta announced.

"I'd only be doing this because you're a guest in this city," I replied. "Normally I wouldn't leave in case a patient had an emergency."

"What could be that urgent in a marriage?" she asked, cheerfully.

I shrugged. "Things."

"Enough stalling, my love. You're coming with me." She grabbed my arm and pulled me through the building.

"Gone for the day?" asked Christy, watching me being dragged away.

"Tell Gus's clients the doctor is away on a house call," Peta remarked as we went outside.

Peta had parked her rental car out front. There was a ticket on her windshield for stopping in front of a fire hydrant. Without bothering to read it, she tossed it onto the pavement and got inside the car. I followed.

The track was busy with patrons risking the family paycheck in pursuit of the big hit, the one that would clear away all the debts and offer them a lifestyle full of the pleasures only those with money could obtain. By the end of the day, most of the men would be going home to drown their sorrows in a bottle bought with the leftover change. Mercifully, I didn't see Peter Daube standing in any of the betting lines.

Peta launched herself into the races. Meticulously, she chose the order of horses before each race. Together we'd sprint up the stairs to place the bet. Then a quick dash back to the stands to wait for the bell. No one yelled with Peta's intensity. Her entire focus was on the thunder of horses. I was caught between watching the race and Peta's facial expressions while she screamed her enthusiasm at the jockeys.

Afterward, we ran from the stadium, holding hands as though we were ten years younger and time had never moved forward. We agreed to stay at my place that night. Peta bemoaned the walls closing around her in the hotel. Also, the maids were noisy each morning, moving carts. She had complained to management twice, demanding a deep discount.

We took the elevator up to my floor. Now I enjoyed the duration over the sweaty struggle with the stairs. I was growing to enjoy Peta's company within my daily routine again. I wondered how much time I had left with her. She kept evading my questions about the nature of her business within Winnipeg.

"I love your apartment," admired Peta, twirling inside the living room. She kicked off her shoes and lay across the couch. "I feel so comfortable here."

"Make yourself at home," I offered, seeing her commandeer my furniture.

"I already have, Gus. Now, how about getting a girl a drink. Betting has dehydrated me."

"You're referring to your yelling," I observed, walking to the kitchen to mix us each a drink.

"Encouragement, Gus. The female voice spurs a horse to greater energy."

"Is that German wisdom or wishful thinking?" I asked from the other room.

"Trust me, Gus. Women possess many ways to influence all creatures."

"Please, you're scaring me." I stirred the drinks, listening to the ice bang inside the glasses. The living room was silent as I carried our drinks inside. Peta was concentrating on a photograph in her hand.

"I hope that's not the one of me taking a dump on the porcelain," I said placing her drink in front of her. "Lonny gets stupid with a camera sometimes when we're drunk."

She shook her head. I looked over. It was the photograph of me and Mitch shot by the riverboat captain. I hadn't seen it since the evening it was taken. Looking at our faces against the dropping sunset, a flood of images came back. It was a different world. Another time.

I suddenly felt very depressed.

"You two look happy," Peta commented. She pointed at the photograph. "This was the one in your clinic today." I nodded. Peta didn't say anymore but continued studying the photograph.

"Listen," I said, taking the picture from her and walking it to another table. "I think I need to call it a night. The week's events have caught up with me."

Peta missed my point. "Then let's go to bed now," she offered, smiling. "I'm ready."

I shook my head. "No, I mean I need some time alone. Sorry."

She looked confused. "You had ten years alone. We were about to have a drink," she said, gesturing to our glasses.

I had lost my taste for the scotch. The photo had evoked abandoned emotions. Now I knew where Mitch's hurt was coming from.

"It's nothing you've done, Peta. I'll be fine tomorrow after an evening alone. I realize you don't want to spend the night at the hotel again. Sorry. But I really do need the time by myself."

She studied my face, searching to see if the real cause was different than what I said it was. She seemed satisfied and stood up to put her shoes on.

"You have worried me, Gus. I have never seen you like this before." She came over and kissed me on the lips. It was tender but did little to alter my decision.

"I'll be okay," I assured her, putting my hand around her waist. "Just a few things I need to work out."

She gave it one last try, boring into my skull with her eyes. "Call me if you change your mind. I will be in my suite." She picked up her purse. "If the maids rattle their carts one more time, I will personally beat them myself." I laughed. But Peta meant it.

She left, and I sat down on the couch that was still warm from her body. I held the photograph in my hand.

What had happened?

Peta happened.

I was in love with Mitch.

And I was in love with Peta—wasn't I?

Was old love like wine, tasting better with age?

Then why was the picture tearing me apart?

I needed a walk. The apartment's silence was beating at my head.

I grabbed a jacket and headed down the stairs. A beer at the King's Head suddenly seemed the right cure.

It took me almost forty minutes, but I arrived to a quiet atmosphere. Robby was off duty. A man with a long, blond ponytail from the flower power era worked the bar in Robby's absence. Three tables were occupied, and two guys in tailored business suits were throwing darts in the back of the pub. The silver-haired guy seemed to be enjoying the thrashing he was giving his younger opponent. I chose to sit by the front window in relative seclusion.

"Scotch, right?" The female voice didn't click, but her face did when I looked up.

"Serena!" I felt a small smile break across my face. She handed me a tumbler of single malt and sat down beside me. The silver stud embedded in her tongue glittered when she laughed.

"Nice to see you with normal skin colour," she said, grabbing hold of my forearm. "I'd never seen a person turn the colour you did after smoking that cigar. First one?" She looked at me slyly.

I nodded, confessing my ignorance.

"Don't worry about it. I've dropped the habit since then. I was developing a hacking cough."

I smiled at her. "I'd have thought after my performance that night you'd have avoided me a second time around."

"Are you kidding? You looked kinda sexy bent over the chair puckering your cheeks with each heave." She burst with a loud, forceful laugh. The two suits playing darts stopped their game to turn around and look our way.

"Bloody hell, mate," I heard Silverhair remark in our direction with a distinct British accent. I ignored them.

"See what working with the public does to a person?" I commented. "You can lie with the most honest face."

"I was actually intrigued by you, Gus. The way things turned out, I wasn't able to get your phone number. I haven't seen Lonny since then either. I was hoping I'd get your number from him."

"He's been preoccupied with the Internet lately. Although I think he'll be returning really soon from cyber to virtual reality."

She placed a pretzel in her mouth, letting her stud balance it.

I was hypnotized.

"Yeah, well," I said, breaking the trance, "my life hasn't slowed its roller-coaster ride since then. I came here tonight hoping to numb some of the seasonal blues."

Her eyes took on a devilish glimmer.

"Gus," she said, taking my hand. "You look like a man who needs pampering."

"I don't understand … ?"

"I'm saying let's go back to my place where it's quiet. I have beer there. And I'll give you a royal scalp massage like you've never had before. In fact, it's guaranteed to eliminate all despair from your life."

"Guaranteed, huh?"

"Of course. I have magic hands."

I studied her manicured red fingernails, which looked tantalizing. I could easily imagine them running through my hair.

"Are you bonded?"

"You'll have to trust me."

"I don't know. You look kind of shifty."

"Do you know the best part of massages?"

"I've never had one, so no, I wouldn't."

"They start on your scalp and end up in my bed."

I choked on my beer. *Where was this offer earlier in the year?*

"Ever feel what a moist tongue stud feels like running up your naked back?"

"I'll bet it feels pretty damn good."

"How about it?" she asked, stroking my fingers suggestively. "We have unfinished business to take care of."

I stopped myself from asking if this was going to cost me. It just seemed too good to be true. And that never happened to me. To score after ten minutes in the King's Head was a feat managed only by the superior male. Brawny men, like Jake.

"No cigars, I promise," she said, grinning. "You'll forget everything that's weighing on your shoulders."

There was the real rub. Maybe for a couple of hours I would, but eventually I had to towel off the oil and face my reality again. I could see my return from the brief distraction being even more painful.

I declined.

Serena was surprised. I could see it plainly on her face. Her hand pulled away.

"I think you might be reading more into this than you have to, Gus. I'm not looking for a boyfriend. I'm talking about a crazy night of sex, the kind of night that takes away everything on your mind. We'll likely never see each other again." She stared at me intently. Sadly, it wasn't even an option.

"I wasn't mistaken, Serena. And you're right, it would make me forget my problems. But just for a few hours. They'd all still be there awaiting my return from bliss. Your magical fingers working my scalp would be a fond but distant memory. I'm afraid tonight I wouldn't be an exciting participant."

Serena actually appeared despondent. I was nearly flattered by her response.

"You're admirable, Gus. I saw that in you when we first met. Whoever the girl is who's possessed your soul doesn't know what she has."

"Thanks. Your remark happens to be the nicest thing someone's said to me in days."

"Only days?"

"Years."

"Now you're being silly."

"My lifelong regret will be missing your tats up close and personal."

"I'll take that you mean my tattoos," she confirmed.

"Of course," I said, shooting her a knowing wink.

"Of course," she replied, provocatively.

"Don't take this the wrong way," I said, pushing aside my nearly empty beer, "but you've done for me what I came here for, and that was to step back and look around. Now I feel ready to tackle my apartment alone."

"Glad I could help out," Serena said, standing up to give me a hug. "Say hi to Lonny when you see him."

"I will."

I stepped outside into the cool night, inhaling as much air as possible. Before I could start walking, a well-worn drunk staggered out of the shadows. His arms waved haphazardly around him.

"Who's your God?" he slurred, unable to focus his eyes on me.

"My friend," I said, smiling, walking past him. "I just turned her down."

I strode the rest of the way back to the apartment.

26

"I'm a professional chef and my speciality is hot fudge all over my body ..."

The morning was wretched, starting the moment my couple parted without a kiss. Bad news. In fact, the woman was already stepping away from the car before it had a chance to come to a full stop. I don't know what kind of mouthpiece he had become to piss her off, but I was sure he had just signed up for a week of walking barefoot on glass shards. *A shitlicker start to his day. A roundhouse kick to my own head.*

I stumbled through work, wincing with each passing hour until it was time for lunch, a meal with Lonny that I had completely forgotten we had scheduled earlier in the week, before the universe had collapsed around me. *A world ago.* Now I awaited our lunch as a needed release. Finally, someone neutral I could talk to. A male, unbiased, uncaring. *The perfect son of a bitch.*

Christy sensed something was amiss and was keeping her yap shut and not ask for details. She had been strangely unquestioning since all my worlds had collided inside my office the previous day. When I told her I was leaving to see Lonny at the Tap and Grill, her raised hand was her acknowledgement.

I walked the block to the restaurant, meeting Lonny in the lobby. Our table was being prepped.

Lonny didn't mince his words. "Do you always walk around with an expression on your face like you're trying to conceal the fact you've launched a big one into your shorts, bro?"

I caught my reflection in the mirrored wall. He was right. I tried to change my demeanor, but it wouldn't budge. I pulled my eyes away.

"Spend a day in my shoes, you bastard, and try to look exuberant," I barked, grateful that I could say it without being slapped. For that single moment, I loved men.

"Give me a break, dude," Lonny replied, slapping me on my shoulder as we were led to our table. "I've never looked like you, even the morning I woke up in the Woodbine Hotel with a woman who had fewer teeth than fingers and with bedbugs in my pubic hairs. So what gives?"

"Troubles afoot in my love life."

He looked at me strangely. "Before, the trouble was finding a lover who didn't have a pimp. What gives?"

I went on to describe the gathering of the hens at my office. He let out a whistle, grinning from ear to ear.

"I call that the type of dream that damages a water mattress." He laughed.

"Yeah, well, last night Peta wanted to stay over, and I was game … until she found a picture of me and Mitch."

"Let me guess," Lonny speculated. "You felt guilty?"

"More than I realized."

"And?"

"I sent Peta away."

"To do what? Cry over a couple of hazy memories? Listen, bud, I've got a closetful, and unless they can reach out and touch me, the herd's moved on."

"I walked to the King's Head, instead."

"That's my boy," he said proudly.

I smiled. "You wouldn't guess who I met."

"You buy this lunch if I do?" he offered.

I looked at him strangely and accepted his bet. "Go for it," I challenged.

"Serena."

I stared at him. "How the hell did you know?" I was astonished.

"Saw her this morning." He sounded matter-of-fact.

"But she said she hasn't seen you since the night I met her at the Shark Club." I was confused.

"Right. Except now it's this morning."

"How's that possible?"

He pointed at his hair.

I didn't get it.

"Needed a haircut, man. Her handiwork."

"She cuts your hair?"

"Don't you talk to these women? It's what she does."

"Of course I know she's a hairdresser," I corrected.

He shrugged. "Needed a trim. Her card was the first one I pulled from my wallet. So I went over there, and she described her experience with you last night. Or should I say, the massage of a lifetime you passed over, you dumb shit."

"I'm committed."

"No, but you should be."

"What'd she say?" I was dying to know.

"Actually, she was impressed by your sincerity. Believe me, it really turned her on. I think she said she settled for a British hump who was playing darts in the pub last night. If it's any consolation, she mentioned she was thinking of you when she was rubbing down his back."

"I wanted to go with her. I finally decided it would only complicate my life further," I confessed.

"No problem. She's not mad. No sane man's ever turned aside one of her famous scalp massages. Trust me." He winked.

I didn't want to go there. Lonny was pure machine.

He pushed back his chair and asked with a large grin, "Who the hell is this German woman, anyway? Serena offers to teach you what she can do with the stud in her tongue and you don't even ask for a rain check. What are we talking about with her? Is she *that* good?" He gave me his best shit-eating grin.

I had the solution for wiping the cockiness from his face.

"Find out for yourself, bud. Here she comes." I pointed down the aisle near the entrance. Peta walked toward us. Actually, she made the fifty-foot distance look like the runway of a Paris fashion show. I heard Lonny moan his approval. For once, I felt I had something over him.

Peta knew black best accented her sleek features. Her skirt contoured her hips and legs and was split up the front. Her brown hair bounced with each step she took in her knee-high black boots.

Lonny was all eyes when she stopped at our table, looking down at us.

255

"Are you here to take our order?" I asked, laughing.

Her white teeth and green eyes shone with her smile.

"What I cook isn't served here," she answered smugly.

"I'll take a double order, then," offered Lonny. I thought I noticed sweat on his forehead.

Peta reached over with her hand. He stood and lightly grasped her hand with its perfectly manicured nails.

"Hello, I'm Peta. Gus's friend." Her accent was a deep purr.

"I'm …"

"Lonny," she finished. "Christy told me where to find you two. Nice to meet you, Lonny."

"If you need cellular phones …"

"Cut the sales pitch," I said in disbelief. Lonny would use any line to impress a woman.

"I do not think you have anything that I need," Peta replied, despite my resistance. "But this guy here, he has it all." She stroked her fingers through my hair.

"Will you be joining us?" I asked, moving over to make room. Her perfume now flooded the area, and I felt myself floating with it.

She shook her head, much to my disappointment. I didn't have to know what was echoing inside Lonny's head either. He looked devastated.

"Why not? Are you ashamed to be seen eating with a couple of common boys?"

She laughed. "Of course not, Gus. I'd love to, but I'm finishing up a business deal in twenty minutes."

"You're already going to be late," I noted.

"I never show up on time. Coming into the negotiations twenty minutes late works everybody up into a frenzy. By that time, I have the advantage. They get blinded by their relief that I showed up at all, making them willing to sign whatever paper I slide under their pens." Her expression was devilish.

"Remind me to bring you along next time I go car shopping," I said, laughing along with Lonny.

"It is just business, Gus," she said, warmly, running her hand along the back of my head. "You've seen the soft side of me." I was becoming uncomfortably hot in my Dockers. Lonny looked poised to take my place in a heartbeat.

I glanced up at her. "So if lunch with Lonny and me wasn't your intention, there must be some reason for your short, but may I add delightful, visit. Would you agree, Lonny?" I asked, and he vigorously nodded his head.

"Do you need directions? A ride? Advice?" Lonny was trying hard.

Peta laughed at his eagerness.

"I had a difficult time sleeping last night after the way we parted," she confessed. Her sincerity was believable. The way I'd called the night to a sudden end had been irrational.

"I know ..." I began to say.

"You have many things on your mind," she continued, "and I am the cause of a lot of distractions for you right now."

"Peta ..." She wouldn't let me finish.

"Therefore, I will not take no for an answer from you this time. You and I are going out tonight. My surprise. I will be at your apartment at nine o'clock, Gus. Do not disappoint me, lover. Be waiting." She ran her fingers under my chin. "You will be very happy with the plans I have made. I promise you an evening you will not forget." Her deep eyes were sucking me in.

"Don't be a fool, brother. Nine p.m." Lonny pointed his finger at me, emphasizing his seriousness.

"Okay," I said, holding up my hands. "I can see I'll be forever scorned if I don't go. I'm in."

"Good!" she cheered. Her hands grasped my head and pushed my face into her cleavage. I heard Lonny let out a tortured groan.

"Lonny, it has been a pleasure," Peta said politely, offering her hand. He enthusiastically accepted.

"Remember, I can set you up with a phone for half price. Unlimited roaming."

I let him finish. It was not like Lonny to live a romance vicariously through my own.

"Do you have a card?" asked Peta, showing no signs of annoyance. She was going to be more than twenty minutes late for her meeting.

He handed her a heavily laminated card. "My cell number is right here," he said, pointing it out. "This one is my home phone. I accept after-hour calls."

Peta smiled. She placed Lonny's card in her purse.

"So, about tonight," she said to me.

"What should I be wearing?"

She was already strutting back down the aisle, but she turned around momentarily.

"Anything you wear is sexy on you, Gus." She left the building.

"Donkey punch me, that is one *hell* of a woman," remarked Lonny. "No wonder your head is up your ass. I need to change my socks. She hits one of those rare nerves in a guy so few women can. Yikes."

I let him rant. My thoughts were on Peta's late-night planning. *What is she conniving?* She had been very insistent that nothing come between us tonight. I felt a surge of excitement rush through my gut. Peta was persistent. I was intrigued.

"Don't let her get away a second time," I returned to hear Lonny say.

"You mean Peta?"

"Yeah I mean her, man. Do yourself a favour and don't overanalyze this opportunity. I can see why you kicked your own ass for the last ten years. Losing her is like running the winning lotto ticket through the washing machine in your jeans pocket. All I ask from you tomorrow is a phone call with details and a few candid photographs."

"What kind of sick perv are you?"

"Don't bust a nut, man. I'm only curious what the urgency is all about. It's good to see my boy back in the game."

"I'll admit she's got my ear. This could also be her way to simply ensure I don't break a date with her again. I'm sure snubbing her last night did not sit well with her."

"It doesn't sit well with me, you idiot! What were you thinking, sending her packing last night!"

"There are moments in every guy's life when he needs a cold beer to help him reflect and Neil Young howling in the background on the stereo. The ladies don't understand this. Suddenly we've become the moody bastards. Let me tell you something. After a night of reflection, it all comes together, baby. It's like jacking on a new set of tires when a hundred miles of fresh blacktop waits for us."

We paid our bills and left.

I made sure I was waiting five minutes early inside the lobby of my building. It was dead on nine when Peta's rental car pulled up outside. My reward for commenting on her beauty was a lasting kiss before we pulled away. The streets were dark, which helped add to the mystique of the adventures Peta planned for me.

Peta was energized. Vibrancy shone from her as she maneuvered the car down Portage Ave toward Main Street. She played an Alannah Myles CD we used to listen to ten years ago. She sang along with the lyrics.

When the car pulled up in front of the Blue Note Café on Main Street, I looked over at Peta, and we both smiled at one another. She had a knack for choosing intimate venues.

The Blue Note held history for us. I guess I could say I learned to love Peta inside the dingy, tight confines while listening to a local band strumming out remakes. It had been late autumn during witching hour, in a booth to ourselves, surrounded by clouds of stale smoke, drinking bitter cups of endless coffee. I'd listened to Peta describe her harsh, solitary upbringing, all her motivations and triumphs unnoticed by her family. Her struggles to define herself, despite outside insistence that a woman did not belong in a man's world. I followed her journey during her tears and laughter, smiling when she did and sharing the pain in her eyes. *Discovery. Awareness.* Afterward, when she bailed out to go back to Germany, I'd reflect on those evenings, sometimes understanding why she may have gone back.

Tonight, we huddled in the same secluded corner, listening to a different band at a different time in our lives. My feelings for her were unchanged, something time couldn't steal from me.

"I once read people can never recreate history," I heard myself telling Peta as our coffee arrived, the waiter then disappearing into the darkness. "Never capture that same moment again." We held hands across the scored table.

Peta brightened. "Why would I wish to bring the past forward," she said, "when I have the future to live?"

I suppressed a smile. "Then why are we here?"

She looked at me carefully. "I loved you back then, Gus. Even if I did not know how much until after I left."

"Why'd you leave?"

She squeezed my hands tightly.

"It was never that simple ..."

"Your boyfriend ..."

"More than that, but all of it does not matter now."

I shook my head. "It matters to me. I can't let you hurt me again." I thought carefully and said, "I don't have the strength to heal again."

Peta's face was crestfallen. "I have made a lot of mistakes in my life, Gus. Choosing to leave you for Lars was the greatest one."

"Don't worry. I've come to terms with it. Honest."

She looked at me with sad eyes.

"But the main thing is you're happy now," I offered. "You obviously made the right choice by going back home."

Peta switched directions.

"We had fun together, didn't we?"

"Are you referring to the times before you left?"

She nodded.

"Sure we did … a lot of them. I didn't want that to change."

Peta leaned forward in an uncharacteristically nervous manner and said, "Gus, I came back here for three reasons …" Her voice trailed off.

I let her finish.

"I had business dealings that needed to be resolved here, although I could have easily completed them from Germany. But I flew here because of my second reason."

I kept my feelings in neutral, waiting to hear her out.

She refused to release my hands as she spoke.

"I thought I would find you and see how you still felt about me. About … us. Especially after the way I left things …"

"And not calling or writing," I added.

"That too. Of course."

I swallowed. "And what did you find?"

She skipped my question.

"I made a mistake ten years ago. Lars convinced me that the right decision was to come home to him. He realized how important I was to him once I was gone."

I really didn't care what son of a bitch Lars felt, thought or did, but I allowed Peta her say.

"He promised me things would be different between us. I would have the freedom and support I needed from him to manage my manufacturing companies. The mistake I made was that I believed him, Gus."

"What do you mean?"

She vigorously shook her head. "The broken promises mean nothing now. You do not need to know all of them."

"I have to admit you've lost me, Peta. I'm not getting where your mistake was if Lars is still in your life. Help me here, will you?"

"Six months had not even passed when Lars again became everything he swore to me was changed. Still more broken promises followed. By then a couple of years had gone, and I was deeply entrenched in my companies. I focused all my energy to make them succeed. I think it was this concentration that allowed me to forget his growing lies. Unfortunately, it also blinded me. But the truth eventually was exposed."

"What happened?"

"I saw the real Lars when I started looking closer. In fact, he had been unfaithful to me for years. Some were models, others those I thought were my friends. It did not matter to Lars. He had everything he wanted. Me. Lovers. His friends. I had been the fool all those years. I gave up the most important person in my life, someone who spoke the truth and cared for me, all for another man made of lies."

"You mean … ?"

"Yes, you are the man of honour I speak of."

She released her grip and held up her hand to stop me from going any further. I let her finish.

She hesitated and then said, "I want you to come back to Germany with me. There is much you can do with me in my companies. We can live handsomely and prosper." She stopped. She flushed. "And I can be your wife." Her eyes didn't move from mine.

I was floored. Peta could see it. She kept silent, letting her offer sink in. So this was her third reason for coming back—it was a big one. *Huge.* Relocating to Germany meant giving up everything I had here, leaving my friends. Not an easy transition when I considered I couldn't speak her language. And it also meant spending the rest of my life with a woman I loved. Craftily, she had made me prove to myself that I still loved her after ten years of neglect. I applauded her creativity. She really did know me enough to make me see things her way.

"Is there any way for you to move here instead?"

"No, Gus, there isn't. My operations require me in Germany. Let me ask you this." She tightly grasped my hands again. "Is solving petty problems for people you do not care about what you want for the rest of your life, or is it waking up beside me in bed every morning? This is what we both want. What we both should have had ten years ago." She held my gaze for a few moments; I was the first to look away.

She was right. Besides my meagre practice, I didn't have a whole hell of a lot here. Lonny? My apartment. A beaten-up Subaru. Crusty Harold smoking his cigarettes. There really wasn't much when I started to make a list. Indeed, wasn't Peta offering me what I had set out to find nearly eight months earlier? I'd found my love in her.

I made my choice.

"Count me in," I said, laughing riotously.

Peta squealed and nearly pulled off my arms. She grabbed me around my neck and pulled my tongue into her mouth. Apparently, my answer was the correct one.

"I guarantee you will never have a regret, Gus," Peta assured me.

"You don't have to tell me. I know," I said. I nuzzled her cheek.

We pulled away and sat back in our chairs. I felt stunned. *I am moving to Germany with Peta.*

"You have made me very happy, Gus Adams," she said in the thick accent I had come to love.

I took a sip of the coffee that had now gone cold. I didn't care. I was going to be with Peta.

Now was the time for details, so I asked, "What's our timetable? I could easily have everything wound down with my practice by springtime. And my lease for my apartment expires then too."

Peta squinted.

"Gus, we are flying out at the end of this week."

I froze. "What? You're joking."

"Not at all." She was serious. "Tomorrow I am booking two tickets for you and me."

"Why do we have to do this so fast?" I couldn't see myself not being here a week from now. There wasn't time to wind down my obligations to my patients in that short period.

"As I have said, this is an extremely busy time for me with my companies. I cannot be away for much longer. Once I am back in Germany there is plenty for me to do."

"I understand all that, of course. But couldn't I come later, once I'm ready?"

"Why, Gus? Taking longer just means doing the things you can get done now. I want us to go back as a couple. And frankly, I could not risk losing you a second time. You could change your mind once I am gone."

"I'd never do that," I shot back.

"I won't take that chance."

"Are you suggesting if I don't go with you now, I'm not welcome at a later date?" It seemed incredible.

"No, I am not, Gus. What I want is for you to come with me at the end of this week. I will help you to prepare in any way. This will not be as difficult as you think. Your clients will understand. I am sure where you live is popular. People will fight to live there. A lease is only a piece of paper. They can come to Germany if they want payment." She smiled, and I began to relax. She was right. Harold always had a waiting list of potential tenants. And it wasn't like I had hundreds of clients in treatment. I'd refer them to other clinics. The hardest would be Christy. She needed the work. I'd see what I could do to help her find another job before I left. I began to feel better. I could do it to Peta's expectations.

"Okay," I said, "I'm getting rid of everything I own except my clothes. Two suitcases are all that I'm bringing. So whatever fits is all that I will have."

"This is great!" Peta said. "I have a car for you in Germany. A nice, new one. You will enjoy it."

I grinned crookedly.

"Let me ask you this, Peta," I said carefully, watching her face cloud over. "What would you have done had I said no?"

She shivered.

"Your question is too cruel for me to answer," she responded. "What you did say is all that matters."

I frowned, and she noticed, asking me, "There is something on your mind? Tell me. We have to be honest with each other. Our relationship will only work with the truth about things on our minds." She made me feel comfortable, and I admired that in her.

"What about Lars? Where does he fit into all this?"

Peta's jaw hardened.

"He does not. I am through with him. I made this perfectly clear to him when I left for Canada. Right now he is living with friends. I have warned him he is never to speak to me again. You have nothing to worry about him."

"Fair enough. I want to arrive in Germany with you and leave all that shit behind us. No baggage."

"No baggage," Peta repeated.

We left the dark, intimate confines of the Blue Note to join twelve hundred withering bodies at the Tijuana Yacht Club on the other side of the city. It boasted the city's largest dance floor. Since Peta insisted we dance, it was the place to go. I loved watching her dance. Her body became magical. It was hypnotic the way every limb became fluid, stroking to the music. We sweated and teased one another until our legs gave out and the lights came on. The drive to my apartment was quick. We hurried to my bedroom to consummate our official reunion. For the first time since the day Peta evaporated from my life a decade ago, I felt incredible.

27

"I like to play. I like to have fun and to try new things. Male. Female. I don't care …"

I woke, and to ensure myself the previous night's events weren't a cruel dream, I moved my head to the left and saw Peta's bundle of hair. *It's real. I am moving to Germany.* My heart battered under my ribs.

A year ago I was alone, bitter and disenchanted with my existence. My only interaction with a relationship involved peering down fifteen floors into a stranger's life inside a car. Now I was in love and preparing to spend my life with an sensational woman.

I gently kissed Peta's forehead. She hardly stirred. I dressed, leaving a note and a key for her. I debated stepping out onto my balcony for a peek at my car couple and quickly decided against it. It was time I respected their privacy.

I had rehearsed what I'd tell Christy when I got to the clinic. She was already there when I burst in the door.

I plunged ahead.

"You won't believe what I found out last night," I began.

She grinned and said, "That sex with a breathing woman can be fun?"

I laughed.

"Good try. How about this? I'm moving to Germany."

Silence.

"I …" Christy's expression didn't change.

I raised my eyebrows.

"Well, if you're going there for Oktoberfest, you're too late. It was last month."

"Nope."

Realization spread across her face. "Are telling me you're leaving with Peta?"

"Bingo."

"Holy crap. That's awesome!"

"I'm glad you're taking this so well."

"Why wouldn't I? This is what you've been looking for, Gus! And to think it's with the woman you fell in love with long ago. *This is so romantic!* God. I'd die for something like this to happen to me, my dream man coming back into my life to sweep me away. This is so Tom Hanks! Wow."

She came over and hugged me. It was the first time we had ever embraced. Because of Christy's support I felt comfortable with my decision.

"Thanks. This means a lot to me."

"Gus, I'm so excited for you. I'm going to plan a huge going-away party for you. We'll celebrate for two entire days." She was really getting into the idea of my leaving. To celebrate, Christy went over to the stereo, and Captain and Tennille rattled our speakers.

"No tears?" I asked. "You may never see me again."

She laughed. "Look around, Gus. We have video, e-mail, chat rooms, discount airlines—distance means nothing. You'll see more of me across the ocean than you do now."

"You make this sound so easy."

"There's nothing more invigorating than a life journey," she said enthusiastically. "Look at the opportunities you'll be having. I'm jealous, Gus."

"Listen," I said apologetically, "we may have to rain check a party."

"Why? I don't mind organizing it."

"I'm leaving at the end of the week."

"What! You're kidding!"

"No. Peta wants me to go back with her. She can't stay any longer because of her business. I don't have a choice."

"Are you going to be able to walk away so fast? Your practice …"

"I think so. Once I thought about it, things seem manageable. Personally, I'd have preferred a couple of months."

"Exactly."

"But at the same time, I want to stick close by Peta while her idea is hot."

"You don't trust her?" Christy remarked seriously.

"Of course I do. I'm looking at this offer as a second chance. I let her get away the first time. I won't allow it to happen again. This time I'm sticking right beside her. The last thing I want is something stupid like procrastination to ruin my future with Peta. I'm packing up my shit and getting the hell out of town."

"You go, stallion!" Christy cheered. She sat down and ran her fingers through her hair. "I'm still reeling that this is our last week together."

I assured her I'd try my best to set her up at another clinic. She declined my offer.

"Don't bother, Gus. This is just the kick in the ass I need."

"What do you mean?"

"Remember when we talked about what I really wanted to do with my life?"

"Sure. You mentioned working on cruise ships."

"Exactly. Now might be that time. I saw a recruiting offer on the Net the other night."

"Then go for it," I insisted. Knowing Christy could survive without me made my sudden departure more tolerable.

She said she'd consider it. I was sure she would. In a lot of ways, Christy was like me. Anchorless, we were able to walk away and set up shop anywhere. We didn't have families or careers, which robbed most people of being mobile and going where their dreams were. And while we could both embrace our current lifestyles, we would never be content until we plunged into the activities that matched our desires.

"I suppose I should stop booking appointments," Christy suggested, studying the schedule book.

I told her to gather all the names of my clients, and I'd make arrangements for alternative clinics.

"So this is it," she said warmly.

"I guess so," I replied, sitting across from her at her desk, as we had done hundreds of times over the years.

"Hey, I've still got a few more days of your whining," she hinted.

"I'll pay your wage for the entire month," I offered. "The least I can do is ensure you have a few bucks for your dates."

"Listen to you," she said. "Now you sound like a person who can shed his cologne collection and drawerful of torn underwear." Her tone was envious.

"Look," I said, turning to my office, "I'm going to make a few phone calls. There's a list of people I've got to tell my news to before they hear it elsewhere."

"You're too late. CJOB's Charles Adler has been broadcasting it since five this morning."

"Damn, he's good," I said laughing.

I sat down at my desk and stared at the phone. Who to call first? My sister Julia won the draw.

I reached her at home as she was leaving for work. She was ecstatic. She wished me all the best.

My next call was to Lonny. I got the biggest reaction from him.

"Are you fucking nuts? I know she's stunning and all, but to leave your job? Are you sure she's worth it? I mean, let's face it, if this don't work out, it ain't like you have a job to come back to. It took you years to build your practice."

I comforted him by saying I felt great with my decision. There was no reason for my relationship with Peta not to work. We both loved each other. I was open to the difficulties a new way of life could bring. What I didn't say to Lonny was his lack of understanding of what it was like to be in love made him biased about my situation. He had no idea how love eliminated a lot of the what-if scenarios. But explaining this to him would be fruitless.

Lonny said one more thing.

"What about Mitch?"

I paused and frowned. "What about Mitch?"

"So what are you going to tell her?"

I stared at my phone. *What am I going to tell her?* This reality punched me in the stomach. *Mitch.*

"I don't really know, Lonny. Geez, I hadn't thought about her."

"Really? The woman admires you like the second coming of Christ and you hadn't thought of what this news is going to do to her? What kind of counsellor are you, anyway, you hack?" Lonny forced a laugh.

"This all happened so fast, Lonny."

"My advice, Gus—be kind, okay? She really fell in love with you."

His words hurt because they were true. *Aren't I doing to Mitch what Peta did to me?* I lied to myself that it was completely different.

"Yeah. I gotta think about that one, Lonny. Thanks."

"Let's get together before you bail out of town, brother," Lonny suggested, and he asked me to call him when I had a couple of hours to spare. I agreed to call once everything was settled.

Now the hard part. Mitch.

She had to know.

I needed to be the one to tell her.

I swore.

For every good action, there is a reciprocal kick to the balls. I had my legs splayed, waiting for my turn.

I told Christy I was cutting out early.

"I guess your attendance doesn't matter now," she remarked as I left the building. I was too preoccupied with figuring out what to say to Mitch to turn back to challenge Christy.

I walked home, enjoying the crisp air. I wondered what kind of weather Germany experienced. I hoped it had the intense blue skies I'd grown to enjoy in Manitoba. In reality, I knew literally nothing about Germany or the culture. There would be lots to learn.

I went straight down to the parkade and got into my car. For a moment, I sat quietly, realizing the time was drawing near when I'd never seeing the car again. It had been my steadfast companion for more years than any woman. I'd miss her.

For old times' sake I roared out past the underground parking gates. Instead of squealing the tires, I fired off a huge clot of exhaust. It still made me feel good.

My attention turned to reality. *Mitch.*

How would I tell her?

Would she care?

If she was smart she wouldn't.

But I knew she'd take it to heart. We both shared the same intense feelings, just for different people.

I owed it to her. I knew firsthand about the fallout to a person's ego when the person he or she loves packs up and leaves without warning. I wouldn't allow Mitch to go through the same thing I did.

Shit. I hated being the cause of another person's grief.

I didn't even know if Mitch would be at home. The faint hope that I'd be able to forestall the inevitable gave me a small window of relief. It was short-lived.

Mitch was tying burlap over a cedar tree in her front yard. She wore boots, baggy sweats and a rugged work shirt. As she struggled to hold the string in place, her gloves looked oversized.

"Need a second pair of hands?" I asked, walking up to her gate.

She glanced at me and returned her attention to the battle of tying a knot.

"Sure."

I moved in close and pulled on the string. She was able to make the ends resemble something like a knot.

"As long as the cats stay off it, this will hold," she said, stepping to the side to admire her handiwork.

"Now you can see why I rent. None of this green thumb stuff," I joked.

She didn't laugh.

"You may look at this as work. I see it as pride of ownership. I also rent, but this gives me satisfaction. Try it sometime. You might be surprised how it makes you feel."

I was caught off guard by her venom. This attack wasn't helping my courage.

"Easy now," I cautioned, "I'm here in peace. Leave the fighting to the neighbours."

"See. There you go again, thinking you're better living on Wellington Crescent. I wouldn't stay there if it was free." She walked around the yard, picking up leaves by hand.

"C'mon, Mitch, where's your sense of humour? You know I'm joking."

"I lost my humour. There hasn't been a whole hell of a lot to be laughing about lately. Sorry."

I chose my words carefully.

"I hate to see you depressed like this."

"Oh, really? You might want to brush up on your observation skills," she remarked. "I'd never let myself get down over a break-up. Certainly not if a guy jumps at shadows from the past. Jesus, Gus, if you wanted out that badly, you didn't have to wait. What was I? A mercy refuge until something better came along?"

I started to reply, and she abruptly cut me off.

"Forget it," she said. "Don't answer. I really don't care."

"I don't believe you."

"Listen, go have your fun with a woman who speaks with a mouthful of marbles. I hope for your sake she doesn't dump you again when it becomes convenient. I know you're a nice guy, just brain dead when it comes to judgment."

I started to get irritated. Now Mitch was getting personal. I took the offensive.

"Peta's admitted she made a mistake by walking away from me years ago. She based her decision on lies. More importantly, she's regretted her decision ever since."

"What a touching story, Gus. Like a reformed alcoholic going back to make amends to all the people she was an asshole to and blaming it on the booze. It was the booze that made me say that. The booze made me do that. Easy out. Believe what you want, I guess. If it was me, I'd tell her to fuck off."

"Well, that's where you and I differ then. No one's perfect. A wrong decision shouldn't mean you have to pay for it the rest of your life. She wants a fresh start. I respect that request."

"Oh, so now it's about respect? She had better hope your high school girlfriend doesn't come knocking, saying she's sorry she didn't put out on prom night, because you'll be gone in a flash."

I shook my head. "You can be really impossible to talk to, did you know that?"

"Funny, but I don't remember inviting you over to talk. I was enjoying myself with my yard work. Shouldn't you be with Marblemouth, sharing a stimulating conversation reminiscing about the past?"

"Soon enough, yeah, I will."

"Well, don't let me hold you back," she spat. "I'm sure you two haven't come close to catching up on the last ten years. She must have years of suffering to get off her chest."

I simmered. Getting angry wouldn't help. I took a deep breath.

"Whatever, Mitch. I didn't come here to fight with you. Or to argue. I wanted to say good-bye."

She'd squatted to pick up leaves, and she turned toward me.

"I thought we already had this conversation in your car. Let me see—oh, by the way, Mitch, sorry, but you're outta here. I've got someone new. Actually, she's a ghost from my past. But she's back now, so you're out. Bye."

She went back to stuffing the black bag.

"Since you're not making this any easier, I'll be up front about it," I said stiffly. "Peta has asked me to move back with her to Germany, and I accepted her offer. I'm leaving the country at the end of the week." *There. It's done.*

I still didn't feel any better.

Mitch's voice quavered. "So that's where this is all going? You're taking off into the sunset." She turned and stood looking at me. She looked pathetic, her face torn with grief. I thought she might cry, but she didn't. I gave her credit for her control. I wanted to move closer and hold her, yet I knew she'd reject me. I stood my ground instead.

"Are you certain about this?" she asked.

I nodded. "Yes."

She winced. Her eyes were hollow. "Okay," she replied, "Have a good journey." She turned back to slamming leaves into the bag. It ripped from her hand, and she kicked it in anger. Instead of picking it up, Mitch hurried into her house, slamming the door.

I was alone.

I turned to go.

Back inside my car, I thought I saw Mitch standing back from a window. I couldn't be certain. The curtain was distorting my view. I waved anyway just in case.

I looked around the neighbourhood one last time. I thought about the evening we walked back from Kelekis, wet, giggling, stumbling along the street drunk from the air of summer that held promises for tomorrow. It made me smile. Mitch had a way of doing something so absurd it'd make me cry from laughing so hard. I'd miss her playfulness. Peta was more pointed. While Mitch was carefree, Peta was aggressive. Designer baseball caps versus designer nails. My preference was stuck somewhere in the damn middle.

My trip to the apartment was uneventful. The sun was gone when I parked. I wanted to savour one of my last breaths of crisp Canadian air, so I walked around the building to the front doors. Harold was smoking beside the shrubs that had long ago shed their leaves. He looked at me and waved.

"Hey, Harold. Snow's not too far off."

He grunted.

"Me goddamn back ain't ready for the shovel. Dis sidewalk getting longer each year. You'd think looking after a hundred suites would be enough for one man. Den the snow comes and the asshole called me when old Missus McCutcheon slips on dis sidewalk. Bullshit." He puffed hard on the cigarette stub, trying to absorb the last remaining bits of tobacco and filter. He tossed it aside and lit a new one.

"Only me wife to go back inside fer," he said gruffly, tossing me a grin.

I nodded and said, "Since I've got you here, Harold, I should let you know I'm leaving the country."

Harold barely raised an eyebrow. He concentrated on the tip of his burning ember.

"Yeah?"

"I'm moving to Germany."

Harold smacked at his cigarette.

"Germany, huh?"

I nodded.

"Never bin der."

"Neither have I."

"Woman?"

"Yeah."

This time he nodded.

"Man will do anythin' fer a fine woman."

"I guess so."

He inhaled deeply, holding the smoke in before releasing it slowly through his nose and mouth.

"I never bin anywhere but dis city. Met me wife here. Never bin with another woman. Don't know if I'd leave fer one." He studied the growing ember.

"Well, for this one I'd move anywhere," I assured him.

He looked at me and winked.

"You leavin' means another 'partment to paint. Goddamn, it'll snow the same day."

"Actually, Harold, I need to leave this week. I know it's short notice, but at least we shouldn't get snow by then." I held my breath.

Harold must have mellowed after two quick hits of nicotine, because all he said was, "Got a lease not due yet. Shouldn't matter. Got a list of names want a top floor. Doesn't need painting, does it?" He cast me a glance.

"Nope," came my response.

He relaxed.

"Leave it with me, din. You always bin good around here. Not like dat goddamn 101 bastard knocking down his wall. Caused me a world of trouble."

I laughed.

"Thanks, Harold," I said, tapping his arm as I walked by.

He kept sucking at the smoldering filter.

28

"I'd like to talk to someone, anyone. I'm totally bored ..."

The week was a blur. Closing up the shop took more effort than I had anticipated. Most clinics I contacted in hopes of relocating my clients weren't accepting new referrals, despite my personal calls. Somehow I managed to locate a new psychotherapist for all my clients. Apparently my reputation wasn't well-known in the community. I couldn't fault any of the clinics. I had withdrawn my membership from the clubs offered by the other therapists years ago. It was a waste of my time—same old bullshit when I did get there. We'd all sit around inside Bailey's restaurant rehashing war stories. I had better things to do with my spare time, like watching foreign movies at the Cinematheque. The invitations had dwindled until they finally stopped. I had officially become disenfranchised.

My greatest fear was the five-year lease remaining on my building. Property managers on commercial real estate had a reputation for being die-hards about broken leases. I was certain they'd hold me to the full contract. I was wrong. The agent was practically salivating while I explained my situation. He even waived the penalty. I discovered they had been hoping for an opening in my building. Apparently the plan was to subdivide my space into four offices. Each monthly rent would remain the same as I was currently paying for my entire unit. No wonder it was so easy for me to break the lease. I couldn't imagine the coffin-sized space the new tenants would have to work with under the new plan. I thought it was robbery, but I kept my cornhole shut. It wasn't my problem.

My parting with Christy was emotional. I had hoped to keep my composure, but I couldn't. She was an amazing kid who I had come to respect. I'd miss the dating fiasco stories we exchanged each morning. We spent our last day laughing about some of our more crazy clients. I promised to give her my e-mail address once I figured out how it worked. Technology was as foreign to me as Germany would be. Peta would be able to help me.

My biggest regret was throwing Christy out of a job. She soothed my anxiety. She had been searching the internet for jobs on cruise ships. It turned out there were plenty of opportunities for anyone with a streak of adventure. It did mean relocating to Vancouver. Leaving her family and the only city she knew was the hardest part for Christy. But she was up for the adventure. I was her catalyst. I could see she was excited about it by the glitter in her eyes. A whole new world was now opening up for her, the carrot of touring an atlas of countries and cultures enticing. Her plans were to drive out at the end of the month. I wished her the best. We hugged. I tried not to cry, but a few tears escaped. She joined me.

Meanwhile, during the free moments we both had, Peta spent the week briefing me on German culture. She spoke about the city we'd be living in, the type of companies she managed and where I might fit in once I got adjusted. She eased my trepidation about the availability of British ales. The crafty German breweries realized they couldn't produce equals and so had spent the last ten years purchasing all the smaller British breweries. Now a good British pint could be had at every German pub and restaurant. Leave it to German ingenuity to stay on top.

German fashion was my second concern. Again, my worries were without merit. European designers were usually two years ahead of clothing trends that eventually made their way to America. I would be able to boast about clothing that would be out of fashion by the time Lonny was buying the latest in dress shirts. I was sold.

I unloaded all my furniture with Goodwill. I think it was the first time they had ever been donated complete sets of furniture that weren't beat to shit. Everything had to go. It took the volunteer movers all day to empty my apartment. In exchange, I was given a plaque of thanks for my commitment to the community.

My only failure was finding a home for my beloved Subaru. Harold offered me a hundred bucks. I held out. He walked away. I was left with a painful decision. A local scrapper came by with a tow truck. I was able to arrange a price of a hundred and fifty bucks for it to be towed away for parts. My victory was short-lived, when I spent a tense twenty minutes with the tow truck driver pleading for my car's value. To his trained scrap eye, my car's rust and age lowered his acceptance price. I recited the quote Sid made over the phone. He ignored my counterattack. Sid worked in the office, he said. It was a take-it-or-leave-it offer. I refused. He climbed back in the truck. I quickly learned that trying to negotiate against the scrap yard bastards was a mistake. I needed their services more than they needed the shit that I offered. I ran after the disappearing truck. Five minutes later I watched my scorned car's taillights glaring at me in hurt disgust as it was hooked behind the truck and taken away. I held twenty bucks cash in my hand.

I viewed the city from my balcony one last time this morning. My feelings were mixed. I had grown attached to the population that was big enough to be invisible in and yet small enough to know someone who knew someone. A native Winnipegger had once given me a sliver of advice shortly after I had arrived. He cautioned me to consider that everything and anything I said to anyone at any time would get back to the person I'd be bitching about.

I heeded his advice.

The canopy of green was gone from the surrounding suburbs. In place was a scattering of bleak grey rooftops and battered streets. This was home.

I made it a point to watch my couple one last time. They kissed. I kissed with them. They were back on loving terms, and I took this knowledge to heart. I would leave them knowing all was well.

I craved a cup of coffee, but my machine was now sitting in a charity warehouse. All that remained were my two suitcases and my bed. And that was being removed in another hour. Looking in from outside on the patio, my apartment looked strange, void of my previous occupancy. I wondered who would inhabit it once I was gone? I hoped they would carry on my morning tradition on the balcony. I contemplated leaving a note explaining at what time my car couple arrived each morning, but I tossed the idea aside, deciding it was up to the new tenant to discover.

During the removal of my bed, Peta showed up. She brought lunch in a bag. My favourite fast food—a George's Fatboy, what seemed like five pounds of delicious burger. Since I was lacking a table and chairs, we ate stretched out on the carpet. We weren't bothered.

"You all right?" I asked.

Peta nodded while taking a bite out of her burger. She seemed distracted.

"I thought maybe you were nervous about bringing a Canadian boy back to your friends," I added. "You seem a little detached today."

"Do not worry about me, Gus," she reassured me, smiling. "My week has been as crazy as the one you had making the final arrangements. Everything is okay. I am just a little tired by it all."

I grinned. "Don't mention it. We'll be able to catch up on our rest during the flight."

"Yes. I never did enjoy the meals and movie they show." She seemed to recover her gaiety.

I felt better.

"So are you sticking around here with me?" I asked. "I know it'll be a boring afternoon while I finalize the apartment."

She wiped her mouth with a napkin. She could only finish a third of the Fatboy.

"I still have more to do, Gus. Sorry. Here is what I thought we could do, if you don't mind."

"Fire away," I said.

"Finish up what you must do here. If you do not mind, I need to meet you at the airport. I'll be out that way on my last stop. Ask for your ticket at the counter. It is already under your name. I'll be waiting past customs."

"No problem. What time?"

"Our flight leaves at seven."

"I'll make it a point to get there before six. They always say an hour ahead of the flight is enough time. Nervous?" I asked, shooting her a smile.

She shook her head.

"Tired. Yes, maybe a little nervous. I will be able to share your excitement once all the arrangements are finalized and we are in the air."

"Good. I'd be worried if you weren't. It still hasn't sunk in for me that I'm moving to Germany. Hell, I'm going to be living with you!"

"Control your excitement, Gus. You might tire of me after a month."

I looked at her. "Are you nuts? I get all fuzzy in my stomach whenever I think about spending every night with you."

She blushed. It was the first time I had ever seen Peta do that. Now she looked around the empty space that once was my home. She flashed me a smile.

"You amaze me with how little you are taking with you," she said. "I've seen the size of your closets. They were all full of clothing."

"I've kept only my very best. It turned out not to be as difficult as I first imagined. A lot of the stuff I hadn't worn in years. Some of it I forgot I had purchased. Hell, I found a suit still sealed in the original bag, untouched!"

She laughed, grabbing my arm.

"You are silly, Gus. Worse than a woman."

Peta and I kissed, and I held her in my arms, savouring the warmth and security of her body. She rested her head on my shoulder, letting me enjoy my moment with her. I kissed her again and told her I'd see her in a few hours. She waved and left for the elevator.

It was time.

Harold inspected each room, ensuring all fixtures remained fixed to where they belonged, no walls held fist-sized holes and that the carpets were no more soiled than after a good party. I passed. He handed over the cash deposit I had given another lifetime ago. He took my key. I felt empty. I was now officially homeless. All ties to the city were nullified. There was no turning back. I had a fleeting urge to grab my key from Harold's nicotine-stained hand. I managed to suppress the reflex. It was like holding back vomit.

Harold allowed me quiet time while I waited for my cab by the front doors. The air was cool enough that I sat inside the vestibule.

Boredom was setting in when Lonny suddenly appeared. I was elated.

"Hey, buddy!" he said, grinning, reaching over to shake hands. "I was in Steinbach today and got a speeding ticket trying to make it here in time. I'll have to slow down tomorrow when I'm on the road to Brandon."

"Sorry. I'm not worth two points on your license."

"Forget it. But I did want to see you before you left. It'll be the only way for me to believe you're actually doing this."

"I'm doing it," I said, laughing.

"Where's all your shit?" he asked, looking at my two suitcases.

"This is it."

"Really?"

I nodded.

"Where'd the rest go?"

"Charity. Gave it all away."

He seemed startled.

"You mean I'll be seeing bums wearing Holt Renfrew jackets now?"

"And Florsheim shoes."

"Are you waiting for Peta?"

"Actually, a cab. She's meeting me at the airport."

He scowled.

"I can drive you. Those assholes will rip you off."

"It's okay, Lonny. Thanks. I've already called for one."

"Shit. I wish you would have told me. I heard the cabbies keep taking their foot off the gas because it adds on three bucks to the ride."

"I'll take my chances," I said.

Lonny leaned against the wall, obviously in deep thought. He asked, "So what are you going to do about the language over there? I mean, how are you going to order a Big Mac and super-sized fries at McDonald's? It'd drive me nuts."

I shrugged. "I haven't thought much about it. Point at the signs, I guess."

"Think about—if you get a shitty meal at a restaurant, how're you going to tell off the waiter?"

"Perhaps I'll get lucky and never have a bad one."

"Yeah, right," he grunted.

"Peta will have to do all the talking for a while, at least until I get down some of the basics."

Lonny's face brightened.

"Guys' night out this evening."

"What's the occasion?"

"We're slamming all the chicks for the worst dates we've been on," he snorted.

I laughed. "This is why I'm not worried about ordering from a menu in a foreign language. At least I won't ever get jammed on any more lousy dates."

Lonny laughed loudly. "Next time I see Zoe and her yellow love truck, I'll tell her you miss her so much you can't sleep."

"As a matter of fact I can sleep just fine. It's my bowels that become bunged up when her name is mentioned."

My cab arrived.

Lonny pointed and warned, "Watch his foot on the gas."

I shook his hand.

"Look me up if you ever travel to Europe," I said.

"Count on it. Find me one of those deviant women with the hairy armpits."

He helped me carry my two suitcases to the car. We shook again before I crawled into the car.

"Cheers, bud," he said, slamming the door shut. "Straight to the airport, pal," he warned the driver though the glass. My cabbie ignored Lonny and drove away.

Winnipeg.

I watched it for the last time through the snot-smeared windows of a cab. I requested that we drive down Wellington Crescent until we hit Corydon Avenue toward Osborne Street. *I want to see the Village one final time.* I wondered if I'd ever walk these sidewalks again. *Probably not.*

The cab pulled to a stop at a red light at the corner of Osborne Street and River Avenue. I looked to my left, and my eyes rested on Starbucks. *Mitch.* We'd shared our first coffee there. I laughed to myself, remembering how I thought I'd been set up and she wasn't going to be there. Our first official "date," and I didn't even know her name when I walked inside the place. I shook my head as the cab began to pull away. It had been the first time I had seen her wearing regular clothing. Simple, but they worked well for her.

We crossed the Osborne Bridge, turned left onto St. Mary Avenue and then left to Portage Avenue. The cab kept up with traffic as we passed car dealerships, low-income apartments and an assortment of strip malls and restaurants.

A&W Restaurant. I laughed out loud, and the cab driver gazed at me through the rearview mirror. *The Bear.* We meet all because some dumbass decided to punch out a mascot bear that knocked over his ice-cream cone. I closed my eyes for a moment. Intervening by tripping the dumbass wasn't something I had ever done before. I preferred to stay out of the limelight. I had no idea what made my foot do what it did. But it was the first time Mitch and I met. She took charge and took my statement. It all seemed so insignificant, yet it was the catalyst that got us together. Her perseverance to keep getting together sparked our relationship. I giggled. *How badly do you want to find someone in the dark with one thousand people watching fireworks!* I noticed the car driver staring at me again through the mirror.

The cab approached Polo Park mall; the lot was full of shoppers. That was another thing about Winnipeg: people loved to shop. Season didn't matter or what time of day; the malls were busy and people were spending money. I smirked when I saw a billboard for Moosehead Beer in the corner of the mall's parking lot. *How many of those did Mitch and I down during those crazy warm summer evenings!* I had to give Mitch credit. She carried home every single case of those beers despite the danger—in her area a case of beer was like a white tail in open deer season. She was tough. She laughed off the element of danger, saying no one was getting between her and her case of Moosehead. I believed her.

The cabbie turned right off Portage and put the pedal down on Route 90. The city was a mess of roadways that often didn't make sense. A driver could go from 50 kilometres an hour to 80 kilometres and back within a three-block period. It had taken me years to realize that when native Winnipeggers spoke about roads like Dunkirk Drive, Osborne Street, Memorial Boulevard, Colony Street, Balmoral Street, Isabel Street and Salter Street, they were referring to Route 62. The cab turned down Wellington Avenue for the final stretch toward the airport. I reached into my pants to dig out my wallet to pay for what was looking to be a forty-dollar tab. I yanked my wallet from my pocket in the confines of the car's backseat. Along with the wallet was a piece of paper. I unfolded it. A napkin. *Kelekis.* The one Mitch gave me. She wanted me to have it as a reminder of our late-night interlude at the restaurant that followed my nutty date with Petulla. My heart beat hard in my chest. I touched the napkin in my hand gently as the car jittered along the road. All those dates I'd had were each followed by feelings of frustration. The women had all been flawed in different ways. I remembered bitching to Christy, "Where the hell have all the *normal* ones gone?"

I looked at the napkin and red lettering on it. There was also a lipstick smear. *Mitch was a normal one. Maybe she seemed too normal after all the goons I had dated.* Except now her "normal" represented the type of stability and loyalty I'd sought when I started my quest to find my other half, the sweater-and-jeans type of girl who liked domestic beer, soap opera TV and late-night walks holding hands. A girl who wouldn't crash a car through a ballpark fence or stiff me for money, without daughters who attempted to rape me on a wheel or put a drug in my drink, a girl who wouldn't *break my heart and come back to steal it again.*

The car came to a stop. My palms were wet. The cabbie looked back at me for his money. I looked at the suitcases beside me. The airport doors were to my right. I closed my eyes and took a deep breath. I handed the driver two twenties and got out. The Canadian air was brisk and this was to be my last breaths of it. I entered the Winnipeg International Airport doors.

Inside, the terminal was an elongated, sterile grey interior, all the registration agents lined against the far wall. The amenities and food shops were on the second floor. I always found this airport the easiest to navigate, since all domestic and international flights departed from the same general area. There were no distinct wings to make a traveler run between terminals to catch cross-connecting flights. In Winnipeg, making a connection meant moving ten steps to the right.

I scanned the airport and didn't see Peta anywhere. I knew she was always prompt, so I wouldn't have been surprised if she had already checked in and was behind the gates. I moved off to the side to go through a suitcase to find the sheet of paper Peta'd given me with the information on the flight and airline I was to board. Peta had paid for the ticket that was waiting for me at the agent's terminal. I dug through the suitcase, pulling aside shirts and underwear until I pulled out a red sweater. I knew what it was before it unfolded. DOWNTOWN BIZ PATROL was stenciled in white across the back. It was the sweater Mitch gave me to wear after my own clothes were rain-soaked following my date with Petulla. *Shit.* Mitch was a kind-hearted soul who literally gave the shirt off her back.

What am I thinking? Is this all wrong? Am I making the biggest goddamn mistake in my life? Everything suddenly shifted. I honestly felt that moving out with Peta was the *right* decision. The *only* decision. But was Mitch right when she said she was here now, and Peta was a ghost? I looked around me. The entire room seemed to sway from left to right. I had given up everything, every fucking thing I owned, my apartment, my car, my practice … my love, Mitch. *My soul mate.* I ran my hand harshly across my forehead. *What the hell am I supposed to do?* I dug back in my bag, looking for the paper with my notes. I couldn't possibly jam out on Peta now. *She came back for me. She promised me a lifetime with her. But she left me ten years ago without a shitlicking care how I felt about it. Mitch truly cares.*

I felt the glossy picture and pulled it out. *The River Rouge.* My body flushed. *The two of us had something the captain had never seen between two people before*—the something that I swore on my thirty-ninth birthday I wanted to find and grab hold of and cherish for a lifetime. *There she was, right beside me all this time. You fucking idiot.* I stood up and my knees popped. I looked around furtively. "Goddammit!" I said under my breath.

This was a dog's breakfast. *This is my life. My life is with Mitch. She is in the here and now. Peta is a ghost.*

I shoved all my shit back into the suitcase, grabbed them both and went back outside into the Canadian air that moments earlier I thought I'd breathed for the last time. *Maybe Mitch is going to do the right thing and tell me this is what happens to guys who chase shadows. Hit the bricks, loser. She has every right to hate me forever. To never open her door to me, to never open her heart again to me. She has every right.*

I had to find out. I needed my Mitch.

A line of cabs waited by the door, and I climbed into a backseat, barking out the address for Lisgar. The car could not move fast enough. What could I even say to her? She'd been so mad, so embittered, *so ripped apart* by my actions the last time I saw her. *She will hate me forever.* I shook my head. This time I had to face my own actions, my own past, my own future. No one could do this but me. *I owe it to both me and Mitch.*

My heart sped up as we got closer to her home. What if she wasn't home? It occurred to me she might be out. *On a date? Do I camp outside her doorstep?*

"Where did you fly in from?" asked the cabbie to break the silence.

"From the land of morons," I said, prompting a scowl from the driver.

The city streets were now dark and void of traffic and pedestrians. By the time we reached Main Street only the drunks roamed. I took strange comfort seeing the familiar homes and in particular Mitch's place when we turned onto Lisgar. Despite abandoning all of my own possessions and attachments to the city, just being back in this location gave me a warm feeling.

Mitch's house looked dark. I couldn't see a trace of light from any of the windows. The front porch light was on. The car pulled up, and I paid the driver and hauled my suitcases from the backseat. I turned around to ask the cabbie to wait until I made sure Mitch was home, but he was already accelerating down the street. It was brisk outside. I was dressed for flying, not standing outside. I had no access to a phone.

The gate was unhinged and I walked up the stairs that creaked in every familiar spot. I put down my suitcases and knocked hard on the wooden door. The doorbell had stopped working back in the fifties, she'd told me.

No answer.

I waited a strained fifteen seconds and knocked again. I felt exposed standing outside. My heart pounded in my chest. *This is not looking good.*

I was quickly losing my bravado. I paced around the porch. I tried peering into the front window, but the blinds were drawn. I walked around to the back of the house, trying to see into any window. There was no sign of anyone inside. It seemed very quiet inside. *Or Mitch is doing a good job of hiding. Ever think of that, moron?*

I didn't want to think about that.

I tried the front door one more time. I realized that if she was home she wasn't coming out or else she was definitely not home. I felt totally defeated. I needed to see her. I needed to talk. I needed to hear her voice.

Maybe this is how my destiny plays out. I removed the photograph from my suitcase and stared at it. My eyes welled with tears. So much emotion jumped out from the photo toward me. I could feel Mitch in my arms, as if I was right back in that moment in the summer heat, dancing on the boat.

The street was vacant, and then I saw a set of headlights coming toward the house. A vehicle stopped out front.

A cab.

This was telling me my destiny—it was all over. I had no idea how the driver knew I needed a lift, but it was my signal to leave. *It's over.*

My nose was running, and it was more than from just the cold outside. I wiped with the back of my shaking hand. I picked up my belongings. Now they felt immensely heavy. My shoulders sagged under the weight. I took a step toward the stairs, and I watched a silhouette exit the cab. The figure straightened out and turned toward me. I took the few steps down toward the walkway, and the figure walked toward me. The person wore a wool hat, light jacket and boots to keep out the chilly air. We walked toward one another on the same narrow sidewalk. We both stopped, facing each other.

Our eyes met and held.

Silence.

Mitch spoke first.

"In case you haven't figured it out yet, you're not in Germany."

I frowned.

"You mean I'm still in one of the most amazing countries in the world?"

"For better or for worse."

"I can handle that. It's exactly where I need to be."

"Really?"

"Really."

"And is that because of the city's high property tax rate?"

"It is all because of one person."

"Really?"

"Really."

"What makes you so sure?"

"Stupidity. It can be the most eye-opening kick to the stomach."

"So what's it telling you?"

"That I'm talking to a woman who believed in me. Who cherished me for who I am. Who was committed to sharing a life together and ..."

"And ... "

"And I felt the same way but was an asshole who got caught by a ghost. And I realize I am probably too late to say I'm sorry. This is where I want to be."

"Really?"

"Really."

"I don't give second chances."

"I'm asking for this." I held up the River Rouge photograph.

Mitch studied the picture.

"What would you give to get that back?"

I held out the Kelekis napkin.

"I'd give you my heart. Well, in this case, this napkin, which represents my heart." Mitch stifled a chuckle.

"You still have that."

"I want what goes with it."

"I'm not a hamburger and fries."

"You can be my ketchup."

"I prefer to be mustard. I like to make eyes water."

"You do that to me just by being next to me."

Mitch took in a deep breath, and her eyes looked pained.

"I don't want any more bullshit. I expect total loyalty from this point on, and I will kill you in an instant if any ghost ever comes back from your past. I fucking mean it," Mitch said, punching my shoulder.

"Friends?"

"Friends."

"For real?"

"For real."

29

". . . To exit the System at any time please press the star button …"

I live with Mitch now in a house we bought along the river. If I was going to survive on ground level, I needed a backyard ripe with wildlife and scenic water. The river holds special meaning for me. It brought Mitch and me together.

I no longer wake up each morning with the need to see an enigmatic couple kiss. I reach next to me and kiss the woman who loves me as much as I love her. It's been four years now, and I never knew happiness felt this damn good. I love that Mitch dresses in flannel and wears a size-ten shoe.

Forty came and went, and I discovered some neat things about it. The first, I guess, is the obvious: age is irrelevant. It's what you're doing and who you're with that matters. And this leads me to my second revelation: leave the past where it belongs—*in the past*. Believe me, it is there for a reason. While I'm at it, never use age as an excuse to find love. It just does not work that way. All you've got to do is open your eyes and love will find you pretty damn fast.

Peta. I've never heard from her again and never cared. In our personal commitment to one another, Mitch and I stopped buying all German-brewed beers.

Mitch is calling me now. She wants to go for a walk along the riverbank. It snowed again this morning and the hoar frost has lined the tree branches. The best part is when we get back. I get to snuggle with her under the blankets. She claims men in their forties are the world's best lovers. I won't argue with that one.